THE RETURN OF THE KNIGHTS

THE DANCE OF LIGHT: BOOK ONE

Gregory Kontaxis

GK

Translation: Sophia Travlos

Cover Design: Miblart

Editing: Taya Greylock

PaperBack ISBN: 978-1-7397294-1-7

Ebook ISBN: 978-1-7397294-2-4

Hardcover ISBN: 978-1-7397294-0-0

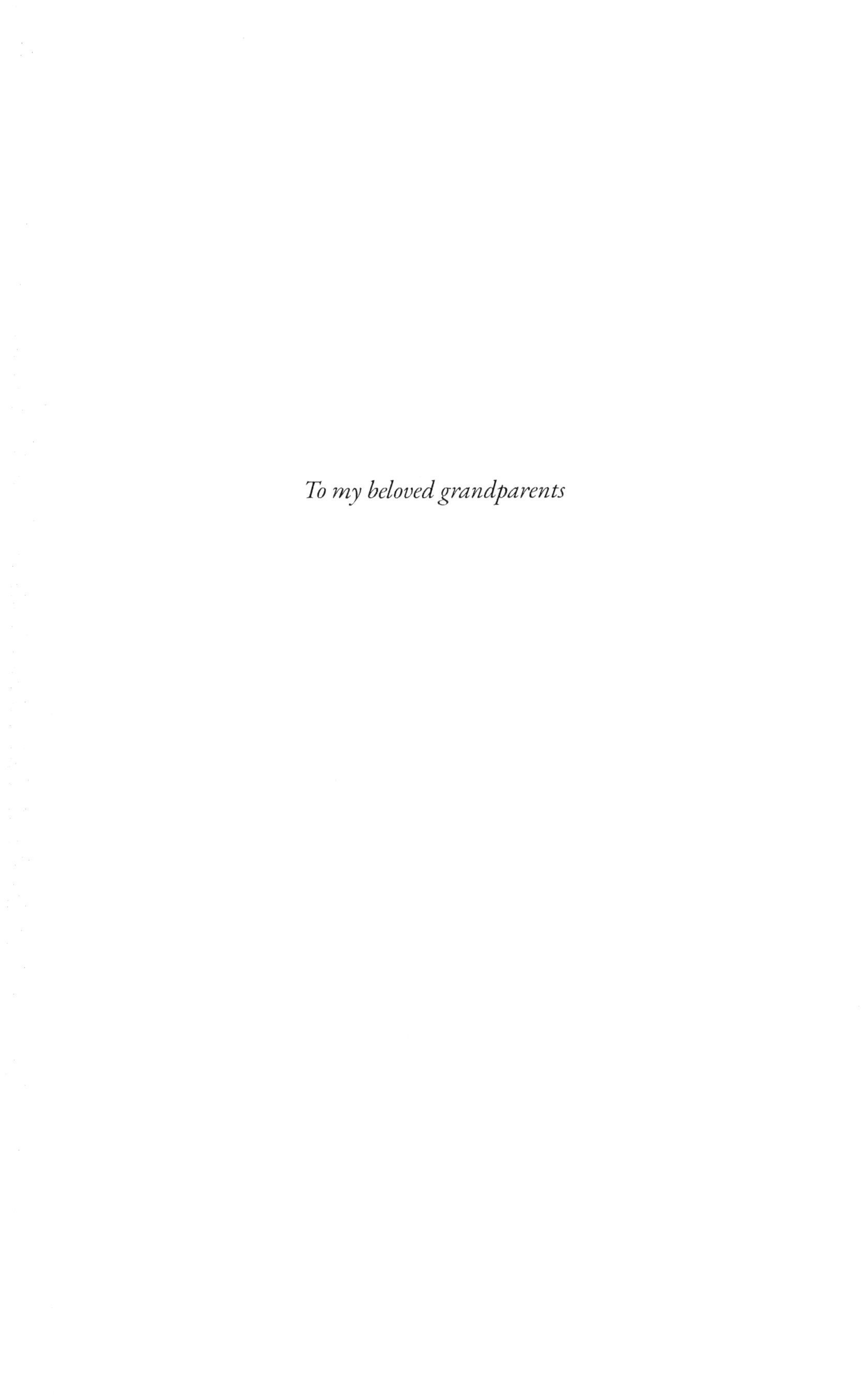

To my beloved grandparents

Contents

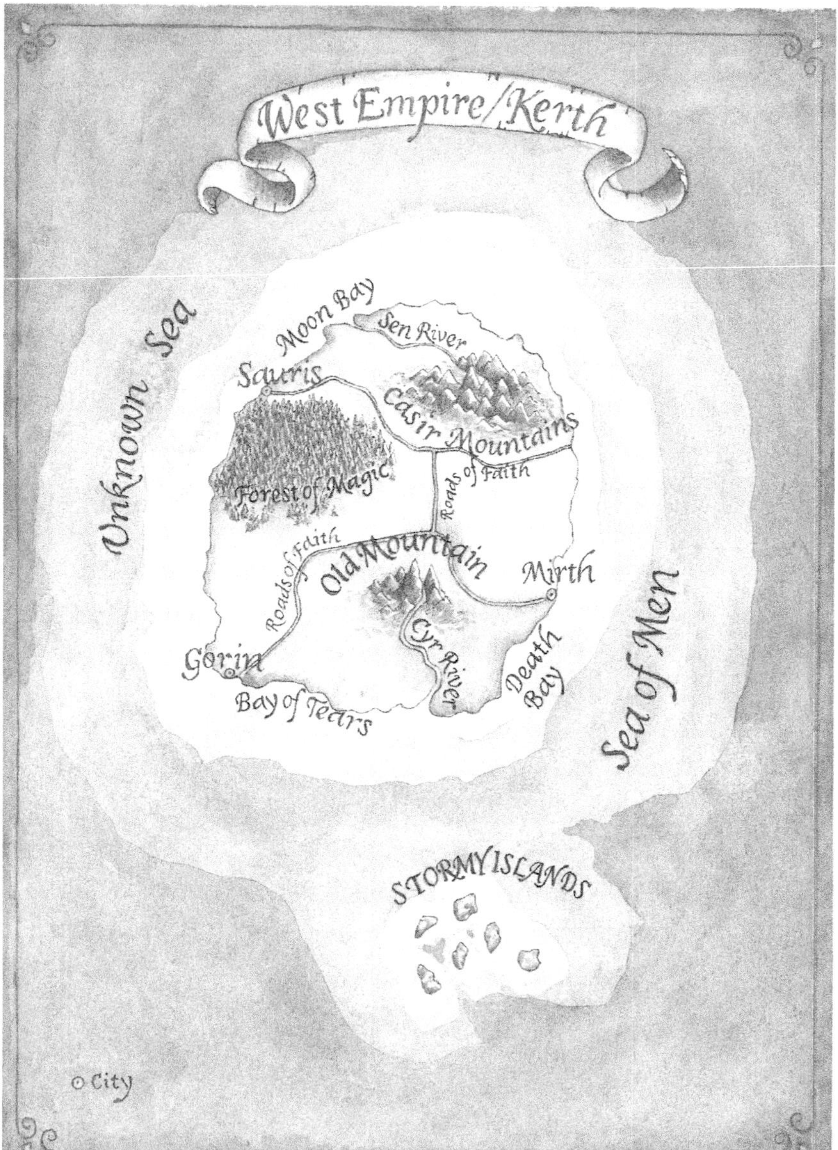

West Empire/Kerth

Unknown Sea
Moon Bay
Sen River
Sauris
Casir Mountains
Roads of Faith
Forest of Magic
Roads of Faith
Old Mountain
Mirth
Sea of Men
Gorin
Cyr River
Death Bay
Bay of Tears
STORMY ISLANDS
City

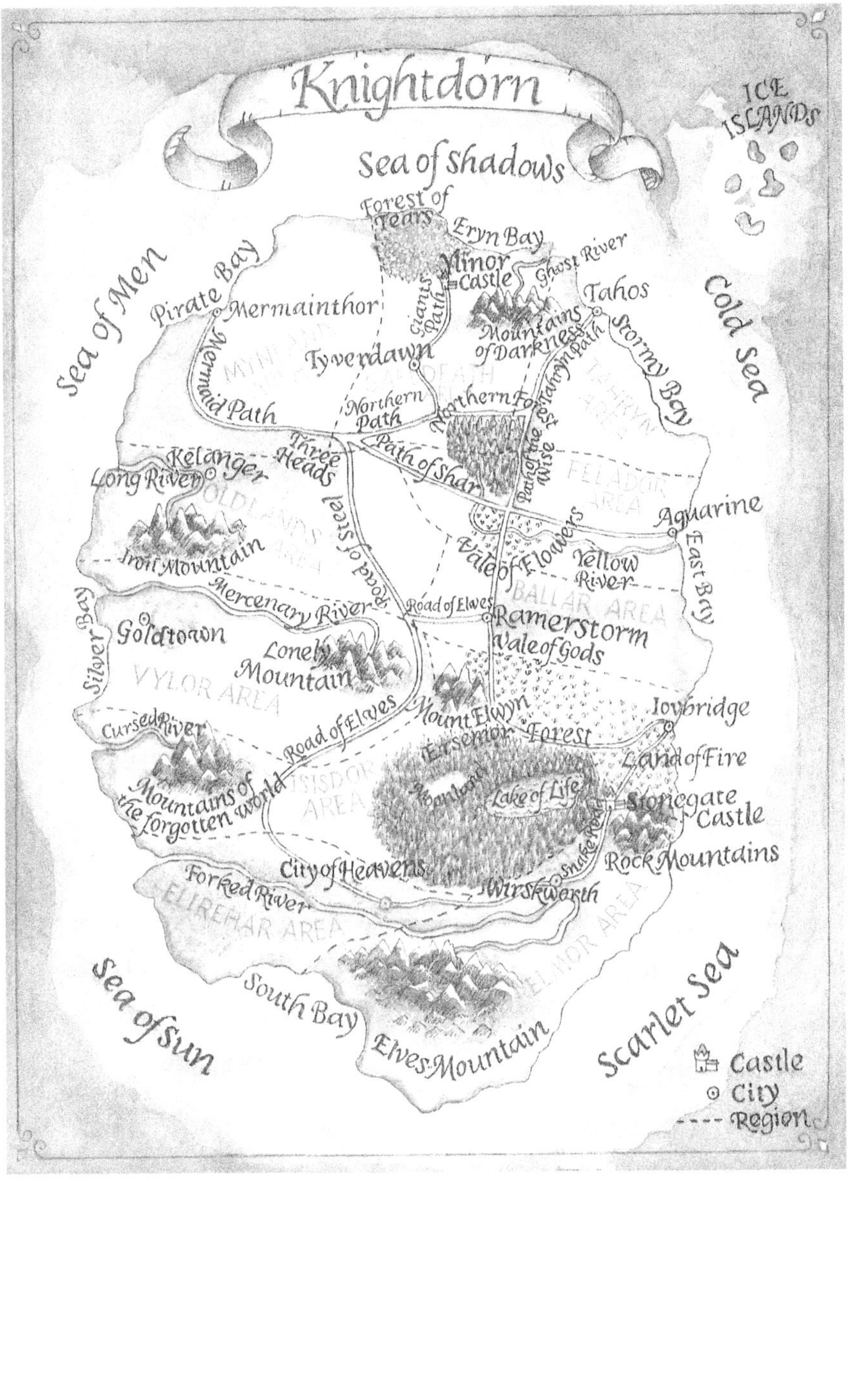

Knightdorn

Sea of Shadows
ICE ISLANDS
Forest of Tears
Eryn Bay
Minor Castle
Ghost River
Sea of Men
Pirate Bay
Mermainthor
Giants Path
Tahos
Cold Sea
Mountains of Darkness
Mermaid Path
Tyverdawn
Tahryn Path
Stormy Bay
MYNLAND AREA
GALDEATH AREA
TAHRYN AREA
Northern Path
Northern Forest
Three Heads
Path of Shar
Path of the Wise
Kelanger
Long River
OLDLANDS AREA
FELADOR AREA
Aquarine
Road of Steel
Vale of Flowers
East Bay
Iron Mountain
Yellow River
BALLAR AREA
Mercenary River
Road of Elves
Ramerstorm
Silver Bay
Goldtown
Vale of Gods
Lonely Mountain
VYLOR AREA
Mount Elwyn
Iovbridge
Road of Elves
Cursed River
Ersemor Forest
Land of Fire
Mountains of the forgotten world
ISISDOR AREA
Moonland
Lake of Life
Stonegate Castle
Snake Road
Rock Mountains
City of Heavens
Forked River
Wirskworth
ELIREHAR AREA
ELNOR AREA
Sea of Sun
South Bay
Elves Mountain
Scarlet Sea
Castle
City
Region

List of Regions, Organizations, and Characters

Kingdom of Knightdorn

Queen: Sophie Delamere
Royal Council: General-Lord of the Knights Peter Brau, Captain Merick, Captain Robyn, Captain Richard Lamont, Captain Hugh, Captain Frederic Abbot, Lord Counsellor Gregory Mollet, Lord Counsellor Patrick Degore, High Priest Leuric
Capital: Iovbridge
Emblem of the Kingdom: Seven swords in a laurel wreath on a white field
Emblem of the queen's House: A golden oak tree on a green field

Regions of the Kingdom of Knightdorn

Isisdor

Governor / Ruler: Sophie Delamere
Capital: Iovbridge
Faith: The Unknown God
Emblem of the region: Seven swords in a laurel wreath on a white field
Emblem of the governor's House: A golden oak tree on a green field

Elmor

Governor / Ruler: Syrella Endor
Capital: Wirskworth
Faith: The God of Souls
Emblem of the region: A snake on a yellow field
Emblem of the governor's House: A snake on a yellow field

Felador

Governor / Ruler: None
Capital: Aquarine / City of Healers
Faith: The God of Wisdom
Emblem of the region: A golden oak tree on a green field
Emblem of the governor's House: None

Oldlands

Governor / Ruler: Ricard Karford
Capital: Kelanger
Faith: The God of the Sun
Emblem of the region: A hammer and an anvil on a brown field
Emblem of the governor's House: An axe on a brown field

Mynlands

Governor / Ruler: Launus Eymor
Capital: Mermainthor
Faith: The God of Youth
Emblem of the region: A mermaid on a violet field
Emblem of the governor's House: A mermaid on a violet field

Gaeldeath

Governor / Ruler: Walter Thorn
Capital: Tyverdawn
Faith: The God of War

Emblem of the region: A white tiger on a red field
Emblem of the governor's House: A white tiger on a red field

Vylor / Black Vale
Governor / Ruler: Liher Hale
Capital: Goldtown
Faith: The Avaricious God
Emblem of the region: A rusty coin on a black field
Emblem of the governor's House: A rusty coin on a black field

Tahryn
Governor / Ruler: Eric Stone
Capital: Tahos
Faith: The God of Rain
Emblem of the region: An old ship, *The Fairy*, on a white field
Emblem of the Governor's House: The tide of the sea on a green field

Ballar
Governor / Ruler: Borin Ballard
Capital: Ramerstorm / White City
Faith: The Goddess of Nature
Emblem of the region: A white hawk on a black field
Emblem of the governor's House: A white hawk on a black field

Elirehar
Governor / Ruler: None
Capital: City of Heavens / City of Pegasus
Faith: The God of Life / The God of Light
Emblem of the region: A white pegasus on a light blue field
Emblem of the governor's House: None

Regions Independent from the Kingdom of Knightdorn

Ice Islands

Leader: Begon the Brave
Faith: The Goddess of the Sea
Emblem: An iceberg in the sea

Castle of Ylinor in the North Beyond the North

Lord of Ylinor: Gereon Thorn
Faith: The God of War
Emblem: A wyvern on a dark green field
Emblem of the Lord's House: A white tiger on a red field

Stonegate

Guardian Commander: Reynald Karford
Faith: None
Emblem: A red-and-black sun, with spears for rays, on a white field
Emblem of the Guardian Commander's House: An axe on a brown field

Western Empire in the Continent of Kerth

Emperor: Odin Mud
Capital: Mirth
Faith: The God of Justice
Emblem: A red sun, with a white field
Emblem of the emperor's House: A shield, covered in blood, on a white field

Characters

Ager Barlow – Deceased. Former King of Tahryn.
Aghyr Barlow – Deceased. Former Governor of Tahryn.

Alan Ballard – Deceased. Borin Ballard's son.

Aleron – The wise of the elwyn.

Alice Asselin – Deceased. Aymer Asselin's daughter and King Thomas Egercoll's wife.

Althalos Baudry – Grand Master of Isisdor. He is presumed dead.

Amelia Reis – Deceased. Lady of Elmor and Sigor Endor's wife.

Anrai – Member of the Trinity of Death. His father was a giant.

Anton Loken – Captain of Ballar.

Arianna Erilor – Deceased. John Egercoll's wife.

Aron – Stonegate's Guardian.

Arthur Endor – Deceased. Syrella Endor's brother and Velhisya's father.

Avery Elford – Deceased. First King of Mynlands.

Aymer Asselin – Deceased. Former Governor of Oldlands who found murdered in his sleep.

Beatrice Egercoll – Deceased. Thomas Egercoll's sister and Queen Sophie's mother.

Begon the Brave – Leader of the Ice Islands.

Bernal Ballard – Deceased. First King of Ballar.

Bert Dilerion – A lord from Felador. Eleanor's brother.

Berta Loers – Ghost Soldier.

Borin Ballard – Governor of Ballar.

Brian the Sadist – Member of the Trinity of Death.

Brom Endor – Deceased. Lord of Elmor and Syrella Endor's uncle.

Byron the Sturdy – Deceased. Great warrior of the Ice Islands.

Daryn Endark – Lord Counsellor of Elmor.

Devan – Captain of Oldlands.

Doran Brau – Deceased. Peter Brau's son.

Edmund – High Priest of Elmor.

Edward Endor – Deceased. Former Governor of Elmor and father to Syrella, Sigor and Arthur Endor.

Edward Ewing – Man of Isisdor's City Guard.

Eimon Asselin – Lord of Oldlands, Aymer Asselin's son and Alice Asselin's brother.

Eleanor Dilerion – A lady of Felador. Bert Dilerion's sister.

Elliot – A lad from a village troubled by his past.

Ellin – Velhisya's mother.

Emery – Captain of Ballar.

Emil Ballard – Deceased. Borin Ballard's son.

Emma Egercoll – Deceased. Thomas Egercoll's sister, Robert Thorn's wife and Walter Thorn's mother.

Eric Stone – Governor of Tahryn.

Erneas – Deceased. Grand Master of Gaeldeath.

Euneas Molor – Deceased. Grand Master of Felador.

Favian Egercoll – Deceased. Thomas Egercoll's brother.

Frederic Abbot – Captain of Isisdor.

George Thorn – Deceased. First King of Knightdorn and Walter's grandfather.

Gerald Thorn – Deceased. Uncle to George Thorn and former Lord of Ylinor.

Gereon Thorn – Lord of Ylinor. Robert Thorn's brother and Walter's uncle.

Gervin Gerber – Royal Guard of Isisdor.

Girard – Deceased. Grand Master of Oldlands.

Giren Barlow – Slave. Aghyr Barlow's son.

Gregory Egercoll – Deceased. Thomas Egercoll's brother.

Gregory Mollet – Lord Counsellor of Isisdor.

Grelnor Lengyr – Lord Counsellor of Elmor.

Hann – Deceased. Grand Master of Mynlands.

Henry Delamere – Deceased. Former Governor of Felador and Sophie's father.

Henry Endor – Deceased. Sigor Endor's son.

Hereweald Delamere – Deceased. Former Governor of Felador and Henry Delameres's father.

Hugh – Captain of Isisdor.

Hurwig – Elliot's hawk.

Jacob Hewdar – Lord of Elmor.

Jahon – General of Elmor.

James Segar – Deceased. Captain of Elmor.

Jarin – Stonegate's Guardian.

John Egercoll – Deceased. Former Governor of Elirehar. Father to Thomas, Favian, Beatrice, Emma and Gregory Egercoll.

John, the Long Arm – Bounty Hunter.

Lain Hale – Deceased. Former Governor of Vylor and Liher's older brother.

Launus Eymor – Governor of Mynlands.

Laurana Brau – Lady of Isisdor. Peter Brau's wife.

Laurent Mill – Deceased. Lord of Oldlands. He died when Lain Hale attacked to his castle.

Leghor – Leader of the centaurs.

Leonhard Payne – Healer of Felador.

Leuric – High Priest of Elmor.

Liher Hale – Governor of Vylor.

Linaria Endor – Captain of Elmor and Syrella Endor's daughter.

Loren Elford – Deceased. Former Governor of Mynlands.

Lothar Hale – Liher's younger brother.

Magor the Terrible – Leader of the giants. He is presumed dead.

Manhon Egercoll – King of Elirehar and brother to Thomyn Egercoll. He was one of the seven riders of the pegasi.

Maris Magon – Deceased. Lord of the Knights and Regent of Elirehar. He served as a regent of Elirehar by the time that Thomas Egercoll became king, and he kept his title after Thomas's death.

Maygar Asselin – Deceased. Former King of Oldlands.

Mehryn – Deceased. Grand Master of Elmor.

Mengon Barlow – Deceased. First King of Tahryn.

Merhya Endor – Captain of Elmor and Syrella Endor's daughter.

Merick – Captain of Isisdor.
Morys Bardolf – A lord from Wirskworth.
Myren Endor – First King of Elmor.
Odin Mud – Self-proclaimed Emperor of Kerth.
Patrick Degore – Lord Counsellor of Isisdor.
Peter Brau – General of Isisdor.
Philip Segar – Peter Brau's squire and James Segar's son.
Renier Torin – Deceased. Grand Master of Ballar.
Reynald Karford – Guardian Commander of Stonegate.
Ricard Karford – Governor of Oldlands.
Richard Lamont – Captain of Isisdor. George Thorn made him captain when he resolved a siege by Lain Hale against the castle of Laurent Mill.
Righor – A centaur.
Robert Thorn – Deceased. Former Governor of Gaeldeath. Father to Walter Thorn and husband to Emma Egercoll.
Robyn – Captain of Isisdor.
Rolf Breandan – Member of the Trinity of Death. He is known as Short Death.
Sadon Burns – Most powerful lord of Elmor.
Saron Gray – Lord of Gaeldeath.
Selwyn Brau – Lord of Isisdor and Peter Brau's son.
Selyn – A lady of Elirehar.
Sermor Burns – Deceased. Sadon Burns' only son.
Shilor Penn – Lord Counsellor of Elmor.
Sigor Endor – Deceased. Syrella Endor's older brother.
Sindel Brau – Deceased. Peter Brau's son.
Sophie Delamere – Queen of Knightdorn.
Sygar Reis – Lord Counsellor of Elmor.
Syrella Endor – Governor of Elmor.
Thindor – The last pegasus of the world. He is presumed dead.
Thomas Egercoll – Deceased. Former King of Knightdorn and Alice

Asselin's husband.

Thomyn Egercoll – First King of Elirehar. He was one of the seven riders of the pegasi.

Thorold – Grand Master of Elirehar. He is presumed dead.

Velhisya Endor – Syrella Endor's niece. Her mother was an elwyn.

Vyresar Tobley – Guard of the City of Heavens.

Walter Thorn – Governor of Gaeldeath who rebels against the Queen of Knightdorn.

Will – Captain of Ballar.

William – A Defender of the Sharp Swords.

William Osgar – Deceased. Lord of the Knights.

Wymond – Deceased. Grand Master of Tahryn.

Zehir – A centaur.

The Endless Night

Elliot walked in the dark, deep in thought. *Am I ready?* The words echoed endlessly in his mind. He had longed for this moment more than any other. He remembered how, a long time ago, he had shouted out that he was ready. But now? He had never imagined that when the time came for him to leave, he would have to bid farewell to the person he loved more than anything else.

He carried on walking, lost in thought. He sometimes wondered why he was unafraid of all he had to achieve. The reality was that he didn't really know how he felt.

A sound startled him out of his reverie. He looked amongst the trees, but the light of the moon was weak that night. He didn't expect anyone to be there. Elliot stood still, listening—sure now he had heard footsteps.

"We must be quick!" a voice came. "If they realise that we abandoned our patrol before the battle, they'll have our heads on spikes."

"It's worth the risk," a second voice spoke. "You know that I fight better if I have women the night before."

His village was the only one for miles. No doubt they were headed there. He was alarmed—he had to run...he had to warn them...

A third voice called out, "Who's there?"

The light of a torch fell upon Elliot as his hesitation and momentary panic kept him riveted in his place. Hurried steps rushed towards him just as the sound of a sword being unsheathed reached his ears.

He took a few steps out of the light and tried to hide—*how many are there?* He crouched and crept through the trees, but the footsteps came now from all sides, and the light washed over him once more, pinning him in place.

"Don't move!" shouted the man holding the torch.

Three men, their swords lifted, approached—he was not armed.

"I'm just a poor villager," said Elliot, raising his arms. "I beg you, don't hurt me."

The men laughed.

"If you have women to give us, we might think about it," the man spoke again. His eyes glinted viciously in the torchlight, matched by the snarling tiger on his jerkin.

"He must be from the village we're looking for, Hick."

Hick threw a look of approval at his comrade and lowered the torch towards Elliot's face.

"Will you take us to your women, or do you prefer to die?" he spat out, laughing.

Elliot remained silent.

"Lads that live in the fields are usually brave. But it looks like you're a coward."

"I've always been a coward," Elliot responded.

"Better a coward and alive, than brave and dead!" applauded Hick. "Show us the way to your village," he added, returning his sword to its sheath.

Elliot lunged, reaching out with his right hand, and pulled the sword from Hick's sheath, then hit him across the face with its hilt. The man fell to the ground, and the torch slipped from his hand.

Wary now, Hick's comrades lowered their swords towards him. Elliot brandished his, then feigned an attack. The two men stepped back in alarm, losing their balance. As they fell, Elliot darted in and slit their throats.

He looked at the blood spurting from the torn flesh, then moved towards Hick, who was struggling to get up.

"Are more on their way to my village?"

"Who are you?" The words were mangled by broken teeth. Hick made an attempt to stand and fell to the ground again.

"Speak up!" Elliot ordered, anger erupting inside of him. For the first time, a man responsible for all he had lost was at his mercy...

"I'll kill you, you cunt!" Hick got up, staggering, and lurched to attack.

Elliot punched him in the face. The man sank to the ground, and Elliot leaned over him, bringing his sword to Hick's chin.

"Nobody knows we are here!" The tone of Hick's voice now revealed his terror. "Let me go! Have mercy!"

"Elliot?"

Elliot turned abruptly, keeping his blade at Hick's throat, and saw a small boy had picked up the fallen torch.

"What happened?" the boy asked, looking at the two bodies and then at the fallen man in front of Elliot.

"Why are you here, Oliver?" The child was the last person Elliot would have wanted there.

"The Master...," Oliver stammered. "He isn't well."

"Go back!" Elliot ordered. "I'm coming."

The boy dropped the torch and started running. Elliot watched him go and was glad he didn't look back—no ten-year-old should witness what would come next.

"MERCY!" Hick begged.

Elliot plunged the sword into Hick's chest with all his might. Blood burbled out of the hole in the jerkin, and Hick slumped, his face growing slack. Elliot took one last look at the lifeless body and began to run towards the village as fast as he could.

The Battle of Ramerstorm

"We're not ready. Our men are not enough."

"Pardon, General?"

Peter Brau hadn't realized he'd spoken aloud. "Nothing. Just an old man's mutters." After years of war, the queen's armies had yet to win a battle against the usurper, so morale could hardly sink any lower. Even considering that, the general in command shouldn't be admitting defeat before the first arrow loosed. He raised his voice so the ranks to either side of him would hear. "Today, we turn this tide. Walter Thorn's army will break on Ramerstorm's walls! On the walls of the White City!"

"For Ramerstorm!" Captain Robyn called.

"For Ramerstorm!" The cry rippled down the lines.

Behind them towered the walls of Ramerstorm, the walls of the White City, the final city in Walter's path to Iovbridge and the throne he'd killed so many to reach.

Peter looked at his army. Blue cloaks bearing the Pegasus beside the Seven Swords rippled under the blazing sun. A little further off, a few black cloaks with the Hawk of Ballar entered the mix. His gaze turned upon his son, tall like his father, dark-haired with Peter's curls and his mother's honey eyes.

"You'll organise the archers on the battlements, Selwyn. You're not needed here."

Selwyn looked at him, bewildered. "I'll fight by your side!" The stubborn look Peter knew so well set his son's jaw and mouth.

Peter shook his head. "You're the best archer our army has. I need you on the wall!"

"You can't keep trying to keep me out of harm's way."

"I'm not trying to."

"My brothers died. Your sons died. Stop pretending they didn't." Selwyn spun around to obey, fury in his stride.

The boy was right. Peter couldn't protect him. The walls would probably not shelter him for long. Peter had built his strategy on the expectation of failure. Why else meet an army twice theirs in size outside the walls of the city? He couldn't allow Ramerstorm to be encircled. There had to be an avenue of retreat.

Peter breathed out slowly, his heart heavy. How could a woman crowned queen when she was still a child contend with one of the most bloodthirsty men to set foot in Knightdorn? Walter would slay her as he had slain every other member of her family.

Peter mounted his horse and tried to order his thoughts. He had to stay focused. "Robyn," he shouted to the captain closest to him, a short, broad-shouldered, long-bearded man, "I want you to keep our troops close to the wall. Let the archers earn their pay."

A general shouldn't be laying out tactics on the day of battle with the enemy in sight. However, if he'd given his officers time to think through their orders, they would realise that the city was yet another sacrifice in a long string of such sacrifices across a game they'd been losing for years. And men with defeat in mind do not fight well. Fear would spread, panic would consume the city. The lie had to be maintained. Victory was not only possible, it was certain.

"Captain Merick, I want the cavalry to hold their position. As soon as the enemy comes closer, flank them. Find Ballar's officers, and notify them."

The two captains nodded and hastened to give orders.

Suddenly, a trumpet call blasted through the stifling air. In the middle distance, innumerable red banners, each emblazoned with a tiger, flapped in the hands of Walter Thorn's slaves. Sixteen thousand men headed for Ramerstorm—twelve thousand cavalrymen along with four thousand foot-soldiers advanced slowly in formation, silver shields reflecting the sunlight. Brown sprinkled the field of red banners—the hammer, axe, and anvil of the former Oldlands Kingdom among Walter's tigers. A thousand men of Kelanger—Oldland's regional capital—sent by Ricard Karford to march beside Walter Thorn's soldiers.

Peter's chest tightened. The enemy's forces were too many for his army. Archers in the rearguard marched with countless arrows in their quivers. Soldiers with swords and shields made of the most expensive steel stood behind the cavalry. Gaeldeath boasted more cavalrymen than any other region in Knightdorn.

Peter waited in the heat, sweating in his armour, resigned to the carnage the day would bring. Hope had long since left him, but duty kept him at his post. He watched the dust rise beneath thousands of tramping feet.

Walter's army stopped out of arrow range. The cavalry split in two, and a gilded chariot charged down the centre like a bolt of lightning. Two jet-black horses with golden helmets drew its load, a blond, long-haired man held the reins, a white tiger by his side. The chariot ground to a halt, and the man shouted for a group of soldiers to follow him, then made for White City.

Fear gnawed at Peter. Even in the midst of his army, with the walls of Ramerstorm behind him, no part of him wanted to meet this challenge, though duty compelled. He shook his reins and left the ranks, motioning for Robyn and veteran soldiers to follow him.

The two parties met halfway between the opposing armies. Walter Thorn greeted them and dismounted from his chariot with an icy smile. The man put Peter's functional battle gear to shame. Walter's armour was ornamented with gold and silver. He wore thick pauldrons studded with colourful rubies, and two jeweled clasps held his long, crimson cloak in place. The tiger dismounted with a roar. Walter hardly seemed to have aged since the war began, though he had been younger than Selwyn's twenty years when the conflict started.

"It's always such a pleasure to see a man I have crushed time and time again on the battlefield." Thorn smiled and offered a mocking bow. "I hope the queen will be prudent enough to avert this battle. It's time Her Majesty accepted my supremacy, or she will soon meet her ancestors."

Peter dismounted and glanced at Walter's four attendants. Their faces were masked, and their dark suits of armour fully covered their bodies. Three wore blood-red cloaks, while the fourth's was black. Peter had met the Trinity of Death and the Ghost Soldiers before—Ghost Soldiers were trained by Walter himself, and the Trinity of Death comprised the three most capable Ghosts in the world. On the right was Rolf Breandan from Mynlands. He was short—slightly taller than a dwarf—with a tiger-seal carved on his dark armour. Next to him stood Anrai, a gigantic man. Many believed the blood of giants ran through his veins. The centre of his breastplate was not ornamented with the tiger but with a single, black, winged creature. Brian the Sadist completed the trio, bearing the white tiger on his breastplate, a clasp in the shape of a ship securing his cloak.

The fourth attendant, all in black, was the most lethal woman ever to be born. Berta Loers was Walter's most trusted Ghost.

"You're a disgrace to your House," Peter retorted. "A murderer driven by greed. You've no honour, no principles, and no right to the throne!"

Walter narrowed his eyes. He was taller, stronger, and younger than Peter, as capable of killing Peter in a duel as he was of defeating the queen's armies in the field. His fingers strayed to the sword glittering at his belt, touching the ornate symbols carved on its hilt.

"One more word, and I'll feed your tongue to Annys!" He nodded to the tiger, who watched Peter with blue eyes that were a match for Walter's. Both held an unnerving hunger. "My father almost ruined our house for the sake of Thomas Egercoll! So, I killed him. You think I would show more mercy to the queen or her family?"

"All of us owe a duty to the Pegasus Tamers—"

Walter chuckled, then burst into laughter just as his tiger roared. "Pegasus Tamers?" His eyes welled with tears of mirth. "A creature that existed four hundred years ago... Where was pegasus when I cut off Thomas Egercoll's head?" he spat. "I haven't come all this way to talk about legends. Will you give up the throne in peace or will you force me to kill every man in your army, along with your beloved queen?"

"A murderer like you will never become king!" Peter met Walter's stare without flinching.

Walter's face contorted with rage. "Brace yourself for battle! In a few days, I'll seize Iovbridge and leave none living. I hope you're ready to bury your last son." Walter let out a sardonic smile and, in one single move, lifted himself up onto the golden chariot. He began to head back to his troops, followed by his attendants and Annys.

Peter mounted his horse and galloped quickly towards White City. He had expected nothing from the parley, and he had got nothing. It was just a veneer of civilization over the slaughter to come. He worried for his son.

The attack started almost before Peter regained the ranks. Walter Thorn's thousands began their march to the beat of drums.

Peter looked up toward the parapets on the wall, finding his son standing by the aging Governor, Borin Ballard, bow at the ready.

The first cavalry formation closed in ahead of the foot soldiers.

"Archers, loose!" Peter yelled, and his officers relayed the order to the walls with the pre-arranged signal.

Arrows filled the sky. A few of the charging horses fell, screaming, spilling their riders. Not enough. Walter's forces were well armoured, arrows spinning away from steel helms, shattering against breastplates. The officers hollered to the archers under their command. "Loose!" And again, "Loose!" as the wave of cavalry devoured the remaining distance beneath thundering hooves.

With Peter's cavalry moving to attempt to flank their adversary, the foot soldiers in the vanguard raised their pikes to meet the charge.

Walter's forces smashed into the front line. Lances pierced flesh, swords rent armour and sliced limbs as more and more men dropped to the ground, blood fountaining from ruined throats. White City's archers continued to feather the enemy whilst Peter's cavalry fought to flank them.

Fiery arrows and huge stones began to hurtle towards Ramerstorm's walls. Walter's allies, Ricard Karford's men, had brought siege engines from their homeland. The eastern tower began to fail within the first few solid hits, while the stones were already crushing the men positioned on the battlements. Peter raised his eyes in terror, looking for his son. Somehow, amid the chaos, he saw Selwyn running towards the western tower of the city alongside a small number of remaining archers.

Most of the defenders in the vanguard had fallen to the cavalry's devastating charge. In the aftermath, the Ghost Soldiers once again confirmed their gory reputation: they killed with ease any man they crossed paths with, while at the same time their fiery arrows covered the sky, enveloping White City in flames.

Time passes in strange ways within a battle, sometimes crawling, sometimes leaping ahead. It seemed only minutes had passed, and already Peter's army had broken, whilst behind him Ramerstorm's walls were crumbling.

In the heart of the fight, Peter struggled to regroup his troops, sending runners to direct his captains. Merick came stumbling away from a knot of men locked in combat, his armour bloodstained. "We've lost all our cavalry, and our frontline has collapsed. We have to retreat."

"We can't lose Ramerstorm so easily!" Peter had expected to retreat, but not like this, not in shambles. He'd wanted the ground before the city littered with the enemy's dead.

"They've crushed us! We can either die here or withdraw to Iovbridge to regroup," urged the captain.

A man in a brown Oldlands cloak came out of the fray, charging towards them on horseback. Peter lifted his sword, threw himself out of the lance's path, and somehow cut the man from his saddle as he passed. "Retreat!" he shouted at the top of his lungs.

Ramerstorm's gate opened with a deafening boom, and the soldiers ran through it into the city as the remaining vanguard became a rear-guard, trying to hold the enemy back long enough for their retreat.

Peter entered the city running, sweating, and breathing hard. The gate rattled shut not long after him. Far too few of his soldiers had made it back behind the walls with him.

He leapt from his mare and ran for the steps to the battlements. Every inch of his passage through the half-ruined western tower was bloodied and strewn with dead bodies. The staircase was in ruins in many places, yet he managed to reach the top, heart pounding. The scene beyond the city stopped him in his tracks.

The spectacle below flooded him with a sorrow so deep it hurt like a physical wound. Hundreds of his men lay dead. Even as Peter watched, Walter passed through the red banners of his troops in his golden chariot. He tugged at the reins and stepped down onto the bloodstained ground less than a spear throw from the walls, the white tiger following behind. Against all odds, his eyes found Peter amid the ruined stonework. A sardonic smile spread across his face.

A lone figure rushed from Ramerstorm's fallen as if seeking to take on Walter singled handedly in the midst of his victorious army. With horror Peter realized it was Robyn. The valiant captain had stayed behind to give them time to retreat.

"No!" Peter shook his head, unwilling to watch, unable to look away.

Walter drew his sword in a flash, and the steel rent the air. Captain Robyn's arm hung from his torso by a thread of flesh, gouting crimson.

Walter glanced at his tiger. "He's yours," he murmured.

The tiger pounced and began to devour the captain. Walter chuckled, glancing once more towards Peter. Robyn's screams choked off, and with a sense of loss and shame, General Peter Brau turned to organize his escape.

The smoke had begun to engulf the twilight air. An elderly man looked up through a hut window and coughed bloodied sputum into an earthen pot. He closed his eyes, weary, burdened by sorrow. How many more would have to perish for his mistake? Still, he couldn't change the past.

The man lay on a straw mattress, every inch of his body in pain. "How did I grow so old and so ill?" he muttered to the straw. Elliot entered the hut holding a wooden bowl. Almost seventeen, broad in the chest, with short brown hair and light green eyes, he stood taller than most men. Too young, the old man thought, to bear the burden that fate had placed upon him.

"How are you feeling?" Elliot asked in a tender voice tinged with sadness.

"I've seen better days."

"White City has fallen."

"I sensed it," murmured the man. "The time has come. You must remember your training. You must bury your rage and pain in order to help Knightdorn. You're a knight, not a simple soldier—don't you ever forget that!"

Elliot looked piercingly at him. "You're the only family I've got left."

The aged man watched him with a gentle smile. "It's time you met your real family... Bear in mind, though, that pain, rage, and anger will never lead you to serenity—only patience, faith, and love can do that. Your father would be proud of you."

"I won't let you down." Unshed tears brightened Elliot's eyes. The man appreciated that—it had been a long time since anyone cried for him, and if not now, on the edge of death, then when?

He held the boy's hand and stared deep into his eyes. The sight of Elliot's face filled him with serenity, even the pain in his chest seemed to fade. His eyelids grew heavy, and a sleep that wasn't sleep reached up for him. The old man stopped fighting it. He met his death with a smile.

Elliot didn't know how long he stood holding the old man's hand. Long enough for his tears to dry and for the hand to grow cold. Finally, he let go. At the doorway, he shot one last glance at the soulless body, then walked out into the dusk. Villagers crowded outside the hut—the people he had grown up with sharing his grief.

"He's gone," he stammered.

The villagers hastened to embrace and comfort him, but he pulled back, asking them to leave him alone. He walked toward the outskirts of the settlement, watching the distant smoke spread across the sky, swallowing stars. An omen. A call to arms. He was thinking of all the things he had to do, all the things he had been longing to do for years. Yet now, he didn't feel the same impatience. It wasn't fear either—he simply felt lonely, as if a huge part of himself had vanished forever, and now that the path stretched ahead, he felt desperately alone. Directly overhead, a single star glowed in the sooty sky. Elliot's hand tightened on the hilt of his sword. He clutched it with all his might and whispered to himself, "The time has come." He was ready to set off on the journey he had long been waiting for.

The Retreat

The soldiers marched towards Iovbridge as fast as they could. Behind them, Walter's forces were still pouring in through Ramerstorm's shattered gate. It would take the enemy some time to realise that the bulk of Peter's army had escaped from the rear of the city, sacrificing it to their invasion.

Peter rode at the front of the column, guiding his men towards the ancient road that led through the Vale of Gods. The general ignored his body's complaints. He was too old for battle, but who else would stand in his place?

He knew the queen would be disappointed when they got to Iovbridge. Peter had left a handful of men behind Ramerstorm's crumbling walls to delay Walter's victory. They wouldn't be able to hold out for long. But they would give the remaining soldiers time to open enough of a lead to reach Iovbridge.

Captain Robyn's death haunted Peter even as he rode. Robyn had been one of his ablest men, and still, he had succumbed to the first swing of Walter's sword. What chance did any of them stand against the man?

The dusk would soon give way to darkness. Behind them, the smoke of Ramerstorm continued to poison the air.

Selwyn's voice broke the muffled tramp of feet. "Father!"

Peter pulled at the reins of his black mare and looked back. Borin Ballard had fallen off his horse. Peter turned his steed around and galloped towards the old man.

"I can't carry on," Borin panted as they helped him to his feet.

"Lord Ballard, we'll be at the palace within the hour. Then, you'll have all the time in the world to get some rest." Peter looked back pointedly at the glow of the not-so-distant flames. "I hardly have to spell out the alternative. We need to reach Iovbridge and inform the queen of Ramerstorm's fate."

Borin was breathing with difficulty. "I can't ride," he whispered.

Selwyn shouted to some men to bring the old man water. "I'll carry you on my horse, my lord," he offered.

A Ramerstorm soldier approached Borin, holding a small flask. Lord Borin reached for the water only for the soldier to lunge at him with a knife—so quick that Peter barely understood what he was seeing. Selwyn reacted quickly, thrusting his sword through the traitor's chest. Lord Borin fell back with a cry, having narrowly missed having his throat slashed open.

Peter jumped off his mare and ran to the dying soldier. "Why did you attack your governor?"

The soldier tried to raise his head, letting out a death rattle. Peter lifted his neck, trying to keep him alive. Selwyn's blade still stood from the man's chest, clearly piercing a lung.

"I'm sorry," the man's words were strangled as he breathed his last. A few metres away, Selwyn was trying to lift the governor. Borin stood up with difficulty.

"What happened?" he mumbled in confusion.

Frowning, Peter stood. "I hope he's the only man with Walter's gold in his pocket. He's been paid to kill you. Walter wants Ballar's council to choose a new governor, one he can control."

"The men on my council are dead!" the old man said. "There's nobody to take my place."

Peter eyed the failed assassin and wondered if there were others paid to kill Borin. When would they have a better chance than in the confusion of a retreat? "Who is this young man?" He nodded at the dead body.

Borin approached unsteadily and looked at the dead lad. "He was one of my personal guards."

Peter's frown deepened. "We have to move on. Merick, you and your most trusted men are to form a protective circle around Lord Borin."

"You think there will be others?" mumbled Borin.

Peter shook his head slowly. It was a terrifying thought. Traitors inside the palace could attempt the murder of more than just Borin. And given Walter's methods, it was a distinct possibility.

"We have to carry on," repeated Peter. "Lord Ballard, can you ride?"

"I will!" said the old man. He raised his voice, calling out to soldiers watching. "I've lost my two sons while fighting this man. I've lost all my counsellors and vassal lords, but I won't die by the hand of my own soldiers! Whoever wants to kill me, a man who shed his own blood to save Ballar, may step forward now. I challenge him to single combat!" yelled the governor.

No one stirred. Peter shot a glance at the men of Ramerstorm. Their black cloaks were flapping gently in the wind. They had a long way to go, and most of them were foot soldiers.

"Selwyn, carry the governor on your horse. Merick, a close watch!"

Merick nodded. "General, you need to be protected too."

Reluctantly, Peter nodded and let the captain assign three men to watch his back.

Several miles remained before Elliot would reach Iovbridge. He was riding at a gallop, hair flying behind him. He could see the walls in the distance. Finally! The home his parents had known.

Even the wind of his charge wouldn't clear his mind. He tried in vain to order his thoughts. He'd spent all his life beside a man who was gone forever. His Master had been both father and mother to him, the man who had taught him everything he needed to know in order to become a knight, all on condition that he never sought revenge.

Elliot remembered his Master smiling at him after a gruelling trial. *"You did great!"*

"You asked me to vow that no matter how powerful I become, I will never seek revenge. I will use my sword only to protect Knightdorn in the name of peace and prosperity, like my parents did... How do you know I will keep my promise as soon as I complete my training? How do you know I won't be blinded by a desire for revenge?"

His Master had looked at him with great affection. *"I know you'll honour your vow, for you are a knight. A knight and defender of peace in Knightdorn is of value only if he has honour. I also know that you want to carry on with your parents' work,"* the Master had replied in a serene voice.

"My parents died so there would be peace in a world in which nobody wanted any peace."

That hadn't been true though, and over the years the drillmaster had shown Elliot that the common folk yearned for a peace denied them by men like Walter Thorn, the rich who wanted more riches, the powerful who wanted more power.

Elliot had sworn to stop Walter, but still the matter of revenge stood between him and his Master.

"Walter Thorn must die. Whether I kill him in order to protect the people of Knightdorn or out of revenge makes no difference."

The Master shot him an intense look. *"It makes a world of difference! Killing a man in order to protect the kingdom is completely different from killing him in order to avenge yourself. Revenge will make you seek him out. Your heart will be filled with rage and hate, so you will risk lives to get to him. A knight's purpose is only prosperity for others—he doesn't duel or drag men into battle for personal gain. You will do it only when the time comes for you to duel with this man in order to protect Knightdorn and its people. This is the most important lesson I can give you."*

As Elliot tore down the road to Iovbridge, his Master's words flashed through his mind. He didn't want to let him down. Ramerstorm had fallen, and he knew the queen's men would come back as fast as they could to organise Iovbridge's defence for the final showdown. A battle Walter had been anticipating for years.

The queen stood no chance of winning this battle. Walter had conquered almost the entire kingdom and would marshal the armies of all his allies before setting off for the Palace of the Dawn. Nevertheless, they had almost twenty days before he would be able to gather all his forces in Ramerstorm. Walter was arrogant yet had never underestimated his opponents. Even now that his dominance was more certain, he wouldn't attempt to lay siege to Iovbridge without his vassal lords' armies.

A while earlier, Elliot's Master had heard that Walter was marching toward Ballar, mainly with his cavalry and some swift foot-soldiers, leaving behind a large segment of the army of Gaeldeath and his allies. An attack timed to disrupt the harvest.

The real purpose behind Walter's attack against Ramerstorm was to cut off Iovbridge before laying siege to it, thus limiting its supplies. Most of Isisdor's crops were in the Vale of Gods, close to the border with Ballar. With Ramerstorm in his hands, Walter could have control over the Vale of Gods, stealing the harvest.

Walter's plan, thorough as it was, at least gave the queen time to act. Elliot planned to be there to advise her. He rode on, not slackening his speed as Iovbridge came more clearly into view ahead of him, bigger than he had ever imagined.

Peter looked behind him. The men were marching wearily across the Vale of Gods. A contingent of the archers who had stayed a while longer in Ramerstorm to create the illusion of a last stand were catching up from behind. Fewer of them than Peter had hoped for. Ahead, Iovbridge waited, and Peter came armed only with bad news. The final stand at the Knightdorn's capital, which had seemed so inevitable for so long, was hard upon them. Within weeks at most, Walter and his entire force would stand before the walls.

The smoke spreading across the sky would have signalled their defeat to the queen. They had to organise and regroup swiftly. Reports and experience suggested they had almost twenty days before Walter's allies reached Ramerstorm.

Peter had to convince the queen to draw up a plan for her escape from Iovbridge in case it fell. *When it fell.* It was a fact that she would never agree to such a retreat, but there was no way he would let her fall into Walter's hands.

As if that were not enough, she had to be surrounded by trustworthy men in case there were traitors in their midst conspiring to assassinate her. Borin, too, was in a perilous position. If he were to be assassinated within Iovbridge's walls, the refugees from Ballar would likely riot. Such internal conflict was the last thing they wanted.

The queen and her council had had the foresight to transfer the elderly and the women and children of Ramerstorm, along with villagers from the surrounding Ballar countryside, to Iovbridge in safety, several days before the battle. Truth be told, there were decrees that protected civilians during periods of war, but Walter disregarded all of these. As soon as his men entered the cities of his sworn enemies, they killed, raped, and razed to the ground whatever they came across.

Before nightfall, the huge gates of Iovbridge slowly came into sight. It was the grandest city in the Kingdom of Knightdorn, the ancestral home of the elwyn, with the famed Palace of the Dawn and its surrounding verdant gardens. Every time he returned to Iovbridge, he couldn't help marvelling at it.

Two concentric walls encircled the city, all the way to the Harbour of the Scarlet Sea. The outer wall was short—seven metres tall—with round, tiled towers, while the inner wall was more than twelve metres high. Many square towers jutted out every hundred yards or so, counting out its length. The stone was an amber colour, and the ornate Aznar's Gate—named after the first wise man of the elwyn race—was ornamented with gold and silver.

The ancestors of Kelanger's men had crafted their most exquisite creation when they reconstructed Iovbridge after the rebellion against the first King of Knightdorn. The idea of this beautiful city, the cornerstone of Thomas Egercolls' reign, falling into a Thorn's hands again was horrifying.

The soldiers approached Iovbridge and went up the stone path leading to the main gate. Peter distinguished a crowd of people jostling against the length of the inner wall's battlements. Although the height made it difficult for him to see clearly, he was sure the queen was there waiting for their arrival.

The gleaming gates opened, and Peter kicked his horse towards the bronze gates of the inner wall that were opened up in turn. Countless families were waiting for them—they wanted to hear about their relatives, most of whom had not come back and never would. Robyn's wife would be waiting. Knowing that he would soon have to tell her what he could scarcely admit to himself unnerved him.

Peter left the foot-soldiers behind in the care of their officers. Accompanied by Borin, Selwyn, and a handful of mounted troops, he pulled ahead, wanting to reach the heart of the city as fast as he could. They were running out of time. He had to call a council meeting. His son followed behind him, together with the rest of the men, while his horse sped through the paved paths and the bronze arches. He crossed the Square of the Elder Races, heading towards Blossom Road—the most commercial part of the city, stretching from the Path of the Seven Swords to the Temple of the Unknown God. A rosy hue spread along its deserted alleys. Even in the Fishermen's Square, which skirted the Harbour of the Scarlet Sea, there weren't hordes of people.

He turned into the Path of the Seven Swords, leading to the Palace of the Dawn. Peter emerged from beneath an arch depicting two crossed swords, and the palace lay in front of him. The House of Egercoll's gold coat of arms adorned its entrance, next to the Seven Swords. The pegasus was so artfully chiselled by Oldlanders that it seemed it would come alive at any moment. The royal building was built out of moonstone, a stone found only in the mines of Wirskworth. The palace glittered like white gold, and a dome the colour of the sky towered over it. The Scarlet Sea lay to the east of the splendid building, many parts of which offered an idyllic view of its waves. It was a work of architecture too perfect, too delicate, for the war that would soon come swirling around its gates. And here was Peter Brau, failed general, carrying his defeat to lay before the queen, burdened with evil news for good people. He sucked in a deep breath and let it out slowly.

Peter tugged at the reins and dismounted, followed by Borin and the rest of the mounted men. Surrounded by lush green gardens, the palace yard was crowded with people. The scent of the cypress trees pricked Peter's nostrils as he walked with heavy feet. Queen Sophie was there waiting for them. Her long brown hair touched her shoulders, and her bright blue eyes looked more downcast than ever. Sophie wore a silk, cherry-red dress, and her cloak, studded with gems and stones, was embroidered with gold thread, but she hadn't put on her crown. Next to her stood her commanders' wives, who waited impatiently for news of their husbands—as was always the case after battle.

Peter felt his stomach knot. He walked ahead, followed by his captains. It was then that he saw her—a dark-skinned woman with almond-shaped eyes, dressed in a dark green cloak, looking at their company, apprehensive. Margaret, her little boy in her arms, was looking for her husband. The sense of dread Peter felt grew in intensity. He approached the woman and boy, pulling out his sword and taking a bow. Already she was shaking, her fingers white where she gripped her child too hard.

Peter didn't need to speak. His pale face and inability to meet her eyes told the whole story. And still he said the words, compelled by duty and the regard of his queen.

"Robyn is dead. I'm sorry," he faltered, trying to hold back his tears. He turned from Margaret's silent, twisting pain, and faced the queen amid her glittering courtiers. "Many hundreds have fallen, and Walter has Ramerstorm. His armies will stand in the shadow of your walls within three weeks."

The Unexpected Visitor

Queen Sophie walked alone, several attendants trailing respectfully. Robyn was dead! She couldn't believe it. Yet another of her best captains had fallen in the battle against her cousin.

General Peter had recounted everything there was to know, and the weight of it had settled on Sophie's shoulders, both as a friend and as queen of the nation. More blood on Walter's hands, more wives and children who would never see their loved ones again. How many more had to die because of the man who had slaughtered all her family?

Sophie wished she was still that child in Aquarine, young and dreamy-eyed. The girl who had wanted to become a member of the Order of the Healers, who dreamt of becoming one of the most renowned healers in Knightdorn, living a happy life by the lakes of Aquarine. But now her business was dealing with the deaths of her people. More every day. And Walter was on his way, the final step of his path to her throne. He would be at her gates within a month.

Sophie thought back to when news had arrived of a much earlier attack, a time when Walter's battles had been far away and her uncle bore the burden of the crown.

That day had been scorching hot. Young Sophie and her mother had returned to the Castle of Knowledge in Aquarine and found it in commotion. On reaching the ancestral home of the House of Delamere, Sophie and her mother found her uncle talking to her father, his voice raised. The two men had turned awkwardly to greet them.

"Beatrice! You're back! The king has just arrived from Iovbridge," her father had announced. *"Your uncle has brought you a present!"*

Sophie had shot a happy glance at her uncle Thomas, who remained stern, while her mother had hastened to embrace him.

"Thomas, what a pleasant surprise!" Sophie's mother had exclaimed. *"I noticed the royal knights outside the castle. Is everything all right?"*

The king frowned at his sister. *"I bring bad news from the north,"* he began. *"Walter's gathering his army in Tyverdawn. My informants say he'll soon attack the northern regions. We must stop him before it's too late. I need Aquarine's men."*

Sophie's heart fell. Her mother was similarly flabbergasted. *"Robert is rebelling against the king?"*

"No." Sophie's father shook his head. *"Robert left Tyverdawn, along with Emma and a few trusted soldiers, and rode toward Iovbridge. He's going to fight with us."*

"In other words, Robert will fight against his own son?" Beatrice was bewildered.

"The situation is critical," the king said. *"Gaeldeath's council accused Robert of high treason. Walter was chosen to replace his father as governor. Robert and Emma fled for Iovbridge and informed me that Walter is planning to conquer the former kingdoms of the north with the intention of controlling their armies and attacking the Crown."*

Sophie couldn't believe that Walter would make war on his own parents. It was bad enough that he'd rebelled against his king and uncle.

Sophie's father grimaced, looking almost as distressed as her mother. A war with their nephew was something neither of them wanted. *"My men and I will move towards Iovbridge, and from there we'll head for the Road of Steel. We must restrain Walter before it's too late,"* her father said.

The king nodded. *"As soon as I come back from Iovbridge, I'll order a guard to transfer Emma here, close to you. She's in a very bad state and fears we're going to kill Walter. Whatever he's done, he's still her son. I think under these dreadful circumstances, the best she can do is stay with her sister."* The king gave Sophie's mother a meaningful look.

Gripped by panic, Sophie had run to hug her father. As soon as she left his arms, King Thomas hastened to hug her. *"Don't worry, my dear girl. Your father will soon be back home."*

Sophie pushed the memory aside. That had been the last time she'd seen her father, and the recollection often haunted her. She shook the feeling off. Focus was required. Walter was close to achieving his greatest ambition: to seize her throne. She would soon face her cousin and was sure he would show no mercy. He had longed to be king for seventeen years. His attack on Iovbridge would be unrelenting. Sophie felt desperate, and she couldn't do a thing. No one could stop him, and the council meeting they were about to hold would just be a waste of time.

Sophie and her counsellors walked a little farther into the Tower of Aimor, which housed the chambers of the royal family. The sound of their footsteps reverberated off the stone floor until they reached a big wooden door with bronze cladding. Two guards pushed against the double doors, revealing a grand hall. Dozens of windows stretched along the room, Sophie was still impressed by the architecture of the place. The ceiling was high and for the greater part was embossed with ancient symbols, and a pegasus had been carved in its center. In the middle of this large room, thick pillars made of black marble formed a circle around a square table with tall oak chairs. Sophie took her place at its head, General Peter beside her. She glanced at the sombre-looking men seated in the rest of the chairs. Many of them were still armoured.

"We've all heard the terrible news," Sophie began tentatively. "I know that none of us have slept for days. Day will break soon, and, though all of you should have been with your families, we need to hold this council." She looked at the chair where Captain Robyn should have sat. "A great man sacrificed himself for us. A man, along with countless others, gave up everything in the hope that we may prevent Walter Thorn's tyranny. Before we continue, I would like to suggest that Captain Robyn be anointed as a knight and awarded the respective honours."

General Peter gave her a surprised look. "Your Majesty, the title of knight has been forbidden in Knightdorn by this very council."

Sophie felt anger every time she remembered the treachery committed by the last members of the Royal Guard who defiled the titles of knight and the lord of the knights, leading to their ban. The Royal Guard had conspired with Walter before the Battle of Aquarine. The day King Thomas Egercoll's armies were defeated, the royal knights stepped aside, allowing his assassination by Walter. The last lord of the knights, William Osgar, had been trained by Althalos Baudry, the same Grand Master who had trained Walter. William and the others were rewarded for their duplicity with death, carried out by Walter while they slept.

Sophie gathered her resolve. "One foul deed should not tarnish an ancient title. It's a drop of evil in the ocean of good that the order has done. Knights have always given us hope, and their restoration might be a ray of hope for our men."

The general looked doubtful. "I'm sorry, Queen Sophie, but the revival of a title associated with treason will not help us. Our troubles are deeper than that. We need to talk about how we are going to handle the siege that's com—"

"Because of Walter, all of Knightdorn lives in fear. The title of knighthood is dead and buried, and the Egercoll name has been debased! We must do something so the people of Isisdor may believe there is still hope. The knights have always represented courage. I wish Captain Robyn to be buried with knightly honours and for you to be sworn lord of the knights and protector of the queen until the end of your days," Sophie said.

Peter stood there with his mouth open.

"It's impossible for General Brau to be knighted! He's a father!" argued Captain Richard Lamont, a bumptious, stocky man with sparse blond hairs sprouting here and there on his scalp.

"Why can't knights have sons or daughters? Can somebody remind me?" Sophie asked, displeased by the man's objections.

"A knight's single sworn duty is to protect the ruler that he is serving—a family might distract him from his oath," replied Merick.

"General Peter lost two sons to protect his queen. He has already honoured his oath of knighthood." Sophie glared around the table, daring anyone to disagree.

"Your Majesty, we need to talk about Iovbridge's defence. Walter is approaching, and every passing moment we become more and more vulnerable. Knighting me won't change these facts."

"My decision is final," Sophie blurted. "It shall be formalised tomorrow. Now, I want to know exactly what happened during your return. From what I have understood, something happened to Lord Borin."

Merick was quick to respond. "One of his personal guards attacked him. Tried to cut his throat." The captain hadn't taken off his chain mail, and Sophie now saw that his face was still speckled with blood.

"Are any of Walter's men in Borin's guard? I'm sure that if there is one, then there are more... if not among his guards, then certainly among the rest of his soldiers," Sophie said.

General Peter nodded. "I believe that the plan was to assassinate Borin and leave his soldiers leaderless so that they would choose a new governor who would support Walter. Thorn must have more men under his command who will sway the others. After the assassination, one would claim leadership, and the rest would support him."

Sophie looked at the faces around the table. Who could she truly trust? "If there are more traitors, they may attempt to assassinate me... We must interrogate White City's captains!"

"I agree with you, Your Majesty," Peter concurred. "But we don't have time for interrogations. We will double your guard, and some Iovbridge men will be around Borin at all times." The general nodded to one of his captains, delegating the task. "Walter won't attack Iovbridge immediately. He will wait for his allies to get to Ramerstorm before he makes his move. We have a few weeks, maybe a month. He knows that the city walls are sturdy. He won't take even the slightest risk of being defeated in front of all of Knightdorn."

Captain Merick took the floor again. "I'm with General Brau. Walter won't move against us before gathering all his forces in Ballar. The Oldlands army, the northern men, and Ylinor's hordes will all answer his call. Iovbridge's forces stand at approximately ten thousand, along with two thousand men from Ballar. They're not enough. We need help"

"Merick's right." The general nodded. "Walter has achieved his goal—he attacked our allies separately, decimating their armies all these years. Only Lady Endor can help, but if her men don't cross Stonegate, they won't reach Iovbridge in time. Plus, her army is nothing like it used to be. Perhaps we could retreat to the south-east, but we'll have to fight Reynald Karford to get to the south."

"We don't have the time nor the men to take Stonegate. Walter will soon be right outside our gates," Merick countered.

Sophie's anger grew as her soldiers discussed surrendering the city. "I would not retreat to Elmor even if I could!"

"We can fortify Iovbridge—the arrows and the hot oil over the gate will keep the siege going for months," Peter suggested, trying to give the council courage.

Captain Richard Lamont glared at the general. "You don't know what you're talking about. You've forgotten that we don't have the supplies necessary to withstand such a siege for months! You've also forgotten about the Shiplords of Tahos. If the Ruler of Tahryn sails on the Scarlet Sea with his thousand ships, we're going to have to fight on two fronts. And if Borin gets murdered, we'll even have to face Ramerstorm's men. We must surrender Iovbridge in exchange for our lives, otherwise, we're all going to die. Walter will slaughter every man, woman, and child if we fight him."

Captain Richard had lived out the best part of his youth. He rubbed at his thick jowls and licked at his yellowing teeth. His words almost always provoked anger among the council, but he had proven his worth in the battlefield. They called him *Richard the Fiend* behind his back.

"The throne is gone. Sadly, none of us can stop Walter, but we can save thousands of lives by surrendering our city."

General Peter looked at Richard—he seemed outraged. "Walter is not going to spare the queen's life, nor the lives of the Royal Army and the counsellors who fought against him all these years! Have you forgotten what he's done so far to everyone who didn't support his claim to the throne?"

Richard didn't respond, so Peter went on.

"Even if Walter spared my life, I'd rather die than serve a king like him. I lost two sons in the fight against him, and I will keep fighting for as long as I live and breathe!"

Richard blinked slowly. "I have a family too, General Brau. We must get away! Walter will torture and kill us all!"

The council members seemed pensive. Sophie looked at the men around her. The Royal Council had long consisted of nine members: The lord of the knights, the general, the grand master, the high priest, two lord counsellors, and three captains. These days, no man bore the title of Grand Master or lord of the knights. The council now had five captains—two more than any other time in the past.

Captain Frederic Abbot, a sturdy, grey-haired man with a long scar between his right ear and his chin broke the silence. "I think you are overreacting, Richard. Walter isn't going to use ships at this time of year. The high winds and the turbulent sea will not allow Shiplords to cross the Cold Sea. We still have enough supplies to hold fast under siege, and a trusted guard will be around Borin at all times. I'm not saying that we can win the battle, but we're not in a position to surrender yet. If our reaction is spirited, perhaps someone amongst our old allies will support us."

Richard got up off his chair. "Nobody has supported us in the last two years! Do you really think they'll help us now, Frederic? Just one step away before our end? Why haven't they done so all this time?"

Frederic Abbot stood up too. His scar stretched as he spoke. "Because it's the final battle! Perhaps our resistance will inspire them to take our side!"

Sophie stood, and the two men sat down in silence. As the only noble-born captains, Richard Lamont and Frederic Abbot had the loudest voices on the council. Being wealthy and long established, the Abbots always had their say, as did the ambitious and troublesome Lamonts. King George Thorn was the one who had given land, a noble title, and the office of captain to Richard when he resolved a siege. Still, despite worrying ties between the Lamonts and the Thorn family, Richard's loyalty had never been in question. General Peter Brau, by contrast, was born in the slums of Iovbridge. His skills in combat had compelled King Thomas to give him a noble title and the surname Brau.

No one spoke for a few moments. Sophie headed to a window, seeking a different view. The worry on her council members' faces echoed her own. The veil of night had covered everything, and she looked at the stars in the sky through the black smoke trailing in from Ramerstorm. Sophie knew they had no hope of defeating Walter. After so many years of war, along with the fight that her uncle had put up in Aquarine, the Royal Army was nearly depleted. The army of Iovbridge had for years consisted of newly recruited city folk and stood no chance against the enemy's experienced warriors. They no longer had any allies either. Her cousin had made sure of that.

Thoughts swirled in Sophie's head. At the beginning of his rebellion, Walter didn't have the support he needed to win. The marriage between Robert Thorn and Emma Egercoll had united Knightdorn, and a long peace had followed. The new king, Thomas Egercoll, had given his sister's hand to George Thorn's only son, Robert. But old ambitions had consumed Robert's son, Walter. And slowly, piece by piece, he had begun his advance towards the throne. Taking control of Ylinor Castle and maneuvering himself into ruling Gaeldeath were important early moves in the game.

Sophie's mind stuck on George Thorn. Walter's grandfather, the First

King, proved to be a vicious man. George was crowned the first king of a united Knightdorn—it was the first attempt at peace after centuries of war. Knightdorn was covered with the black veil of death for decades. So, the nine kings, who for centuries had held dominion over the continent, agreed to surrender their crowns and adopt the title of governor—thus, the kingdoms united, and one from amongst themselves was chosen king above all. George Thorn earned the central kingdoms' trust and had the northerners on his side, so the rulers of the south accepted him on the throne. From then on, George was known as the *First King*.

It was George's delusions of grandeur that soon brought about tensions between him and several governors. His noble friends pillaged towns and castles, while he himself imposed unreasonable taxes on the former kingdoms, sinking them into poverty. Then, in a skirmish at the Palace of the Dawn, during the Harvest Festival, the First King killed Brom Endor. Sophie had been taught what happened next. That act enraged the south in its entirety, and even George's sworn allies in the north turned their backs on him. The Egercolls raised the war banners even faster than the Endors and the Pegasus Rebellion had shrouded everything in Knightdorn until Thomas Egercoll managed to take Iovbridge and put an end to George's tyranny.

Sophie stopped thinking about the past; the only important thing was the present.

"Unfortunately, we cannot hope to receive help." Sophie looked away from the dark landscape. "I'd like to hear the lord counsellors' opinions too."

Patrick Degore and Gregory Mollet were both stern men with velvet jerkins and cloaks sewn with gold thread. Gregory Mollet watched her with a serene expression on his wrinkled face that seemed to suggest he knew something good that she didn't. That, or he just had enormous faith in her. Patrick Degore was younger. Blue-eyed, thick-nosed, and pockmarked. He touched his blond beard in an agitated manner, then fiddled with the bunch of parchments in front of him.

"Your Majesty, the lords of Iovbridge have contributed their utmost to the war," Patrick said. "But after the fall of White City, we have been cut off. Our harvests are enough for about thirty days, and sharp steel is now hard to find. If the enemy besieges Iovbridge, hunger will rack the city. And...," he hesitated, "the Crown's gold does not suffice to pay the Royal Army or the nobles for their harvest. The debt has been growing since your late uncle chaired this council. Perhaps it would be wise to discuss a potential surrender with amicable terms."

Merick gave an ironic smile. "I expected nothing more from the lords!"

Patrick turned red. "I guess you're forgetting our contribution to the war over almost two decades. We surrendered our men, our harvests, and even our gold to the Crown. King Thomas took our soldiers, and after some years, he demanded our gold to pay them. We risk losing not just our wealth but also our lives! This council has deprived the lords of dozens of privileges without ever rewarding them for their contribution to the war after all these years."

Gregory Mollet spoke in a serene voice. "We are on your side, Your Majesty. The House of Mollet along with all noble houses of Isisdor have given an oath of devotion to the Crown. We will do whatever the council deems necessary."

"Perhaps Your Majesty should reconsider the prospect of an alliance with the Western Empire," Patrick interceded, glaring at Gregory.

Sophie gave the lord what she hoped was a piercing look. "Are you asking me to marry the self-proclaimed *emperor's* son, my lord?" She kept her voice calm, letting the heat of her stare tell him how strongly she objected.

"A marriage would be the only way to find new allies. The emperor always wanted—"

"I'm not going to sell Knightdorn, along with its queen, to the *emperor*, Lord Degore."

"We need to ask for help from Elmor." General Peter raised his voice.

"How?" retorted Richard. "Even if they agreed to help us, the Vale of Gods is now guarded by Walter's men, and the Southern Passage through the Land of Fire belongs to Karford. And if you're suggesting our emissaries go through Ersemor, you've lost your mi—"

"Even if I could send messengers, I wouldn't do that," Sophie interrupted him. "I don't want Elmor's men to march to Iovbridge for me. I don't want anybody else to sacrifice themself for me. Captain Richard, you are free to leave the city. You have my word that nobody will stop you." Her eyes locked with the captain's, but he stayed where he was.

Sophie drew a deep breath and hoped she'd hidden her relief. She knew that her only hope of survival was a new alliance with Elmor. However, the Governor of Elmor, Syrella Endor, would not easily decide to fight for her. As if that weren't enough, Stonegate was yet another obstacle. Stonegate Castle, the *South Passage*, was the only eastern road that headed south. Nevertheless, the command of Stonegate belonged to one of Walter's men, and so, the Guardians of the South were her opponents too.

Sophie had thought that conquering Stonegate was the best way to try to seek a new alliance with Elmor. With the South Passage under her command, her emissary would arrive fast in the south, and Syrella's men could easily march to Iovbridge. However, there was no time for any of this. Even if there was, Sophie didn't want to ask anybody else to die for her.

"It's time we got some rest. At first light, Captain Robyn will be buried with knightly honours, and General Peter will be sworn in as lord of the knights. He will also choose four more royal knights, and a new general who will be presented to the council."

The counsellors looked surprised at Sophie's decisions. Peter opened his mouth to speak when there was a knock on the chamber door. All eyes turned to the entrance, through which Selwyn Brau emerged. He had taken off his chain mail and now wore a crimson jerkin.

"Selwyn, what are you doing here?" roared Peter.

"I apologise, Father," said the young man humbly. "I've just been informed that a man has arrived in the city. He's asking for permission to see the queen as soon as possible."

Peter's brow furrowed in anger. "Why would you interrupt a council for that? Is it an emissary from the enemy?"

"No, Father, just a lad from a village. However, he said that he was trained by a Grand Master"

"A Grand Master? Grand Masters are dead!" Sophie said.

Selwyn shrugged as though he shared her skepticism. "He said that his Master told him '*The time to fight for the queen has come*'."

Ghosts in the Dark

The news of a Grand Master training candidates for knighthood stunned Peter. He hardly dared to believe it. Suspicion spread across the room. The captains glanced left and right as the queen looked on stupefied.

"Selwyn, describe this man to me," demanded Sophie.

"He's very young, Your Majesty. Not much more than a boy. He has a sword, nothing else," Selwyn continued hesitantly. "The guards took his blade and held him at the gate."

"Bring him to me," the queen ordered.

Selwyn quickly left the room. The council rumbled with concern.

"Your Majesty, are you sure that you want to hear this lad out?" Peter asked, thinking it likely to be a waste of her time. It was too much to hope that a knight might come to their aid.

"I want to know why he's here," she said decisively.

There was silence for what felt to Peter like eternity, time that could have been spent planning. Finally, the door opened.

The lad escorted into the chamber was tall and sturdy with brown hair and light green eyes. His clothes were shabby, and his cloak tattered. The young man's gaze immediately found the queen. He seemed puzzled at the sight of her.

Peter nodded sharply at the guard, who hurried out of the Council Hall with his blue cloak waving. Selwyn moved to go too.

"Stay, Selwyn!" Peter called, and his son stood still.

The boy kept looking at the queen as if he couldn't believe his eyes. "Thank you for agreeing to see me in the middle of the night."

"When you address the queen, you must refer to her as *Your Majesty*," said Merick.

Sophie shot a look at the captain, and he stayed silent. She looked the boy in the eyes. "What is your name?" she asked.

"Elliot." His voice was hoarse. "I have come to fight on your side, Your Majesty."

Sophie looked closely at him, visibly curious. "Which city do you come from? Who is your father?"

"I come from a small village next to Mount Elwyn, a half a day's journey from here. I never met my family. The villagers in the village where I grew up found my mother shortly before my birth. They helped her, but she died right after giving birth. Before she died, the only word that came out of her mouth when she saw me was *'Elliot.'* No one ever found out who she or my father were."

Peter remained suspicious. The boy could be one of Walter's agents. Still, any talk of a Grand Master needed to be explained. "Why do you want to fight for the queen now? Why not sooner?"

"I couldn't fight before my training was over. I rode to the city when my Grand Master deemed I was ready."

Captain Richard laughed out loud at that. "Grand Masters are dead! These days, it's almost impossible to find a simple drillmaster even in the cities."

"What was his name?" asked Peter, wondering if there was any shred of truth here, or if the boy was simply delusional.

Elliot gave him an appraising look. "Roger Belet. He lived in Tyverdawn for years before Walter Thorn's ascent."

"Erneas was the last Grand Master of Gaeldeath!" said Peter

"My Master would have taken Erneas's title after his death. However, he decided to leave Gaeldeath's capital when Walter became governor."

"Then your Master never became a Grand Master... Where is he now?"

continued Peter.

"He died yesterday," Elliot answered, his voice full of sorrow.

Richard's face hardened. "I've never heard that name before," he shouted. "I don't know if you're telling the truth, but I think it is of no concern to this council. You're just a boy! We appreciate your offer of help, but unfortunately, it's not enough."

Elliot looked at the queen again. "I have a plan. I believe that we can face Walter Tho—"

"On whose authority are you talking to the queen about war plans before her council?" Richard yelled. "Just because you think you have some training doesn't mean that we should listen to you! Selwyn shouldn't have interrupted us with this nonsense!"

Elliot slowly turned his head and faced the captain. "I could defeat anyone in this room in single combat. I could defeat anyone in all of Iovbridge, I dare say. If you think my training deficient, you would lose nothing by accepting my challenge."

Everybody froze for a moment. Peter was shocked both by the lad's inappropriate challenge and by his confidence. He wouldn't mind seeing the captain beaten, but they had more pressing matters to attend to. The queen raised an eyebrow. Richard unsheathed a long sword from his belt and moved toward Elliot.

The queen stood up at once. "Captain Richard," she snapped. He glared at her and begrudgingly sat back down.

She turned to Elliot. "I don't know who you are, Elliot, but I admire your confidence," she began. "You should be glad to have the honour to speak to the queen on the day of your arrival at Iovbridge. If I'm not mistaken, you are the only unknown guest to have received this honour. But challenging my counsellors to single combat is the ultimate insult."

Elliot bent down in shame. "I apologise if my behaviour insulted you or your council, Your Majesty," he responded. "It is an honour that you have allowed me to speak to you." He looked around at all the attendees. "But we don't have much time. I'm begging you to listen to me! Everybody in Knightdorn knows that Walter Thorn will soon attack Iovbridge. You have neither alliances nor a sufficiently large army, and the smoke in the sky shows that White City is now in your enemy's hands. I suspect that none of the strategies that you've thought of leaves you satisfied, so what do you have to lose if you hear me out?"

"Elliot," the queen's eyes met his again. "Our time is precious. Why would I spend it listening to you in place of my general and his captains?"

Peter could see that the queen was ready to dismiss their visitor. And yet the boy was right—they had no plan. At least no good one. "Your Majesty, forgive me for intruding, but I'm curious to know what Elliot has to suggest. He has impressive knowledge about the current state of Knightdorn for someone who grew up in a village. A village with a drillmaster who lived in Tyverdawn, yet one whom none of us has heard of. I'd say that he's an informer for Thorn, but he'd be a fool to try and convince us with such a story!"

The queen leaned toward Peter. "Why do you want to hear him?" she whispered.

Peter frowned. The truth—that he had no better hope than this wild story— was not one he wished to burden his queen with. "Nobody would try to convince us of such a story if it weren't true. Perhaps a drillmaster survived Walter's massacre and found refuge in that village under a different name. If the strategy this boy brings comes from a Master, I'd like to hear it."

The queen sat back from Peter and observed the lad. "I will allow you to share your thoughts with us."

The lad took a deep breath. "Walter Thorn is going to gather every single man amongst his vassal lords before attacking Iovbridge. Unfortunately, his army cannot be defeated without powerful allies. The only region that can help is the former Kingdom of Elmor. I will head south as a messenger of the queen and ask the region's governor to unite her army with ours. I'm certain that the governor wants to fight. She is just waiting for a sign from you, Your Majesty."

Peter had to admit they needed allies, but asking for them was hardly a stroke of tactical genius. He held his tongue and waited to see how Elliot would convince the others.

"I will need four men for that journey," Elliot said.

Richard had turned violet. "That's your masterplan? You don't think we've sought allies?" he growled.

"Even with Elmor's men on our side, we wouldn't be able to face Walter's forces," Captain Merick added.

Elliot smiled. "Maybe not. But nobody will expect their involvement in the battle. Walter will siege Aznar's Gate with all his forces, while a few thousand men will be guarding the city's South Gate. He will prevent the queen's soldiers from attacking him from the side by riding around the city, using the South Gate, while he'll also want to keep any man from trying to run toward the Land of Fire to save himself." The boy's confidence was growing as he spoke. "If Elmor's soldiers march east and attack the South Gate, they will surprise Walter's men. The Royal Army will have the chance to get out of the city and attack them from behind, thus surrounding them. Undoubtedly, we will lose many soldiers, but nobody will expect Elmor's men and if many of them manage to enter Iovbridge they'll be able to help us with the siege."

"You may indeed be right, Elliot." Peter tried to picture the strategy in his mind's eye. There was a certain undeniable logic to it. "But even if the Governor of Elmor agrees to fight, there's no time, neither for you to reach her and ask for an alliance, nor for her armies to get to Iovbridge. This would only be possible if we had Stonegate in our charge, but we don't have enough men to conquer it. The only alternative way of getting to the south-east so fast without crossing the South Passage is to go through Ersemor, but neither you nor Elmor's men, were they to decide to help us, can cross that forest."

"I have no intention of riding through Ersemor. It is true that we won't be able to make it without Stonegate's passage," replied Elliot. "The only solution is for me to defeat its Guardian Commander in a duel.

This way, I will take the castle's leadership and choose a new Guardian Commander, asking him to swear that Stonegate passage will belong only to Sophie Delamere and her allies."

Peter looked to the queen, who seemed about to speak. Before she could, thunderous laughter shook the room.

"If you are such a great swordsman, why don't you challenge Walter himself to a duel?" Richard's voice boomed over the sniggers of the other officers and lords.

Elliot looked at the artful pegasus on the chamber ceiling. "I'm not ready for that," he replied.

A smirk appeared on the captain's lips. "But you're ready to defeat the Guardian Commander of Stonegate?" His eyes had narrowed, making him look like a chubby cat. "Reynald Karford has never lost in single combat."

Elliot gazed thoughtfully at one of the windows at the end of the chamber. "I'm ready for that. The commander of the castle is going to accept the combat, and if he fails, the castle's passage will be ours without losing a single man."

"How do you know he will accept the duel? Stonegate's laws don't apply to foreigners. He might order your execution on the spot. Besides, how are you so sure that the new Guardian Commander will honour his oath?" asked Peter as the laughter subsided.

Merick looked at him, stunned. "That's your concern, Peter? Stonegate's men always honour their oaths. If somebody defeated Reynald in single combat, he would have the right to choose a new Guardian Commander, if he chose not to stay in the castle himself. And if the new commander swore to allow passage only to the queen and her allies, he would honour his oath. Besides, the Guardians of the South would gladly obey a new leader in opposition to Walter. Reynald is lucky their oaths are held sacred, otherwise they would have assassinated him years ago. As for whether Reynald would accept the duel, he's certainly clever and wily enough to consider his alternatives, but I believe that he wouldn't want to appear cowardly before a boy he can kill with a stroke of the sword."

The queen looked from one man to the next. "Do you believe this boy could defeat Reynald? A former member of the Trinity of Death?"

Peter did not respond, and the queen leaned toward him. "Your question was foolish! I believe that you know the laws of Stonegate," she whispered.

"Of course, I do," Peter said. "I wanted to know how much he knew. A boy who grew up in a village, familiar with all the politics of Knightdorn..." Peter spread his hands. "I'm convinced he had a drillmaster, someone who experienced the wars of recent years from up close. And only one vanished without anyone ever finding out what happened to him."

The queen's eyes shone. "That's impossible! Do you believe Althalos raised him? Do you truly believe Althalos survived and stayed in a village without helping us all these years?"

Peter was troubled. He faced the boy again. "Elliot, do you know what the Trinity of—" Before Peter could finish his question, a bugle call sounded, and the counsellors jumped up in a panic.

Peter instinctively unsheathed his sword and stood next to the queen as the captains got up off their seats. Selwyn hurriedly approached his father.

The chamber door opened with a thunderous clang, and a burly guard along with another man of the Royal Guard barged in. "There are invaders in the city! Somebody climbed up the wall's western tower by Aznar's Gate and killed a guard."

"Selwyn, run at once to Borin's chamber!" Peter ordered. "The rest of you, guard the queen! We must escort her to her chambers in safety."

The queen shook her head. "Only a Ghost Soldier can climb that wall! My chambers are on the other side of the tower. Borin's chamber is much closer. Take me there and run to the wall. If Walter has men in the city, they are going to act now."

"Walter must have men in Iovbridge," Elliot spoke up, uninvited. "It would be impossible to climb the inner wall without help from the inside..." The boy's eyes stared into the void for a moment. "Moreover, a man of Walter's would have had to have left White City immediately after the battle to get to Iovbridge so fast."

Peter glared at the boy, but he was right. Perhaps someone could climb Iovbridge's outer wall, but it would be impossible to make it over the inner wall.

Merick glanced from the door to the windows. "There may be more of Walter's men in Borin's guard. It will be dangerous for the queen to wait with him."

Peter agreed, but unless the traitors were truly great in number, likely they were not yet inside the palace but rather were outside, helping the Ghosts to scale the wall.

Queen Sophie spoke up. "Only two of Borin's men are guarding him right now... But I have two men of the Royal Guard, and three more city guards are outside his chamber. They are enough to stop anyone from getting near his chambers."

Peter looked at her for a long moment, impressed that the young woman had kept her focus despite the panic. He turned to his son. "Selwyn, you will stay close to the queen."

Peter led the way, followed by his captains and the council, the queen safe in their midst. They wound through torch-lit corridors to the governor's chamber. Two men of Borin's guard stood at the door with their swords raised. Three palace guards rushed to speak to Peter.

"General Brau, we heard the bugle. Do you know what is going on?"

"There are intruders in Iovbridge. The queen will remain in the governor's chamber together with her guards. I also want a guard to escort this young man to a chamber next to the Royal Hall. See that he stays there until I come back." Peter pointed at Elliot.

Captain Frederic, his ugly scar white against the red of his face, grabbed Peter by the shoulder. "This boy might be hiding much more than he said. It wouldn't be wise to keep him in the palace."

"He's unarmed." Peter pointed to Elliot's empty belt, then removed the captain's hand from his shoulder, meeting his anger with a sharp stare.

"Maybe that was his plan all along: to remain inside the palace while we leave to confront the intruders," insisted Frederic.

"I won't send him to the dungeons, and I won't waste men to transfer him to the thieves' cells. I want all men out of this cham—"

"Let's have him follow us," said the captain forcefully. "If I find out that he's one of Walter's rats, I'll feed his beautiful head to the dogs."

Peter simply nodded.

They left the queen in Borin's chamber and ran to the courtyard and then the city beyond. The streets were restless. Soldiers prowled, hunting for intruders, while common folk watched with worried expressions, the bugle call having alerted them to danger.

Peter looked into the distance at Iovbridge's wall. "We must go up the western tower. The Path of the Seven Swords is the shortest way," he urged.

Captain Richard nodded. "If someone managed to climb the wall, they must be hiding there. It would be impossible to pass through the entire guard ... unless they were disguised."

"We need to find the man who sounded the bugle." Peter ran along the path and reached the western tower with the others behind him. To his surprise, he didn't find a single man of the City Guard at the entrance. He ran inside, went up the stairs to the heart of the building. Along with Elliot, the rest of the counsellors climbed up for quite some time until they reached the top of the tower, and with a clamour, Peter jerked open a wooden door to the walkway that ran behind the battlements. Smoke still filled the sky above Iovbridge.

The autumnal gusts of wind whipped at Peter as he walked the top of the wall, the others behind him. He spotted a crowd ahead, illuminated by lanternlight. As he drew closer, he could see a number of guards had gathered around a fallen man. Peter rushed towards them.

"General Brau!" a soldier acknowledged him. "This guard was found dead. We found him moments ago. There's a rope." He pointed to their right.

A thick rope had been secured to allow an intruder to scale the wall. Peter looked over at the drop and felt immediately nauseous, the height made him dizzy.

A young guard hazarded a guess. "Perhaps he fell asleep, and the intruder killed him in his sleep."

"So, the rope was tied on its own, you idiot?" yelled Richard. "Some accomplice in the city tied it after murdering the guard." He looked around at the men. "Who blew the bugle?"

"I don't know. As soon as I heard it, I ran toward the sound. When I got here, there was no one around except for the body, so I sent someone to notify you."

"One of the guards used the bugle and I don't think it was the killer," said Captain Merick. "I don't think the traitor wanted us to rush to the point where the intruder would climb."

Peter tried to put his confused thoughts in order. He saw Elliot examining the point where the rope was tied. Soon after, the boy took a look at the dead man.

"This man was killed by someone he knew and didn't consider a threat," Elliot said. "His sword is in its sheath, which means he didn't try to defend himself. It would have been impossible to get close to him at this point without him noticing. Who was on guard with him?"

Peter was impressed. It was obvious that Elliot was clever.

"The boy is right," mumbled Richard. "But I still think he's a spy," he declared pointing at Elliot. "He appears suddenly, on the day we have intruders in Iovbridge, while Walter is almost right outside our walls. I don't believe in coincidences!"

Peter saw Frederic reaching for his sword's hilt. "How did the intruder manage to climb down, unnoticed, from the tower? A guard could pass by the rest of the City Guard, but they'd be asking questions if a stranger were with him," noted Peter pensively. "They didn't take the dead guard's clothes to dress the intruder, and they're not here now, unless you can spot a stranger."

The guards were confused and looked around. Merick began to speak. "Was this guard on his own?"

"No," answered the guard that Richard had earlier called an idiot. "He was keeping watch with Edward, but I didn't find him here when I came."

"The man who was standing guard with the dead man is missing, and you haven't mentioned it until now?" Peter yelled. "We must get to the queen right now!"

Men from Ballar approached along the wall, weapons and armour clattering as they headed towards Peter and the others.

"We heard the bugle call and came to help," shouted a tall, dark-haired man with Ballar's hawk sewn on his black cloak as the newcomers approached.

Peter eyed the six men suspiciously. "There are intruders in the city. Who are you?"

"My name is Anton Loken. I'm a captain from Ramerstorm." His tone was pompous, his features prideful.

Peter turned his gaze to Elliot. The boy looked down carefully, took hold of the rope, and started pulling it up slowly. Peter looked back to Anton. "How did you know where to find us? Who told you to come to this tow—"

Before Peter could finish his question, one of Ballar's men unsheathed his sword. Elliot was much faster. Unarmed, he pulled Peter's sword from his belt and stabbed through the soldier's neck. With shouts and whispers of steel, chaos ensued.

One of the Ballar men clad in black proved very adept. A single sweep of his sword felled two City Guard men. Richard pounced on him with a holler, while Peter picked up a dead guard's sword to help the captain. The rest of Ballar's men were fighting furiously with the guards when arrows struck several of the enemy.

City Guard swarmed the area, drawn by the sounds of battle. Peter hounded the last traitor from Ballar, Richard on his knees nearby, bleeding after taking a blow on the shoulder. The man in black made a sudden move and almost thrust his sword into Peter's throat when an arrow pierced his chest. He dropped his sword. Peter bent towards him as the man knelt on the cold stone.

"How many spies did Walter send?" he demanded.

The man looked him in the eye and laughed weakly. "For our sovereign king," he whispered, his gaze searching the stars and the smoke above. His eyes remained open but couldn't see anymore. Peter stood up, and Frederic joined him, supporting the injured Richard.

"The queen!" exclaimed Peter. There was no time to waste.

Merick looked around as Peter moved to the stairs. "Where's Elliot?"

Peter met Merick's gaze. The boy had vanished.

"TO THE QUEEN!" they all screamed at once.

Selwyn waited inside the chamber with the queen, along with Governor Borin and a royal guard named Gervin Gerber. Two Ballar guards, another man of the Royal Guard, and three more soldiers of the City Guard stood outside the chamber ready to challenge anybody who approached. Selwyn felt they were more than capable of dealing with whoever had found their way over the wall, even if they did reach the queen's door.

Selwyn looked at Sophie. The queen sat in a corner, lost in her thoughts, while the governor looked out an ornate window. He felt sorry for the young queen, not much older than he but with the fate of a crumbling kingdom in her hands.

"Your Majesty, I apologise for us having to remain here," said Selwyn humbly, taking a look at Gervin. "It would be dangerous for you to be left alone,"

"Don't worry." The queen's brown hair hid most of her face, but it couldn't hide the pain in the tone of her voice. Torchlight flickered round the chamber, leaving shadows licking against the stone walls.

A commotion outside the chamber froze them all. Screams and shouting broke the silence, followed by a loud thud on the door. Selwyn and Gervin unsheathed their swords together. The door opened with a resounding thud, and three men rushed in. One wore the uniform of Iovbridge's City Guard, but Selwyn didn't know him. The other two were dressed in Ballar's black cloaks.

Borin seemed perplexed as he looked at his men. "Will? Emery? What's going on?"

Unlike the governor, Selwyn already knew what was going on. He stood ready for the attack. The Ballar men smiled, but there was nothing friendly in their faces. The Iovbridge guard seemed elated. "We don't have much time. Kill them!" he shouted.

Borin seemed unable to grasp the extent of his men's treachery. The three men raised their swords and approached Selwyn and Gervin.

"You stand no chance," blurted the Iovbridge guard, looking at Selwyn. "Move aside and save your life."

"I'd say that *you* stand no chance," said a calm voice behind them. Elliot had entered the room. "Your plan was very clever, Edward," he said to the guard.

Puzzled, the three men looked at the boy, who started moving in a circle around them. Selwyn stood his ground, equally surprised but willing to let the lad occupy the traitors, buying time for help to reach the queen.

"You killed your watch partner on the western tower and tied a rope to make us think an outsider had entered the city. You also used the bugle to summon the council and the City Guard to the wall, leaving the queen and Lord Borin alone inside the palace." Elliot seemed unruffled, speaking with no trace of fear. "Then, you met the rest of Ballar's traitors. Some ran to the western tower to hold up the captains, while the rest of you moved toward the queen and Lord Borin's chamber. Nobody entered the city. The rope wasn't long enough to reach the ground..."

Edward—how Elliot knew the guard's name was beyond Selwyn—shook off his surprise and smiled. "I've been trained by Walter himself, boy. I was under his command for a long time before I got to the palace. I've waited for this moment for years..." Excitement shone in his eyes. "You don't have to die," he said. "Just step aside, and I will spare your life. I will show mercy. Once Walter gets the throne, I'll make sure that he rewards you."

"I'm sorry, Edward, but the only mercy that counts right now is mine," retorted Elliot firmly.

The three men looked at him, dumbfounded. "Kill him!" shouted Edward.

The Ballar men darted forward. Selwyn moved to intervene, but Elliot shouted, "Stay where you are, Selwyn!"

Selwyn bristled at the order. He was under no obligation to listen to this lad, but protecting the queen, not Elliot, was his duty. He remained where he was, in front of the queen and Borin, Gervin by his side.

The first of Borin's guards, Emery, attacked Elliot. The boy raised his sword and parried, forcing his opponent to his right. Will followed his comrade, but Elliot warded off the blows easily, astonishing both foes. Edward ran to the fight, swinging at Elliot with all his might. Elliot avoided the blow with a swift sidestep and continued to counter all three with admirable speed.

Selwyn had to admit he was impressed. He knew himself incapable of matching the lad's remarkable display. It lent a lot of credence to the story he had told.

"Throw down your swords, and I'll make sure that your life is spared despite your betrayal." Elliot spoke calmly, as if there was no duel. Selwyn watched the boy closely, realizing Elliot was passing up opportunities to deal fatal blows.

"You are going to die!" roared Edward and attacked, spit flying. His strike found only air as Elliot swiftly moved to the right.

Edward's swordplay might not be troubling Elliot, but Selwyn recognized the man's skill. Even if it had been Edward alone, Selwyn was far from sure that he and Gervin could have kept the soldier from the queen.

Shouts and pounding footsteps approached the chamber. Selwyn tensed, but soon the open doorway was filled with familiar faces—his father among them. Relief flooded through him, but then everything changed. Gervin was moving, his sword arcing to strike the queen—Selwyn lunged, his father's shout of fear ringing in his ears. His blade deflected Gervin's no more than a hand's width from the queen's heart.

Gervin recoiled, ready to lash out at Selwyn, who now stood between him and the queen. But Elliot moved too quickly, slashing throats and then cutting off Edward's right arm with a single slice.

Elliot spun in a flash, throwing his sword toward Selwyn. The blade hammered into Gervin's back, the point emerging bloody from his chest. He fell at Selwyn's feet. For a moment there was stillness, everyone in the room frozen, the fight over.

Selwyn bent and freed the sword, which he now recognized as his father's. Edward writhed on the ground, soaking the floor with hot blood.

Weaponless, and ignoring both the dead and the dying, Elliot went to one knee before the queen and bowed his head. "I beg of you to trust me, Your Majesty."

The Last Grand Master

Elliot watched General Peter walk back and forth in the room. The general looked dishevelled, and Queen Sophie had thrown herself onto a chair, exhausted. There was silence in the Council Hall. The sun would soon rise, bringing with it all the troubles of a new day. The rest of the counsellors tried not to make themselves known from their corner.

"What you did earlier, Elliot—" General Peter paused mid-sentence. "—it was something few men can do," he finished off, putting his fists on the wooden table.

"I have experienced the Pegasus Rebellion up close... I have fought for years against Walter Thorn..." He hesitated again and closed his eyes. "You are asking me to trust you, but to do that, you must tell me the truth." His gaze returned to Elliot. "From the very first moment, you made me suspicious—a boy, having grown up in a village, trained by a Master, rides to Iovbridge with a plan that he could not have devised without years of experience and knowledge." The general exhaled loudly. "Most counsellors thought you were Thorn's spy, but now it's certain you don't want the queen dead. I want you to tell me if the man who trained you was Althalos Baudry," he asked and stood tall and upright.

Elliot remained unperturbed, observing the room with curiosity. It was the first time he found himself inside such a building, a far cry from the humble homes where he grew up. He gazed around drinking in every detail.

"Elliot! Do I have your attention?" asked Peter, a little frustrated.

"I'm sorry, General. I've never met that man, but my Master told me that he was one of the greatest Masters of all time."

"One of the greatest? Perhaps an understatement. Drillmasters are many. But each Knightdorn region had only one Grand Master. Do you know why that is?"

Elliot shrugged. "I assume because they were the best."

"You are not wrong... Grand Masters only trained one man at a time and picked boys who were, let's say, more special." He paused for a moment as if hoping Elliot would say something, then continued.

"Grand Masters forged the most well-rounded warriors. Every man who had that title also had a seat at the royal council or the governors' councils. They could also choose any boy they wished as their apprentice in their regions. But Althalos had been given the honour to be able to choose men from all Knightdorn regions, even from the independent Ice Islands," said Peter.

It seemed to Elliot that the general's speech was for the benefit of his audience. Perhaps not the queen, who seemed to be well versed in the ways of the old order, but maybe for some of her advisors who had forgotten or never known.

"Sounds like a great man," he said a few moments later.

"He even managed to convince the centaurs to fight for Thomas Egercoll! However, I am sure they regretted this decision." Peter's mouth twisted into a frown.

"Why?"

"What do you mean?"

"I'd never heard that the centaurs fought alongside King Thomas. Why did they regret it?"

Disbelief was reflected in Peter's gaze. "Because Walter butchered them!"

"How? I thought centaurs were superior to humans."

Peter smiled at that. "The centaurs' plan was to surround Walter's army alongside Thomas's allies. Meanwhile, Walter had realised the trap and he sent Reynald Karford and Vylor's men to attack the centaurs while he marched to Aquarine, whose army was in Ramerstorm with the king. Once Thomas's informers notified him about what had happened, he immediately rode to Aquarine—his sister and niece were there. The king didn't send an army to help the centaurs nor, so agitated was he, did he send a warning. The centaurs were slaughtered."

Elliot felt sorrow on hearing those words. "I have heard that Althalos opposed George Thorn, disgusted by his tyranny... I never understood why he decided to train Walter."

"He believed that Walter was more like his father than his grandfa ther... Walter was the last boy he ever trained—no one else trained by Althalos is alive these days." Peter made a step toward Elliot. "However, after seeing you fight, I'm not so sure about that..."

"About what?"

Peter gave him a piercing look. "Do you know what happened to Althalos?"

Elliot was divided as to how much he should say—he wished he could speak the full truth, but it might put all of them in great danger. "I have heard that he died many years ago," he said at last.

The general remained silent for a moment. "The truth is that we never found out what happened to him... I remember the last time I saw him... That day he gave me his last advice."

"What advice?"

Peter's eyes wandered in the void for a few moments. "It was one of the worst periods of my life. King Thomas was dead, Robert Thorn was dead, even Sophie's parents hadn't survived. Just a few days after the Battle of Aquarine, Althalos reached Iovbridge together with Sophie, who was presumed dead too. Her mother had delivered her to the Grand Master trying to save her, and Althalos and the girl managed to escape from Aquarine. Then, the Grand Master asked me to support her ascension to the throne—I thought he had lost his mind. It seemed inconceivable to me to crown a little girl in times of war. Althalos was adamant. He gave me that last piece of advice and disappeared with two women: Queen Alice Asselin who, according to rumour, was pregnant, and Walter's mother—Emma Egercoll." The general's features had grown sorrowful as he recounted his memories.

"He disappeared?" Elliot asked.

Peter nodded.

"Did he ever mention where he would go?"

"No."

"Why did he do that? You needed him more than ever." Elliot had decided to ask a lot of questions. That would prove he didn't know anything.

"I don't know." Peter sighed heavily. "Many people believed that Queen Alice's pregnancy was nothing but a rumour as she had been married with King Thomas for almost eighteen years without bearing a child. Nonetheless, others were certain that the rumour was true and that she left Iovbridge with Althalos and Emma in order to save her baby from Walter—maybe Althalos tried to protect Alice."

"What happened to her?"

"She died," Peter replied. "Walter started looking frantically for Althalos and the two women. After he found them, he said they had ended their lives by drinking poison when they heard he was near. Walter claimed that Alice's body didn't show any signs of a pregnancy. Many didn't believe him."

"What do you believe? Do you think Walter murdered Alice together with his own mother?"

The general seemed pensive. "Yes... He murdered his father in the Battle of Aquarine—killing his family members was never a problem for him."

"And Althalos was never found?" Elliot asked.

"No," said Peter. "Walter spread a rumour that he had died of old age, but he never offered any proof, and I never believed him. Althalos was well-loved, and after so many murders, another would only strengthen the riots against him at the time. I always thought that he had killed Althalos and hid the truth. However, I was secretly hoping..."

Elliot couldn't understand. "For what?"

"That Althalos had escaped and hid from Walter." The general's eyes opened wide. "I expected that one day he would suddenly appear in Io vbridge... But I was wrong... I followed his advice and supported Sophie for the crown. I even convinced the council to disallow the votes of those governors who had allied with Walter in the Aquarine atrocities. I did everything he asked, but he never came back."

"I am sorry, General," Elliot said, meaning it.

"If you are really sorry, maybe you can tell me the truth..."

"What tru—"

"I don't believe Althalos to be dead! A boy appears in the waning moments before our final crushing defeat, from a village with an unknown Master, and I am to believe it coincidence?"

Peter stared at him, leaving the counsellors ill at ease. Their attention turned to Elliot.

"I told you before—my Master's name was Roger, not Althalos," Elliot said. He knew Peter was angling him into admitting more. "With all due respect, General, I believe that you should interrogate the guard who almost assassinated the queen and not me." Though he would likely die from the loss of his arm, Edward's wound had been tended to enough to keep him alive for the time.

"I don't need your advice," General Peter shouted. "I'm trying to win the war in which I sacrificed my own two sons. I won't take orders from a boy!"

"There is only one way you can hope to survive this war, and I have explained it to you." Anger curled in Elliot's stomach—why couldn't they just listen to him? His plan was their only hope.

"You want me to follow the plan of a boy who hasn't told me an ounce of truth?" the general snarled. "You will be imprisoned until you decide to speak."

"I believe that my imprisonment will be to the queen's detriment," Elliot said, feeling irritated. He had just saved the queen, and they treated him like a common thief.

The queen stared at Elliot. "General Peter will be the new lord of the knights. He has the right to decide your punishment. Selwyn, take this man to the thieves' cells!"

Selwyn startled upon hearing his name. A moment later, he grabbed Elliot by the arm and pulled him out of the Council Hall. Elliot started walking without protest—he might have had many doubts about his Master's plan, but he had decided to follow it. He spoke only as he left the room, raising his voice so none of them would miss his words. "I must admit that I deem your decision to name General Peter the lord of the knights wise, Your Majesty."

Selwyn walked behind Elliot and in the company of two more guards. They had tied Elliot's hands behind his back.

The fracas that followed the sound of Edward's bugle had died down, and the smoke had cleared from the sky by the time the first light of dawn arose. They crossed several small, cobbled roads linked to the city's majestic commercial street. Elliot noticed the merchant stalls were slowly filling up. Blacksmiths with their apprentices, bakers and merchants who sold everything from flour and spices to silk and perfumes, ran here and there. The guards marched him onwards and soon they could make out the magnificent Temple of the Unknown God from afar.

Elliot felt tired and frustrated as he walked. His fears had proven true; he had failed to make the queen and the general listen to him. He looked around—he had been so intent on telling his plan to the queen when he set foot in the city that he hadn't noticed how beautiful it was. He observed from afar the entrance to the Temple of the Unknown God which had several artful columns around it, on a round portico.

Elliot knew the gods were part of Knightdorn's bloodstained history. The Wars of the Gods had lasted over five years when King Maygar Asselin mocked the God of Rain and protector of Tahryn's Shiplords during the spring tournament. His knights, worshippers of the God of the Sun, put King Ager Barlow's knights to shame by defeating them. Having had his God insulted by Maygar, Ager then attacked him, leading the knights to conflict. The feast turned into a battle, and countless men breathed their last on Kelanger's soil. The Thorns were looking for pretexts for another war, so the Wars of the Gods, also referred to as Wars of the Sun and Rain, succeeded the Wars of the Winds' dark days.

Elliot had heard that with the advent of the one king, conflict in the name of the gods was prohibited. The unknown god denoted human's ignorance about the one true god's identity, conferring honour on every god worshipped in the world.

Iovbridge both surprised and impressed Elliot. It seemed a great pity that such a beautiful city was enveloped in pain and death again, as it had been so often in its history.

Some wooden shacks with smoking chimneys appeared to his right. Further off, a dozen manor houses were visible on the east side of the city, near the Scarlet Sea port.

Selwyn pulled him by the shoulder, and they turned into a dim, dirty alley. The city streets appeared to be giving way to a neglected and overgrown park. Elliot noticed some small structures among the trees that looked like metal caves with iron bars covering their narrow entrances. A prison of some sort... Most cells were vacant, but in some he could make out sleeping figures on the ground.

Selwyn opened the door of a vacant cell and pushed Elliot in. He then locked the gate with a rusty key and nodded at the two guards behind him. They started walking, but Selwyn turned back, meeting Elliot's gaze through the bars.

"You saved my life. I tripped after Gervin's attack, he would have killed me. Thank you."

Elliot stretched his neck. "You offered me something too."

"What do you mean?" Selwyn looked taken aback.

"I'm new to this city, to this world. I need men who are loyal to the queen, whom I can trust. After what happened, I know you are such a man."

Selwyn stared in surprise. "Do you believe they'll let you ride to Stonegate?"

"I think that I need some rest."

Selwyn weighed him up for a couple of seconds. He turned his back to leave but again changed his mind. "I want to ask you something, if you can tell me the truth."

Elliot waited patiently.

"You could have finished off Thorn's men earlier than you did. Why didn't you?"

Elliot smiled at that. "Why do you think?"

"Honestly, I have no idea."

"I waited for the queen's council," Elliot said. "I wanted them to witness with their own eyes what I can do, so they'd be convinced to hear me out. If I had killed them quickly, I would only have had your word. And before you ask what I would have done to earn their trust if Walter hadn't placed traitors in Iovbridge... I don't have the answer." He sighed, tired. "Sometimes, fate plays tricky games... Please, don't think that I had anything to do with the treachery in order to earn the council's trust."

"Earning trust by promising to fight Reynald and preventing an attempt to assassinate the queen would be too reckless for anyone who didn't mean it," Selwyn said. "If I thought you were one of Walter's men, you'd already be dead—a bit of revenge for my brothers would please me." He lowered his gaze.

Grief settled on Elliot's shoulders. "The dead don't care about revenge."

Selwyn took one last look at him, turned his back, and walked away in silence.

Blood in the Flames

Down in the dungeons of the Tower of Courage, Peter tapped his leg impatiently. This part of the palace was not adorned with gold and silver. Nothing there was redolent of the Tower of Aimor's prestige. Peter looked around—the royal knights used to live there, but after the title of knighthood was banned, and the last royal knights died, the tower was occupied by immature youths who bore the title of defender and constituted the queen's Royal Guard. Peter admired every corner of this aristocratic building, but the dungeons in the Tower of Courage were one of the areas he didn't like visiting. George Thorn had used them for torture. It was common knowledge that countless souls had flown out of tortured bodies desecrated in the most horrific ways, made all the worse because the elwyn had once buried their dead there. That such a sacred place had been turned into a torture chamber made him nauseous.

Peter stared at the queen—his thoughts never straying far from her decision to revive the order of the royal knights. For centuries, the title of knighthood had held sway over human history. Kings and lords named capable men *knights*, thus giving them lands and social prestige. As the years went by, the kings of Knightdorn decided to confer the title of knighthood upon only a small portion of great warriors. So, the old title *knight* was replaced with that of *defender*, and the new knights were turned into select personal guards of the kings. *Until the dark days...*

Peter looked at the iron door of the freezing cold room. The walls were chipped here and there, the stench of mould and damp hovered in the air, and his nose twitched as the strong smell reached his nostrils. The traitor of the City Guard would be brought before them at any moment.

The queen had ordered Borin's transfer to a room next to the royal chambers. Only her men guarded him now. Unfortunately, they could not trust any soldier from White City. *We cannot trust anyone in all of Iovbridge*, Peter thought, saddened.

The council's men lined the dungeon. A wooden table with all kinds of torture tools stood by a mouldy wall. Only the high priest and the lord counsellors were absent. Peter would have preferred to have been absent too, but he had to be there with the queen, as they would soon interrogate one of the most valuable prisoners they had had captured during the years of the war.

Peter felt exhausted. They hadn't managed to get a moment's sleep after the battle in White City. The dungeons didn't have windows, but he knew the sun had started rising in the sky of Isisdor's capital. The queen stood by him, silent. She had straightened her back, chest upright. She always took this stance when she was angry.

The door opened, iron grating on stone, and two guards in blue cloaks came in, holding a scrawny man. Where his right hand should have been, there was only half an arm, covered with stained bandages.

"The healer did the best he could so that he doesn't pass out from the loss of blood. He cleaned the wound with wine and covered it with honey, but he's going to need herbs and rest soon, otherwise you will only interrogate him once," said one of the guards quickly.

"Thank you. You can go," said Peter.

The men left the captive, who, unable to stand, collapsed on the floor. Captain Richard loomed over him and looked at him in disgust.

"Raise your head and face your queen, fucking traitor!" yelled Richard.

The man didn't move.

"You are going to tell us everything... I want to know how you conspired with Walter to kill the queen and if there are any other traitors in the city," said the captain.

Edward didn't seem frightened. "I won't say a word. If you're going to kill me, then do it," he said with a quick, short breath.

The scar on Captain Frederic's cheek stretched so much that it seemed about to bleed. He unsheathed his sword and stood in front of the treacherous guard.

"Do you know who I am?" he spat, eyes full of hatred. "I'm Frederic Abbot, and I've been a member of this council since King Thomas's time. In the last twenty years, I've lost two brothers in the wars against your leader. I have so wished to get my hands on one of his men, alive..." His face contorted with manic obsession.

Peter glanced apprehensively at the captain, but he didn't speak. Frederic raised his sword and struck the maimed limb. A horrendous wail burst from Edward.

"It will be my pleasure to keep going for a long while to come." He was about to strike again.

"STOP!" screamed Edward. "SHOW SOME MERCY!"

Frederic laughed dementedly and struck again. "I've just begun!" he mumbled with a hint of enjoyment.

The traitor howled wildly, and his body had started to shake. "What do you want to know?" The words came out of his lips in a whisper.

"Everything," hissed Frederic.

Edward sat up weakly. "I was under Walter's command for years until he ordered me to ride to Iovbridge and follow a plan for Lord Borin's assassination. My lord believed that the Ruler of Ballar would retreat to Iovbridge, together with most of his officers and his people, before Walter attacked Ramerstorm. White City is weak, and your army has neither the men nor the horses to face my lord's army... Walter anticipated that a small army would try to delay him at Ballar's capital, as surrendering the city without a fight would reveal cowardice, and the queen has proven that she's always willing to let her men die purposelessly. However, my lord did not expect to find Borin with officers from the palace there.

But even so, you managed to get away without losing all your men." The man's words came out with difficulty. He drew a ragged breath and continued.

"Walter had ordered me to act as soon as Borin and his captains arrived at the palace—I was not to waste time, as my lord believed that you would soon increase Borin's guard with Iovbridge men," he continued. "I didn't know how many or which Ramerstorm men conspired with Walter, except that they were captains. My lord had ordered me to wait for the day Borin and his soldiers would be in Iovbridge. Then, I would blow the bugle somewhere along the wall and run to the palace. And so I did. The captains waited for me in front of the palace gate. When I met them, the two most skilled swordsmen followed me, the others ran to the wall to delay you. It was expected that you would run to the battlements as soon as you heard the bugle," he muttered, holding his bloody limb.

The captain struck him again at lightning speed. The fallen man convulsed with pain. He would soon faint. Peter began to feel queasy at the spectacle.

"You give us nothing we cannot deduce for ourselves. I told you I want to know everything. I'm going to give you one more chance, otherwise I'll cut off your other arm." Frederic's eyes had narrowed into a terrifying stare.

The maimed man's breath came out in short gasps. "My name is Edward Ewing. I was born in Kelanger and lived there for years. My father was not one of Oldlands' powerful lords but had the undying appreciation of many rich nobles. He sold slaves until the House of Egercoll came to power. My family lost everything when Thomas sat on the throne. Slavery was banned, and most of the nobles lost their castles and men." He paused briefly. "When Aymer Asselin was assassinated and Ricard Karford took Oldlands, everything changed. The day the new governor opened the gates to welcome Walter Thorn, I was still a child, but my excitement was immense. I had been trained by the city's drillmaster and was ready to put myself under his command. And so it happened. Walter honoured my devotion and completed my training before assigning me this mission," the traitor had begun to pant, but joy was reflected in his eyes as he uttered the last words.

"I rode to Iovbridge a few months ago and enlisted in the City Guard. When I arrived in the city, I claimed to be from Aquarine and offered to fight for the queen. The guards asked me if I had any letters confirming my origin, but I didn't—Felador has been without a governor or council for years. The guards consulted the captains and allowed me to join the Royal Army. Iovbridge needed every man who could fight." Edward took a deep breath. "My lord wanted to get Borin out of the way. I knew that Ballar's captains would know where their governor was. As soon as I found them, they told me something I had not foreseen—one of the captains had run to Borin's room to see if the queen had increased his guard with her men. The captain informed me that the queen was in his room with eight other guards. We didn't want to kill the queen ..." He exhaled. "After Aymer Asselin's death, Walter didn't want to take Iovbridge by fraudulently murdering its ruler, unless there was no other way. He wanted to destroy the city, a show of might for all of Knightdorn to see... But we had no choice. We had to kill every witness and leave the chamber quickly, otherwise we'd be sentenced to death." The man seemed about to faint.

"Your death was a given, since we knew you killed the guard on the western tower," murmured Richard.

"I saw him tie the rope and attacked him. Then I blew the bugle and ran to the Palace of the Dawn to inform the officers—that would be my defence," came the man's response. "I had to decide whether to abandon the plan. It was my only chance, as you would then increase the number of guards. I decided to carry on. My lord would rather I took the lives of two of his enemies than do nothing," the traitor went on. "So, we ran to Aimor Tower. The guards didn't expect us to attack them, so we easily crushed them. When we entered the chamber, we found the queen and Borin, along with two more guards."

"Why did the captains want to kill their lord?" asked Peter.

"Ballar's captains worship Lord Thorn. They had sent a letter to express their support."

Frederic was about to hit Edward again upon hearing these last words, but Peter stopped him.

"A few months ago, my lord found out about their devotion and organised the plan," mumbled Edward.

"It'd have been wiser for the captains who rushed to the western tower not to have revealed themselves," remarked Peter. "If Borin were assassinated, the officers would have had the power to give Ballar's rulership to whomever they wanted."

"We needed men to delay you, and they were willing to sacrifice their lives," said Edward. "If we succeeded, one of the two captains who followed me could claim Ballar's command. My lord knew that Borin's death, combined with the killing of his captains by Iovbridge men, would end in rioting. The men of White City would suspect several plots. It wouldn't be hard to persuade them to fight for Walter," he concluded.

"How was Gervin involved in all of this?" asked Peter again.

"Gervin comes from Mermainthor—most Northerners were always on Lord Thorn's side."

"He had been in the queen's personal guard for five years... Why now?"

"He left Mermainthor and came to Iovbridge as a spy years ago. Walter knew that he'd manage to get to the Royal Guard. My lord gave me a message for him, and I passed it on... Gervin would remain close to the queen until Iovbridge fell. If Walter failed to take the city, Gervin would kill her," croaked Edward. "My lord was certain that it wouldn't be necessary, but he always wants to have a back-up plan, and I would help Gervin, if needed... Gervin had orders not to leave his post under any circumstances."

"Then why did he attack the queen?" asked Peter.

"I think he panicked," came the answer from the wounded man. "He knew that we were going to kill Borin, but he didn't know when, and he did not expect the queen to be in his chamber. When we entered the chamber, we found only one other soldier, though the one who took my arm came soon after. I'm sure Gervin believed that we would kill them easily. So, he didn't reveal himself, as he didn't know what we intended for the queen. When you reached the chamber," he raised his eyes to the counsellors, "it was all over... Gervin should have stayed put. It was foolish of him to reveal himself... I think he was afraid that Walter would punish him if he found out that he hadn't helped us. He was wrong."

"If you had succeeded, what would have happened to Gervin? We would've questioned him about what happened," said Richard.

"I would have killed him. I thought about it when I headed to Borin's chamber," muttered Edward. "He could have claimed that our faces were covered, but if you hadn't believed him and had tortured him, he might have betrayed us."

"What would you have done if Borin and his men had never come to Iovbridge?" Merick asked.

"I would have stayed in the city and, if necessary, helped Gervin kill the queen."

"Are there other traitors in the palace?" asked Peter, speaking up for the first time.

"Not that I know of. But my king never reveals his entire plan."

Frederic stabbed down into Edward's leg, and the man writhed in such agony that his voice began to falter.

"Do not call that man a *king* ever again!" he screamed.

"Did you know that a man from White City intended to attack Borin shortly after the fall of Ramerstorm?" Peter took the lead again.

The prisoner was white as a sheet. "No, Ballar's captains told me about that when we got together—nevertheless there are many who would give their lives for my lord. The truth is that this man's stupidity hampered us, as it made you suspicious about there being more conspirators, and you increased the governor's guard faster than we expected." For a moment,

Edward seemed pensive. "Maybe he was a man of Walter's, but I doubt it," he said mostly to himself. "My lord usually makes sure that his spies are kept hidden to ensure that if one gets caught, he will not reveal the rest. But a betrayal of the governor in front of his men would rally Ballar against Walter... His assassination attempt doesn't fit my lord's tactics," he concluded.

The prisoner's every word frightened Peter more and more. Walter's followers jumped out of every corner, and as if that weren't enough, they were armed with tremendous patience, like their lord himself, waiting for the right moment to act.

Peter tried to smother his worry and went on. "How did letters from Ramerstorm get to Walter? I thought he had banned the reception of letters from his enemies' territories."

Edward laughed with what little strength he had left. "That's what you think. Only letters with the queen's seal or those of her allied governors have been banned. All other letters are received by my lord's guards, in every capital of the regions under his rule. The messages are read by Walter's trusted men before they reach their recipients, and some are even read by him.

"Only nobles and some officers are literate... Reading the letters, Walter learns about his high-ranking supporters in regions where the leadership is against him, acquiring spies and accomplices. Of course, the letters from Walter's enemies are destroyed, and their recipients are punished by death."

Peter gazed upon the traitor in astonishment. When Walter's rule grew to include most Knightdorn regions, he spread the word that he forbade his allies to receive letters from rival territories. It was rumoured that he feared the Crown and the alliances that might be rekindled. Walter propagated the idea that if Sophie and her ally-rulers wanted to be loyal to him and conceded the crown and their regions to his rule, they could send messengers to convey their words, without letters. Until then, his regions would not receive any letters from his enemies' territories, and his guards would interrogate every man who reached his lands. Once again, he had deceived them. Still, every letter could reach Walter's lands, as long as it was not sealed with the coats of arms of his enemy-rulers and the Queen. *The trick was simple and clever,* thought Peter.

"If that's true, we would have known... How did Ballar's captains know and we didn't?" asked Peter.

"Anyone who is loyal to my lord can find out what he needs to know... Nevertheless, these secrets rarely reach his rivals' ears," said Edward. "Walter was sure that you would discover the secret, and the queen or her allies would try to send letters with different seals. So, he ordered the guards to read every letter that reached his territories thoroughly. However, you never discovered the secret..."

Silence enveloped the dungeon until a hoarse voice came from its depths. Frederic seemed untouched by the revelation. "Is there anything else of use that you could tell us?"

Edward looked at him in surprise. "No," he murmured softly.

Frederic plunged his sword into the wound he had opened in Edward's leg.

The man's cries were so strained that his voice would soon leave him. Frederic continued unabated and the prisoner, writhing and screaming, uttered four words, "BLOOD IN THE FLAMES!"

Peter grabbed the captain by the arm and pulled him away from the fallen man. "What does that mean?"

"Walter has found Leonhard Payne. He has him under his command," cried Edward, his remaining hand useless pressed against the wound. "One day I was passing outside Lord Thorn's chamber and heard Leonhard shouting, more carried away than ever. Curiosity got the best of me, and I tried to eavesdrop—the only thing that came out of his mouth was *'blood in the flames'*."

"Leonhard Payne? Did you learn what he discovered? Did you learn what *blood in the flames* means?" asked Sophie.

"No. I don't know, I swear!" said Edward almost in a whisper.

"Have you told anyone else?" blurted Peter.

The man looked terrified. "No, Walter would have killed me if he'd found out I had spied on him."

Peter felt disgusted. "Was your lord not afraid that you or someone else might reveal information to us if Borin's assassination attempt failed?"

Edward searched Peter's eyes. "My lord will take the throne soon. There is no information that can help you stop him," he murmured. His eyes wandered in the void for a few moments. "The honours that awaited those of us who lived were going to be priceless. My House would have become one of the greatest in the kingdom."

The queen's glare dripped with poison. The counsellors watched the prisoner, disgust and fear mixing in their features.

The traitor swayed and said, "Who is the boy who fought us? I haven't seen such abilities in a long time."

The queen looked at him with revulsion and hurried out of the dungeon. The men of the council began to leave the room, and Edward lay on the stone floor. For a moment, he seemed to think that he'd be saved.

Peter silently raised his sword, and the man jerked as the hard steel pierced his flesh. His body shuddered for a few moments, then he went still.

The Pegasus Brotherhood

Sophie was exhausted. Captain Robyn's death had poisoned her dreams, and she couldn't get the traitor's words out of her mind. The marble tub with the various scented bath oils was the only place where she could find peace. A young maid started rubbing her back as the steamy water caressed her breasts.

B*lood in the flames...* What could that mean?

Her mind began to wander. Leonhard Payne was one of Felador's greatest healers. He had discovered cures for several ailments that had plagued Knightdorn for centuries, and he was renowned for his knowledge about the properties of herbs. Sophie's father was the one who discovered the truth about Leonhard's experiments and sentenced him to death, but the healer managed to escape from Aquarine before his execution. Her father had discovered that the famous healer was experimenting on dying soldiers, orphans, and desperate villagers, unconcerned for their lives; the price for his discoveries was pain and death.

Henry had heard that Leonhard had taken refuge with the First King, but after the Pegasus Rebellion, there was no trace of him. *Leonhard Payne must be very old now...* Years before, a merchant reported that Leonhard was experimenting on mermaids and had told her father. Sophie remembered laughter echoing around the table. *"I feel sorry for the man who tries to capture a mermaid,"* a man from her father's court had shouted.

Sophie never became one of Aquarine's healers but she knew many stories about mermaids. Legend had it that the God of Wisdom lay with the Goddess of the Sea, and she gave birth to a son and a daughter; the boy was the first centaur and the girl the first mermaid. Life endowed the boy with intellect and wisdom, the girl with youth and beauty. The stories also said that mermaids lived for centuries in the depths of the sea, ageless and invincible.

The words that Edward had overheard kept reminding her of the rumours about Leonhard, but she could not piece them together. *What could a mermaid have in common with 'blood in the flames'?* Those thoughts made her dizzy. There was some fruit and cheese on an oak table by the tub, but she wasn't hungry. Innumerable questions combined with fear of the impending siege distracted her from all else. *Who was that lad who had reached her doorstep? Who was that lad who had saved her from certain death...?* Sophie mulled over these thoughts again and again. She didn't believe in luck, nor in fate. A soldier with such special abilities looked like a gift from the gods, and she had learnt that no gift came without the expectation of something in return.

The sky was clear that noon, and the arched windows let the sun's rays brighten the room as she wallowed in the water. For a moment she wished she were a mermaid. How carefree it would be to swim along the shores of Knightdorn, free of worries.

Without warning, the door opened wide, and a young man appeared. Sophie screamed, and the maid jumped out of her seat. The man pulled his head back behind the door, startled.

"Forgive me, Your Majesty," shouted the young man behind the wooden door, frightened.

"Fuck!" screamed Jocey.

Philip Segar—General Peter's squire—stayed hidden.

Sophie hurried out of the tub, and Jocey briskly wiped her dry, then dressed her in a violet tunic. Her hair still dripping, Sophie walked to the door.

"The next time you invade my chambers, I will order your execution," she said, gritting her teeth when she saw the squire.

Philip Segar was tall and sturdy with white teeth and golden hair. He was the son of Captain James Segar, who had fallen in the line of duty in the siege of the City of Heavens. Philip was a childhood friend of Sindel Brau, Peter's eldest son.

"Forgive me, Your Majesty," Philip whispered humbly, his face red with embarrassment. "The guards let me through as I bring an urgent message from General Brau. In my haste, I forgot to knock."

She looked into his big, black eyes, waiting to hear the rest.

"The general wants to speak with you as soon as possible. He sent me to ask that you meet him."

"Very well, I will meet him in the Royal Hall."

The man nodded and, with a bow, left the room running, his blue cloak billowing behind him.

She watched him go, considering his handsome features, the sort of face her maids whispered and giggled about. A different queen might take a young man like Philip to her bed, but Sophie had not felt the slightest spark for anyone since Bert. She was only twenty-six years old, and she had begun to feel as though desire had left her forever, never to return.

Sophie stripped herself again, and Jocey scented her body with various oils—a few drops to her wrists and ankles, to her breasts and to her thighs. She chose a silver-coloured silk dress and allowed Jocey to settle a golden circlet in her hair before heading to the Royal Hall.

Sunlight was streaming into the Royal Hall as she entered, filling the majestic space under the dome with both warmth and grandeur. Her uncle may have destroyed Iovbridge and the palace as soon as he'd entered the city during George Thorn's reign, but the stonemasons of Oldlands had renovated the Royal Hall after the war. The throne they had carved was an elevated, ornate seat made of moonstone, two golden pegasus wings protruding from its edges. Behind the throne, the stone wall bore Isisdor's emblem, the seven swords in the laurel wreath symbolizing the bloodstained gift of the Elder Races to the seven riders of the humans. Flanking the wreath were two blue banners bearing the pegasus of the Egercolls. The golden oak of the Delamere's, Sophie's House, was not present, overshadowed by the Egercoll blood in her veins. Sophie liked the fact that each region had its own emblem. The First Kings had given their kingdoms the coat of arms of their houses as sigils. Those emblems were held sacred by Knightdorn's people and never changed through history—and a ruler's personal coat of arms was never given pride of place over a region's sigil on banners.

Footsteps were heard from afar. The general emerged from between two columns and approached Sophie.

"My scouts brought unpleasant information," Peter said.

Sophie knew he had sent a handful of men to observe the enemy's movements through the forests that stretched into the Vale of Gods.

"Walter used a battering ram to break through the gate of White City."

"That was to be expected," she muttered.

Peter was about to go on, but something stopped him.

"Is there anything else I need to know?" said Sophie, letting her irritation show.

"My scouts said that Walter's soldiers stacked the dead from the battle in the Vale of Gods but did not burn them... They put them in carts."

"Why?" she asked, horrified.

"I can hazard a gruesome guess." Another moment of hesitation. This time Sophie did not press him. "I think he wants to sling the corpses into Iovbridge with catapults," he said at last.

Sophie's stomach clenched, and she wanted to turn away from her general. She swallowed, unable to find words.

"Your Majesty, I would like to keep this information from the council. I believe that the counsellors, already scared, will panic."

She nodded. "I agree."

Peter looked worn out, with black bags under the wrinkled skin around his eyes. His green cloak was askew on his shoulders, his hair unkempt. It was obvious that he had not been able to sleep.

"What could *blood in the flames* mean?" Peter asked suddenly.

Sophie had no answer. Much as she had tormented her mind, she had found no explanation. "Perhaps the traitor made up that story, hoping we would spare his life."

"I doubt that," he murmured. "It is very hard to make up a lie with enough truth as to be convincing while in so much pain."

"Do you need something else, Peter?" Sophie wanted to be left alone.

"I have an idea. Maybe... maybe we could..."

"Speak freely."

"Maybe we should consider giving Elliot a chance," said the general.

Unexpected, Sophie paced a few steps away and then back. "What made you change your mind?"

"Your Majesty, I have thought about it a great deal. We have nothing to lose by letting him ride to Stonegate."

"Do you want us to send a lad to his death, like a sheep to the slaughter?"

"Honestly now, do you believe that?" he stared at her. "The boy has unique skill. It is a huge waste to keep him imprisoned next to drunkards and petty thieves."

"You asked for his imprisonment."

"I know," admitted Peter.

"Fortunately, you didn't send him to the dungeons," she said. "A lad who saved my life..."

"He also saved my son's life," Peter added. "I tried to get him to tell us more about himself. But it doesn't really matter."

"He didn't ask for an army. Just four men. In the unlikely event he succeeds, he may be able to bring help to Iovbridge," Peter said.

"I doubt the Ruler of Elmor will fight for the Crown."

"I think Syrella Endor will help us. With the Poison Masters, maybe we stand a chance... Their help would be more valuable than that of the city's lords; Lord Degore seems constantly disgruntled..."

Sophie mulled over Syrella and her soldiers. Elmor's men were known as Poison Masters because of their extensive knowledge about poisons and their antidotes. With Elmor on her side, she knew they would be stronger. However, the truth was that even together, they couldn't stop Walter.

"Lord Degore...," she groaned. "Even now that death is closing in on us, he will be in some brothel in the company of young boys."

Peter sighed heavily. "He's not the only counsellor having fun in brothels."

Sophie looked at her general. "How many men are left in Wirskworth? Ten thousand? Maybe fewer? They still wouldn't be enough."

Peter reflected for a moment. "The boy is right—they will surprise Walter's forces. If his soldiers in front of the South Gate fall quickly, Elmor's army will be able to enter Iovbridge and help defend against the siege."

"What if Syrella throws Elliot out of her city instead of throwing her men into the war? Why fight for the queen who betrayed her? And sending a peasant? She will see it as an insult."

"No lord or officer will travel to Elmor through Stonegate. No one will trust Elliot and his plan."

"I know! But sending a villager to ask for a new alliance from Syrella will only show disrespect,"

The general closed his eyes. "We will name him a knight."

Sophie shivered and fixed Peter with a harsh glare. "Do you know what might happen if Wirskworth is left without an army? After taking Iovbridge, Walter's men will head to Elmor and attack every village in their way, killing children and raping every woman."

Sophie didn't want to send an emissary to Syrella. She didn't want to be responsible for the death of every man, woman, and child in her land. Too many had died for her all these years. Deep in her heart she knew that even together they couldn't beat Walter. Sophie would prefer to leave Elmor in peace and die alone. She couldn't bear the responsibility of more people's lives. Not anymore.

"I know you want to protect the people of Elmor, Your Majesty, but... but this plan may be our only hope—not just for us." Peter suddenly raised his voice. "If Walter takes Iovbridge, will he let Elmor live in peace? We all know that he'll kill anyone who did not support his claim to the throne. Elmor's absence in the final battle for Iovbridge will not spare them. Only when united can we have hope..."

Sophie sighed and looked the general straight in the eyes. After a few moments she gave an elusive nod.

Elliot stood up. His body was numb, and his stomach was rumbling. He took two steps and grabbed the iron bars of his cell. The trees hid the sunlight. This place was not at all like the beautiful gardens of the palace and the ornate alleys of the city.

Several hours had passed since the previous night's events, and no one had visited him. He was sure that someone would come, even if only to ask for his help for the coming siege. He hadn't expected to easily convince them to send him to Stonegate, but he had hoped for more than just a filthy cell. He threw a punch at the nearest bar. Pain spread from his fist and down his forearm.

His Master had made a mistake. How could they listen to him? A council with experienced officers and lords wouldn't just go along and follow a stranger's plan. He had tried countless times to convince his Master of this, but he always answered with the same phrase. *"This is your challenge, Elliot. To make people trust you."*

Elliot had been lucky that Walter's conspirators had acted on the day of his arrival. His skills seemed the only way to earn trust, and keeping the queen safe against four opponents was the best he could ever have hoped for. The truth was also an option, and perhaps the best one... But that would require him to disobey his Master and break his oath, never mind the little voice in his head asking *what is the value of an oath, if we're all going to die?* The thought nested in his mind.

It would be easy to escape, but his Master had advised him, if he found himself in such a position, to wait three days before doing so. So, he sat in his stinking cell, stewing in his growing anger, anger with himself, at his master, and at the people who had put him there.

"Nonsense!" he shouted and punched at bar again.

Footsteps approached, and he stepped backwards, waiting.

A stocky soldier appeared before him holding a large ring with dozens of keys. He wore chain mail and a frayed blue cloak. The man looked left and right with unusually round eyes, then his gaze settled on Elliot.

"Come closer," he said hurriedly as he pulled a set of manacles from his belt.

"Where will you take me?" Elliot asked with suspicion.

"Stop asking questions, and come closer."

Elliot obeyed, turning his back to the bars. He felt the cold steel on his wrists as the manacles were clamped in place, and his heart began to pound. The guard opened the cell door with a deafening clang.

"Walk forward!" he ordered.

Elliot began to walk. His eyes fell upon the snoring man lying on the floor in the next cell, his head resting on a mountain of excrement.

The queen sat on the throne when Elliot was escorted into the hall. The golden wings springing up behind her made her look like a fairy. General Peter waited at her side, a pensive look on his face.

Elliot looked up at the dome. The faces of countless gods looked back at him. Beneath their gazes, he felt small and filthy. Straw and mud decorated his clothes, and he was sure he didn't smell good.

"Remove those," Peter said to the soldier, indicating the manacles. "Then leave us."

The general took a step toward Elliot after the guard had left. "I'd like to ask your forgiveness for sending you to the cells," he began. "You saved the life of the queen and my son. It was a mistake on my part to ask for your imprisonment."

Elliot folded his hands in front of him and looked at Peter. "There is nothing to forgive. It was my duty to protect the queen and her men."

Sophie peered at him. He thought he saw curiosity and gratitude in her blue eyes. "Thank you," she said softly.

He smiled, and Peter began to speak. "I would like to talk to you about some things that should not leave this r—"

Elliot spoke before the general could complete the sentence. "I swear my silence on my family's memory."

Sophie and Peter looked at him, surprised.

"All right," acquiesced the general after a moment. "But first, I have to ask you one more time." He held his breath. "Who was your Master?"

"I haven't lied to you," Elliot protested.

The general exhaled wearily. "So be it," he said.

"How sure are you that you'll succeed in bringing Elmor's army here?" Peter asked.

A thrill of anticipation rushed through Elliot. Finally. Finally, the game had begun. "I can take Stonegate, and I am sure that Syrella Endor will fight for the queen. Everyone knows the Endors have always been the Egercolls' most loyal ally. And Egercoll blood flows in the queen's veins."

"The Governor of Elmor won't take her armies to Iovbridge because of an old alliance. There is great bitterness," said Peter.

"I understand. However, I would like to discuss something else before we think how to persuade Elmor."

The general and the queen shared a glance, then the general nodded for him to continue.

"The truth is that I didn't share my true plan before the council."

The general's eyebrows rose in surprise. Anger narrowed the queen's gaze.

"Did you think such an act would be prudent?" asked Sophie.

"Prudent and necessary. A dozen Ramerstorm captains turned out to be traitors, and Walter even has men in your personal guard. If there are spies in the council, information may reach the enemy much sooner than it should." The general made to speak, but Elliot went on. "I don't trust any man on the council except you."

Peter opened his mouth and closed it.

"If I make it to Stonegate, I'd like the news of the Guardian Commander's fall to reach Walter, and I'd also like him to know that the queen's messengers are heading south-east," Elliot said.

Sophie shifted on her throne.

"Have you lost your mind?" asked Peter. "If Walter finds out that the queen and her allies are free to cross Stonegate while Iovbridge messengers are heading to Wirskworth, he will assume that Elmor will be involved in the battle! He will increase his forces at the South Gate, and once Syrella's men reach the city, he will crush them... They will stand no chance against Walter's soldiers without the element of surprise."

Elliot looked at him unperturbed, and the queen sat back on the throne. "Why do you want the news to reach Thorn?" she asked.

"What do you think Walter will do when he hears such news?"

Sophie sat in silence while the general scratched his chin, then spoke. "Walter will get angry when he hears Stonegate has fallen into our hands, and he will assume Lady Endor will march to Isisdor... He knows Syrella hates him, and a defeat of Reynald Karford will be a great victory for the Crown, the first against him—the Guardian Commander's fall will leave the southern path open for every ally of the queen while strengthening the Crown's prestige in Elmor."

Elliot nodded his approval.

"All Walter would really want to do is slaughter Syrella's men before they could reach us here," concluded the general.

Elliot smiled. "Exactly!"

"But that would be impossible," said Peter.

"Would it?"

"With Stonegate under a new leader who would not concede the South Passage to him, Walter would have to try to retake the castle or cross the Road of Elves. He has no time for any of those."

"Gaeldeath's horses are the fastest in Knightdorn. If Walter rides on the Road of Elves night and day, with horsemen only, he'll be on Snake Road in five days."

"But—"

Elliot continued, "If he hears about Reynald's fall at the right moment, he will have time to ride south quickly and attack Elmor's men before they cross Stonegate."

The general didn't seem to understand. "Walter is waiting for his allies in Ramerstorm. He won't ride south as long as they march toward Ballar. Even if his horses managed to reach Snake Road so quickly, it would take weeks for him to return. His horses will be dead tired and won't be fast on the way back. His allies will reach White City before he returns, and it will be impossible to wait for him there. Ramerstorm cannot accommodate that many men. Also, it will be a huge waste of Walter's supplies just before the siege of Iovbridge."

"I agree. That is why he will send a messenger to his forces and order them to wait on the Path of Shar. It is the most fertile land along their journey."

"But—" It was the queen who tried to speak this time, but Elliot continued.

"Walter's allies will meet on the Path of Shar before marching together on the Path of the Wise. He must learn quickly about Reynald's fall before his men cross the fertile land... If they move away, he won't ask them to return. It's the only place with plenty of food where they can wait without wasting their supplies."

"Do you think that Walter will decide to delay the siege of Iovbridge for so long in order to attack Elmor's army?" Sophie objected. "He won't even be certain whether Elmor will march into battle."

"With the South Passage under the queen's orders, Walter will assume that Lady Endor will ally with the Crown and that this is the only way to easily slaughter Elmor's army, along with that of Iovbridge," Elliot said.

The queen seemed skeptical. "If you're right, then it's foolish to let Walter know the news about Stonegate... Why send him in Elmor's way? Why put Syrella's army in danger?"

"As soon as I arrive in Wirskworth, I will advise Syrella to gather all the villagers at the regional capital, along with all the crops and animals on her land. I will also urge her to dump waste around the Forked River, destroying its soil... I will explain the plan to her and ask her to wait in Wirskworth for six days before we march to Iovbridge."

"Six days?" asked the general.

"Walter will need five days to ride along the Road of Elves and attack on Snake Road. He will leave behind the siege weapons and every cart and mule dragging supplies for his armies. That is the only way he can head south fast. Once there, he will look for Elmor's men. He will rush to villages to find out if the soldiers have crossed the road. When he discovers that there are no people or crops on the land, he will be surprised, assume that Elmor declined the call, and will ride to Wirskworth. That is the only land in the region with water and crops for twelve thousand men and horses. Then, he will realise he was trapped and will be forced to go back to Ballar."

Peter seemed to finally understand his plan. "It'd be impossible for Walter's riders to invade Wirskworth... Even without the destruction to the land, they could not take the city without siegecraft."

"Perhaps Walter could leave some cavalry on its doorstep until the siege of Iovbridge was over," Elliot said. "Nevertheless, if he finds no food in Elmor's land, he will be forced to retreat with all his soldiers."

"As the queen said—why do you want to send Walter to Elmor?" wondered Peter. "What is the point of all this?"

"Once Walter leaves Elmor, accepting his defeat, Wirskworth's men will march undisturbed to Iovbridge. They can even carry supplies, since we will then have enough time before the enemy attacks the royal capital," replied Elliot.

"Even then, Thorn can return to Ballar before Elmor's men get to Iovbridge. His horses are very fast, but most of Elmor's soldiers are on foot," said the general.

"His men and horses will be exhausted, and the rest of his allies will be miles away," rebutted Elliot. "He won't try to attack Elmor's men on the south-eastern path. It is too dangerous with the Royal Army lurking at the South Gate. He needs more soldiers for that. He would attack Elmor's army in the open fields of the Snake Road but not so close to the city."

Another glance between Peter and the queen.

"And if Walter and his cavalry leave Ballar, Iovbridge will have enough time to retake the Vale of Gods and attack Ramerstorm. Only the infantry of the enemy will be in White City—about four thousand men."

The general almost choked upon hearing Elliot's last words. "You want us to attack Walter's men in White City?"

"I'm sure Iovbridge doesn't have supplies for many days, and the enemy's soldiers will collect every crop from the Vale of Gods for themselves. You can take back these crops... and, it would be wise if you had collected the food from your land before Walter arrived in Ballar..."

"News of my cousin's arrival came late. We had to support Ballar and didn't have time. The turmoil made us neglect Iovbridge's supplies," admitted the queen.

"When you heard that Walter was going to be in White City, you ought to have gathered every harvest in Iovbridge, along with the soldiers and people of Ramerstorm," remarked Elliot. "A battle outside White City was foolish."

The queen looked at him, angry. "How dare you!"

"I'm sorry I disappointed you, Elliot," said the general. "Ramerstorm is a small city with weak walls. If I had let Walter besiege it, he might have set up guards at every gate, preventing a retreat, and as soon as he invaded the city, we would all have been dead. Thus, the council decided to meet them in front of the walls. The archers were to prevent the enemy forces from approaching. If we failed, we could retreat from a secret gate before the enemy got wind of it."

"Why battle in Ramerstorm? Even if you had made it, Walter would have come back with a bigger army."

The general didn't seem to expect that question. "To protect an ally of the Crown."

"The last ally," added Elliot. "Wouldn't it have been wiser to ask Lord Ballard to retreat to Iovbridge, bringing his soldiers to the city without losing men in Ramerstorm? If you had failed, how many men would have had to be sacrificed for you to be able to retreat?"

"A queen who doesn't fight for her allies is a coward!" shouted Sophie.

"It's better to be a coward and protect your people than to be brave, pushing them to death..."

The queen flushed—with both anger and embarrassment, Elliot thought.

"If Walter leaves Ballar, it will be a unique opportunity to attack White City," Elliot insisted.

"We don't have siege weapons like Walter's, nor men to waste in a siege!" said Peter.

"You have Ballar's Governor! I'm sure he will know of some way for you to enter the city quietly."

"We cannot keep Ramerstorm," argued the queen.

"Of course," concurred Elliot. "We don't need White City. A victory over the enemy's men, together with their defeat at Wirskworth, will be enough to hurt Walter's prestige among his allies. We will take back the food, and we will show the kingdom that we still have a chance against Thorn. This is all we want. Nevertheless, nobody can know the true plan until Walter leaves Ballar—Iovbridge is full of traitors."

A crease appeared between Peter's eyes as he considered. "I will think about it," he said. "However, we must be sure that Walter will believe the news of Reynalds's fall," he added, hastily recounting what they had learnt from Edward's interrogation.

Edward's revelations seemed insignificant to Elliot. "Once I take Stonegate, I'll dispatch a messenger to Ramerstorm to inform Walter of what happened."

Peter pondered for a moment. "Walter won't believe the news. I'm sure he will think it's a trick. The queen's first victory right before he attacks the throne... and a victory over a former Trinity of Death member at that."

"Perhaps we could give the messenger an item of Reynald's, something only he could have," said Elliot.

Sophie's face shone. "Reynald carries the Sword of Destiny! A famous sword that has no equal."

"Then the messenger will ride with the sword and hand it over to Walter," finished Elliot.

"This might work," Peter said. "But still, Walter will think it's a trap... Why inform him of our victory and our plans? He will wonder why we didn't prefer to keep the element of surprise."

"Maybe. But he will conclude that it's impossible for it to be a trap."

"He may think it's a ploy for us to retreat!" said Peter.

"Walter knows the queen won't surrender the throne of Knightdorn without a fight. If she wanted to retreat into Elmor, she would've done so a long time ago."

At last Elliot saw something other than despair in the general's eyes. "Then, we must take advantage of this truth," he murmured. "If Walter leaves Ramerstorm, we can retreat to Stonegate. When we reach the castle, we will send some outriders to observe Snake Road up to the Forked River." The general's excitement grew. "You'll inform Syrella of our arrival in Elmor," he said, looking at Elliot. "If your plan succeeds, then we'll march to Wirskworth undisturbed. Behind Wirskworth's walls, we'll have the combined strength of two armies and Ballar's men."

Elliot listened carefully to his words but didn't speak. His gaze turned to the queen.

"I'm not giving in to Elmor," she said.

"Wirskworth's walls are the strongest in Knightdorn, and the city is huge. It can accommodate the people of Iov—"

"I've told you countless times—I won't ask Lady Endor for her hospitality! I already feel uncomfortable sending messengers to her doorstep, asking for her men, and I wouldn't do it if I had other options... I was hoping that—" Sophie cut her sentence off with a sigh. "I won't go to Elmor unless Syrella asks me to."

"Your Majesty—"

"Don't say a word, Peter," Sophie barked. "What will happen if Lady Endor doesn't allow our entrance? Do you want the people of Iovbridge to die on Elmor's soil and my name to go down in history next to cowardice? The cowardly queen who died without allies in the south-east, begging for help!"

"Elmor will not leave the people of Iovbridge unprote—"

"And if it does, it will sentence its people to death. Walter won't stop until he takes my life, and I won't give in to Elmor. I don't care if Walter attacks their land after my death. I won't sentence them to certain death by retreating there!" she blasted.

Silence spread across the hall.

"Walter will think that it's a game of power," Elliot said, breaking the awkward silence. "Once he receives the sword," he added.

"A game of power?" spluttered Peter.

"The sword may make his allies doubtful about Elmor's involvement, as well as curious about the identity of the man who defeated Reynald. His alliances are built on fear. He'll be sure that the queen is trying to sow discord among his men just before the battle, so his desire to head to Elmor will become stronger."

"What will happen if he doesn't take the bait?" asked Peter.

"If Syrella Endor decides to fight, I will lead her army to Iovbridge," said Elliot.

Peter exhaled wearily. "As I said before, if Walter doesn't ride to Elmor, we will lose the element of surprise."

"Our best chance is to fight with enough supplies and two large armies from behind the walls of Iovbridge. But if Walter decides to stay in Ramerstorm, you have to hold the siege for about eight days until Elmor's army reaches Isisdor."

"I believe we can do it!" exclaimed the general.

"If Lady Endor refuses to fight, I'll return to Iovbridge by myself," Elliot added.

"Don't come back," said the queen. "Save your life."

Elliot nodded. "I'd like to ask for four companions for this journ—"

"Wait a minute," interrupted Peter. "We need to talk about what you'll say to Syrella if you manage to get to Wirskworth. The Governor of Elmor will not welcome you with open arms when she hears that you dragged Walter to her capital."

Elliot looked at the elaborate ceiling. He had momentarily forgotten that detail.

"There is discord between Elmor and Iovbridge, and the Poison Masters' leader is quite stubborn."

"Why?" asked Elliot. He always wondered what had happened between Syrella and Sophie.

Peter seemed troubled. "When Walter was going to attack Elmor, the council of Iovbridge decided to send the entire Royal Army to Wirskworth. We would fight Walter in the city with the strongest walls in the world. Then, I rode south to inform Syrella of Isisdor's decision. As soon as she confessed her intentions to me, I lost my mind—she intended to line up her men at the Forked River, hidden behind the trees.

"When Walter arrived in Wirskworth to besiege it, she planned to attack him—I explained to her that the plan was dangerous, that if Walter got wind of it, he would kill us all. *'Everyone knows that our walls are powerful, and everyone expects us to face Walter behind them. No one will expect this trap.'* Those were her words...

"So, Iovbridge decided to keep its army in Isisdor, refusing to take part in this madness. Unfortunately, Walter realised it was a trap and attacked at the Forked River, killing most of Elmor's forces..." The general's voice reflected his pain. "Wirskworth's men were slaughtered, and Syrella accused the Crown of treason."

Elliot sighed wearily.

"I'm sure that a letter from the queen asking for an alliance won't suffice," added Peter.

"There must be a way!" said Elliot. "What do they respect the most in Elmor?"

"The great warriors," came the answer from the general.

The queen looked at the general, an unasked question in her eyes.

"Maybe... if they learn that you were trained by Althalos and defeated Reynald Karford in single combat, maybe they'll listen to you."

"Are we going to ask them to fight on our side using a lie?" asked the queen.

"It's the only way," insisted the general.

"No one will believe him!" she lashed out.

Peter glanced at the queen. "Only a dozen men could beat Reynald in combat... such a victory might be enough to persuade Syrella to accept a new alliance."

Sophie frowned. "The only witnesses will be your companions, while Reynald's sword will be in Walter's hands," she murmured, turning her gaze to Elliot.

The general seemed to sag slightly, then his eyes lit up. "Syrella must see Reynald's fall with her own eyes."

The queen didn't seem to understand, but Elliot felt a tingle of fear in his spine.

"Will you invite Lady Endor to Stonegate to watch the duel, Peter?" Sophie's voice revealed sarcasm.

"No, he means for me to take Reynald to Elmor," whispered Elliot, and the woman's eyes opened wide.

"You don't need to carry him—his head will be enough!" retorted the general.

Elliot turned his gaze to the man. "I'm not going to kill him."

The queen and the general were stunned into silence.

Elliot stared at the queen. "He would be a valuable prisoner. Isisdor must not mimic Walter's cruelty. If I kill or maim him, I'll be the same as Walter."

"So be it," said the queen after a few moments of silence. "I will give you a letter for the governor in which I will name you a knight. She must see a man of prestige to agree to listen to you. But I can't anoint you now while everyone thinks you're a prisoner... It will be formalised later."

Annoiting and ceremony was of no consequence to Elliot.

"I can help you find some companions," added Peter. "Do you want warriors or—"

Elliot stopped the general. "I have someone in mind for this role," he said.

"Who?"

"Selwyn," said Elliot hesitantly. "I'd like him to help me find three more companions and follow me to Wirskworth."

"I think it's time for you to go back to your cell." Peter's jaw clenched. He was damned if he was sending Selwyn off at a time like this.

"It was just a suggestion," exclaimed the queen, half-rising from her throne.

"He's the only other man I trust in Iovbridge. I need him to follow me," explained Elliot.

"Selwyn is Peter's son! You can't take him with you on a suicide mission!" Sophie said.

"He's the son of the queen's most important military leader! Do you believe that the Ruler of Elmor will be satisfied with four random testimonies? I need men with prestige," Elliot continued steadily. "Selwyn lost his brothers in the war," the boy looked Peter in the eye. "The love for his lost brothers will always keep him away from the lure of a power like Walter's. He is the only notable man I can trust."

Tears pricked in Peter's eyes at the mere idea of letting his last son leave on such a mission.

"He'll be safer in Wirskworth than in Iovbridge," Elliot continued.

Elliot wasn't entirely wrong. If Peter's son stayed in Wirskworth, he'd be safe. *If Elliot fails at Stonegate, Reynald will kill him and his companions*. Peter knew these thoughts would drive him crazy. "You will give me time to think about it," he declared. "You'll stay in your cell until you leave the city. Nobody should suspect a thing."

Elliot nodded. "You must decide quickly. The Sword of Destiny must reach Walter no more than eight days from now! It will take two days for his messenger to reach the Path of Shar—his allies will be there in ten days. He must hear the news before his armies cross the Northern Forest."

Peter glanced at him, nodded, and headed to the door, admitting the same stocky guard, who returned the manacles to Elliot's wrists and pushed him from the room. Peter was left with the queen, lost in his thoughts.

Sophie broke the silence. "It's your decision."

"I'll talk to Selwyn and Laurana," he said helplessly. Sophie got up from the throne and walked towards him. She touched him gently on the back.

"It's been years since the last time messengers, with a knight among them, followed a royal order to pursue a war alliance."

Peter laughed softly. "The First Kings used to give different names to those envoys."

"I think the Pegasus Brotherhood would be a good name for this company."

He looked at her in surprise and nodded. "No one can know that you approved such a plan."

"Only you could reveal it, so I have nothing to fear. You are the only man I would trust with my life." She smiled.

Sophie left him then, her brown hair dancing down her shoulders as she left the Royal Hall. Despite all the concerns that tormented him, he could think only of her. Sophie Delamere, the woman who had lost everything, the woman who had never stopped fighting for Knightdorn, trusted him with her life. But he had betrayed her, and he would soon become the second lord of the knights to desecrate an ancient institution of courage.

Whispers in the Dark

Selwyn observed Peter pacing furiously in the chamber of the Counsellors' Tower, his green cloak waving over his velvet jerkin.

Selwyn was determined. He felt anger welling up, an anger that had been simmering inside of him all these years. Selwyn had already become one with his anger. He could never put it aside but had learnt to bridle it, not succumb to it, except for when it was needed. Sometimes anger was a useful emotion; it kept him focused on the battle while rescuing him from the grief that made him feel trapped and incompetent.

Grief changed people, turning them into stone statues stuck in the past and with no direction for the future. But the thought of revenge motivated him; Selwyn felt its flame slowly burning in his chest, waiting for that moment—the moment when he would take revenge for his brothers he'd loved so much.

The truth was that he was tired of waiting all these years, and the opportunity he had now was unique. Elliot offered him his heart's greatest desire: adventure and blood. A journey full of risk and danger. No one could stop him. He may have felt guilt about leaving his father, he may have imagined his mother's terror, but he would not back down.

"My decision is final," Selwyn declared.

Peter's fear showed on his face. "Selwyn... you don't understand... It's almost impossible for the boy to succeed," he cried. "Iovbridge's army needs you."

"Really?" Selwyn smiled. "My absence will cost our army so much, but

Elliot's won't? A lad who killed four men with two swings of his sword!"

His father raised his voice. "He doesn't want to stay in Iovbridge."

"You can keep him in his cell if you want."

"He saved the queen from certain death and... and—" Peter couldn't finish his sentence.

"And he saved me too," Selwyn added firmly. "I think I owe him."

Tears rolled down Peter's cheeks.

Selwyn walked over to him and held him tightly by the shoulder. "I know you're scared," he murmured. "I know you fear losing me as you lost Sindel and Doran. But you can't protect me forever. I want to be the same man my brothers were," he continued. "I'm scared for you too... for my mother. Maybe this plan is our only hope."

Peter looked into his eyes. "Your mother cannot know the truth. If she does find out, she'll be terrified, and, in her panic, she might say something. No one can know." The general was serious now. "Until we hear from Stonegate, only the queen and I will know where you actually are," he added. "At the council, I will maintain that you and three other men rode to Elliot's village with him to find out more about his origins. I'm sure the counsellors will be furious, but not as much as they'd be if they knew the truth."

The general looked at the sunrays dancing happily on the chamber's stone walls. "If something happens to you, Laurana will hate me," he whispered.

"It's not your fault. It's my choice," declared Selwyn.

The man breathed out wearily, then said, "I'll talk to her later."

"We'd better tell her together," replied Selwyn.

Peter didn't seem to believe this was a good idea. "Elliot will stay in his cell until you set off. No one must suspect anything." He was more confident now, speaking with authority. "You'll help him find three more men. You must choose wisely. The absence of capable soldiers will infuriate the council. You must be sure that your companions will keep their mouths shut. Watch them, and if they try to talk, kill them."

Selwyn did not object. "Elliot may want to meet the men who will follow us, but it'll be dangerous to bring them to his cell. The city has many indiscreet eyes."

Peter breathed out heavily again. "I have an idea." He did not seem happy. Selwyn waited for him to continue, but the general suddenly took on a profoundly serious expression. "You have to promise me," he said.

Selwyn didn't speak.

"You will keep me posted on the plan's progress, and from the moment you leave Iovbridge, you'll obey Elliot. Don't take any risky decisions on your own."

Selwyn smiled. "Don't worry, Father. I've been ready for this for a long time."

His father's face grew stern. "No, you're not, but neither is Elliot," he retorted. "Skill in battle is not as important as you think. If you really were ready, you would only feel fear and not excitement."

Peter cast one last look at Selwyn and left the chamber, leaving him confounded by those last words.

The rain had covered the long and narrow path with mud, and Selwyn walked with difficulty, trying to avoid the deep puddles into which his boots sank. Thousands of thoughts spun in his mind, making him impatient for what was to come.

Selwyn held a torch that softly lit the dark path. He may have been in this world for twenty years, but he was still afraid of the dark. His gaze wandered up the tall trees that moved as the wind grew stronger. He continued walking until he began to see the cells in front of him. Several figures were lying on the dirty straw, and their snoring drowned out the rustling of the leaves.

"Good evening, Selwyn." Elliot lay on the straw, his gaze lively as Selwyn's torchlight filled his cell.

"I bring you news."

"I'm glad you'll be travelling with me," Elliot said with a smile.

Selwyn frowned.

"Well, you wouldn't have come here in the middle of the night if you didn't intend to follow me..."

"Be quieter, Elliot," murmured Selwyn. "Someone could be eaves-dropping."

"The thieves in these cells have been sleeping since sunset," the lad reassured him.

Now it was Selwyn's turn to smile. "My decision angered my father," he blurted.

"I'm sure."

"No one, not even my mother, knows where we're going."

Elliot got up and walked to the cell's steel door; the flames lit up his face. "The most difficult thing is not to face your biggest fears but to face them alone. Your father did the right thing to hide the truth, so you shouldn't be hard on him."

The stranger's insight unsettled Selwyn. It seemed the young man understood more than Selwyn had intended.

"My father informed the council that I, along with three other men, would accompany you to your village to discover what we could about you and your Master. The counsellors were outraged." Selwyn didn't bother to hide his annoyance. "They argued that we could use you in battle and considered it madness to waste men for such a purpose while Walter's men are guarding the Vale of Gods. The queen insisted that she had the right to use her men as she wished and said that we would cross the valley carefully. Despite the frustration, no one objected. Her Majesty promised that we would return before Walter's arrival, so that not a single man would be wasted. No one will know the true plan—the queen will only reveal it if Walter leaves Ballar. The nobles think that my father is forcing me to flee, so that I might survive Walter's arrival," Selwyn continued. "My father wants us to cross the Land of Fire carefully, without the Guardians becoming aware of our presence too early. He ordered me to wait outside Stonegate until you fought Reynald, but I—"

"And that's what's going to happen," interrupted Elliot.

Selwyn looked at him for a moment but didn't protest. "I'll help you find three more companions. If they try to tell anyone the truth about our plan, they'll have to die."

Elliot nodded in agreement.

"We cannot take the best soldiers with us, but I know some—"

"Soldiers are not what I need."

"What do you need?"

Elliot smirked. "I want someone who has travelled to every corner of Knightdorn, who knows every road, forest, and valley in that land. I also need someone from Wirskworth."

Selwyn nodded as he thought about Elliot's demands, then spoke, "As you said, we must approach Stonegate without the Guardians noticing us in the Land of Fire. A guide will be helpful," said the lad. "Also, if we get to Wirskworth with someone of their own, they may be more inclined to believe us. Someone local is always more trusted than a stranger."

Selwyn thought for a moment. He himself hadn't travelled much in Knightdorn. His brothers had travelled with their father while Selwyn had been posted to Iovbridge. But he knew men who fit Elliot's description. "Long Arm John has travelled all over the world. He was a pirate and a bounty hunter. And Morys Bardolf comes from a small noble house of Elmor. He left Wirskworth for Iovbridge two years ago," he said. "Morys is a good swordsman and a man of honour, but John is a drunkard and wayward. He's not from noble lineage. Gold and prostitutes are all he seeks."

"*Long Arm*?" wondered Elliot.

Selwyn laughed. "They call him that because he never once failed to capture an outlaw."

"I think he's just what we need," said Elliot with a tone of satisfaction.

"I will get them alone at first light. John will be easily convinced. I'm sure he'll want to leave Iovbridge now that Walter's approaching. He may hate Walter, but he wouldn't risk his life in a battle against him. In fact, he wouldn't risk his life for anyone."

"Courage and devotion are not what I'm looking for."

"Morys will not be happy to return to Wirskworth, but he'll do it to help the queen," Selwyn continued. "After the battle and the massacre that followed at the Forked River, he was exasperated with Syrella Endor and left his city to join the Royal Army. The queen welcomed him to the city and honoured him with the title of defender."

Elliot listened to him in silence, then nodded briefly.

"We need one more man," Selwyn remarked. "Maybe a good swordsman would be useful."

Elliot seemed to ponder for a moment. "We want a young soldier, not a veteran swordsman," he murmured. "Such men are hard to tame."

Selwyn thought that Elliot was wise beyond his years. "You could watch the trainees in the courtyard," he suggested.

"I do not think it prudent for me to leave this cell until we depart the city."

"My father has an idea..."

Elliot seemed to notice the hesitation in Selwyn's voice, yet he didn't ask anything else.

"I have to go back to the palace," Selwyn spoke. "We'll meet again tomorrow."

"Hold on," Elliot said. "You must promise me something..."

The boy's words sounded the same as his father's, and Selwyn stood in front of the cell, waiting.

Elliot's eyes met his. "You'll swear to me that you'll obey me. I know that you've lost loved ones in the war, but you'll have to bury your anger and rage if you want us to succeed."

Selwyn frowned, and then a sound came from behind the trees. He turned in a flash, dropping the torch as he drew his sword. In the guttering light, Selwyn felt a presence approaching. He raised his sword, prepared to strike, then light spread again into the gloomy night as Elliot reached through the bars to grab the torch. A black dog halted at the edge of the light, then trotted off. Selwyn closed his eyes and let out a sigh of relief.

"You have to stay calm. Panic will never be your friend."

"We are conspiring about secret plans in the night, next to criminals in a city full of spies... You should get scared when you hear sounds in the dark."

Shadows danced across Elliot's features. "No," he replied. "You must learn to curb your fears. There's nothing in the dark that should scare you. It's only the unknown that frightens you. When you become one with your fears, only then will you be able to tame them and use them as your weapon."

Selwyn felt his cheeks flush in shame. He'd been afraid of the dark since he was a kid. He remembered running, panic-stricken, through a forest, unable to hear his brothers' voices, unable to find their tent. It was the first time he had gone hunting with them, and he had gone off on his own in search of a rabbit, wanting to impress them. Hours passed before they found him crying, sitting by the roots of a tree, while snow had covered the ground in the icy night. Now, he felt like he was still that embarrassed child.

Elliot looked at him as if he could see through him, as if he was reading his thoughts. "When I was a child, I was terrified of the dark," he said. "My Master wanted me to overcome my fear, so he asked me to stay in the forest by myself for as many nights as needed until I killed a hyena."

Selwyn was stunned. This was very harsh punishment for a child.

"I sat on a rock for two nights, thinking I was going to die. On the third night, I was so overwhelmed with fear that I began to hear whispering in my head. It was my subconscious. It was shouting at me that I should run, go back to bed, and tell my Master that I couldn't do what he asked.

But slowly, I began to calm down, and other voices came to me. There was a part of me that was afraid, but another part of me wanted to prove my worth. I moved silently, like a shadow in the dark. I waded into a muddy swamp to diminish my human odour. Then I killed a ferret and left its dead body next to my hideout. When the hyena appeared and heard the rustling behind it, when my spear tore its flesh, then I was the fear. And the darkness was now my weapon and not my weakness."

Selwyn wasn't sure what to say to this young man, so self-possessed and calm. He took the torch from Elliot's hand and put the sword back in its sheath. "I will visit you soon," he murmured. He moved to leave the gloomy park, then took one last look at Elliot. "You have my word," he said. As he walked away, he could not help but think this was both the strangest and the scariest conversation of his life.

The Girl with the Veil

John stood on a deserted pier, looking impatiently around him. He didn't like being kept waiting, especially now. This cursed city was smothered in melancholy and fear, and he should have left it long ago. The sky was gloomy, dense clouds hiding the dawn that was blooming in the east. A few small waves broke onto the anchored ships in the Harbour of the Scarlet Sea

John had never in his life longed for death the way soldiers seemed to. The restless heartbeats, hunting in an unknown forest, the anxiety of sailing in unknown stormy seas that lash a galley's bow... those were the things his soul yearned for. The battles of soldiers and kings aroused his revulsion. Now the once beautiful city of Iovbridge, the city of promises and dreams, seemed to choke him more and more. He had given up on adventure in recent years, finding refuge in the taverns and brothels in Knightdorn's capital. But all good things eventually come to an end. It was a truth he insisted on forgetting as he got older.

Strange rumours had reached his ears in the last few days. In every alley you heard whispers of revolt or, rather, a conspiracy against the queen after the annihilation of her army in White City. John did not intend to die in Iovbridge. He had to leave the city as soon as possible.

The hour was so early that fishermen hadn't even started setting up their haul in the Fishermen's Square. The Harbour of the Scarlet Sea was quieter than a deserted forest. John kept looking around, wary. He had thought of ignoring the invitation. What could the son of Peter Brau ask of him? He also wondered why Selwyn Brau hadn't come himself but had sent a little boy to convey the message.

John heard footsteps. He hid behind an overturned boat and peered over it, catching sight of a dark-skinned, young man, about twenty-five, walking on the pier. John knew him, but this was not the young man he was waiting for. More layers. More reason to be suspicious. John crept away, keeping behind the hull, but he tripped over a loose plank in the pier. As he sprawled on hands and knees, he heard the sound of a sword being drawn, and the footsteps hastened in his direction. John made an effort to get up, but it was too late.

"One would expect that a bounty hunter would be more careful... What are you doing here, Long Arm?" asked the man. There was a threat in that voice—but there often was. His eyes were darker than ebony, his curly hair the same. He had a flat nose, a thin chin, and he filled out his scarlet jerkin more thoroughly than most.

"Don't stick your nose into my affairs, Bardolf, 'cause you'll regret it," cursed John, trying to get up.

"Are you spying on me?" Morys Bardolf raised his sword, aiming at John's throat.

"I'm warning you," snarled John. "If you don't put the sword down, the Scarlet Sea will become even more scarlet with your blood."

Morys sneered. "It's strange you're still here, John. Cowards like you beat it when war approaches."

John was about to launch himself onto Morys when a voice called out.

"Enough!"

John and Morys both turned—and saw Selwyn Brau with a smile on his lips.

Selwyn had approached them quietly as they quarrelled. Morys lowered his sword, and John stood up, his anger clear.

"Why so much secrecy, Lord Brau? One would think you're hatching a conspiracy."

"That would be a good assumption," admitted Selwyn.

Morys's eyes widened in surprise while John's narrowed in suspicion.

"Is the son of the lord of the knights conspiring against the Crown?"

Word had spread quickly, then, of Selwyn's father's new position. "No," he said. "Only against the Royal Council."

Morys spoke up. "I don't understand."

Selwyn took a deep breath. "First, I must warn you that only a few know what I am about to say," he began. "No one can know what I'm going to tell you. If you talk," he paused, "you'll die."

John's expression was tinged with fear, but Morys put on a sober face.

"You can leave, if you want," continued Selwyn.

Morys didn't move, clearly proud in his stoicism, and Selwyn eyed John. He was sure the bounty hunter was tempted, but John held his ground. Secrets and conspiracies always drew the interest of corrupt men.

"Very well," sighed Selwyn. "The reason I called you here is that I want you to travel with me to Wirskworth to deliver a message—"

"I think I've heard enough," shouted John before Selwyn could finish his sentence.

"Don't interrupt me."

"I don't intend to die for the queen, Brau!" John said. "I'm sure you want to seek an alliance with Elmor's ruler." He was almost laughing now. "The Vale of Gods is held by Walter Thorn, and Reynald Karford guards the Land of Fire. If you think I'll cross Ersemor or the dry fields to the western path, you've probably drunk too much wine!"

Selwyn's anger surged. "Aren't you forgetting who you're talking to?"

"Forgive me, my lord," said Long Arm with a theatrical bow.

Selwyn only glared, then continued, sharing the details of the traitors and Elliot's plan. He knew it was risky revealing everything. A wiser man would lie and tell them about the true plan only after they left the city. However, no lie would convince John and Morys to ride towards Stonegate. To counter any possible treachery, Selwyn had decided to have men follow them. If they talked, they would be killed.

"Once we get to Wirskworth," Selwyn finished, "we will ask for a hearing with the governor, and we'll have a royal letter with us."

Morys opened his mouth to speak, but John beat him to it. "Wonderful! It's been years since I last heard such an intelligent plan," he mocked. "Five men will seize Stonegate, drag Reynald Karford to the south, form a new alliance with Elmor, and force Walter's armies to retreat. If we had thought of it earlier, we would've saved ourselves twenty years of wars."

"I know how it sounds," Selwyn said, trying not to sound defensive. "But with Elliot's help, I believe we can succeed."

"With Elliot's help?" growled John. "Some lad killed four men, and you're ready to worship at his feet? Reynald will kill him. And if somehow the boy survives, Wirskworth will never welcome us. Not now."

"No one knows Knightdorn better than you do, John. I need you to lead me south as quietly as you can. Once we get to Wirskworth, you're free to leave," replied Selwyn.

"What if the boy is defeated in Stonegate?" argued John.

"We will take care to cross the Land of Fire without being seen by the Guardians of the South. Once we get close to Stonegate, Elliot will approach, seeking single combat with the Commander. We will wait in hiding until their fight is over."

Long Arm growled something incomprehensible. He was around forty years of age. His boots were old, and his eyes were the colour of chestnut. Some greasy tufts of thick hair stuck out here and there on his head. His belly had grown in recent years, and his body exuded an odour of red wine.

Morys had yet to voice doubts, but he did not seem convinced. He looked at Selwyn intently. "Do you trust this boy?"

"Yes."

"Then I will do what my queen orders," Morys declared.

John's contempt for this loyalty was obvious, but he said, "I'll help you get to Wirskworth. I don't intend to fight anyone, and if there's a battle on the way, I won't stick around to watch you die."

Selwyn nodded, pleased.

"I'd like to think that I'll get paid for my services."

Selwyn's patience snapped. "We are at war, you idiot. Perhaps you'd prefer the queen's place on the battlements when the siege begins?"

John scowled but held his tongue. It seemed Selwyn's threat of violence was not taken lightly. He had won the battle.

"Remember, all you know is that we're going to travel to the village where Elliot lived—nothing more," growled Selwyn.

The two men nodded in agreement.

"I'll meet you again later to see to our preparations. At dawn tomorrow, we're leaving."

John turned sharply and walked the length of the pier, his steps hurried. Selwyn followed more slowly, Morys with him.

"Selwyn, I didn't want to challenge you in front of Long Arm, but," Morys hesitated for a moment, "do you think this plan can succeed?"

Selwyn sighed, unsure how to answer that question. "There's something special about Elliot."

Morys nodded at this vote of confidence. "You are a worthy soldier and a man of honour. Your word is enough for me," he said after a few moments. In the distance, John bellowed a pirate song.

Elliot was quite pleased with Selwyn's account of the meeting. "Thank you. I couldn't have hoped for anything better," he said.

The general's son smiled. "It's time to go," he whispered. Selwyn glanced to the left and right, and Elliot followed his gaze. The park was deserted, and the other three prisoners were curled up in their cells. The sun was scorching that morning. The guards brought bread and water twice a day, but they would not return for hours.

Still, Elliot was worried. "Are you sure we will be safe?"

"Stay calm. No one will notice you," whispered Selwyn. "Come closer," he snarled suddenly, raising his voice to be certain none of the thieves, if any were awake, suspected conspiracy between the two.

Elliot brought his hands to the bars, and the young man clasped manacles on his wrists. Then he grabbed a brass key that hung from his belt and put it in the rusty lock. The door shrieked open, and Selwyn grabbed Elliot by the arm, dragging him out.

Once out of sight of the cells, Selwyn pushed Elliot behind a tall pine tree and hastily released his hands. Elliot stretched his body and looked around. He saw a guard's uniform tucked between the tree's roots.

"What if someone recognises me?" Elliot asked.

"Trust me—your face will blend with all the others. No one knows all the guards."

"And the lords and captains on the council?"

"They have no interest in a boy who came to the city just a few days ago, no matter the circumstances of your arrival. Especially at this moment in time."

Elliot put on the uniform and threw his rags next to the old pine tree. He wore a breastplate with the Pegasus next to the Seven Swords, his light blue cloak fluttering behind him. His boots were made of leather, and a thin blade hung from his belt. Selwyn was dressed in a fig-coloured silk jerkin but didn't carry a sword. Only an elaborate dagger hung from his belt.

They left the park and crossed the narrow streets of Iovbridge's slums. At a busy intersection, they passed several merchants setting up stalls and shops, and a baker was making fresh bread. The road smelled of spices and oils. Elliot saw the Temple of the Unknown God looming ahead.

"The young apprentices are trained next to the Fishermen's Square," said Selwyn. "I'd rather go through the alleys than cross Blossom Road."

Elliot hesitated, then nodded. He would love to see the interior of the temple, but they didn't have time for this.

The Scarlet Sea soon appeared before them, and Elliot marvelled at the magical landscape. The water looked like blood under the red-gold sunlight, and some galleys swayed on the calm waves under a soft breeze. His breastplate enhanced the warmth of the sunlight, a welcome change from the chill of his cell. Nevertheless, hardship didn't bother him. He had grown accustomed to much worse during the years of his training.

Commotion from a big square ahead of them reached Elliot's ears, but Selwyn turned into an alley heading in the opposite direction. They turned again and then again, and then began to walk on a cobbled road that seemed to touch the dreamy seawaters. The ringing of steel on steel soon reached Elliot's ears, a sound he hated and loved with equal measure; it masked the splash of the waves, and he and Selwyn approached a small courtyard full of apprentices training.

Elliot's gaze fell on a few dozen apprentices clumsily wielding their swords. Some fighters used steel, others wooden training weapons. The spectacle was worse than he expected. The young boys held their swords either with fear or with indifference, and their movements were awkward and blundering. An old man watched the pairs of fighters and shouted instructions here and there.

"Unfortunately, there aren't enough men to train these lads. Few drillmasters have survived in recent years, and every Grand Master has been killed," Selwyn said.

"The queen's officers could train these boys," Elliot replied.

"We're at war," Selwyn countered. "Officers only train their squires and some young men of noble lineage. They don't have time for every boy in Iovbridge."

"These young men are the future of the Royal Army," said Elliot emphatically.

"These young men are just what's left. Hundreds of young men have died in the battles of recent years. The defenders are not involved in the training of lads, and all the captains are swamped. The only drillmaster left is old Tristan."

Elliot walked to the courtyard. Wooden swords and bows were thrown here and there on the stony ground. *These young men would look like sheep in a battle against Walter's armies,* he thought. Tristan was walking around the perimeter, supervising the fighters with a bored expression. Elliot followed Selwyn and then saw two men lingering on the edge of the courtyard.

As they approached, Selwyn whispered, "These will be our fellow travellers: John of the Galley Villages and Morys Bardolf of Wirskworth."

The two men nodded, their faces uncertain.

Elliot looked them over. "It's my honour that you'll follow me on this journey; I promise you—"

"Keep your honour and your promises, lad," the one called John said, his skepticism clear. "I'll show you the way to Elmor to leave this damned city and nothing more. As soon as we reach Wirskworth, I'll be leaving."

Elliot laughed. "Of course. But after you help me, my sword will always be there to protect you even if it costs me my life. I promise to protect every companion who accompanies me on this journey."

John stared and started laughing. Mory's gaze held disbelief, and even Selwyn looked at Elliot in surprise.

"You're crazy. If you knew this world, you'd know that no one can protect anyone," countered John. "Someone who seeks to duel with Reynald can't even protect himself."

Elliot turned to Morys, waiting to hear his thoughts. The man returned the attention, sizing Elliot up. "I don't trust you," Morys said, puffing out his chest, "but Lord Brau and my queen do, and that's good enough for me."

Elliot nodded.

"We must hurry," Selwyn said. "You should choose an apprentice."

Elliot glanced again at the pairs of fighters. These young men were not ready for the task; John and Morys would have to be enough. "These lads can't fight," he said.

Selwyn avoided looking at him. "We don't have the army we once had," he mumbled.

"They don't hold the sword properly, and their bodies are weak. The armour's weight would prevent them from moving. They will be like sheep against wolves in a real battle."

"Master Tristan is doing what he can. He's the last drillmaster," Morys said.

"He's not enough! Perhaps the officers should have figured that out," snapped Elliot.

"The officers will fight for Knightdorn's freedom!" Morys blurted. "We won't be judged by a boy who's never fought for the Crown!"

"You were like these lads once. You became a good soldier because a capable Master trained you," Elliot pointed out.

John snorted contemptuously, but Elliot's attention was elsewhere. At the edge of the courtyard, one trainee was swinging wildly, her long, black hair covering her face as she frantically tried to hit her opponent. He avoided the blows, laughing mockingly. Elliot moved closer. No more than twenty years old, the young woman's face was determined. Her brown eyes were fierce as her slender body moved, but her blows were weak. The lad in front of her seemed to be amused.

"You have to try harder if you want to hit me, Eleanor," he shouted sarcastically.

"I'd say that it'd be quite easy for her to hit you if someone showed her how to do it," said Elliot.

The lad who was duelling with the young woman turned slowly and looked at Elliot. "And who are you?" he snickered.

"Nobody," Elliot said calmly.

Master Tristan approached them, looking disgruntled at the interruption. "What's going on here?" His eyes fell on Selwyn, who still watched from the other side of the courtyard. "I did not expect to see you here, Lord Brau."

"We were merely passing by," Selwyn said. Elliot thought he looked nervous. The fewer people who saw the four of them together before leaving the city, the better.

"I'd say you need to teach them more about movement, Master," said Elliot. "They stand almost motionless."

Selwyn signed to him to hush. Tristan turned toward Elliot, his mouth set in a stern line. "You're not a Master, young man. You'd better leave the training to me."

"This lad's sitting so still that even a dog could disarm him."

The trainee turned red, and the young woman laughed. "I'm an archer, not a swordsman," he muttered.

The courtyard was quiet around them now, all eyes fixed on Elliot.

"Why don't you try to hit me with an arrow?" suggested Elliot, slowly lifting a discarded shield and a wooden sword next to his boot.

The lad glanced at a bow on the stony ground, then back at Elliot.

Elliot gave him a nod of encouragement.

"Lower that bow at once, Arnott," yelled Tristan as the young lad raised the weapon and aimed at Elliot. "You are aiming at a man of the City Guard!"

Arnott, his eyes darting from one man to the other, lowered the bow a few inches, but his finger kept stretching the string.

"I order you to hit me," Elliot shouted.

Tristan screamed as the arrow streaked toward Elliot's chest. He swiftly raised the shield, and as the arrow drove into it with a sharp thud, he hurled the wooden sword. Arnott let out a cry of pain as the sword struck him in the face, the bow slipping from his hands. The apprentices looked stunned at the spectacle, while the young woman, Eleanor, seemed merely curious.

"You have to be faster with both the sword and the bow," said Elliot calmly. "In battle, no one stands still for you to aim. And never underestimate your opponent. One mistake against a steel blade will be enough."

Tristan stared at Elliot. "I haven't seen something like this in a long time," he stammered.

"He's one of our best men." Selwyn had approached.

"What is your name?" asked the Master.

"Lore," replied Elliot calmly.

"I don't know you."

"I'm not popular."

"We won't bother you anymore, Master," Selwyn said, pulling Elliot by the shoulder as Morys and John followed. The four men left the courtyard hurriedly and continued on, until they were lost from sight in an alley.

"I risk everything for you, and you show off before the entire courtyard!" roared Selwyn. "If someone speaks... if someone understands what happened... the council will be furious!"

"An old Master and some poor lads. None of them would dare approach a lord or a counselor of the queen." Elliot was unperturbed. "They're scared. Death is approaching the city day by day. Whatever happened will give them courage. They'll believe that perhaps someone can protect them. Every good soldier can do what I just did."

"Few men can do what you just did." Sarcasm had left John's voice.

Elliot wasn't paying attention. "I think I have found our last companion."

John snorted.

"You mean that bully?" Morys said "You just humiliated him in front of the entire courtyard."

"No... not him. The young woman."

Morys stared. "I lived in a city with great female warriors, but that girl is not one of them. She won't stand the journey, and if she falls into our enemies' hands, she will be raped and killed."

"Determination is everything if you wish to become great," said Elliot. "The boys are full of fear, but this young woman fought like nothing else was happening in the world—that is a warrior's mightiest strength."

No one spoke, and Elliot took advantage of the silence.

"Do you know who she is? Does she have any family in the city?" He looked at Selwyn.

The three men weighed him up, troubled. *They all know who she is,* realized Elliot.

"Her name is Eleanor Dilerion, and she's an orphan," Selwyn said. "Her parents died in the Battle of Aquarine, but her brother managed to get out of the city with her in his arms, and they travelled to Iovbridge. Eleanor was only three years old." The young man paused for a moment. "Her brother was Bert Dilerion..." Selwyn trailed off, not quite meeting Elliot's gaze.

"And this matters why?"

"Bert Dilerion loved Queen Sophie from the moment he met her. His father was a childhood friend of Henry Delamere. When he arrived in Iovbridge, he was only twelve years old, and Sophie was nine, but they adored each other and were inseparable. The queen wanted to marry him when she turned sixteen, but the Royal Council opposed her will, insisting that she should seek a strong military alliance through marriage. Sophie never accepted that. She relented enough not to wed Bert, but they never separated—not until he died. Illness. He was only twenty-two." Selwyn hesitated. "The queen never got over it. She remains unmarried, and they say she hasn't taken a lover, despite her youth. Eleanor was always her protégée, the only thing left of her lost love."

"Why isn't she trained in the palace?"

Selwyn shrugged. "None of the officers wanted to take on a woman as a student, so she decided to train alongside the common boys in the city. The queen reprimanded her for her stubbornness."

Elliot smiled, this young woman reminding him of himself.

"Despite the reprimand, the queen thinks the world of Eleanor. She won't allow her to leave Iovbridge," Selwyn said.

"Convey my desire to Her Majesty," persisted Elliot.

"Very well," Selwyn agreed.

"We will set off at dawn with or without her."

"We have to go," murmured Brau Jr.

Elliot nodded, and the men hurried forward.

In the dim cell, Elliot shuddered against the wind, the muddy straw offering no warmth or protection. Dusk had fallen, and the park was deserted. The guards had freed the petty thieves at sunset, so he was alone. A light bobbed through the growing darkness, and Elliot came to his feet as lilac-colored skirts came into view.

"Your Majesty, I did not expect to see you here."

The woman was holding a torch. No guard accompanied her. The lace on her sleeves and at her neckline ruffled in the wind. Her blue eyes were bright in the light of the flickering flame.

"I want to talk to you," she said abruptly.

"It's dangerous for you to wander alone in a place like this."

She grinned. "A place like this is the safest for me—no one would expect me to be here."

"Walter could have spies watching you."

"Don't worry about me," she retorted. "I was informed that you want Eleanor to join you. I thought you were looking for soldiers," she said, scowling.

"Courage and dedication are sometimes more important than a capable soldier. Eleanor also lost her parents in the battles against Walter. Her love for them will dull the lure of power like Walter's. This girl won't betray me. Just like Selwyn," Elliot said softly.

The queen's expression did not reveal her thoughts. "I love this girl as if she were my sister," she suddenly whispered. "If you fall into the hands of Walter's men, they will," she bit her lip, "they will torture her, rape her, and kill her!".

"No one will touch my companions."

The queen's light filled the cell as she leaned close to the bars. "Of course, Eleanor wants to follow. She was always stubborn. She doesn't know how dange—"

"You have made your decision, Your Majesty," Elliot cut her off. "Otherwise, you wouldn't be here."

Sophie sighed heavily. "I'll hide this from the Royal Council." Another sigh. "If they find out about Eleanor, they'll think Peter and I conspired to get our loved ones out of the city. They were already outraged when they heard that Selwyn would be leaving." She closed her eyes for a moment. "You ask for too much. No other king or queen would agree to such a plan!"

"And they would be wrong!" Elliot approached the cell's bars.

The woman didn't show fear. "Maybe Eleanor will be safer away from Isisdor... They'll protect her in Wirskworth," she said more to herself. "Iovbridge has so many traitors and spies that she's more in danger in the city than outside of it."

Elliot remained silent.

"You have to promise me," cried Sophie. "You will leave her outside of Stonegate with Selwyn until you win the duel. Order her to return to Iovbridge if you lose," she warned.

Elliot nodded sharply. He would follow Sophie's orders.

"And if you make it to Wirskworth, order her to stay there and never return to Iovbridge. No one will recognise her in Elmor—perhaps she'll be able to live a beautiful life there."

Elliot leaned close so their foreheads nearly touched between the iron bars. "As you wish," he said humbly. He wanted to say so much more.

Sophie held his gaze. "Thank you for saving me," she said after a while. "Thank you for fighting for me... even if I never gave you anything." Her eyes seemed to sparkle in the torchlight.

"I'll fight for you until my eyes can no longer behold the light of the moon."

The queen's lips parted—she knew the story, of course, knew the words of the Knight of the Moon. Tears welled in Sophie's eyes and then rolled down her cheeks. She pushed back from the bars and made to leave, but she stopped before his cell was in darkness. Looking back, she said, “Good luck, Elliot.”

Elliot watched her go away, feeling a slew of emotions. The torch’s flames looked like a veil over her hair. A memory suddenly flashed through his mind—the little girl in the white veil stared at him from afar, screaming, while he could only sob.

The Sword of Destiny

John's rear end was growing numb. His horse followed Elliot's black mare with a swaying gait as the sun caressed the cloudless sky with its golden rays.

The path they followed was parallel to the Path of the Elder Races. They had decided to be prudent, as the Land of Fire hid many dangers, and take a less-used road. Copses of trees and muddy fields lined their way. John felt tired already. He would rather they had taken the more comfortable Path of the Elder Races—an easier journey that would have risked an early encounter with the Guardians of the South.

Selwyn, Eleanor, and Morys rode silently next to Elliot. Soon, they would be close to Ersemor, and thousands of thoughts poisoned John's mind as he rode. An old fear had awakened in him, and no matter how hard he tried, he couldn't tame it. He had travelled to every corner of the world—from the Western Empire to the Ice Islands and from Gaeldeath to the Elves-Mountain—but the Ersemor Forest was the only place he feared. He remembered the first time he saw a wyvern—the size of a pirate galley, with thorns on its wings and tail longer than a dagger. He had also seen mermaids swimming in stormy seas and giants resting on rocky slopes, but Ersemor frightened him more than anything.

He'd been young and boisterous when he'd first set foot in Ersemor, eager to see the world. He had heard the stories before riding into the notorious forest of the centaurs. Rumour had it that Ersemor's huge trees, which grew beside rivers with crystal-clear waters, looked the same in every part of the forest, indistinguishable from each other. It was said the forest imprisoned anyone who tried to cross it, the centaurs' ancient magic turning it into a maze. Legend had it that only men with pure intentions or blood with the pegasi magic could cross this place. The stories claimed that the Egercoll line was the only one touched by the same magic that wraps the pegasi.

John hadn't believed the legends. His younger self had dreamt of riding in the forest and seeing the centaurs up close. But when he reached the shadows beneath Ersemor's trees, he had immediately felt a strange aura around him, and his horse had grown restless and wild. As the forest closed in around him, John had carved marks into the tree trunks to see if he was crossing the same land over and over again. He never saw one of his markings again and he knew he was lost. Fear had begun to nest inside him, and one night he felt a black cloud engulf him in his sleep. He remembered it approaching him like a hot breath, his eyes opening wide under the dark sky. Shaken, John had ridden his mare wildly through the night and escaped—and he had never returned.

As the fear and the memories of that night waned and years passed, John grew convinced that centaurs and their magic were a thing of story only—until he saw two centaurs in Iovbridge with his own eyes. King Thomas had ridden alone to Ersemor, seeking an alliance against Walter Thorn, and the centaurs had agreed to fight on his side. John never learned how the king had managed to cross Ersemor and gain the strange creatures as his ally. Pure intentions or blood with the pegasi *magic*, he had thought countless times. Not that John believed in such things. No matter how powerful the man might be, Thomas Egercoll's blood wasn't more magical than John's. He may not have been literate, but he knew that logic, not legends, could explain most things. Logic was the best defense against myths and gods and priests, he'd found.

John shook himself from his thoughts of Ersemor—there was no reason to think about it since they didn't plan to cross it. They now rode a small trail he had chosen that would take them to Stonegate.

Though he had travelled with pirates, smugglers, deserters, and petty swindlers, the truth was that this company was the strangest he could remember. He looked at the lad, Elliot, in the old armour given to him by Selwyn Brau—the Pegasus and the Seven Swords glistened on the young man's chest, and the blue cloak fluttered gently behind his back. Something strange was going on with that lad, something John didn't understand. He was a stranger, and yet here he rode with two capable soldiers, one the son of the lord of the knights, and a young woman who was friend to the queen.

As for Peter Brau's son, Selwyn rode proudly, bearing an expensive, glittering plate with the same symbols as Elliot's. The young man was a worthy soldier, but he would die at Reynald Karford's hand nonetheless. As would Elliot. What frightened John the most was that those involved in this plan were the only people he believed had an ounce of logic in this accursed kingdom.

They continued riding until the sun began to disappear from the sky, giving way to darkness.

"I think we should rest and continue at dawn," Elliot suggested.

"Aren't you used to riding and the sting in your thighs?" mocked John. "I thought you wanted to get to Stonegate quickly."

Elliot didn't return the smile. "Everyone is exhausted, and we have a long way to go until Wirskworth. We'd better rest."

John turned his gaze and saw, a little further back, the two young men and the girl—they looked tired. He stopped and got off his horse. The land was a few miles away from the Path of the Elder Races, but the mud was deep around it. The rains of the last few days had left their mark, signalling the end of the summer. Wildflowers dotted the landscape, with oaks and pines standing watch. Moss and yellow leaves lay on the muddy ground, while hundreds of stars adorned the sky above their heads.

As they made camp, Morys coaxed a fire to life to cook the hares he had shot with his bow. The others passed bread around while John tied the hares to two branches over the fire. The meat began to cook with a tantalising smell as his belly began to rumble.

Elliot was so hungry he could barely see. He took a bit of rabbit meat, then washed it down with a sip of wine—they had water and plenty of wine with them, the latter being John's inviolable condition for travel-ling.

"You say that you wouldn't give your life for the queen, Long Arm. But if Walter Thorn takes the crown, what will you do? I don't think you'll like Iovbridge with him on the throne," Selwyn broke the silence.

John snorted contemptuously. "I'll leave, you idiot! I'll get to the Ice Islands, farther if necessary. I don't think Walter cares about me, and I don't care who will rule over Iovbridge palace."

"I don't think you would like the Ice Islands," Morys spoke for the first time since making camp.

"I don't think you've ever been there," countered John.

"I don't need to have been there to know that the people of the Ice Islands are a bunch of barbarians." Morys's breastplate lay next to him. The Isisdor emblem was engraved in the centre, but a snake was sewn on his yellow cloak.

"You're stupid and narrow-minded, Bardolf. You've only ever lived in Iovbridge and Wirskworth, and you think you know the world?

"The people of Ice Islands are unique. There's a place for everyone in their land, and they share a way of life: to bow to a leader of their choosing, not a king or queen on the other side of the world."

"You sound like you love them, John. Why didn't you live there al-ready?" scoffed Morys.

"Because I hate the cold. But I'll take it over fighting for the Crown."

"Of course, cowards suit a coward."

John glared at Morys. "Are they cowards for not fighting on the queen's side?"

"I thought the Ice Islands accepted King Thomas and asked to join Knightdorn some years ago," Elliot said.

"That's true. Thomas Egercoll was the first King of Knightdorn to travel to their land and speak to their leader. On the Ice Islands, Thomas envisioned the great changes he would bring to Knightdorn in the years to come."

"King Thomas's ideas for the future were just and noble," Elliot said, "unlike the lords and kings who imposed their will on the weak."

Morys grunted, seemingly annoyed. Elliot frowned. He had been taught that only Walter's supporters were against Thomas Egercoll's decrees.

"So some say," John said. "Many believe that Thomas tried to give more power to the powerful, while others think he tried to fight injustice. I think he wanted to do the right thing, but his decisions were too short-lived to change centuries-old habits."

"The king's decisions were unfair to the noble families who honoured their kings and people for many generations," said Morys, his voice taking on an edge. "He took their men, the defenders of their lands, and he would have asked for their gold, too, if he'd lived long enough."

"The king was confronted with one of the greatest warlords ever born in this world!" cried Selwyn. "He made difficult choices to defend his people."

John laughed. "I knew you'd defend Thomas, Lord Brau. Like I knew that Bardolf would grimace like an old goat. You, boy, why do you support Thomas Egercoll?" he asked, looking at Elliot.

"Every virtuous man was in favour of Thomas." Eleanor spoke for the first time. She had said little, keeping to herself as they began their journey.

"We don't care what you think, *girl*. Women have no sense about those things," blurted Morys.

Eleanor's cheeks flushed with anger. "I did not expect such narrow-mindedness from a man of Wirskworth—a city with a female ruler, a city that was the first to give women equal rights to claim any office in the kingdom, before Thomas did the same."

Morys snorted, disdain in his eyes.

"I wonder if you know the whole story about what King Thomas did," John said, looking Elliot in the eye. "I wouldn't think folk from a rural village would understand."

"On the contrary, Long Arm! They know what it means to live in a world without slaves," Elliot said.

"Of course!" John mocked. "However, this change was not the one that angered most people. Maybe you should listen to the whole story."

Elliot frowned. He didn't want to talk about Thomas Egercoll but was curious to hear what John had to say. Everything he knew he had learnt from his Master. It'd be interesting to hear the facts from someone else.

"Then tell me," he said, and Long Arm's smile revealed his dirty teeth.

"As I said, when Thomas was finally made king, he travelled to the Ice Islands and met a ruler chosen by the people of that land. Thereafter, the king envisaged the kingdom he wanted to build and changed many laws in Knightdorn. Thomas forbade slavery and imposed payment for every servant in a lord's service. Then, Thomas forbade the inherited succession of any office in Knightdorn. The king, as well as the governors, would be chosen after the death of their predecessors. Thomas knew it was difficult to grant every man in the kingdom the right to vote, so he decided to charge the councils in each region with the task of electing their leaders. Thomas also didn't want his council to be comprised of nobles only, so he changed the Royal Council's structure—he gave several seats to men of humble descent, while he kept only two counsellors of noble birth. Thomas believed that men who had ascended from slums and villages would represent the common people's voice in the vote for a king."

"Thomas was unfair on that matter," Morys interrupted John.

"What happened next?" asked Elliot.

John frowned. "The king didn't require the governors to adopt this structure for their own councils. He asked them to form their councils as they wished and hoped that they would take inspiration from his choices. However, the rulers and many lords were furious; the former because their houses had been ruling their regions for centuries and now were in danger of losing that role, and the latter because they would lose one of their most significant privileges if the governors didn't appoint them to the new councils."

John seemed amused with his narrative. Elliot was sure he had welcomed the second king's decrees and applauded the blow to the powerful.

"But the lords didn't yet know the last change that the king intended to bring to Knightdorn... Thomas Egercoll hated the idea that every lord had an army in his possession." John grinned. "Some lords had more soldiers than their governor, so any strife between them could lead to immense destruction. To counter this, Thomas imposed a heavy tax on every lord who had over two hundred soldiers. When the lords threw a fit, since it would be impossible to pay so much gold, he asked them to hand over the rest of their men to him or to their governors in exchange for various favours. That decision angered every nobleman in Knightdorn. But the king didn't change his mind."

Selwyn and Eleanor listened in silence, but Morys glared and said, "You talk too much, Long Arm—it's time to shut up!"

Elliot mulled over the differences between what John had said and what he had learned from his Master. According to his Master, King Thomas only tried to fight injustice in the kingdom. However, Long Arm's recounting illuminated many weaknesses in his plan; using taxation to make demands would always be problematic, and it was certain that many lords, even the loyal ones, would revolt.

"Two hundred men isn't enough to protect most castles," Morys spoke again. "The king was leaving them exposed."

"Many said so to Thomas," admitted Long Arm, "but the king wasn't convinced. He said if any lord faced a serious threat, the governor would send help. Of course, the nobles insisted that help could arrive too late, so the king suggested they relocate to their regional capitals. He promised them that the rulers would, by royal decree, build towers for them as long as they handed over their soldiers. The regional capitals were vast but sparsely populated—they could accommodate every lord of their region, along with his soldiers.

Selwyn seemed pensive. "My father told me that most lords refused to surrender their men, but the taxes made them give in."

"It's true," John muttered.

"Lady Endor was against that decision," Morys said.

This Elliot knew. His master had mentioned that Syrella disobeyed some of Thomas's decisions and covertly flouted the law. Thomas knew about her actions but chose to turn a blind eye because of their old friendship.

"Many nobles learned to appreciate the decrees," John said.

"Why?" Elliot asked.

"They became incredibly rich! The towers in the capitals no longer needed many servants, and without the cost of soldiers, more of the income from their lands reached their pockets." John took a long swallow of wine.

"Then why did they decide to follow Walter?"

John sighed heavily. "They're a fickle breed. They may have appreciated their increased wealth, but they never forgave Thomas for depriving them of their castles and soldiers. However, not every noble followed Walter. At the beginning, it was mainly the lords of Gaeldeath who did," he said. "They were wary of Walter for some time—his mother was an Egercoll—but they quickly discerned his hatred for his grandfather's opponents and supported him. Then, Robert Thorn was accused of treason by the council of Gaeldeath, which granted the region to Walter. Walter had promised the lords that he'd change Thomas's decrees when he became king."

"Thomas should have attacked Gaeldeath when Walter became governor," Selwyn said.

"It wasn't easy—he needed time to gather his men and march to Gaeldeath. At the same time, Walter used single combat to quickly conquer many northern and central regions, feeding those soldiers into his armies," John said. Then, he attacked Tahryn's capital and took its soldiers too." John argued.

"Walter managed to get revenge on all the northern rulers who had turned their backs on his grandfather in the Pegasus Rebellion. He killed most of them before he attacked Thomas," Morys pointed out.

"Thomas couldn't stop Walter when he had all the north on his side," Eleanor said, looking thoughtful. "He was too powerful while Knightdorn was mired in debt due to the huge costs of the armies now maintained only by royal gold... Thomas was trying to impose a perennial peace through his decrees, but he underestimated the gold he would need for his plan to work."

"Thomas shouldn't have demanded the lords' soldiers," Morys insisted. "That brought his end. He gave the governors enormous power—if one chose to disobey the king, he'd have had a huge army in his possession."

"If a governor chose to disobey the king, his vassal lords would have been forced either way to give him their men. The only question that matters is this one: What is more dangerous for peace in Knightdorn? An army under an overlord or ten armies under ten vassal lords? It is a question that even history finds hard to answer," noted John.

Morys' scowl deepened as John looked pleased with his philosophizing.

"I thought you didn't like Lady Endor, Bardolf," said Long Arm sarcastically. "But here you are, welcoming some of her decisions."

"I may disagree with her on many things, but her decision to retain the power of the lords which had fought for her House for generations was fair."

John smiled. "The Leader of the Ice Islands was the only one to welcome all the changes of the second king! Begon was so impressed with Thomas that he decided to include the Ice Islands in Knightdorn. Thomas gladly accepted, but his death ruined the deal. Begon, however, initially agreed to ally with Sophie."

"Begon's decision not to fight Walter, after the fall of his champion, only shows cowardice," huffed Morys. "No matter the rules of the single combat."

"The people of the Ice Islands always keep their word," cried Long Arm.

Elliot was impressed with the bounty hunter's considerable, and unexpected, knowledge.

"An oath is insignificant compared to Walter's death," countered Morys.

"No one hates Walter more than I do," Elliot said. "However, true leaders must keep their word." Elliot hadn't spoken for some time. Silence followed his words.

Long Arm raised his wooden cup, commending him. He looked drunk, and Selwyn glanced at him with disdain. Cold enveloped them as the fire flickered, and they made ready to sleep. Elliot had taken first watch.

"I didn't expect I might see one of the legendary swords again," said John as he lay on the icy moss.

"Legendary swords?" Elliot asked.

"The Sword of Destiny!"

"I thought they were just famous, not legendary," Elliot said with a laugh.

Faces around the campfire turned toward him.

"Many believe that the Seven Swords have powers that no other sword has. The elwyn, the giants, and the elves ensured it was so," murmured Selwyn.

Elliot had never heard such a thing. Had his Master kept such a secret? He knew about the Seven Swords that the Elder Races had given to the humans, and he remembered his Master saying that the Elder Races had disappeared as soon as they handed over those great weapons to them, but he had never heard of powers. "Why did the Elder Races gave the Seven Swords to humans and then disappear from the world?" he asked.

"Disappeared?" scoffed John.

"They left this world," insisted Elliot.

Long Arm stood up. "Only fools think that the Elder Races are gone."

Elliot didn't speak, and John continued loudly. "It is known that the Elder Races never intended to give the Seven Swords to humans. Their promise was to the Egercolls alone. When the Elder Races betrayed that bloodline, they were drenched with the Egercolls' curse, but they never disappeared or left this world." Elliot frowned, and John stared with a slack jaw for a moment. "Don't you know the most notorious story of our world?"

Elliot hunched his shoulders, unsettled by all the eyes on him and by his own ignorance. "No," he replied, trying to keep his voice even.

"According to legend," John began, clearly relishing the opportunity to keep talking, "the elwyn, the elves, and the giants were the first races to live in Knightdorn. The Age of the Elder Races was the most peaceful in this world, without war for over three thousand years. Then, four hundred years ago, came the Black Death Age... This era was one of the most devastating the world has ever known. The giants started attacking the elves while the wyverns covered every corner of Knightdorn with death. The elwyn hated war, and they never involved themselves in the fights between giants and elves.

"At the time, there were only two major cities in Knightdorn—Iovbridge, the home of the elwyn, and Wirskworth, the elves' city. The giants lived in the Mountains of Darkness in distant Gaeldeath. The rest of Knightdorn was just pastures and fields with a few elves and elwyn cultivating the land, away from the two big cities. The giants used to attack those places, showing their barbarity, but the elwyn didn't want war and so persuaded the elves not to attack the giants. Until Magor the

Terrible became the leader of the giants' tribes and began to spread death throughout Knightdorn.

"In the Black Death Age, the first centaurs arrived in Knightdorn and settled in Ersemor. Soon after that, humans crossed the Sea of Men, reaching the continent of Knightdorn for the first time in history. From the moment they arrived in Knightdorn, the giants slaughtered humans for pleasure while burning the villages and the farm land where they lived. The giants also attacked Ersemor, riding on wyverns and killing several centaurs. When the elves grew fed up with the elwyn's tolerance of this destruction, a horde of them attacked and killed Magor. Some legends say that they never managed to kill him, that he just disappeared, but the giants were certain that the elves had assassinated him."

"We can't possibly know that this is all true, Long Arm," Morys scoffed.

"I want to know the rest of the story," Elliot said.

Morys turned his gaze away with a sigh, and John smiled.

"After Magor's murder, the giant tribes descended on Wirskworth with their wyverns," Long Arm went on. "This battle left behind so many corpses that, according to legend, the God of Death became omnipotent and defeated the God of Life.

"Both races limped away from that battle, nearly exterminated. The giants returned to the Mountains of Darkness, and the elves left their city and travelled to Iovbridge, seeking the elwyn's hospitality. The story goes that they couldn't bear to live in the place where almost their entire kind had died.

"The end of the battle marked the end of the Black Death Age, giving way to the Age of Men. When the giants got decimated, they were isolated on the Mountains of Darkness, and thousands of humans began to arrive in Knightdorn. Then, the first nine kings created the nine kingdoms of Knightdorn, and the elwyn retained Iovbridge. The elwyn and the elves considered humans a primitive race that needed their wisdom to evolve—until they saw the pegasi flying in the sky. That creature enchanted the elwyn more than anything..." Long Arm paused for a moment.

"So, three hundred years ago, our age and the story of the First Kings began with the first war between humans in Knightdorn. Most of the First Kings opposed Myren Endor as soon as they heard about the gold, metal, and silver hidden in the mines of the ancient city of the elves, in the depths of Wirskworth. When the nine kings divided Knightdorn, they had no knowledge of the treasures of Wirskworth that had fallen into the first King of Elmor's hands by pure chance. Most felt that Myren didn't deserve these treasures in conjunction with Knigthdorn's most magnificent city. King Thomyn Egercoll and the rest of the Egercolls supported Myren. So, the war began—Endors and Egercolls along with the centaurs against the other kings. The centaurs never allied with humans but faithfully served whoever the pegasi followed, as the latter were for them the symbol of life."

"But the centaurs allied with Thomas Egercoll, and he had no pegasi," Selwyn said.

"According to history, that was an exception."

Selwyn glanced at John with a doubtful look.

"Who won the war?" Elliot asked.

"The armies of the seven kings may have been three times those of their opponents, but no one could defeat Thomyn and the rest of the Egercolls. Legend has it that the pegasi's magic gave them mythical powers, allowing them to overcome every enemy in battle. It wasn't long before the seven kings accepted their defeat and returned to their kingdoms. Rumours proliferated in Knightdorn, and Aremor, the wisest elwyn, rode to Elirehar and saw the pegasi's power with his own eyes. Aremor was dazzled by those magical creatures and made the Egercolls an offer—one that brought the Elder Races' destruction." John paused for a moment and took a sip of wine.

"What offer?" asked Elliot, eager to know more.

Long Arm smiled again as the red drink dripped from his lips. "He offered to make seven legendary swords for the seven riders of the House of Egercoll using pegasus blood. These swords would be peerless, mighty beyond all others. The Egercolls were blinded by the promise of these terrific weapons and gave pegasus blood to the Elder Races.

"The elwyn and the elves travelled to the Mountains of the Forgotten World, where the first generations of the elwyn used to forge their weapons. Even the giants travelled south, wanting to see the blood of the creatures whose fame had spread all over Knightdorn. The Elder Races knew how to handle metals better than anyone else and forged the most wonderful swords ever made, drenched in pegasus blood. But then envy pierced their souls..."

"Envy?" Elliot was puzzled, and Long Arm grinned again.

"The Elder Races envied the Egercolls for their bond with the pegasi—they believed that mere humans were incapable of controlling the power given to them. Aremor might have admired the pegasi, but he thought they were dangerous as long as they served the Egercolls—so, prompted by him, the Elder Races sold six of the Seven Swords to the enemy-kings of the Egercolls. Those swords were the only ones that could kill a pegasus, and the seven kings wanted to avenge themselves on the Egercolls."

Elliot was dumbstruck by what he heard. The pegasi's legend had fascinated him ever since he was little, and now he felt that the winged horse would suddenly fly into the sky before his eyes.

"The seven kings attacked the Egercolls again and defeated them, killing six of the seven pegasi, along with their riders on the battlefield. Then Manhon, the last remaining Egercoll, realised what had happened and rode to the Mountains of the Forgotten World. He was ready to attack the Elder Races, alongside the centaurs and the Endors, but Aremor gave him the seventh sword, the Sword of Light, which was the most powerful of all. Manhon took it but couldn't forgive them for the death of his siblings, so he killed Aremor. And with the centaurs' help, he cursed the Elder Races with a curse so strong that they could never again leave the Mountains of the Forgotten World... Only the Sword of Light can liberate Aremor's soul and break the curse," concluded John with a silent burp.

"What happened to the last pegasus, Manhon, and the sword?" asked Elliot with bated breath.

"All that is just legend," cackled Long Arm. "There's never been a winged horse—"

"What do the legends say?" insisted Elliot.

"Manhon avenged the seven kings for the death of his siblings. He died of old age years later, and the last pegasus disappeared after his death," said Selwyn. "As for the Sword of Light, it was passed from generation to generation and reached Thomas Egercoll."

Elliot almost jumped up. "So Walter Thorn has the sword?"

"No, Thomas didn't have it at the Battle of Aquarine. No one knows what happened to it. Many believe that the king gave it to Althalos shortly before the battle," blurted Selwyn.

Elliot could not take in the overwhelming information pounding in his brain, and Long Arm seemed to notice.

"Don't be taken in by nonsense, lad," John said. "There were no pegasi, curses, or magic swords. The Elder Races forged seven magnificent weapons, but they don't hold power. As for the Elder Races, I've seen them with my own eyes in the Mountains of the Forgotten World. They never disappeared, and no curse has haunted them. They just prefer these mountains more than the world humans have built—or, rather, destroyed."

"My brother used to tell me that the Elder Races are despised because of that story," murmured Eleanor. "They are considered decadent, unreliable, infected, filthy, full of curses from the gods. However, I don't agree. No race should be despised."

"Of course. Just as anything different from humans," commented John.

"What happened to the other swords?" asked Elliot.

"They've been passed down in some of Knightdorn's oldest houses," Selwyn said. "Although the Blade of Azar, the Blade of Silence, and the Sword of Light are now lost."

"I don't think the Elder Races deserved that fate," Morys broke in. "Manhon shouldn't have cursed them."

"You're a fool if you believe these fairy tales!" cried John again, holding back a burp. "But humans are all fools, if you ask me. What drives a man to take the Seven Swords as the symbol of the Kingdom of Knightdorn—a symbol that represented the power of the Elder Races' gift to humans, a symbol inherently tied to betrayal? Foolishness, that's what. Intoxicated by power, humans have never taken anything else into account."

"Enough," Morys said. "Fairy tales or no, we have to rest. We have a long road ahead of us."

The others accepted his words in silence. After a while, the tremor of their snores began to shake the serenity of the night. While everyone was asleep, Elliot trembled with insurmountable anger, as if someone had poured all the poison in the world into his body. The man who had raised him, the man who was his only family, had hidden countless truths from him... His whole life was a lie.

And then joy stirred within him—soon, he would let out the rage that nested deep inside his soul.

The Land of Fire

Selwyn watched Elliot out of the corner of his eye as they rode. The boy looked different, brow furrowed, ice in his eyes. He hadn't spoken yet that morning. The silence made Selwyn uneasy, a feeling intensified by Elliot's ignorance about the Seven Swords and the Elder Races. Surely a Master would have educated his charge on such things. Questions kept turning in Selwyn's head, but he couldn't find any answers.

The sun was intense this morning, and the five travellers' horses were whinnying. Morys and John were ahead, on their brown horses, with Eleanor close behind, her black hair fluttering over her cloak which had Isisdor's characteristic blue colour. Selwyn was last, with Elliot next to him. Stonegate would darken the horizon that day. John had informed them that they'd reach it shortly after dusk.

"Is everything alright, Elliot?" Selwyn asked suddenly.

The lad didn't answer.

Maybe he's scared, thought Selwyn. As charismatic as Elliot was, he was still a youngster who would soon face a very powerful man.

"Yes," Elliot's answer came after a while.

"Are you looking forward to fighting Reynald?"

A smile formed on Elliot's lips. "I think so," he responded, which did nothing to quell the unease in Selwyn's stomach.

The path they were crossing gave off an inhospitable feeling. John could see the narrow Path of the Elder Races beside them. A strange aura had enveloped the party, the tall trees lining the way hiding the sunlight. Memories began to haunt John as he led the way—the Pegasus Rebellion had begun in the Land of Fire. He remembered; he had been spying from afar to see who would prevail in the battle for the throne. The Guardians of Stonegate, along with the Endors, were the only ones to have fought alongside the Egercolls in the first battle against George. Lord Ballard hadn't had time to prepare his armies. Kelanger and Aquarine were too far from Iovbridge. Nevertheless, the southerners didn't want to wait. The blood of Brom Endor and his family had soaked Iovbridge palace, and their passion for revenge had blinded them. Thus, the Pegasus Rebellion began, and Gregory and Favian Egercoll lost their lives on this soil, leaving Thomas and his sisters as the last descendants of their family.

After the deaths of Favian and Gregory, the armies of the central cities reached Isisdor, and together with Elmor's men and the Guardians of Stonegate, they invaded Iovbridge. George Thorn and his wife committed suicide by drinking poison, and Thomas was chosen king.

So much death... So much war... thought John as he glanced at his companions. Maybe he should have stayed in Iovbridge. Maybe he should have slunk off in the night and left the party. Elliot's horse shied away from a branch swaying in the wind, but the boy didn't react, his features stony. *Who the fuck is this lad?*

The trees looked gloomier as they went on, and the pleasant smell of flowers had faded. Eleanor noticed a jasmine bush on her left; she pulled her mare's reins and headed toward it. Her thighs hurt more and more, but she didn't want to show weakness, surrounded as she was by men who already considered her weak. On top of that, her stomach was bloated, and the blood would come soon.

She plucked a jasmine blossom and wondered how such a beautiful flower had grown in such an inhospitable place. She inhaled its light fragrance as she brought it to her face.

"I did not expect an aspiring warrior to admire the forest flowers." Morys had approached her quietly.

"And who are you to judge me?" she retorted. "At your age, you should be an officer, yet you're only a soldier."

Morys's face flushed with anger. "I've only celebrated my name twenty-four times, girl."

"Your name? I thought you should be counting the years of your life."

Morys glared at her. "In Elmor we celebrate our name. Counting the years since birth is *your* custom, not ours."

Eleanor chuckled softly. "Elmor has many traditions, the most renowned being foolishness. All of Knightdorn found out this truth at the battle in the Forked River."

She expected an angry reply, but it was not forthcoming. Instead, Mory's features softened, and he glanced away.

"I love the place where I grew up and its people," he murmured, "but Lady Endor disappointed me."

Eleanor felt a pinch of affection. She knew that Morys longed for his land, as she longed for hers, and it wasn't easy for him to speak badly of it or the people who lived there.

"Do you remember Felador?" he suddenly asked her. "I know you left when you were still a baby."

She felt pain upon hearing the name of her birthplace. "No, I don't remember anything... Neither my land, nor my parents."

Morys seemed to understand the hidden pain in her voice, and they rode on in a companionable silence. Perhaps they had more in common than she thought.

Elliot pushed the party hard, not allowing them to stop beyond watering the horses in a small stream. He was tired, his body aching, but the cold anger lodged in his chest wouldn't let him relent even as the sun began to set.

A voice pierced the air. "Stop!"

John got off his horse and looked intently at the dark spruces and pine trees in front of him. The sun was slowly giving way to darkness, and Elliot saw John turning his gaze to the west.

"Stonegate is this way," Long Arm shouted, pointing away from the trees. "We have to head to the Path of the Elder Races to reach the castle gate."

A muffled noise came from the forest to Elliot's right, just as the wind blew more fiercely. The horses whinnied restlessly, and John swallowed hard.

"We must be next to Ersemor," said Selwyn.

John looked at the young man. "You're not wrong, Lord Brau."

"Only men with pure intentions or with the pegasi magic in their veins can cross Ersemor," Morys burst out.

John turned to him with a look of disapproval, but Elliot's attention was drawn elsewhere, and he angled his horse toward Ersemor's trees. The air whistling in his ears sounded like a voice. Calling to him. He felt an urge to run into the heart of the forest.

"We will ride next to the Path of the Elder Races and spend the night near it," said John hurriedly. "At first light, you can ride to Stonegate's gate," he mumbled, looking at Elliot. "And I'll drink my wine until Reynald dispatches you," he cackled. "Remember, we can still flee," he added.

Elliot pulled his mind away from the forest and looked at Long Arm. "I can see the fear in your eyes, John," he said with grit. "I can see the trembling of your hands, I feel the terror in your voice. But I'm not afraid. Neither of the forest nor of Reynald."

Surprise fanned across Long Arm's face, and Elliot was astonished by what he had just uttered. A strange sense of power, an unknown force, seemed to pierce his body.

Selwyn broke the silence, insisting they move on. The five companions rode away from Ersemor, approaching the Path of the Elder Races. Cold air caressed Elliot's face, and stars began to appear in the sky while a thin fog covered the landscape. They selected a tall tree with spreading branches as their shelter for the night. The ground was flat and dry around the roots. Morys set to work lighting a fire with his flint while Selwyn saw to the horses. Set apart, Eleanor spread her cloak over icy moss and sat down.

Elliot sat close the young woman, and she turned her gaze toward him, pensive.

"Why did you bring me along?"

Elliot smiled. "Why do you think?"

"I can't find a reason. I am neither a good warrior nor a good guide."

"You are someone who lost loved ones to Walter."

The woman turned pale. "What does that have to do with anything?"

"Did you love your parents?"

"Of course!"

"Then you will never betray me." Elliot saw the question in Eleanor's eyes. "Would you ever fight for Walter?" he asked.

"Of course not! He and his men killed my parents!"

Elliot grinned. "I trust you. I know that your love for your parents will always prevent you from betraying a man like me—a man that fights to stop Walter. I don't trust any man in Iovbridge, but I can trust you".

Eleanor's features softened.

"Do you think Sophie is a good queen?" Elliot asked.

"Yes."

"Why?"

"Everyone believes that powerful warriors or wealthy lords make good rulers, but they are wrong. Compassion is what makes you a good ruler, and Sophie is the only queen who leads with compassion."

Elliot smiled, pleased by this assessment and by Eleanor's confidence.

A few moments passed, and the smell of the hare slowly spread through the air.

"I need to hunt," Elliot declared.

All eyes fell upon him.

"We still have enough rabbits," noted Eleanor.

"We'll need supplies to get to Wirskworth," he responded indifferently.

John was already holding a bottle of wine under his jaw. "If you take Stonegate, you'll be able to ask the Guardians for as many supplies as you want, boy," he said dryly, as if he were talking to a child. "If nothing else, how are you going to hunt in pitch darkness?" he added, bringing the flask to his lips.

"Darkness makes you invisible," countered Elliot. His companions continued to give him puzzled glances, but he didn't care. The invisible power of Ersemor's breath was still in his soul, and he now knew what he had to do. It was the first time in his short life that he could decide his own fate. He was about to slip into the darkness when he heard a voice behind him.

"I remember the promise I made to my father but also to you," Selwyn said. "Nevertheless, you won't be alone tomorrow."

Elliot turned and looked at the young man, feeling his eyes grow hot with tears. He blinked them away, but warmth lingered in his chest. For the first time, he felt like he had people who believed in him, who would even follow him to their deaths. He wasn't sure if his feelings were true, but looking at them, he felt love, even for John.

"Thank you, Selwyn... but I will be alone," he said slowly. He turned and walked between the pines.

A loud snort, like a thunderbolt, woke John from sleep—Selwyn, jerking awake as Morys spoke into the darkness.

"Where's Elliot?"

John had fallen asleep, letting the fire flicker, and, though the stars were still dancing in the sky, the green-eyed boy hadn't returned.

"I don't think he has lost his way," Eleanor murmured.

Selwyn's eyes narrowed, glinting with firelight. "He left," he snapped in a strange voice, as if he didn't want to believe his own words.

Morys let out something like a screech. "He left?" he shouted.

"He got scared," growled Selwyn.

"Silence!" John stood up, a tremble in his legs.

Selwyn turned his gaze, ready to cuss.

"Everybody quiet," John whispered again, and the young man obeyed.

John listened to the sounds in the still night—he had found himself in every nook of this world chasing outlaws and hijackers, and now he was certain that something wasn't right. He made to grab a burning branch from the fire, but the touch of icy steel on his neck brought him to a standstill as a blade slipped out of the darkness. And then the firelight flashed off the heads of a dozen or more spears aimed between pine boughs. They were surrounded.

The Guardians of the South

Eleanor was walking with her head down—her arms were bound by thick chains, and her legs trembled with fear. The Guardians had taken her sword, along with her companions' weapons. The queen had warned her that this journey might not have a happy ending, but she had insisted. *"Do you think I'll be safer here? I want to fight for you! I want to fight for my family!"* Those were her last words to the queen. Sophie had looked at her with sorrow. Eleanor was sure that she felt guilty for not being able to protect any of the people she loved.

Eleanor tried to control her fear—she didn't want to start crying in front of so many soldiers. She knew that some men liked to rape girls and women, and fear gave them a sense of power. She tried to observe her surroundings, learn what she could about her captors. Anything that would keep her calm. Eleanor glanced at the Guardians who escorted them—they held long spears, and swords hung from their belts. She knew that Stonegate men guarded the South Passage on Walter's behalf, defying several of their old oaths. Even if the Guardians hated Thorn, their oath to the Commander of Stonegate was paramount, and Reynald had been Walter's man for a long time.

She kept looking at the Guardians. The main purpose of Stonegate's men was to reverently keep the Oath of the South. According to that oath, Elirehar and Elmor—together with the castle of Stonegate—would always be united against any enemy of the southerners. The Guardians would also guard the castle's passage from non-southern peoples.

Her brother had told her many stories about the Guardians. They had shed their blood to protect the south from invaders several times in the past. However, after the election of George Thorn as king of the whole of Knightdorn, they were forced to allow all travellers to cross their castle. Eleanor had heard Sophie saying that at the time of the Pegasus Rebellion, the Guardians immediately took the Egercolls' side, fighting beside them and resealing Stonegate's gates.

Eleanor's hatred for Walter and his war flared as she remembered her parents. This man had brought so much pain to so many people. He was the only man in history who managed to get Stonegate to defy the Oath of the South. After Thomas's fall, Reynald Karford rode to the castle on Walter's orders, and challenged the Guardian Commander to single combat. The Commander fell dead, so Reynald took Stonegate while cutting off its ties to Isisdor and the south.

The Guardians should have killed Reynald long time ago... But they always followed stupid laws. Stonegate laws even required its leader to accept a duel for the command of the castle if a Guardian challenged him. That law didn't apply to foreign challengers. However, Eleanor had heard people saying that the Guardians' leaders were so arrogant that they seldom said no to combat.

No one could disagree that Stonegate was of great geographical importance, but many were surprised by Walter's decision to send Reynald, a member of the Trinity, there. Reynald was one of his most loyal and powerful soldiers, and surely Walter needed him on the battlefield. Nevertheless, Reynald had held to his post, not leaving Stonegate for almost seventeen years.

Eleanor looked at her companions—hunched and chained as they shuffled along. John's face seemed like an amorphous mask. Morys and Selwyn kept their heads down. Ahead, two men led their mares. There had been no sign of Elliot during their capture. But her hopes of rescue had faded as they were marched onward, and Eleanor thought less of Elliot and more of her family—she missed them so much. *The time has come*, she said to herself—she would finally meet again with her loved ones. She took a deep breath and wished she could take her own life instead of becoming chattel to Karford's men.

Selwyn was terrified. The memory of his brothers nested in his mind. He had sought vengeance for them ever since he could remember. But now he had missed any chance of that, and all he felt was fear—he had always feared death.

The sun had now risen in the sky, and the Guardians walked silently alongside the prisoners. Their armour was old and rusty, with silver steel helmets, and their long, white cloaks had a red-and-black sun sewn at the centre, its rays pointed like spears. Selwyn knew that long spears were one of the Guardians of Stonegate's favourite weapons, and their skilfulness in phalanx formation was unparalleled. The narrow Path of the Elder Races around their castle—combined with the formation in which they fought—created many problems for their opponents, regardless of numbers.

Morys stumbled on the uneven ground, falling to his knees, and a Guardian picked him up, cursing.

"Be careful, you fool! If you stumble again, I'll do you in before we reach the castle!"

Morys found his balance and continued in silence, while Selwyn found himself on his right. "Don't be afraid," he whispered, more in an effort to inspire courage in himself than in Morys.

The man looked at him sternly. "I'm not afraid of death."

Selwyn didn't believe him—no matter how brave a man is, death cannot leave him untouched. *I will soon meet my brothers*. This thought calmed his soul. But then Elliot's image pushed aside the faces of his brothers. Selwyn had believed in him. He had thought that only Elliot could give Knightdorn hope. He felt a fool.

They walked until Stonegate appeared—dozens of banners with red-and-black suns at the centre shone on the wall's embrasures. The wall was long and wide. Square towers built out of grey stone stood sentinel over the wall. Their battlements were guarded by vigilant guards. Selwyn kept walking—Stonegate seemed huge under the bright sunlight, and the tall towers seemed to caress two white clouds that adorned the sky. A small moat flooded with mud stretched around the castle, and a drawbridge stood in front of the gate. The bridge was lowered, and two turrets surrounded the majestic wooden entrance.

The iron-banded wooden gate opened with a deafening thud. Two men on horseback approached, crossing half the distance of the drawbridge. They held long spears in their hands, and large triangular shields hung on their backs.

"What do we have here, Rowan?" Suspicion was painted on one horseman's face. His beard was dense, his face rough.

Selwyn's escort nodded at him. "Jarin. Found them camped next to the Path of the Elder Races," replied a tall Guardian, taking off his helmet. "They must come from the palace, judging by their armour."

The mounted Guardian's gaze fell on the Pegasus and the Seven Swords on Selwyn and Eleanor's chests, then on the bloodthirsty snake on Morys's yellow cloak.

"Pegasus and snake," he murmured. "The Guardian Commander will be thrilled. Bring them in."

Selwyn crossed Stonegate for the first time in his life. A thick cobblestone floor covered most of its interior. Selwyn noticed a few tufts of yellowed grass sprouting here and there through the stones' recesses. The shape of the shadow cast by the wall reminded him of the stories his father used to tell him as a child. The first Guardians were called *Shadows*, as they moved silently in the dark, like the gods of the night. Selwyn knew that the Guardians of Stonegate found these stories amusing. They didn't believe in any higher power, mocking the gods that were worshipped in Knightdorn and the regions beyond.

The four companions continued to walk into the inner part of the castle as the gate closed loudly. Some women and young children looked at them with wonder, as if they had never seen a stranger in these places. Selwyn tried to forget his fear—Stonegate consisted only of stone and earth, and its soldiers were men like any others.

The man called Jarin stopped his horse next to a tower with large windows and called for the others to wait. He dismounted and went inside the tower as a crowd began to gather.

Selwyn waited, trying not to shuffle his feet, trying not to look afraid. At last the door to the tower opened, and Jarin reemerged, his face grim and full of pride. A man in a silver suit of armor followed, the plate gleaming in the morning light. Selwyn felt his mouth grow dry. Reynald Karford. He was no longer young, but he wore his experience well. A large sun dominated his chest, but his cloak was brown, not white, and a hammer and an axe next to an anvil were sewn at the centre. Oldlands' coat of arms next to that of the Karfords—Reynald Karford may have been Stonegate's Commander, but he hadn't forgotten his true origin. The Guardian Commander's face was wild, his hair black and thick, and his eyes were a vivid blue. A small scar stood out on his left cheek, and his crooked nose protruded well above his thin lips. The rubies on his sword's hilt shone over his belt as if they kept the elixir of life. The Guardian Commander stopped in front of the captives and looked at them with cold eyes that held a promise of death. Terror flooded Selwyn's soul.

Reynald felt anger pouring out of him. "Invaders from Isisdor on my doorstep... Do you know what happens to invaders, girl?" he asked, looking at the young woman in the blue cloak.

She stared back at him with such hatred that he couldn't help but admire her courage.

"We are not invaders, Guardian Commander," she shouted, her black eyes sparkling.

Reynald smiled. "Just exploring the Land of Fire? Out for a pleasant stroll?" he said sarcastically.

"We are headed to Wirskworth and hoped to use the Stonegate passage," explained the eldest of the men.

"Under what jurisdiction would you cross my castle?"

No one spoke, and he slowly approached the four companions, his eyes fixed on the older man who wore no armour or emblem to mark his allegiance. He seemed the most frightened, and Reynald intended to take advantage of that. "What were you doing outside my castle? Were you spying? Is Isisdor planning to attack me? Tell me everything, and I promise to grant you a quick death," he said.

The man's gaze was like that of a dead man. "We are not spies, my lord," he whined. "The coming war in Iovbridge made us leave the city to seek our fortune in the southern parts of the kingdom."

Reynald frowned and the man withered further under his gaze. Whether the man spoke true or not, it was clear these strangers were cowards. He paced around them, one hand on his sword's hilt.

"Maybe you aren't spies. I'd say you are deserters, and at Stonegate, deserters are punished even more severely than invaders." He turned to Jarin. "Put the men in the dungeons until I decide their punishment, and send the girl to my chamber."

Eleanor let out a shaky breath as Morys took a step forward in Reynald's wake. Dozens of swords rose around him.

"I challenge you to single combat for the castle's leadership." His words froze the air around them. Eleanor looked at the young man with a mix of consternation and admiration. Reynald turned slowly, a dangerous gleam in his eyes, and opened his mouth to speak, but another voice drowned out all else.

"This combat is mine, Morys!"

Eleanor turned and saw a Guardian threw down his helmet, the steel clanking off the cobblestones, and then Elliot's green irises settled on Reynald with hatred reflected in them.

The Path of Wishes

Power surged in Elliot as he looked into the Guardian Commander's eyes and saw surprise.

"Who are you? Where did you find this armour?" Reynald demanded.

Elliot smiled. "I heard your men approaching my party in the night, attacked one of them, and took his armour," he replied dispassionately.

"Did you kill a son of Stonegate? Your screams will fill the nights for many days, foolish boy."

Elliot took a step forward, and the Guardians' swords turned toward him at once.

"I didn't kill anyone. I left him unconscious in the forest. I believe he will have recovered by now."

The Guardian Commander walked towards him. "An attack on a Stonegate son is punishable by torturous death—prepare the boat!"

A soft murmur came from the crowd surrounding them. Elliot knew about boat torture. The victim was forced to consume large amounts of honey. Their body was then anointed with it and tied to a boat that would float in soiled water for days. The diarrhoea that the honey provoked in the victim—combined with the golden, sticky liquid on their skin—attracted beetles and maggots which devoured them slowly and torturously until they died of rot.

"I challenge you to single combat, Guardian Commander! Do you reject my challenge?"

Reynald came closer. "Someone who attacks my men cannot have the honour of combat. You will die in a lake, and no one will ever hear from you again!"

The Guardian Commander turned and gestured to his men to proceed, but Elliot shouted with all his might. "You're one to talk about honour, Karford! How many innocent people has your sword taken? How many civilians have you tortured and killed fighting on Thorn's side? Nevertheless, I'm not surprised—only cowardice could bring you to this place, and you just proved that you're a coward!"

The silence that followed was heavy and absolute. Elliot was fully aware of the gravity of his words but had no choice—he had to infuriate the Commander. Only then would he accept the combat. The Guardians may have been notorious for their arrogance and stubbornness, but Reynald was not a Stonegate son.

The man stood still for a moment, then drew the Sword of Destiny from its sheath in a flash, the rubies shining in the light of the morning.

"You will beg me to kill you, you fool! Your limbs will be eaten by the dogs, and I will keep you alive without arms and legs so that you can see their teeth devour them." Saliva flew from the Guardian Commander's mouth as he spoke.

Elliot smiled at his words.

"Give me a spear and a shield!" screamed Reynald, sheathing the Sword of Destiny. Jarin swiftly complied. "Choose your weapons!" he shouted, hefting the spear.

Elliot drew the sword at his waist. He had left the sword Selwyn had given him in the woods, taking the blade of the man he had captured. He walked slowly between the bristling swords of the Guardians and extended his hand to a stocky soldier who held a rusty shield. After glancing at the Guardian Commander, the man handed over the shield. The guards pulled back, pushing the four prisoners, as Reynald began to walk around Elliot.

"Have you learnt to fight, boy? I hope you weren't trained by some drunkard old general." Reynald laughed sardonically.

Elliot stood still, unwilling to take the bait.

"Do you want to honour your queen? Now, she's even more insignificant than the ants digging holes in the ground!" The contempt in Reynald's words ignited a flame in Elliot's chest. The strength he had felt when nearing Ersemor's borders hadn't left him yet.

Reynald attacked with incredible speed, his spear directed at Elliot's left leg. Elliot lowered his shield and avoided the blow. Reynald aimed for an opening to his head, trying to hit him in the face. Elliot's reaction was so quick that the Guardian Commander tripped; he had bent in a flash, and his sword had struck the Commander's steel shield at the tip of his hand. The man's shoulder swayed as Elliot ran towards him. The Guardian Commander struck his spear at his chest, but Elliot stuck it between his shield and his sword and, with a swift motion, cut it in half.

Reynald looked at him with eyes that sparked, throwing away the remnants of wood and pulling the Sword of Destiny from its sheath. Elliot attacked again, aiming at his opponent's feet, but Reynald anticipated it; he avoided the blow and swung his blade. Elliot repelled him, but Reynald's strength was staggering. He stumbled backward, then reset his sword and shield in a defensive posture. The Guardian Commander rushed at him like a savage, and struck the shield again and again as Elliot deflected, his arm burning from the power in Reynald's blows.

The man smiled. "That was all you had, little boy?"

Reynald swung for Elliot's head, but he avoided the blow. Reynald attacked again, striking Elliot's shield. Then he went for his right foot. Elliot swerved and raised his sword to retaliate, but his opponent was faster. Reynald's shield gripped his as he tried to cut off the hand holding it. Elliot let go of the shield instantly and pulled back, raising his sword.

"Now you'll die!" Reynald said, kicking the fallen shield.

Elliot returned the smile. "For years, I heard legends about the Trinity of Death, their skill in battle and the fear they sowed during the Knightdorn wars! But as it turns out, you are nothing special, Karford!"

Reynald eyes widened, and then he attacked, bellowing in rage. Elliot repulsed the blow with a nonchalant movement of his sword.

"I wanted to see that skill before I beat you! I am not at all impressed!"

Reynald's eyes narrowed, his sword slashed through the air again and again, but Elliot repelled his blows comfortably. The Guardian Commander moved gracefully, trying to find angles and finish him off, but Elliot matched him, keeping the man at a distance as their swords met in great, clanging strikes.

Reynald attempted a blow with his shield, but Elliot was prepared. His sword struck the man's hand, sending the shield spinning away. As the duel continued, Reynald's fury erupted like lava, and he swung with new savagery, missing more and more. Elliot attempted a counter, but Reynald grabbed his hand and swung his sword in an arc that would sever Elliot's head from his neck. Elliot dodged, hearing Selwyn scream, then switched his sword to his left hand and cut deep into the flesh at the back of Reynald's leg. Reynald stumbled backward, trying to stay upright. Elliot pressed his advantage, his chest thundering with rage. Reynald tried to find his balance, but it was too late. Elliot grabbed his hand and wounded his right palm. The legendary sword fell to the ground, and Elliot aimed his blade at the beaten man's neck.

"Kill him," screamed Reynald. "Kill this bastardly deserter."

Elliot turned his head—no one else moved. The Laws of Stonegate were inviolate, and the Guardians now owed their allegiance to him.

Reynald seethed. "Kill him, traitors!"

The Guardians remained motionless.

"COWARDS, RASCALS, DISLOYAL DOGS!" Incensed, Reynald spat saliva as he shouted, his gaze pinned on Elliot. "Who are you? Who taught you to fight?"

Elliot felt his lip curl in disgust. "Guardian, approach!" he shouted, looking at Jarin. The man obeyed.

"Who's the most capable man in the castle?"

The Guardian looked at him in astonishment. "You, my Guardian Commander." He made a slight bow.

"Among the rest of the Stonegate men."

"I am, Commander."

"Is there anyone who disputes this?" Elliot cried, looking at the mob.

Nobody spoke.

Elliot looked at Jarin. "Then I name you the new Guardian Commander of Stonegate!"

The man's eyes grew wide with surprise. "What? Why?"

"I have other plans, Guardian. I can't stay here. But before you take the office of Commander, you must give me an oath before your people."

Jarin seemed to know what he would ask of him. "I can't," he muttered. "Stonegate will not fight for the queen. The Guardian Commander must put what's good for his people above all, and such an oath would bring death to my people."

"What does the Guardian Commander's oath say?" asked Elliot.

"The Guardian Commander must put the sons and daughters of Stonegate over every governor or king in Knightdorn. The Commander's oath to his people and his people's oath to him are inviolable."

Elliot smiled, pleased with the man's sense of honor. A cunning man would swear anything in order to take command of the castle.

"I don't want Stonegate to fight for Iovbridge."

"Then what are you asking of me?"

"I want the queen and her allies to be able to cross Stonegate peacefully. I also want you to guard the passage against Queen Sophie's enemies, whether she sits on the throne or not."

The man seemed thoughtful, and Reynald began to laugh out loud, penetrating the silence. "Walter will kill every man in the castle if such a condition is accepted."

Elliot slowly turned toward him. "Stonegate showed devotion to the Oath of the South for centuries until you forced them to break their oath—you even forced them not to get involved when Walter invaded the former southern kingdoms! The Guardians shed their blood on Thomas Egercoll's side to overthrow the First King, but you commanded them to bow before a Thorn. I'm not asking them to defy any oath—just to guard the passage for the queen and her vassal lords." His words resounded in the Guardians' ears, and he turned to Jarin. "Only Stonegate's men know who their real enemy is."

Reynald grimaced, one hand trying to stem the blood flowing from the wound Elliot had given him. Jarin walked toward where the Sword of Destiny lay. Hesitating for a moment over the rubies in the hilt, he picked it up. "What's your name?" he asked, turning to Elliot.

"Elliot."

"If you concede the castle's rulership to me, I'll let you cross the South Passage," Jarin said. "I also swear to allow the queen and her allies to cross Stonegate and to obstruct her enemies from entering. You have my word."

Elliot weighed him up as Jarin approached.

"This sword belongs to you." The man extended his hands offering Elliot the legendary blade.

"I don't want it."

"Elliot, this sword is—"

"I know," he murmured. "I want a Stonegate man to hand it over to Walter."

Jarin's arms pulled away as his expression hardened. "Why?"

Elliot leaned toward the man. "Walter must hear about what happened here, and only this sword will convince him of the truth."

Jarin seemed hesitant. "If he finds out what happened, he might attack us!" he exclaimed.

"Walter wants to take the throne. He's not interested in Stonegate—at least not right now."

The man frowned, puzzled. Elliot was sure that Jarin didn't understand the real purpose of such an act, but he couldn't reveal more.

"Very well!" Jarin's voice came out like a loud roar. "But I want to ask something of you, too."

Elliot waited for Jarin to continue.

"If Walter Thorn ever attacks my castle, Sophie Delamere won't leave us to defend ourselves alone, and Stonegate's sons and daughters will always have a place under her protection."

The request was unexpected. He didn't have the power to make such a promise but was sure that the queen would accept the new Guardian Commander's condition. "You have my word," he said vigorously.

"You're a fool, Jarin." Reynald had stood up, holding his bleeding arm. "This boy has no jurisdiction over Isisdor or Delamere's vassal lords. He can't give that oath—he can only tell you what you want to hear."

Jarin gave him a brooding look.

"He's nothing but a deserter," continued Reynald.

"A deserter who defeated a former Ghost of the Trinity," Elliot murmured.

Selwyn spoke up. "We are carrying a letter sealed by the queen for the Governor of Elmor. We are not deserters but messengers who intended to cross Stonegate peacefully."

"And why did you hide this truth when I asked you why you were on my land?" screamed Reynald. "You hid the fact that you were carrying a letter from the queen to Syrella Endor. You knew such a letter would mean your death. You never had any peaceful intentions, and I'm sure this lad doesn't have the slightest jurisdiction to give an oath on the queen's behalf."

While he spoke true, Elliot knew the Guardians held to a code all their own. Strength was everything to them, and in their eyes, a warrior worthy of overthrowing Reynald Karford would certainly have enough influence in the queen's ranks to give an oath on her behalf.

Jarin looked at Elliot in silence. After a few moments, he extended his hand, ignoring his former Guardian Commander.

Elliot shook his hand, then hurried toward his companions.

"What will become of the former Commander?" Jarin asked abruptly.

Elliot turned, observing the blood-stained former Trinity of Death member. The man had fallen to the ground again, unable to support his weight, though his gaze simmered with vengeance and rage.

"With the new Commander's permission, Reynald Karford will be taken to Wirskworth where he will be tried for his crimes," he replied.

Jarin seemed puzzled but nodded in agreement. "You may rest here and continue your journey at dawn."

"Thank you, Guardian Commander, but we don't have time. We must continue before it gets dark. May our horses be returned to us?"

Jarin nodded to his men. The Guardians freed the prisoners from their shackles, and a blond-haired Guardian gave them their horses.

Elliot and his companions filled their stomachs with food and their haversacks with supplies. Then Selwyn presented the new Guardian Commander with the queen's seal on the letter to the Governor of Elmor. Jarin dispatched a Guardian north, tasked with finding Walter and presenting the Sword of Destiny. Elliot would trust few men to guard such an heirloom, but the Guardians of Stonegate had proved to be true to their ideals.

Meanwhile, the Guardian Elliot had rendered unconscious had returned bearing Elliot's armour, cloak and sword. Outfitted in his own armour and in the Iovbridge blue again, Elliot rode next to the chained Reynald as they departed Stonegate. The man's wounds had been bandaged and a gag inserted into his mouth. The new Guardian Commander of the castle accompanied them beyond Stonegate, and Elliot was pleased to know that the inhospitable, wild place from the stories was in fact a refuge for honour.

Their horses continued for a few moments, crossing the castle. A gentle breeze caressed Elliot's face and for the first time, he felt he could push through with his plan.

The sun was setting, giving way to the stars, when a trumpet sounded loudly from the tall towers of Stonegate. Jarin stopped and turned his horse as a Guardian raced across the ground to catch them.

"Commander, we have visitors," the Guardian panted.

Jarin looked surprised. "Are they holding a banner?"

"Yes, the white tiger. Walter's men."

The Guardian Commander's eyes widened in fear, and he glanced to Elliot before turning back to his man.

"How many?"

"About two hundred. They wish to speak with the Guardian Commander."

Elliot looked at Reynald, his mind working feverishly. He had to assume that Walter had sent an army to Stonegate for reinforcement in case the Ruler of Elmor tried to take the castle while heading towards Iovbridge. The final battle for the throne was near, and no doubt Walter anticipated that perhaps Lady Endor would put aside her differences with the queen. These men must have travelled for days on the west road. Walter would have ordered them to travel on the Road of Elves, as it would have been dangerous for them to get anywhere near Iovbridge where numerous soldiers kept watch due to the imminent siege.

"I will refuse their entry," Jarin muttered.

"I can't cross Snake Road with Walter's men in my way! I can't fight two hundred men!" said Elliot.

Jarin's eyes grew wild with fear. "You said that you didn't want us to fight by your side!" he countered. "I can guard the South Passage against the queen's enemies, but if I attack Walter's men without them attacking my men or my castle, it will be like declaring war on him. If Walter decides at some point to attack the castle, I know that he'll kill every Stonegate soldier, but the Guardians do not fear death," he stated. "But if I kill his men unnecessarily, he won't be satisfied with the soldiers. He'll take the life of every man, woman, and child he finds in these lands!"

Elliot was looking for a way to escape. Even if he waited at Stonegate until the following dawn, he was sure to meet Walter's men on his journey. It would take a while for him and his companions to ride to

Elmor's capital without being noticed, and they had to get there as soon as possible. "I must get to Wirskworth as fast as I can," he said. "Jarin, you must help me."

Their eyes met, and Elliot saw a flicker of determination. "There is only one way—I hope you can make it," the Guardian Commander said.

"We won't cross Ersemor." John brought his horse in front of Jarin's. "Even if we attempted to do so, it'd be very hard to avoid Walter's men without a huge delay in our journey," continued John.

"Commander, I can't delay an answer to them," said the Guardian with impatience in his tone.

"We have no time, and there's only one way you can make it," growled Jarin. "You must cross Ersemor to the west, until the Centaurs-Land, and then head south toward the Road of Elves. Once you get there, ride south of the road, alongside the Forked River. That path is almost always deserted, and its trees offer good cover for travellers who don't want to be seen. However, don't attempt to move south before reaching the Centaurs-Land because the forest will be so inaccessible that you won't make it. Unfortunately, there are only two paths in Ersemor that lead south. The one leads to Snake Road, which you want to avoid, and the other starts from the Centaurs-Land"

Elliot glanced at John—a shadow of fear lurked in the bounty hunter's eyes, but they had no choice. "Lead us on!" he said hurriedly.

Jarin nodded to the Guardian to his right. "Take them to the path! I will take care of the visitors!" He glanced at the travellers, gave a nod to Elliot, then rode back to the castle, the other Guardians following suit.

The five companions, along with Reynald Karford, rode at speed as their prisoner struggled to free himself of his shackles. The Guardian guided them in silence as the night had already spread its veil around the castle. The ground grew muddy and wet. After a while, the Stonegate man stopped and dismounted.

"Here!" he shouted, waving his torch, and Elliot approached him to see an underground passage behind a small opening in the inner wall of the castle.

"How are we going to get out of here?" Eleanor's voice shook as she spoke.

"You'll continue until the end of the path," the Guardian spoke quickly and grabbed a torch resting in a bracket on the wall, then lit it with his own. "Hold the fire high! The horses get frightened in this place."

Elliot took the torch from his hand and saw John's frightened face behind the flames.

"Morys, stay close to him!" Elliot indicated Reynald with a nod of his head and then urged his horse forward.

His companions followed him hesitantly. Their breath and the horses' footsteps broke the suffocating silence under the torch's dim light. Elliot took in the overstretched spiderwebs, mouldy walls and carved symbols adorning the underpass's interior. He lost his sense of time until a cold wind whipped his face and the moon emerged in front of him like a pale sapphire . He pulled his horse to a stop by a towering tree. He saw Eleanor's black hair fluttering as she passed in front of him. Selwyn seemed fatigued, but Morys looked more alert as he rode next to Reynald. Stonegate's former leader rode hunched over. Long Arm approached Elliot. The moonlight illuminated the rage and fear on his face.

"I told you we cannot cross Ersemor!" John screamed. "Even at the edges, the forest will pose countless obstacles! Do you think we'll be able to reach the Centaurs-Land miles away from here?"

"Why are you so afraid of this forest?" countered Elliot.

The man looked at him with eyes full of indignation. "YOU DON'T KNOW ANYTHING! I HAVE TRIED TO CROSS THE FOREST, BOY, AND I ASSURE YOU THAT IT'S IMPOSSIBLE!" The echo of his voice covered every other sound.

John was panting, and Elliot listened to the leaves' rustling. Suddenly, a white light flashed before him, flickering among the trees, and he felt the urge to run towards it. He slowly angled his mare that way. John followed in silence, also observing the bright glow. And then the darkness gave way to a new path, unfolding, luminous, the most magical thing Elliot had ever seen. Trees with golden leaves glistened on all sides, and small, pearl-shaped flowers shone under the soft night light. The ground was as red as blood, and the sky looked blue with the light of stars.

"Where are we?" Elliot searched Long Arm's face, enchanted by the scenery.

John's eyes had widened in surprise. He swallowed hard, and then his voice came out in a whisper. "On the Path of Wishes."

The Lake of Life

"John, what is this place?" Elliot couldn't believe what he was seeing.

John seemed charmed by the magical landscape. The golden leaves looked like bright stars, and the colourful sky exuded a magical serenity.

"It's the path to the Centaurs-Land. Many know the centaurs' home as Moonland," replied the man.

Elliot gazed in wonder. "But how has it come to show itself to us?"

"Legend has it that the path only appears to pegasi or to travellers with pure intentions. The only humans who are thought to have had pegasus magic in their blood were the Egercolls. I, however, never believed in that balderdash," stammered Long Arm.

"There are countless stars in this place," Selwyn spoke, his voice seeming too loud for the place.

"According to old folk tales, the stars above the Path of Wishes reflect humans' wishes... I have never had faith in those stories, but I think I've changed my mind now," responded John.

Their horses continued walking slowly, and Elliot felt an immense serenity flooding his heart—and then a second sensation. "I have the feeling we're being watched," he whispered. Elliot looked around carefully, and then a pair of eyes appeared among the trees. He slowly drew his sword.

"I would advise you to put your sword away," said a voice among the thick trunks.

Elliot's instinct told him to obey, and the blade returned to its sheath in a whisper. "Who are you?" he asked.

"The real question is who are you..." The voice pierced their ears, and then a slender figure appeared on the path before them.

The newcomer was quite tall, like Elliot, but his demeanour was that of an elderly man, and his hair was silvery-blue and long, caressing his bony shoulders. He may have been old, yet his face was so well-shaped that it looked like it had been sculpted by a craftsman. His eyes had a starry blue colour Elliot had never seen before. Elliot was sure that the creature in front of him was not human.

John slowly approached the newcomer, as if he couldn't believe his eyes. "An elwyn!" he exclaimed. "I did not expect to find an elwyn in such a place."

"What did you expect, John?"

Long Arm's eyes opened wide in surprise at the sound of his name. "How do you know my name? And what is an elwyn doing with the centaurs?" His question sounded like an insult, and the starry blue eyes scoured his face thoughtfully.

"The right question is what are *you* looking for in this place. From what I remember, you left in a scurry the last time you visited."

Long Arm shied away from the elwyn.

"We want to cross the forest as quickly as we can," Elliot said. "We have to get to the Road of Elves and then head to Wirskworth."

The creature looked at him piercingly, as if he could read his thoughts. "Why do you want to go to Wirskworth?"

"I have a plan to prevent Walter Thorn from taking over Iovbridge." Elliot had not expected to reveal so much—but he felt he could trust the creature before him.

A sigh came out of the elwyn's lips. "Many believed they could stop this man, but they all failed."

"You don't know who I am—I'm not like the others." Elliot's words sounded childish.

"Indeed," admitted the creature. "But I wonder if you know who you really are."

Elliot frowned, not understanding those words.

"How come an elwyn is far from the Mountains of the Forgotten World? I thought the elwyn were cursed," Morys spoke out.

The elwyn's face stiffened in anger. Long Arm cast a look at Morys, full of contempt. "Human's curses hold no sway over me, young man! I'm the wisest of the glorious elwyn race!" he growled. "No curse is worse than the existence of your kind."

"I didn't know that a race of traitors could be glorified," Elliot said, letting anger lace his voice. The story John had told them had taken root in his soul.

"My race is the oldest of this world, human. A world that your kind almost destroyed," retorted the elwyn. "The human race is our world's biggest sin."

"Envy is a sin too!"

The creature looked at Elliot and closed his eyes wearily. "A sin sufficient to punish entire races for centuries, when the sins of men destroyed a whole world."

What does he mean? Are the legends about the curse true? Elliot thought.

"What is your true purpose, human?" the elwyn spoke again, looking at Elliot. "What is your heart's deepest desire?"

"To fight for the salvation of Knightdorn and the freedom of its people," he replied.

The elwyn took a deep breath. "Hatred has enveloped your heart... a hate as black as the shadows of the forest," he cried out.

"I thought only travellers with pure intentions could find this path," replied Elliot. "If you see hatred, why did you let us cross Moonland?"

"I didn't reveal the path to you—the forest itself did. I don't know why." The elwyn's eyes suddenly shone bright. "Nevertheless, I won't decide whether you'll cross the Moonland," he remarked indifferently and, with an invisible nod, moved forward under the colourful starlight.

Elliot glanced at his companions and hesitantly began to follow the elwyn, riding slowly. After a time, a lake appeared to their left. Its waters looked like colourful crystals under the bright sky.

They paused, and Elliot reluctantly approached the elwyn, but then something drew his attention—the lake waters had suddenly lost their azure colour, a greenish hue spreading over the surface instead.

"I've never seen silver waters before," Eleanor said.

Elliot turned in surprise.

"Silver? In the name of the Seven Swords, Eleanor!" cried Morys. "These waters are red like blood!"

Selwyn looked at them, confused, and then Elliot understood—they were each seeing something different.

"What do you see?" The elwyn's voice sounded low in his ears.

Elliot would rather not have answered. "I see green waters with a blue tinge on the lakebed."

The elwyn glanced sharply at him but didn't speak.

"Why do we see different colours?" asked Elliot, raising his voice.

"The lake takes on a different colour for each creature. Each colour symbolises something for the soul of the beholder," a voice came from behind him.

He turned and looked at John. The man had proved again that he knew much more than Elliot expected.

"This is the Lake of Life. The centaurs study its waters under the moonlight and read the future," Long Arm continued.

The elwyn scoffed. "Read the future," he repeated, laughing. "If you could imagine how complex the future is, human, your species would be far superior to what it is. All you can read are the signs of fate, which constantly change over time."

Elliot and his companions continued on horseback as the elwyn walked beside them in silence. At last a vast plain appeared before them.

"Aleron, I didn't expect you to have company." A new voice greeted them as a centaur came out of nowhere. His bearing was regal, his hair silver and his eyes were a bright violet. His human torso was pale, fit, and muscular, while his horse body was larger than that a typical horse and covered with a pitch-black coat of hair.

Elliot eyed the centaur—his face was beautiful though wild. His violet eyes fell on the companions and the captive.

"Good evening, Zehir," replied Aleron lazily. "I found these travellers on the Path of Wishes. The forest allowed them to pass."

The centaur seemed surprised. "I haven't seen humans on this land for a long time," he muttered. Suddenly, his horse tail twitched, and his gaze fixed on the figure on Morys's right. "I didn't expect Reynald Karford to visit us!"

Reynald regarded the centaur with a look of disgust. Zehir approached the bound man and examined his bloodied limbs, then stretched out his hand. Reynald tried to pull away, and his horse snorted, but the centaur looked at it sternly. The mare calmed, and the centaur examined the man's wounds.

"I'd say someone slashed you, Reynald," murmured Zehir maliciously. Then the centaur raised his gaze and looked at the visitors once more. "Follow me!" he said.

The phrase didn't sound threatening, but Elliot felt compelled to obey. They continued riding for a few moments, with Aleron leading beside Zehir, until a vast field stretched before them. Its grass seemed silky soft, and the sky grew even clearer. Suddenly, Elliot noticed countless centaurs appearing from all sides. A small creature passed by—a baby with a human face and a horse's body.

The heat of this place was suffocating, and Elliot felt the leather vestments under his breastplate stick to his skin. The newcomers' presence had already been sensed, and a crowd began to move toward them. They did not seem pleased by the presence of strangers.

Zehir continued walking without a care in the world, and then Elliot realised where he was leading them. A huge fire burned at the edge of the field, lighting up the night landscape. Its white smoke billowed like a swan that had spread its wings. The flames hopped in the sky like thirsty spirits. Elliot expected to feel the warmth of the fire setting his bone-weary body alight, but as they approached the flames, he felt lighter, as if the fiery hyenas were about to cleanse the soul of whomever approached. He was stunned to see there was not a single piece of wood or kindling at the base of the fire. *This place is truly drenched in magic.*

Zehir suddenly stopped, and his tribe began to gather quickly around the fire, like a herd. Thousands of pairs of violet eyes were fixed on the newcomers, and a centaur taller than the others approached Elliot. The tall centaur had silver hair and black coat. His face was handsome, as were the faces of all the centaurs, but it was also coarse and wild. A long beard protruded from his slender chin. "You have no right to transport captives through our land," he declared.

John glanced at Elliot, as if asking him to keep his mouth shut. "We didn't intend to violate your land, Lord Centaur."

The huge creature's eyes weighed up Long Arm with disgust. "Then why are you here? I thought you wouldn't try to cross my land again after your last visit!" A smile was painted on the centaur's lips.

John seemed to carefully choose his next words. "The queen, along with Knightdorn's last hope, rely on our mission, Lord Centaur. I have to lead my companions south, to—"

"Knightdorn's last hope lies on a drunkard, an old man like you?" The magnificent creature laughed mockingly.

"This captive must get to Wirskworth, and Snake Road isn't safe. We must cross your land on our way toward the Road of Elves, Lord Centaur. It's our only hope against our enemy," repeated John, ignoring his words.

"It's not my enemy, human!" growled the creature and turned his eyes to the captive. "Reynald Karford, I never expected to see you chained at my doorstep."

The captive squirmed in his shackles.

"A murderer, a man without honour who became a Guardian Commander at the South Passage. Fate is the mystery of life, after all," said the centaur as if to himself. "Remove the cloth from his mouth!" he ordered.

A white-furred centaur moved quickly and pulled the gag from Reynald's lips as he swayed on his grey horse. He looked at the large centaur and started laughing out loud.

"I'm not afraid of you, Leghor. I have fought your kind in the past, and if you freed me from my shackles, I'd do it now, you filthy nag."

Many hooves beat on the ground all at once.

"Lord Leghor," John spoke again, now using the centaur's name. "You must let us continue on our way! Iovbridge doesn't have time for—"

"Where was Iovbridge when this man led an attack against my race in the Mercenary River?" interrupted the centaur, who still stared at Reynald.

John looked nervous. "The second king only tried to protect his family."

Leghor snorted contemptuously. "The second king gave my race death only. This man belongs to me. I'll let you cross my land, but I'll keep this prisoner—it's the least humans could give my race for their betrayal."

"You have no right to hold him, centaur." Elliot raised his voice, and thousands of violet eyes turned toward him.

Leghor turned his head and smiled, revealing a row of white teeth.

"He's just a stupid boy," said John quickly, trying to smile too.

The centaur ignored him. "I'd be careful of what I said, human," Leghor muttered, looking at Elliot.

"I'd watch what I said if you had kept your oaths, centaur." Elliot's words were met with a frosty glare.

For a moment, it seemed like Leghor would attack him, but his voice sounded calm when he spoke. "What oath are you talking about, stupid boy? Your mouth hadn't stopped suckling when humans betrayed my race."

"King Thomas did not betray your race. All he did was try to save his family, but you broke your oath. You swore to aid him and his allies until

Walter Thorn's fall."

The centaur expression grew steady and unreadable. "I swore to fight on the side of Thomas and his allies until Walter was defeated, but Thomas also swore that he would always be by my side until we were successful. I *kept* my oath, while the king violated his when he walked into Aquarine, ignoring the death that would fall on my race." Now his face hardened with anger. "This prisoner is your race's debt to mine."

Elliot's rage was ineffable; he had never expected to be in this place, and now it was too late to restrain himself. "You don't understand, Leghor. This prisoner belongs to me and will cross the Moonland with me, whether you like it or not. But this is not my only request."

The centaur's eyes became two slits. "Oh, really? What are your other demands?" he sneered.

Elliot fixed his gaze on him. "Walter will soon attack Iovbridge, and the centaurs will have to fulfill their oath by fighting on my side."

Leghor glanced away, into the fire, as silence spread. Then he moved closer to Elliot. "A boy thinks he will force my glorious race to fight on his side," he remarked. "Turns out, humans are even more stupid than I thought. Your words and disrespect are punishable by death." His eyes sparked, and the tone of his voice showed that he would keep to every word he had uttered.

Elliot weighed him up, dismounted, and approached him, anger simmering inside of him. Suddenly, the bonfire flared, its flames rising higher in the sky, taking on the colour of blood. Leghor looked at the fiery hyenas in surprise, and then Elliot's voice sounded like thunder.

"I'm Elliot Egercoll, son of Thomas Egercoll and Alice Asselin! The time has come for you to honour your oath, centaur!"

The Forgotten Oath

The flames in Moonland subsided. Elliot observed the centaurs' gaze and avoided looking at his companions. He knew they wouldn't appreciate that he had hidden the truth from them while they risked their lives for him. Despite his resolve, his gaze slipped to his right—Selwyn's eyes were filled with surprise. John, Morys and Eleanor looked puzzled. He glanced at Reynald Karford, whose expression was the one that surprised him the most; Reynald's face showed no hatred or anger, but embarrassment and obvious curiosity.

"Liar!" howled Leghor after a while. "King Thomas never had a son."

"My mother left Iovbridge shortly after the second king's fall while she was pregnant." Elliot felt a pinch of panic, uttering those words. His anger had carried him away, and he knew it. This information was one of the biggest secrets in Knightdorn. He wasn't sure whether he should have revealed it.

Leghor looked at him strangely. "Alice Asselin was pregnant and gave birth? How is that possible?" he wondered. "Walter found her and killed her shortly after Thomas's death, along with his own mother! He may have propagated the rumour that Alice and Emma committed suicide, but anyone with a grain of common sense did not believe this nonsense."

Elliot didn't want to say more, but it was too late. "My mother gave birth before Walter could find her," he cried. "And the rumours are true. When my mother and Emma learned that Walter knew where they were, they ended their lives by drinking poison."

The centaurs' leader took on a pensive look. "And where did you grow up?" he asked after a few moments.

"My mother knew that Walter would find her. Thorn had heard people say that she was pregnant and would not rest until he had found out the truth and had killed her along with her baby. So, after my birth she sent me to a village in Isisdor where I lived all my life."

Leghor looked at him intently. "How did Reynald Karford fall into your hands?" he burst out.

Elliot was surprised by the change of subject. "Why are you interested in this?"

The centaur scoffed. "Why wouldn't I be? In fact, several more questions come to mind," he murmured. "You see, I couldn't understand why Ersemor's magic allowed you to cross the forest, since your intentions are not so pure. But it all makes sense now—pegasus magic flows in your veins," Leghor continued. "Still, I wonder, how has this information not reached every corner of Knightdorn? The queen wouldn't have kept a truth such as this in the dark, and that kind of news would certainly have reached our ears. I also see a man that few could beat in single combat in chains. I think it is unlikely that the Stonegate men attacked their leader, and Iovbridge didn't send an army to the Land of Fire—we would have noticed that."

"No one knows the truth about me," replied Elliot.

"Interesting." Leghor's eyes shone. "But you haven't told me: how did you capture this man?" he continued, pointing to Reynald.

"I defeated him in combat."

"Reynald Karford fell to a villager?" scoffed Leghor. "This man slaughtered worthy warriors of my race! I saw that with my own eyes! He can't possibly have been defeated by mere a boy."

"And yet, it's true," Elliot said calmly.

The centaur glanced at Elliot's companions and Reynald; none of them had reacted to Elliot's words. "You must have had a great drillmaster!" Now, his voice revealed suspicion. "Who trained you?"

"Roger Belet," came Elliot's response.

The centaur took on a strange look, as if trying to hide his thoughts. "I have never heard that name before," he said.

Elliot gave no answer, and Leghor observed him for a while with eyes that still sparked. Suddenly, a strange emotion stirred in Elliot's soul as for a moment he felt that Leghor knew more about him than he showed.

"I don't know if this young man is telling the whole truth, Leghor. But one thing is for sure—Egercoll blood flows in his veins."

The centaur turned his gaze to Aleron. The elwyn's skin shone under the colourful stars.

"As you said yourself, Ersemor revealed its passage to him, while no human without the Egercolls' blood could see the true face of the Lake of Life." Aleron's starry-blue eyes looked at the centaur with a curious expression.

Leghor's black tail swished abruptly as he listened to his words. "So be it," he said as if to himself after a few moments. Silence spread around the fire, and then the centaur turned his gaze to Elliot. "I'll let you cross the Moonland together with your prisoner," he pronounced at last.

"Thank you," Elliot muttered, "but I'd like you to fulfil my other wish too."

A female centaur with silver hair and a brown coat stood behind Leghor and glared at him. "Even if you are Thomas's son, do you think we owe allegiance to the Egercolls?"

"The centaurs' oath to the second king was eternal." Elliot knew he was trying his luck. Visiting Ersemor had never been part of the plan; his Master had ordered him to avoid it, but fate had brought him here. By now, he had already revealed more than he would have liked, so he thought it was worth trying to gain another army.

"You're new in the world, Lord Egercoll," Aleron said. "No oath is eternal! Oaths are based on trust and respect," he continued. "Humans have shown disrespect to the centaurs' race, and that's not the way to call for a new alliance."

Elliot's anger turned to shame upon hearing those words.

"I will fight Thorn by your side." A voice came from within the crowd, and many pairs of eyes shifted.

A grey-coated centaur stepped forward—his hair was longer than most, and his violet eyes were benevolent. Elliot noticed that his face had several scars from past battles, and a large scar covered his human chest.

"You still haven't learnt your place, Righor?"

"I can fight for whomever I want, Leghor."

"You have an obligation to obey your leader! This enemy is not ours!" shouted Leghor.

"Isn't the one responsible for the slaughter of half our race my enemy?"

Leghor pulled out a long sword from a scabbard on his back. "You shall obey my command."

Elliot drew his own sword, and the centaurs growled menacingly.

"Enough." Aleron's voice drowned out their murmuring. "The world is already plagued with enough fighting. Everybody put your swords away."

To Elliot's surprise, the centaur obeyed, and so he too sheathed his blade. Leghor's paced on the soft grass, his hooves digging divots in the ground; his rage hadn't subsided.

"I don't know who you really are, lad, but you certainly lack wisdom." Aleron's eyes were fixed on Elliot's. "Unsheathing your sword in front of a centaur who allowed you to cross his land is an insult. Know that power is a quality that many before you possessed, and they have all been dead for many years."

Elliot wanted to protest, to defend his actions, but Aleron continued.

"Only a tyrant forces others to fight for him. A true leader doesn't ask anyone to fight for him, but everyone wants to follow him to their death... Choose what you want to be, and forget the oaths of the dead."

The elwyn's last words struck him like icy steel—his arrogance and anger had blinded him. Elliot was in the home of a race that had lost husbands, fathers, and sons in the battles of men, and he had demanded that they follow him in battle, without offering the slightest thing in return.

"I apologise if I offended you, Lord Leghor," Elliot said after a moment. "It is my honour that you allow me to cross your land," he concluded with a deep bow.

Aleron nodded approvingly, and Leghor seemed to calm down. "The Moonland is yours if you and your companions want to rest," responded the centaur.

"Thank you, but we don't have time. We must be on our way," Elliot responded.

The centaur nodded sharply and glanced at the herd of centaurs around them. The crowd began to disperse.

Leghor approached Elliot with Aleron behind him. "Continue south and you'll soon get to the Road of Elves," advised the centaur. "The Paths of the Elder Races are not safe these days. Follow the path south of the Forked River on the way to Wirskworth and be careful, Elliot Egercoll!" said Leghor, who then turned away from the travellers.

As Elliot watched the centaur gallop away, Aleron uttered one last warning. "Remember what I told you, lad! I'm not sure about you yet, but I believe our paths will cross again!" With these enigmatic words, the elwyn walked away.

Elliot had avoided looking at his companions for quite some time, and John rode over to him, anxious. "We must continue!" he urged.

Elliot nodded sharply, mounted his horse, and they began to move away from the magic fire that hadn't stopped leaping into the sky. Thoughts swirled in Elliot's mind. *"The difficult thing is not to learn to fight; the difficult thing is to inspire those around you to fight for you."* His Master's words struck him now in a way they had not before. In the end, he had learnt nothing all these years, and a kingdom's fate hung on his shoulders. He felt the need to leave, to vanish from this world. He was reminded, then, of a wolf he had encountered as a child. That year's winter was harsh, and on top of that, countless sheep had been slaughtered in their fields. The villagers were disillusioned until the day Elliot found the stealthy wolf that attacked their flocks. The wolf had approached with snarling jaws, eager for Elliot's flesh, but he had wounded the animal with a sword wielded with remarkable force for a twelve-year-old. The animal howled bitterly as its blood stained the snow red, and Elliot made ready to strike again. He didn't feel anger for the beast, but he had learnt that quick death was better than a slow and torturous one. The Master had approached, and as he was about to strike, he grabbed Elliot by the shoulder. *"I'd say that maybe we could help this hapless animal."*

Elliot had been surprised. *"But it killed our flocks, Master."*

The old man approached the wolf and looked at the wound in its lower abdomen. *"It did what its nature commanded it to do, nobody having shown it anything different. Maybe its nature can no longer change... but maybe it can, so we'll earn a new ally."*

Elliot hadn't understood but had put the sword back in its sheath. His rage toward his Master had erupted like a storm when he'd been ordered to tend to the animal's wounds, but soon affection for the wolf grew in its stead, and he named it Greyfoot. When Greyfoot healed, they set him free. A couple of days later, as Elliot was walking in a valley bordering his village, he'd seen another huge black wolf approaching their flocks. He'd started running as fast as he could, but the big animal had already noticed him. Elliot had hurried to attack but had tripped and fallen. The wolf's jaws had opened with fury. Before he could raise his sword, Greyfoot attacked the wild beast, tearing its neck. His Master had taught him that he could build an alliance even with someone whose very nature ordered them to be his adversary.

As they rode, the centaur named Righor approached and joined. "My heart's greatest desire is to fight Walter Thorn, but I can't defy my leader," he said, panting. "Still, I want to give you a gift."

Elliot didn't understand, and then a white hawk tore through the air. The bird slowed abruptly, approaching Elliot. He was frightened but didn't move, and the hawk landed on his shoulder.

"Many legends say that some animals obey centaurs," John said. The tone of his voice showed that he hadn't believed in those stories either, but that perhaps now he was less certain.

"This hawk will obey only you from now on, Elliot."

Elliot was puzzled. "Do centaurs force other animals to serve humans?"

The violet eyes fixed on him at once. "I'm not giving you a servant but a companion," clarified the centaur. "You're not alone in the path you're crossing, but the afflictions and suffering will not be few. Be patient, Lord Egercoll." With these words, Righor turned and galloped away.

The hawk spread its wings and soared, Elliot tracking its path for a brief moment. Shortly afterwards, he urged his mare forward, and they continued to cross the vast countryside until the centaurs disappeared from sight. They rode for some time, leaving behind the Centaurs-Land. Their steeds pressed on through some wild trees.

"It won't be long before we reach the Road of Elves," murmured Long Arm. "We have to get to the City of Heavens. It's close to our path, as things have turned out, and the only safe place to rest before we reach Wirskworth."

"We don't have time," countered Elliot. "The Sword of Destiny will soon be in Walter's hands. We must talk to the Governor of Elmor, and the road we have to take now is longer than Snake Road."

"We can't get to Wirskworth without resting," said Morys, looking at Eleanor. The girl looked exhausted, and Selwyn didn't look any better. "Perhaps it'd be wise to stop in the forest for a while, before heading to the City of Heavens. I haven't taken that path before, but I'm almost certain that the time to reach Elirehar's capital is about a day, and we're all exhausted. A little rest in Ersemor and the City of Heavens won't delay us much."

"He's right," sighed John.

Elliot breathed out wearily—in truth it was already midnight. It had been hours since the Guardians of the South had captured his companions, and they hadn't had a chance to rest for too long. He pulled back his mare's reins and jumped off his horse. "Let's rest a while, but we'll set off before dawn," he said curtly.

Selwyn dismounted and hurried to light a fire. Morys got the prisoner off his horse and seated him on a small rock next to Eleanor. They held their silence until John yelled out as though he had been holding in his ire for a long time.

"Are you insane, you idiot?"

Elliot realised that John was looking at him and was taken aback.

"You ordered one of the proudest races in the world to fight for you!"

"I made a mistake," he admitted in a low tone.

"Who trained you?" Selwyn's voice sounded steady.

Elliot exhaled wearily. "You know the answer, Selwyn."

"I don't know if I can trust you anymore, Elliot," replied the young man. "A few days ago, you told my father and the queen that you never knew who your parents were. You said these words to the queen—gods above, your cousin—" Selwyn shook his head at his own words "—but you decided to reveal the truth to the centaurs."

"Iovbridge is full of spies. If that information had reached Walter, it might have ruined the plan." Elliot spoke loudly. "The truth could have only brought harm to Isisdor, while here it might have earned us another ally. I thought the centaurs would fight for an Egercoll."

"Do you know the history of the family you say you come from?" John seemed furious.

Elliot looked at him without speaking, giving him a chance to go on.

"I don't know who trained you, but he truly trained a fool," muttered Long Arm. "You used a name that for many symbolises the rebirth of freedom in Knightdorn, but you used it to try to force a race that paid for the consequences of our wars with blood to fight by your side. I don't know if this name is really yours, but you certainly don't have the right to tarnish it."

Now Elliot was sure that they had been unfair to Long Arm, thinking that he was merely an uncouth drunkard. His knowledge was unique, and the respect he showed to every creature that was different from humans was something Elliot had never seen before.

Ashamed, Elliot looked down at his hands—a stranger had just honoured his family with his words more than he had ever done.

Suddenly, a grunt broke the silence, and Elliot jumped up like a bolt of lightning. A hyena leaped from the trees, baring its large teeth. Elliot lashed out, piercing the animal's chest as it jumped onto Selwyn. Such was the force of his blow that the beast collapsed at once. A second hyena rushed Morys, who dodged it with a quick leap. Selwyn hurried for his sword, which lay on the opposite side of camp, as Elliot saw one more pair of yellow eyes glowing in the dark. Everything happened very quickly. The one hyena attacked Elliot, who thrust his sword into its mouth just as John tossed his own blade to Selwyn. The lad grabbed it and impaled the second wild animal in the back with a swift movement.

The chaos seemed to be over, but Elliot turned back to the campfire and fear flooded his soul. Reynald Karford had wrapped a chain around Eleanor's neck. His smile revealed his rotting teeth as he pulled the chain tight. Eleanor squirmed but did not let out a sound of fear.

"Throw me the key," he said calmly, rattling his chains. "Or I'll strangle her."

Elliot was paralysed. His sword hung from his hand, but he couldn't use it. Not without risking Eleanor's life.

"I SAID, THROW ME THE KEY," Reynald yelled.

Selwyn tried to slink around Reynald, but the other man only laughed. "Don't be an idiot!" said Reynald. "I'll take this pretty little one's life before you come anywhere near."

Selwyn stood still, and Elliot read the truth in Reynald's eyes—he'd kill Eleanor if they didn't obey. A sadistic smile twisted Reynald's face. He knew he had won—and then his body went limp, and he dropped like a corpse.

The Lost Master

Reynald felt dizzy—he had a terrible headache. For a moment, he tried to open his eyes, but his eyelids felt heavy. *What happened?* he asked himself. He made another attempt to open his eyes, but the sunlight was strong, and his body felt stiff. He could see that he was on the back of a slow-moving horse. His hands were tied so tightly he felt that the slightest movement would break them. And the pain from his wounded limbs was terrible. He took a few deep breaths—fortunately, they hadn't put that awful cloth in his mouth.

"Where am I?"

His voice sounded hoarse. He forced open his eyes, blinking against the sun.

"Look who woke up." Morys stopped his horse and peered at him.

"If you don't take care of my wounds, they'll fester, and I won't get to Wirskworth alive," said Reynald.

Elliot looked at him strangely, as if the boy wanted to both kill him and help him. He moved toward him, riding proudly. "They'll take care of your wounds where we're going," he said.

"What happened?" stammered Reynald. "I had her," he murmured, and his gaze searched for Eleanor. She was on his mare's left, and she was looking at him with pure hatred.

"You're forgetting that you're just a man," taunted Elliot.

"None of you could have approached me." Reynald was trying to remember the scene, but his brain was fuzzy.

Suddenly, a hawk sat on Elliot's shoulder, and a smile formed on his lips.

"This disgusting, filthy bird attacked me!"

"No, it just dropped a stone on your head from above," said the boy, and Reynald understood why the pain in his skull was so acute.

"Where are we?" Reynald continued his questions. His eyes had now adjusted to the environment and the daylight didn't seem so strong. The sun would soon set.

"In Elirehar," replied John. "Soon, we'll be in the City of Heavens."

It was true—from afar he could see the low walls with the blue flags adorned with pegasi. Round towers with tiled roofs stretched from one end of the wall to the other, and two more large towers rose in the city centre. These towers belonged to Pegasus Castle. To the left he could see the waters of the Forked River. The river stretched south of the Road of Elves, from Wirskworth to the City of Pegasus and from there, to the Sea of the Sun. It was the main source of water in Elmor and Elirehar.

Thoughts swirled in Reynald's mind. Legend had it that the first King of Elirehar, Thomyn Egercoll, built the city with low walls so that the pegasi take off more easily from its interior. Naturally, this was risky if they were under attack, but no one dared attack the city of the pegasi, the mythical creatures who accorded their riders with strength. Reynald had scoffed at such nonsense.

"How long have I been unconscious?" he asked.

"For about a day," replied John.

They were getting closer and closer to the city, and Elliot was in awe seeing his ancestors' home for the first time in his life. They continued to ride toward the City of Heavens until their horses approached the steel gate. *This gate must be very old*, thought Elliot. Nevertheless, that didn't stop him from admiring it. Some carved symbols were at the top, in an unknown language, and the frame was made of gold.

"Who are you?" a loud voice came from above. A man aimed at them with a bow from the battlements.

"We are messengers of the Queen of Knightdorn. We're heading for Wirskworth and looking for a place to spend the night," John called out. They had agreed that Long Arm would speak.

"Messengers who carry a prisoner?" cried the man, indicating Reynald with his bow.

"The Queen of Knightdorn has ordered us to transfer this prisoner to Wirskworth," said Selwyn aloud.

"Who are you?" hollered the archer.

"I'm Selwyn Brau, son of Peter Brau and defender of Isisdor."

"Selwyn?" The man suddenly lowered his bow. "The last time I saw you, you couldn't get on your own horse," he said, smiling before disappearing from sight.

The gate creaked open to reveal a lush, green place. The companions rode inside, and Elliot gaped at the greenery. Backstreets made of white cobblestones seemed to glow in the light of dusk. Small houses led towards the towers in the centre of the city, but something else caught his attention—the statue of a huge pegasus carved out of white stone stared at him from a distance.

"Why are you here, Selwyn?" The guard approached, looking over the party, accompanied by a few more men. His forehead was wrinkled, and his eyes looked tired under his curly hair, which had begun to turn white.

Selwyn looked at the guard, flustered. "I'm sorry, but I can't remember who you are," he said hesitantly.

The man cackled. "Of course you can't! You were still a baby the last time you saw me! It's been years since my last visit to Iovbridge." Suddenly, the man's gaze froze, and Elliot was startled.

"How did he get here?"

The city guards drew their bowstrings back in an instant, all arrows trained on Reynald Karford.

"He's our prisoner," Selwyn said hurriedly.

The man could not believe his eyes. "For the sake of the Seven Swords! How did you catch this man?"

"What is your name, son of Elirehar?" asked Selwyn.

"Vyresar Tobley. I fought on your father's side when Walter Thorn attacked Elirehar."

"Vyresar, I think you know that Iovbridge will be attacked soon. The queen has assigned a very important mission to me. I must get to Wirskworth as soon as possible with this man," said Selwyn, pointing to Reynald. "But before I cross the road on the way to Elmor, my companions and I need a place to rest."

Vyresar held Selwyn's gaze, then sighed. "You are welcome in the City of Heavens," he conceded.

The men of the city lowered their bows, and Elliot and his companions dismounted their horses while a groom hurried to catch their bridles.

"Follow me," ordered Vyresar.

As they walked, Elliot eyed the shops and homes where craftsmen, labourers, and grooms worked, each seemingly content. This city didn't have great towers and buildings like Iovbridge, but it exuded a unique serenity. The foliage on the ground, along with the calm breeze that caressed Elliot's face made this place seem magical.

The walked, Vyresar leading them, until the castle in the city centre sat in front of them. A majestic temple with a round turquoise dome, as large as that of the Unknown God Elliot had seen from afar in Iovbridge, stood to the right of Pegasus Castle. The columns around its entrance were tall and white, and a large emblem was carved just above the wooden door—a pegasus next to a man. The man seemed omnipotent, with large arms and a long beard, and extended his hand toward the creature's head. This was the God of Life, the chosen god of the Egercolls, but also the god of the elwyn and the elves.

At the temple entrance, Vyresar spoke quietly to a priest, who whispered in Vyresar's ear, then Vyresar turned back to Elliot and the others.

"The Grand Master wants to speak with you. The prisoner will remain in the cells."

Selwyn seemed surprised. "Is there a Grand Master?"

"Yes, Lord Brau. After the last battle with Walter, we may not have a governor or an army or a council, but we still have the Grand Master and high priest of the temple."

"Grand Master *and* high priest?" wondered Selwyn.

"Yes, he has both titles," replied Vyresar.

"How does he know about our arrival?" Elliot asked.

"The Master knows a lot, my lad," whispered Vyresar enigmatically. With these strange words, he left them at the entrance to the imposing temple, pushing Reynald with force. Despite the sense of mystery Vyresar cultivated, Elliot did not doubt the guard had sent a runner ahead to inform the Grand Master of their presence.

The companions looked at each other, but after a few moments Elliot proceeded to the entrance and gently pushed the wooden door. It creaked open, and he entered the temple with the rest following him. A huge, dark room lay before him. The temple's large windows were covered with thick textiles, so the light of the sunset didn't reach the interior. Torches imparted a yellowish hue to the walls, which depicted faces and creatures. A series of columns, austere and cold, loomed over them. Inching forward, Elliot began to discern images of battles as he walked.

"I see war everywhere!" cried Eleanor, frightened.

"Because our world is plagued by it," whispered Elliot and drew his sword so fast that John stumbled while the steel shone under the firelight.

"Put down your sword, soldier! No one will harm you here." The serene voice penetrated the silence, and a soft light appeared at the back of the temple's main hall.

Elliot advanced slowly, the others behind him.

"Who are you?" he called out.

"Follow the light and you'll find your answer."

He lowered his sword a few inches as he got closer and closer to where the voice had come from. As he approached, the depictions on the walls became more and more dramatic, as if trying to keep death etched in his memory. Elliot reached the end of the room and noticed a small opening in the wall. He hesitated for a moment, then recovered his courage and hurried through the opening.

The faint light greeted him again, and he lifted his sword, protecting his chest. He spun as the sound of breathing echoed off the walls, at last catching sight of an aged and ragged man who was smiling. His face was so creased with wrinkles that it was as if his vital organs had been drained of life. His clothes were torn. "You're not in any danger here, my lad," he said in a kindly voice.

Elliot weighed him up carefully as the other companions slowly passed through the opening.

"Who are you?" The words escaped from Elliot's lips hesitantly.

"The Grand Master and high priest of the temple of the City of Heavens."

Elliot took in the interior of the room, realising that the walls depicted the most famous legends in history. The God of Life blowing breath into the first pegasus and the elwyn, while they in turn touched the heads of many other creatures. The first giant rising, the first mermaid swimming in a whirlpool, and the first elf emerging from a white smoke cloud. A little farther along, another figure looked like it was being sculpted: the first man.

"I'd swear that the depictions in the temple's great hall frightened you," said the old man seriously.

"One would say that these here are less chilling," replied Selwyn.

"Of course. You are in the Hall of Life, Selwyn Brau. Here, you can view the cycle of the creation of this world," explained the old man. "Outside this room, there are only the achievements of our kind."

His words seemed to surprise Selwyn.

"I'm sure you don't remember me. It's been many years since you last saw me... but I'm sure John, Long Arm, has not erased me from his memory."

Elliot looked at John, who seemed not to believe his eyes.

"Master Thorold?" John stared at the old man as if seeing a ghost. As for Selwyn, he was taken aback at the name John used.

"I don't blame you," said the Master, smiling. "It's surprising that I've lived so many years."

"Where have you been all these years? Why didn't you tell the queen you were alive?" Selwyn now looked angry.

"There was nothing an old man like me could offer Iovbridge apart from one more reason for Walter to want to besiege it."

Selwyn seemed dejected. "You could have trained young lads! You could have given our allies hope! You could have helped the queen who has Egercoll blood flowing through her veins!" His words came out like a sharp blade.

The old man closed his eyes, sighing deeply. "I've lived ninety-eight years, and my time had come to an end. No boy I would train could overthrow Walter, and I couldn't watch any other lads I looked on as sons fall by his sword."

"You hid here like a coward." Selwyn now raised his voice. "Althalos would never have forgiven you if he had known."

"I think Althalos was never able to even forgive his own self... You're too young, Selwyn—someday, you will understand."

"How did you survive? When Walter attacked Elirehar, everyone thought you were dead." John's voice was hushed.

"Walter may have power, but he lacks knowledge," said the elder.

"The queen gave everything for Knightdorn, and I saw my brothers die, while you hid here without training a single soldier in the City of Heavens?" Selwyn spoke again.

"The death that covered Elirehar will never be overcome, my good child. Those who stayed and grew up here after Walter Thorn's attack never wanted to fight or learn to fight." Now the Master's eyes looked tearful.

"You said that no lad you could train would beat Walter. Do you think he is invincible?" Elliot didn't know why he asked that question. It was hard to look at this man and not see anything other than his old Master resurrected—and the pain of that loss and the lies he had begun to understand pulled at him still.

The old man looked at him with benevolent eyes. "No one is invincible," he murmured. "I don't know you, young man... nor the lad and the girl next to you, though my memory betrays me these days."

"My name is Elliot, and next to me are Morys Bardolf and Eleanor Dilerion."

"Dear Eleanor!" exclaimed Thorold. "The last time I saw you, you were a baby! I've heard of the name Bardolf, but I've never met anyone from that House," he continued, looking at Morys. "But the name Elliot doesn't ring any bells." When Elliot didn't answer the unasked question, Thorald went on. "What are you doing here? From what I've heard, you're travelling to Wirskworth on the queen's orders, and with a notable prisoner in your hands."

"We are carrying out orders of the Queen of Knightdorn in an attempt to save the kingdom from Walter. We would like to rest in the city before continuing at dawn." Elliot didn't want to give out any other information. Their adventure in the Centaurs-Land had reminded him that he ought to keep his mouth shut. He did not expect the answer to be satisfactory, as was prepared to withstand a barrage of questions.

"Very well. My men will give you what you need."

Elliot looked at him with wonder mixed with suspicion.

"If you don't mind, I'd like to be alone," Thorold said, suddenly nodding toward the opening in the wall.

It had only been a few hours since their visit to the city's temple. Elliot was idly watching Morys and Eleanor train, but he also felt drowsy. The moon had made its appearance, softly lighting the night.

"Should we not be resting?" cried Selwyn.

"If you ever find yourself in a siege, you'll have to fight vigilantly. Next to you, there may be the bodies of your loved ones. Supplies will dwindle day by day, and the sword will weigh more and more heavily in your hand. If this journey is difficult, how will we survive a battle against Walter?" Elliot glanced at the young man, who swallowed down his protest.

They were in a secluded, grassy courtyard in the City of Heavens, and they trained under the starlight. John had remained in the room he had been given in a small house next to Pegasus Castle since he didn't care about training. The castle itself was unoccupied. Elliot had learnt that after Walter looted the city, the residents had initially decided to repair the castle, but then abandoned their efforts. Elliot felt a strange relief that he hadn't entered the castle. For some reason, he didn't want to be in the place where his father had lived.

Elliot turned his attention from the stars to his companions. Morys was undoubtedly skilled with the sword in his hand, but Eleanor's passion fascinated him. After a pause in their bout, the young woman raised her sword again and walked toward Morys, who looked bored.

"How can a woman disarm me?" he chipped in, looking at Elliot, who had urged him to train with Eleanor. "The sword is so heavy that she cannot even raise it."

Elliot smiled and got up with a swift motion. He walked toward Eleanor and whispered something in her ear. She nodded and stepped forward with a smile of her own.

Morys waited for her attack, but that didn't come, so he approached Eleanor nonchalantly. He made a move, trying to hit her on the shoulder with a light blow, which she avoided. He arced his sword in a circular motion, but Eleanor was faster as she pulled out of his reach. He attacked again, turning the steel to her left shoulder. She skilfully pulled back her arm, and her sword passed through Morys's stance and marked his chest. The man blinked and looked at the icy steel on his chest. The young woman had beaten him, and Elliot smiled at the sight. Eleanor withdrew her sword and looked at Morys with a sparkle in her eyes as he glared at her.

"Elliot, you should be sharing your secrets with everyone," Morys cried.

"Sometimes your blows are predictable. You must learn to improvise," replied Elliot, and Morys looked at him, both offended and curious. "If you observe your opponent's body, then you will know where they'll hit," he continued.

"Interesting move." Thorold's voice echoed around the courtyard. He had emerged from the darkness unnoticed. The old man was looking at Elliot with twinkling eyes.

"It is right to teach the secrets of battle to your friends," the Master said. It was obvious that he had been watching them for some time. "Who taught you to fight?"

"Roger Belet," replied Elliot.

"Old Roger did a good job."

Elliot observed him. "Have you ever met him?"

"I think not, but my memory often betrays me lately. He certainly did a good job, though," said Thorold. "Are you ready to fight the queen's enemies and take your opponents' lives?"

"I don't want to take my opponents' lives. I just want to protect Knightdorn's people. No one will die by my hand if I have a choice," stated Elliot.

The old man watched him as if trying to read his thoughts. "Prudent and wise words," he muttered. "But when you go on the battlefield and see your opponents impale the hearts of your loved ones, your hatred will find you."

Elliot was ready to answer, but movement caught his eye. A blonde-haired young woman approached, her hair shining in the moonlight.

"Grandpa, you must eat before you go to bed," she said sternly.

The girl grabbed the old man by the elbow and began to maneuver him away. In the moonlight, her eyes appeared turquoise as if they carried the sea within, and her lips were ruby-red. She wore a silver gown, rich with embroidery.

Elliot swallowed hard as her blonde hair brushed across her shoulders. Her face looked familiar. He felt like he had known her all his life as she glanced at him, smiling.

"My granddaughter takes good care of me," said the Master, chuckling. "Selyn, these are the queen's messengers from Iovbridge."

The girl smiled again, then she and Thorold walked away. Selwyn stared after them.

"I didn't know Thorold had children, let alone grandchildren," the young man murmured. "If I remember correctly, he was named an Elirehar knight at a very young age, so it would have been impossible for him to have kids."

"He has lived for almost a century. Maybe he got kids when he retired," guessed Morys. "Knights often resigned their positions to younger men."

Selwyn nodded in agreement. "Perhaps."

Elliot was still watching Selyn when Eleanor's voice reached his ears. "I think you should stop looking, Elliot," she said.

He turned to her and noticed the sly smile on Eleanor's face.

That night, as they rested their weary bodies, Elliot was restless. When he finally slept, his dreams were flooded by colourful lightning that struck a stormy red sea.

The Howl of the Wolf

Sophie gazed at the Scarlet Sea. She enjoyed watching the wild waves under the moonlight. The sea brought to mind a carefree youth, the kind she had never experienced. The weight of the throne had fallen on her shoulders when she was a child, yet she had never wanted this throne.

She remembered meeting disconcerted soldiers and officers on her first day in Iovbridge. A good-natured man had approached her, putting his rough hand on her shoulders—it was Peter Brau. *"Knightdorn needs you,"* he had told her, looking her deep in the eyes. Nevertheless, she didn't know then the weight of the responsibility she would have to carry, a weight that few could bear... knights, generals, and captains had baulked in the face of her cousin, and she had had to fight him since she was a little girl.

The years passed, and as she grew older, she knew what the future held for her. Her death would be violent and demeaning. She would be raped and humiliated, then hung in the middle of the capital, though her only sin was that she had tried to protect the people of Knightdorn ever since she could remember.

She had lost hope of another outcome after Bert's death. While he was alive, Sophie had felt there might be a chance to persevere, but after his death, it was as if darkness had swallowed her soul. The only lover left in her life was war, whilst no one really cared about her.

But now another young man had become a focal point in her life, though of a different sort. She still could not fully comprehend that fate had sent something akin to hope in the moment the end was approaching. *How is it possible?* The question never left her. She had pinned her hopes on a stranger, risking the remaining fragments of trust between her and the Royal Council. Four whole days had passed—and the fifth would soon dawn—since the boy had left Iovbridge. The council had been shocked by her decision. Most of Elliot's companions could have gone unnoticed in their absence, but not Selwyn. The new lord of the knights' only living son was an important figure, and in conjunction with Elliot's disappearance, the council had asked many questions. Peter had explained that Elliot's origin was a mystery that had to be explored as his abilities were unique and his Master unknown to everyone. The tension in the Council Hall had risen sharply after these words.

"I never expected such a foolish decision from you, Peter. Walter will be on our doorstep in a few days, and you're sending valuable men on a useless quest? You could have just used the boy in battle. How could you have agreed to send Selwyn to a village with a dangerous stranger?" Lord Counselor Patrick Degore had shouted these words, and even Frederic would not sanction the queen and the general's decision, which was unprecedented.

Nevertheless, Sophie and Peter found themselves in a fortunate position. The emergence of the traitors had united the council against Walter. They would not ask her to give up the throne. Moreover, her decision not to reveal to the council that Eleanor had followed Selwyn on this mission proved wise. Such a truth would have imbued the council with doubts about her and Peter's true motives in the face of the coming war. They would believe nothing else but that they had sent their loved ones away from the death that would soon plague Iovbridge.

Sophie turned away from the sea and walked slowly into her chamber. Her gaze fell on a silver tray on a wooden table. She had asked for meat and cheese along with some figs and gooseberries, yet she hadn't touched her dinner, not even a morsel.

Perhaps Elliot abandoned the plan, overwhelmed by fear of fighting Reynald as soon as he reached Stonegate. Terror washed over her soul at this thought. She hoped that Selwyn and Eleanor were safe. She knew she should have dismissed Elliot, but his battle for her life had filled her with emotions that had prevailed over her logic. No one had declared his loyalty to her as effortlessly as he had in several years; it was hard to resist such earnestness. But she knew she had sent him to his death. He could not take Reynald Karford down in a duel. Guilt flooded her soul. And if Reynald's men caught the others, the Guardian Commander wouldn't spare Selwyn, while Eleanor would suffer at his hands. A sigh escaped her lips. She wouldn't be able to sleep for another night as anguish ate at her inners.

"Why me?" she repeated the question that she asked herself more and more often as of late. She tried to understand why it was she who had to take the throne, why she had to sacrifice her life fighting a man no one could defeat, why she had to be tortured and humiliated for a world that had turned its back on her. Fate was a cruel thing. That was the bitter truth. She made an effort to bring to mind a happy memory. It seemed impossible at that moment, but she had to persevere. A howl broke the silence, prickling Sophie's skin. The wolves had been singing since Elliot left the city, their packs approaching Iovbridge more and more often.

Sophie couldn't think of anything happy, and many events of the past suddenly intruded in her mind. After a while, she felt desperate—every defeat of the last years swirled in her head. She wondered what she could have changed from the past. What she could have done differently. Walter had managed to take the northern regions before she even took the throne...

After Thomas's death, Felador was left with only a few soldiers. So, Sophie couldn't hope for any help from her birthplace. Then, after Thomas's fall, Walter marched on the Egercolls' hometown, intending to destroy it. Back then, Sophie was but a little girl, and Peter advised her to send help. Sophie had listened to her general, but Walter pillaged the region's capital, killing everyone in his way; Peter was one of the few who had managed to escape.

Sophie remembered what happened next. She expected that after the fall of the Egercolls' birthplace, Walter would attack Elmor. However, she was proven wrong. Walter avoided a battle with Elmor, recognising its military prowess at a moment when his army was exhausted from the continuous battles. As if that weren't enough, a plague brought the north to its knees, decimating his men, so he halted all attacks for seven years. When his forces were fit for war again, he focused on Oldlands. Claiming this region was Walter's burning desire as Oldlands's men were the best armourers in the world. Walter marched his armies to Oldland's capital and besieged it for three whole years but failed to subdue it. Sophie had sent her general to help. Peter was formulating a plan to counter Walter when the Governor of Oldlands was found murdered in his sleep. A man loyal to Walter assumed power, and Thorn's entire army, alongside that of Oldlands, attacked Sophie's forces and trounced her men. The general was again one of the few men who managed to get away, but his own two sons died. Sophie had failed again.

The Mercenaries popped into her mind. When Oldlands was added to Walter's allies, Vylor seceded. Vylor's rulers always asked for payment in order to ally with other armies, earning its soldiers the title of Mercenaries. Sophie hated the Mercenaries; they were notorious for greed, torture, and rape. Even the First King had, many times, been outraged by their actions. Nonetheless, Thomas Egercoll was the only one who punished their disobedience by barring their current or any future governor from voting for the election of the King of Knightdorn.

The Governor of Vylor didn't wish to fight by Walter's side. Then, Walter marched to his city and challenged him to single combat for the conquest of Vylor. The governor underestimated him, and when his duellist fell, Liher Hale—the governor's brother—assumed power. Walter executed the former governor and promised Liher a good amount of gold if he agreed to fight for him, and Liher agreed. However, the years went by, and Sophie heard that the Mercenaries were never paid for their services. After Thomas's death, Liher took his soldiers back to Vylor and never took part in the war again.

Furthermore, the Ice Islands had reneged on their promise to fight for her. Sophie was hoping that their leader would sail to Iovbridge and fight on her side. However, Walter reached his land and, knowing how conceited he was, challenged him to single combat. Walter didn't want such an undisciplined army on his side, so after beating the leader's champion, he allowed him to keep the islands but also demanded that his men stay out of every battle in Knightdorn in exchange for his victory. *One more defeat...*

Sophie consequently lost every ally except Elmor. Walter knew that Elmor was an extremely dangerous rival, which made him avoid attacking Wirskworth before his armies greatly outnumbered those of Syrella Endor. When he finally attacked, the devastation was substantial. Sometimes Sophie blamed herself. Maybe she should have sent help to Elmor. She sighed heavily—she had lost every alliance, the old ones and the fleeting hopes of new ones alike.

Sophie walked toward her chamber window again. The wolves' howls could still be heard in the middle of the night when a light knock sounded on her chamber door. Sophie shivered and hurried to the entrance, fear flooding her soul—maybe bad news had reached Iovbridge.

She opened the door to see Peter silhouetted on the other side. "I'm sorry to bother you at such a late hour, Your Majesty." Peter's tone of voice seemed strange. He held himself stiffly, his hands tucked inside his silk robe. Sophie swung the door open for him to enter.

"A Stonegate Guardian arrived at our doorstep a moment ago," Peter said. "I had given explicit orders to the guards to inform me of anyone approaching the city."

Sophie's held her breath as terror swept through her body. Selwyn was dead, Eleanor was dead—the news would pierce through her heart like a sharp knife.

Peter took a step forward, his face solemn—and then he swept his arms open, the Sword of Destiny shining like a pearl in his hands. Sophie gasped and beheld the ornate heirloom, hardly believing her eyes. And then she felt it, something she hadn't felt for a long time. Hope kindled in her chest, and the wolves' howling now sounded more like a roar of courage to her ears.

The First King

Giren Barlow was laboriously cleaning an imposing, carved wooden table while a scrawny old man carefully placed several platters of food on the tabletop. The men in the great hall of Hawk's Nest seemed frightened, though the marble floor shone in the warm morning light. The great hall of Ballards' Castle in White City, though not immense, was imbued with grandeur. With a white hawk carved at the top, its ceiling had an elaborate round shape. Giren stared at the ceiling for a few moments. He had heard that Ramerstorm was named White City after this hawk.

A thud shook the floor as the door opened, and a man entered the great hall, looking drowsy. Giren glanced at him—his red cloak fluttered loosely behind him, while a heavy sword hung from his belt.

"Bring wine and cheese quickly," he shouted at the slaves, without even looking at them. He sat in one of the chairs, his legs propped on the table, and yawned. The old man hurried to him, carrying a plate with all he had asked for.

"Bring bread too," the newcomer spoke again, a demeaning tone to his voice.

Giren felt his stomach clench—he abhorred all the Trinity of Death's Ghosts, but he hated Brian, the Sadist, more than anyone. His anger flared as he watched the old slave try to run on weak legs, but he knew that if he said the slightest thing, he'd lose his hands, his tongue, or even his life. Giren knew he wasn't particularly brave. His only purpose was to serve the future king, the sovereign who would conquer Knightdorn.

If there was one thing that he felt lucky about, it was that his sister and mother had managed to escape from Tahos during Walter's attack by sailing to the Ice Islands. His father had been less fortunate, hung and then beheaded. He was sure that he would never forget such a sight.

Giren finished cleaning the table and hastened to help the old slave who was carrying a few more trays. Around them, several more slaves were cleaning the great hall, paying attention to the smallest detail.

The door to the great hall opened again, and a huge man crossed its threshold. His body resembled a thick pine trunk, and his boots thudded deafeningly as he walked. Anrai had a savage face and harsh features. Rumour had it that his father was a giant who had slept with a human. Giren had heard that Anrai's mother had died in childbirth. If the rumours were true, Anrai was probably the last creature with the blood of giants in his veins, as the Elder Races had been lost to the world many years ago.

The giant man sat down next to Brian and started eating like a ravenous lion. He wore a yellow silk jerkin, and his boots were covered with wolfskin.

"I didn't expect to find you here so early, Brian."

The man looked at him, laughing. "We have a lot of preparations to make," he replied in a voice full of impatience.

"The throne will soon be in our hands, old friend," murmured Anrai.

After a while, the door to the great hall opened a third time, and a dozen soldiers came in. But it was the tall, sturdy man in a scarlet cloak with long blond hair who drew all eyes. He walked next to a woman dressed in black, and his beautiful face exuded a raw evil.

Every man in the room stood up and bowed deeply, facing the newcomer.

Walter sat at the head of the wooden table, Berta Loers, the woman in black, at his side. His blue eyes looked around the great hall. Giren saw him staring at the hawk that was carved onto the ceiling.

"By first light tomorrow, I want there to not be a single white hawk in this city. The tiger will be the only emblem to adorn Ramerstorm," Walter shouted, looking at the slaves left and right.

One of the slaves protested, "But Your Majesty, the white hawk is Ballar's emblem. It would be disrespectful to destroy these carvings."

Walter turned to him. "What's your name?" he grumbled.

"Edan, Your Majesty."

"I've never seen you before. When did you become one of my servants?" asked Walter.

"A few days ago, Your Majesty. I'm a son of Ballar. My life was spared when your men took White City."

Walter got up slowly and approached him with a smile. Edan bowed, and as he stood back up, Walter plunged his sword through the man's neck. The slave made harrowing sounds as he breathed his last. Giren watched the spectacle, trying not to vomit.

Walter wiped his blade on the dead man's tunic, put the sword back in its sheath, and returned to his seat proudly, Berta watching him in adulation.

"We spared this wretched traitor's life, and instead of bowing to his merciful king and satisfying his every wish, he objected to orders. We won't miss this filth," Walter's voice dripped with disdain and disgust. Giren couldn't understand how he could be so cruel.

"You have heard your king," cried Anrai, and some slaves hurried to inform the craftsmen of the changes that had to be made in the city. Anrai then turned to Walter. "My king, perhaps it'd be wiser not to desecrate the symbols of Ramerstorm," said the giant man with some hesitation, looking at the corpse that was leaching blood. "If Borin is assassinated, and Ballar's new governor allies with us, it'd be better to leave his capital untouched, otherwise the people of Ballar might revolt."

Walter looked at him with narrowed eyes. "I don't need to leave Ballar's emblem intact for them to serve me. If they don't, they'll all die, along with Delamere."

Anrai nodded silently.

"I can't believe I left a Delamere on the throne for so many years. That's blasphemy for Knightdorn," continued Walter.

"As soon as we've invaded Iovbridge, I will bring you her head, my lord," Berta spoke humbly.

Walter smiled at her, though he seemed indifferent to her words. Giren and the rest of the slaves removed the dead man's body and continued to serve Walter and his company.

The door to the great hall opened for the umpteenth time that morning, and Giren saw a short man, clad in black, hurrying inside. His hair had thinned out at the top, and his nose was crooked and large. Rolf Breandan, the third member of the Trinity of Death, walked quickly toward Walter. He was not a large man, but his hands were known to be lightning-fast. Giren had heard that he used to carefully cut his opponents' legs, marking the arteries leading to the heart, to drain them slowly of blood and strength. He specialised in leaving them crippled. He had become known as Short Death, a nickname that few dared utter in front of him.

"Your Majesty," he said with a bow.

"Sit, Rolf," ordered Walter.

The man remained still. "Your Majesty, Stonegate has sent us a messenger."

Walter was surprised. Reynald hadn't sent a messenger for a long time. It had only been a few days since he had sent a handful of men to Stonegate to reinforce its guard. He hadn't expected to hear from Reynald unless Elmor attacked, as Iovbridge had no men for such a thing. Nevertheless, the information he had received indicated Syrella Endor had decided to stay out of the battle for the throne.

"Bring him to me," Walter ordered.

Anrai and Brian shared a glance, and Walter stood up. After a few moments, Short Death returned with a flush-faced man. The sun with the spears was sewn into the Guardian's white cloak.

"What's your name, Guardian?" asked Walter.

"Aron," replied the newcomer.

"What news does Reynald send me?"

"Certain things have changed in Stonegate," the Guardian muttered.

Walter's patience was running out. "What news does Reynald send me?" he roared.

"Reynald Karford is no longer the Guardian Commander of Stonegate."

His words froze the room. Brian looked at him in disbelief as Walter felt anger rising in his chest. He tried to restrain himself, if only for a little while longer. "Did Reynald concede the command of the castle?"

Aron avoided looking into Walter's eyes. "Reynald fell in a duel and thus lost command of the castle."

Anrai almost choked, while Brian burst from his seat, enraged. "Who dared challenge Reynald to a duel? Tell us exactly what happened, otherwise I will rip out your tongue," he yelled at the emissary.

The Guardian looked at Brian but didn't seem scared. "A boy from Iovbridge arrived at the castle with four companions and challenged the Guardian Commander to a duel," he began. "He accepted and was defeated. Then the boy appointed a new Guardian Commander in Stonegate and headed south to Wirskworth along with his companions, holding Reynald captive."

Walter's sword flashed, slicing into Aron's leg, and the Guardian fell onto the floor, eyes wide, mouth open in a silent scream.

"Some boy from Iovbridge defeated Reynald and took him captive to Wirskworth? I think it'd be wise to tell the truth if you want to leave here, even if only with half your limbs," Walter said.

"I'm not lying," Aron spoke.

Walter stepped on wound, and now Aron screamed out loud. "Who was this boy?"

"I don't know." The man writhed in pain. "He was unknown to Stonegate. His name was Elliot."

Walter took a step back.

"And he imposed a new Guardian Commander?" Anrai now spoke.

"He let us choose the most capable soldier and gave that man the castle on oath that he would guard it on the queen's behalf. Even so, he didn't ask us to defend Iovbridge."

Walter started pacing slowly, carefully mulling over what he had just heard. His scouts had informed him of a man with the Stonegate emblem on his cloak having entered Iovbridge from the South Gate the previous night. This hadn't concerned him. A villager with ancestry from Stonegate may have inherited the habiliment. There were more than a few who had hurried to leave their villages for Iovbridge, fearing looting and enslavement. Nevertheless, the Land of Fire had no villages in its path, and the Vale of Gods was cordoned off by his men. So, it would be hard for anyone to sneak out from the Vale of Gods and head toward Iovbridge. Stonegate was the only inhabited place to the south of Isisdor, and the man had entered the capital at the South Gate, which suggested he might indeed have come from the Land of Fire. Walter realized he should have attached more importance to this information.

Who would be capable of defeating Reynald in a duel? Maybe some of his men could, but no one in the adversary's camp would have the skills to do so. He turned abruptly and stepped on the injured man's limb again. "You're lying," he shouted amid the messenger's screams. "No man from Isisdor would be able to defeat Reynald."

Aron reached for a sword hanging from his belt. Walter laughed and stomped on his arm. "Do you think you can fight me?" he scoffed.

"The sword," gasped the Guardian, groaning.

Walter looked at the hilt and felt a jolt of surprise in his stomach as he took a step back. This hilt could only belong to one sword. He put the Blade of Power back into its sheath and with a swift motion raised the

Sword of Destiny, not believing his eyes.

"What happened to my men?" he asked after a few moments of silence.

The Guardian looked at him strangely through his pain. "Which men?" he mouthed.

Walter weighed him up with his gaze. "I sent soldiers to Stonegate a few days ago to reinforce it."

The messenger seemed confused. "No one had reached the castle when I set off for Ballar. No one except for the lad from Isisdor who rode with three other men and a woman."

There seemed to be no lie in the man's eyes. His men must have arrived at Stonegate by now, but perhaps Aron had already left the castle. That meant Reynald had already fallen upon their arrival. Nevertheless, he didn't believe that the Guardians would attack his soldiers. They may have agreed to guard the South Passage on behalf of Sophie, but they wouldn't fight for her, and two hundred soldiers were not a threat to the castle. Common sense meant that his men would return as soon as they were denied entry and that the Guardians wouldn't bother them. They knew the fate that awaited them if they did and no doubt hoped he would spare their people's lives if they showed respect to his men. *Fools*, he thought. He would kill them all—men, women, and children—as soon as he took the throne. It was time to leave only those who supported him in Knightdorn. There was no reason to form new alliances with his enemies, as they could no longer overthrow him.

Walter thought carefully about what the Guardian's words meant. After a while, he felt an insurmountable rage welling up inside of him. He wanted to kill them all, everyone around him. Only then could he vent some of his anger. He was the best, the worthiest warrior the world had ever known and also the greatest commander. No one had been able to get the better of his armies on the battlefield since he was a youngster, yet he had waited almost twenty years to take the crown from a woman! The thought of a woman on Knightdorn's throne made him sick to his stomach. Old alliances, rebellions, disloyal nobles and governors had delayed him for so long, leaving the crown to his prostitute cousin. *Cousin*, he thought, disgusted. The only bond that tied them was Egercoll blood, and his hatred for the Egercolls was so great that he often couldn't believe his father had married one. His grandfather, the First King, had taken the throne with the consent of all rulers, and the House of Egercoll took the crown by force, violating the laws of Knightdorn. His father had to rebel, form new alliances and attack, but he preferred Thomas's sister as payment for the throne that was stolen from him. But he was different, and the fact that his mother had been sold to his father to forget the First King's fate, wouldn't stop him. Even if it took fifty years, he would get his revenge.

Walter paced away, no longer interested in the Guardian on the floor. He had to carefully consider his next move. Now that Stonegate had passed into the queen's hands, Elmor could more easily become embroiled in the war against him. He was sure that the emissaries were headed towards Wirskworth in the hopes of forming a new alliance. If the Poison Masters marched to Isisdor, that'd mean considerable aid for Iovbridge, and his battle for the throne would become more difficult. If Wirskworth decided to take part in the war, its men would arrive during the siege—that was certain. He and his allies would be outside Iovbridge in thirteen days, while Wirskworth was about fifteen days away from the capital for an infantry regiment. Adding the day or two it would no doubt take for Syrella Endor to contemplate her options and set her orders in motion, Elmor would not be able to aid Iovbridge for at least seventeen days.

"When did the Iovbridge emissaries arrive at Stonegate?" he asked the Guardian.

"Two days ago," Aron replied. "I left Stonegate shortly after Reynald's fall and exhausted my horse to get to Ballar as fast as I could."

It was obvious, thought Walter. The Guardian looked like he hadn't slept for days. Sophie's envoys would have already reached Elmor if they had ridden fast... If Syrella Endor agreed to fight, she would arrive in

Iovbridge around the fourth day of the siege. *Bad timing*, he thought. The South Passage led quickly to the South Gate of Iovbridge—an inaccessible place to attack as the trees created a narrow passage that extended from the South Gate to the front of the city. He had already considered leaving soldiers at the South Gate, preventing the army of Iovbridge from emerging from behind their walls and attacking him from the side, but now that wouldn't be enough. He needed more men, mostly infantrymen, to stop the Royal Army along with Elmor's soldiers at that point, as his archers wouldn't have easy lines of sight, and the cavalry would lose their mobility in the trees. If his armies at the South Gate fell, perhaps his enemies would ride in a circle around the city and attack his lines from the side. But that was not the scenario that scared him the most. He feared that Elmor's men would try to enter Iovbridge. If they killed his soldiers and succeeded in entering, they'd extend the siege for long time.

He continued pacing in the great hall. He couldn't use Tahryn's galleys at this time of year when the seas were turbulent. Thus, he had lost his naval strength. He racked his brains to find a solution. He didn't want a protracted siege. The conquest of Kelanger had taken him three whole years, and he had been forced to murder Aymer Asselin in order to succeed. He knew that many in Knightdorn whispered that he had never managed to take Oldlands. Not without using deceit. He needed to destroy Iovbridge swiftly and decisively, proving that no one could stand against his insurmountable power. Removing Sophie from the throne by subterfuge was an option to be explored only if he hadn't another choice. He had to finally show Knightdorn he was so powerful that no army and no wall could stop him.

For a moment, another machination sprang up in his mind. The plot to assassinate Governor Borin Ballard must have failed, for if his men had succeeded, he would have known by now. However, he wasn't concerned. He knew that this plot could not easily come to fruition.

He tried to put his thoughts in order. The Iovbridge walls were not as strong as those of Kelanger, and now he had the Armourers from Oldlands by his side. Moreover, the capital of Isisdor had almost three times the population of Kelanger, and its supplies would not suffice. He had made sure of that by conquering the Vale of Gods. On the other hand, if the siege lasted a long time, supplies would be a problem for his own army as well. Even so, the odds were largely in his favor—especially if he removed Elmor from the equation. He thought it likely Syrella would be convinced to fight. His spies in Wirskworth reported that several people in Elmor wanted to help Iovbridge, but the governor hadn't agreed to send an army. But now the situation had changed. With the Stonegate open and Reynald Karford in her cells, Syrella Endor would easily change her mind. Sending Reynald to Wirskworth, using the prestige of that victory, had been a clever move by Sophie.

But then Walter knew what he had to do—it was one of those moments when he felt invincible, as if the God of War were blowing power into his soul. He would wipe out Elmor's army before it reached Iovbridge. *Yes, that is the only solution.* Momentary joy stirred inside of him. He had the largest cavalry and fastest horses in Knightdorn. If they rode vigilantly, without siege weapons, on the Road of Elves toward Snake Road, they'd be there in five days. If Elmor decided to fight, its men should have left Wirskworth by then, but wouldn't have managed to cross Stonegate. No one would expect him to go through Snake Road. He would catch Elmor's armies off guard and destroy them before they passed through the castle—he knew that if they passed Stonegate, it'd be impossible to stop them before they reached Iovbridge. He didn't have the time to attack the Guardians of the South, and he would never attempt to get his men to go through Ersemor. He'd also never give a battle in the narrow paths of the Land of Fire, reducing the mobility of his cavalry. He thought through his plan carefully—Elmor didn't have a large army anymore. His cavalry could thrash the Poison Masters in the wide-open plains along Snake Road. His infantry would be kept safe in White City.

A new thought held his joy in check. His allies would arrive in Ballar before he could return—it was inevitably so. If he exhausted his horses to cover three hundred miles in five days, they wouldn't be fast on the way back, and White City wouldn't have supplies to house nearly fifty thousand men for long. But there was a solution, an alteration to his plan—his allies would soon be on the Path of Shar, between the Yellow River and the Northern Forest. That place was an ideal site for an extended camp.

The adjustments would result in delaying the siege of Iovbridge for about a month, but this would eliminate all his rivals at once. After his coronation, he would march to Stonegate and burn it to the ground. However, he had to send a messenger to his allies fast. If he was late, they would cross the Path of Shar and he didn't want to order them to march north again. If he sent one of his fastest horses, his messenger would be there in less than two days. His heart fluttered with joy, but then he stopped short and spun on his heel to face the Guardian.

"On your way to Ballar, did you stop at the royal capital?" he asked the bloodstained Guardian.

Aron shifted. "Yes," he whispered.

"Why is the queen sending me this news? Why is she allowing me to know this?" he asked, suspicion flooding through him.

Aron looked him in the eye. His gaze may have been overwhelmed with pain, but his expression showed that he had asked himself the same question several times. "I don't know," he replied.

Strange. Sophie had achieved a great victory against him, the first in two decades. She could have kept her dominance in Stonegate secret, bringing Elmor's army to Isisdor without warning. She had intentionally given up the element of surprise. *Why?*

He looked at the fallen man once more and tried to put aside his anger. Emotions were for the weak. Perhaps Sophie and her counsellors were waiting for him to leave Ballar. Maybe that was their plan. *But why?* It was impossible for them to retake White City—they had no more men to waste. Even if they did, they could not hold it. Perhaps they wanted him to march to Elmor in order to attack him in the open fields of Snake Road with two armies, as they knew he'd never fight them united in the Land of Fire. No, no, that would be absurd. For one, the Royal Army would take too long to reach Snake Road, and if they succeeded, they'd be foolish to fight him in the open field. Even if they joined forces, his cavalry outnumbered their three to one. He could wipe out their armies with ease. Peter Brau had proved himself brave and stupid at White City, fighting outside the walls. But the General of Iovbridge wouldn't make the same mistake again. Furthermore, the queen couldn't be sure that Elmor would follow her call, thus, this strategy seemed foolish.

Perhaps it is a trick to allow them to retreat. With his men watching their moves at the Vale of Gods, they couldn't travel to Elmor with civilians at their side. So, if they hoped that he would march south to defeat Elmor's armies in the open, they'd leave Iovbridge as soon as he left White City. *Clever*. The queen's messengers could inform Syrella Endor of the plan, so she would stay in her city, while Sophie would be waiting at Stonegate. It would be impossible for him to breach Wirskworth's gates with riders only, thus he would be forced to return to Ballar. Then, the road to Wirskworth would be left open for Sophie. His idea was not crazy, but he knew his cousin would never agree to such a plan. If she had wanted to give the crown to save her life, she would've done so years ago. Furthermore, assuming that Sophie and her officers had predicted that he would march south was to give them too much credit.

In the end, there was only one plausible explanation. The news was conveyed to him to wound his pride shortly before the battle. It was the only thing he found reasonable. His alliances were built on fear. Thus, the unification of the south shortly before the final battle, combined with Reynald Karford's defeat, would send a resounding message to Knightdorn about the strength of his rival. Moreover, the men of Oldlands—many of whom blamed and despised him for the murder of Aymer Asselin—hated him more than any of his other allies and could perhaps rise up against him. That was his enemies' aim: to win over a new alliance with Elmor as well as to sow discord among his troops before the battle for Iovbridge. He smiled again. How stupid they were. Even now, after all these years, they hadn't learnt that no one could defeat or defy him. He would destroy all of them and take the crown once and for all.

Walter brought his hand to his chin—his plan was so good that it would bring him victory whatever the case. There was the chance Elmor wouldn't decide to fight for the queen, and he would have lost time for nothing. Still, it didn't matter. He could leave a few thousand horsemen at the Forked River to oversee Wirskworth, and if Syrella dared walk out with her army, they'd attack her. The land was fertile around the Forked River, and he had over sixty-five thousand men in his armies. He could sacrifice a few thousand cavalrymen who would serve him little in the siege.

Satisfied, Walter turned back to those assembled in the great hall. Sunrays streamed into Hawk's Nest, and, with a single stroke of the Sword of Destiny, Aron's head left his body.

"Send emissaries to our allies immediately! They'll wait on the Path of Shar until we send them new orders. And prepare the horsemen—we leave Ballar at dawn!" ordered Walter, looking at Short Death.

Rolf seemed surprised by these orders but raised no objections and left the room quickly.

Only one question remained to torment Walter. *Who could have defeated Reynald? A boy?* An old concern loomed in his mind. *Impossible.* Whoever that boy was, he would soon get what he deserved.

Walter felt the need to be alone, so he nodded sharply to Berta, Anrai, and Brian, and headed out of the room.

"Make sure their dinner is the remains of the dead," Walter said, indicating the slaves as he called back to Brian. "Traitors must know the taste of a traitor."

The Snakes of the East

Elliot and his companions rode steadily. Wirskworth was less than half a day away, and they had to get there as fast as possible, as they were behind schedule. The trees had begun to thin out as they continued south-east, scrubby bushes and weeds taking their place.

John was singing, a dull tune, his wine skin never far from his lips. His hiccups sounded like the squawking of a hen, and he grew silent, swaying on his horse's back. Ahead of Elliot, Morys and Selwyn ate apples and bread as they road, Eleanor at their side.

Elliot's stomach gurgled, and he reached into his knapsack for a meat-filled pie from the City of Heavens. His breastplate weighed on him, and his body was sweaty under the leather undergarments. He and his companions had been wearing the same clothes for days. Fatigue enclosed him in its vortex, but he had to keep moving.

A cry broke the silence, and Hurwig spread his wings over Elliot's head. Elliot had given this name to the white hawk gifted to him by Righor the centaur. A snore shook the air. Long Arm had fallen asleep on his horse, as he had already drunk two skins of wine, a gift from the men of the City of Heavens. Morys poured water on John's face, who punched out at an invisible enemy as he woke.

"What the heck?" he screamed. His curses continued for some time, as they continued on the path south of the Forked River. The Road of Elves was a few miles north. The trees rising on the left provided the company with good cover.

It was getting dark when Elliot could see a mound rising on the horizon. He squeezed his mare with his knees, and the horse picked up the pace. "Which is this mountain?" he asked.

"It's not a mountain, you fool. It's Wirskworth," snorted John contemptuously.

As they reached the Forked River, the companions crossed a small bridge carefully and continued north of the waters.

Elliot stared at Wirskworth as they drew nearer, convinced the place could not have been built by humans. Forts and tall, square towers rose through the rocky mountain that shone under the dim light of dusk. The whole city was built from immense, pearly-white blocks of stone, similar to those he had seen in the Palace of the Dawn, and was sculpted into the side of the mountain. *This city would be impossible to besiege*, he thought, observing the moonstone that made up every part of Elmor's capital. Towers grew on each side of the front wall around the tallest gate he had ever seen, and golden snake heads stood above the majestic iron entrance. Anyone battering the gate would be drenched in scorching oil pouring out of the reptiles' mouths. A majestic castle stood at the highest peak. The House of Endor's banners, which also constituted Elmor's emblem, hung on every corner of the wall, yellow and black like bees, a huge snake adorning their centre.

"This entire city is a fortress," Elliot said, gaping.

Morys laughed out loud. "The elves fought the giants astride the wyverns behind these walls."

"I have never seen a wyvern," said Elliot.

"They're as big as ten elephants, and their wings are full of poisonous thorns, so sharp and strong that they could even pierce iron," Long Arm said.

"Have you seen a wyvern?" asked Selwyn, disbelief in his voice.

"Of course," boasted John. "They live in the Mountains of Darkness, in the North beyond the North. It's been years since my last visit."

"North Beyond the North?" Elliot was puzzled.

Long Arm grinned. "It's a part of Gaeldeath. All the lands north of Tyverdawn belong to the North beyond the North."

As they drew closer and closer to Wirskworth, Elliot glanced at Reynald, who had been very quiet since his failed attempt to free himself. Though they hadn't replaced the gag, he hadn't spoken for hours.

Morys stopped his horse and shouted, "Don't move!"

Elliot looked around for danger, then noticed the thousands of arrows pointing at them from the slits in the stone towers.

"We'll wait," whispered Morys.

After a few moments, a trumpet blast rang out. The gate opened slightly, and several horses and riders burst forth, raging as they approached, black-and-yellow cloaks streaming from the riders' shoulders. They encircled Elliot and his companions, one horse penetrating the ring to confront them. Its rider wasn't wearing a helmet, and her skin was darker than Elliot's. The woman's eyes were amber, and her lips were thin like two lines. She carried a long spear and dozens of earrings sparkled in her ears.

"What are you doing on Elmor's soil?" Her nostrils flared with the ferocity of her speech.

"Good evening, Linaria." Morys's voice showed no sign of fear.

The woman seemed not to believe her eyes when she caught sight of him. "Morys Bardolf," she said. "What brings a man like you to Elmor's land?"

"I'd like to speak to Lady Endor. I come as a messenger of the queen, carrying a letter for your mother."

Elliot glanced at the woman with new eyes. He hadn't expected the daughter of Elmor's ruler to look so wild.

"She should be more than a lady to you," the woman said threateningly, but Morys did not respond to that. "Who are your companions?" continued Linaria.

"Selwyn Brau, son of..."

"Selwyn Brau?" The woman suddenly smiled. "The last time I saw you in Iovbridge, you were still at your mother's breast, and I had pigtails."

Selwyn returned the smile with a slight bow.

"Eleanor Dilerion," continued Morys, pointing to the weary girl.

Linaria didn't show much interest in Eleanor and fixed her gaze on the man beside Morys.

"I didn't expect you to start wandering in the south again, Long Arm," she said, looking at John who tried to bow awkwardly.

"This is Elliot—"

Linaria suddenly raised her spear. "A Karford on my doorstep!" she thundered. Her horse pranced close to Karford, coming to a snorting stop before the mounted man.

The captive's eyes were swollen with fatigue, and he kept his gaze on the ground as the spearpoint angled toward his groin.

"I would be honoured to take away your manhood, Karford," Linaria said with a smirk.

"This man is our captive," Morys said firmly, bringing his horse between them.

The woman's eyes narrowed menacingly.

"I must speak to the Ruler of Elmor," repeated Morys, calm and composed.

Linaria's face didn't reveal her thoughts, and Elliot weighed up her escort. The soldiers wore full plate armour with sharp daggers hanging from their belts. Helmets obscured their features. They looked powerful, but Elliot had never liked to wear full plate, preferring speed and agility.

Linaria was not the only woman in the group, though the other was not armoured. Her lips were ruby-red and her skin white, so white that it looked like moonlight on a cloudless night. Silver-blue curls fell below her shoulders, and two gold earrings adorned her ears. The dress under her cloak had a silver-embroidered collar with a lilac hue. Elliot noticed her eyes—they looked like flaming moons, sculpted by a white-blue fire. Then he understood what they reminded him of—her eyes were like Aleron's. He felt he could lose himself in those eyes. He was sure he'd never seen a woman more beautiful.

"Very well." Linaria's voice brought Elliot out of his reverie. "Follow me!"

She turned her horse around and headed toward the city, her comrades keeping Elliot and his companions penned in. Elliot felt like a sheep surrounded by wolves as they approached the gate. He marvelled at the snake heads. They looked so real it seemed their jaws would come alive at any moment.

They were herded inside, the gate shuddering closed behind them. Dark would soon fall, and torches bracketed on the walls let off a soft light. Elliot glanced around as they began to climb the slopes of Wirskworth—a fat butcher was carrying a dead ox on his shoulder, his clothing stained with blood. A little farther off, a blacksmith struck glowing steel with a large hammer as his apprentice pumped bellows. The road was getting narrower as they climbed to the top of Wirskworth. The newcomers and their entourage rode fast through the narrow streets. The higher they went, the more stately the houses became, though none overshadowed a huge temple on the middle hill. Its entrance was positioned above an enormous portico shaped like a half-moon; an imposing dome, the colour of the sea, rose to the top.

They continued to ride until the majestic castle at the top of Wirskworth appeared in front of them. Elliot surveilled the castle carefully. The wall was easily defended; the parapet had so many apertures that at least a thousand archers could aim at an enemy from above. Pointed towers delineated its outermost boundary east and west of its centre, with the House of Endor's banners waving on each side. Their horses stopped in front of the castle's eastern tower which was built of white raw stone and had tiles shaping its pointed peak. As he gazed up, Elliot imagined giants riding on winged monsters, attacking from the sky.

The companions dismounted, along with the guards who had escorted them to the top of the city, and a pair of young boys ran quickly toward them. The boys started leading the horses towards stables in a small courtyard to their right. Linaria dismounted gracefully and headed for the centre of the castle. The companions followed her, along with some guards, and they reached a small entrance. Linaria nodded to the watching guard, and he stepped aside. Elliot was sure that this was not the main entrance to the castle. They wound up stairs and dark corridors until they reached tall double doors. A guard opened one as soon as he saw Linaria, revealing a majestic hall illuminated by candlelight. Thousands of preserved animals, hunting trophies, hung on the walls alongside skulls and skins. In the centre of the room sat a woman in a tall stone seat framed by two golden snakes.

The governor wore a turquoise velvet dress and had gold buckles on her belt. A diadem adorned her tar-black hair, and her brown eyes observed the visitors. Her face was wilder than her daughter's, with a scar starting from the skin under her left eye and reaching down to her upper lip. Around her stood five men in thick steel armour. The black and yellow cloaks they wore over their shoulders had two crossed swords in the middle, and they held helmets with a golden snake engraved over their visor. A girl with brown hair wearing a long silk tunic was watching Linaria approach. Judging from her face, Elliot guessed she was Linaria's sister. To the ruler's left, six men in velvet jerkins stood grimly by a carved table. Some of the men looked old, but some were still gifted with youth.

There were others in the hall, petitioners, and they craned their necks to get a glimpse of the newcomers. Elliot thought it strange that the guards hadn't taken his and his companions' weapons, though with so many soldiers surrounding them, anyone with malicious intentions wouldn't get far.

The woman got up from the stone chair and advanced, looking at her daughter and the guests. Then the City Guard stopped, and Morys took a step forward.

"It's been a long time since we last met, Lady Endor," he pronounced.

"I thought you'd remember, Bardolf! The sons and daughters of this city call me *Your Majesty*."

The man's face looked stony, and he remained silent.

The governor looked at him. "What brings you here?"

Elliot weighed up the bystanders near Syrella. The five armoured guards around the ruler were probably her personal guard, and the men in the expensive jerkins looked like her council, which undoubtedly consisted mostly of nobles.

"I'm here on the orders of Sophie Delamere, Queen of Knightdorn, to deliver a letter."

The governor's eyes narrowed as she looked at their company. Her daughter approached and whispered something in her ear. The governor glanced at her daughter once more before turning to look at the newcomers. "And why didn't the queen send an officer instead of sending you?" she asked.

Morys seemed annoyed. "Iovbridge is at war, as I imagine you know."

Syrella Endor approached him slowly.

"I know what the queen wants, Bardolf. Her counsellors should advise her not to send messengers to these lands."

"Perhaps it would be wiser for the governor to read the queen's words before rejecting them," Morys said loudly.

"If I were you, I'd pay more attention to my words, Bardolf!" replied the woman, her eyes bright with indignation. "There's only one thing the queen could want of me!"

Silence spread across the room for a few moments.

"How did this man get here?" asked the governor suddenly, looking at Reynald.

Morys looked to Elliot, then said, "He fell in combat."

"Iovbridge conquered Stonegate and sent an important prisoner here," the ruler murmured, smiling. "If the favour you're asking is for me to kill him, I'd gladly do so."

"Iovbridge did not attack Stonegate," Morys said, his voice firm.

The governor's anger slipped for the first time. "What do you mean,

Bardolf?"

"Our captive was defeated in a duel," the man spoke again, and the ruler started laughing out loud. Some of those around her followed suit.

"The queen has no soldier capable of such a thing. Even I could kill those in her service. Which Iovbridge man could defeat Lord Karford in a duel?" she asked loudly, and Morys looked at Elliot as if he didn't know what to say.

"I defeated this man." Elliot stepped forward, knowing that this battle could not be won with lies.

Syrella gave him a look full of disdain. "Who are you?"

"I'd rather we talked alone, Your Majesty." Elliot used the title she preferred and which local custom dictated.

She studied him for a moment and then gave an elusive nod. The crowd was ushered out, most of the guards leaving with them. The silver-and-blue-haired young woman remained next to Linaria.

"So?" Syrella said once the hall was quiet.

Elliot glanced at the remaining people in the great hall.

"You can't expect to talk to me without my personal guard and council present."

"My name is Elliot," he began, but hesitation took hold of him as he remembered his Master's plan.

The governor looked at him, waiting for the rest.

Elliot took a breath. "My name is Elliot Egercoll," he spoke, his voice loud now. Whispers rushed through the council, and Syrella Endor features grew harsh.

"Watch your tongue, boy, because your words can condemn you. Lying is severely punished in Elmor."

"Then I'm glad! My tongue only said the truth."

"Who was your father?" asked Syrella.

"My father was the second king, Thomas Egercoll, and my mother was Queen Alice Asselin."

Elliot's companions shifted behind him, no doubt surprised by his honesty. He had made his decision, though. He would do what he thought was right.

Syrella Endor seemed to pale upon hearing his words. "King Thomas never had children," she countered, but there was no conviction in her voice.

"King Thomas had a son after his death," Elliot corrected her.

"Do you have proof?"

"No, but I am telling the truth."

"Impossible!" Syrella seemed lost. "Did Alice Asselin give birth without anyone knowing?" she thundered.

"My mother decided to keep it a secret," came Elliot's reply.

"What happened to Alice?" Now there was a pinch of sadness in Syrella's eyes.

"My mother poisoned herself, along with Emma Egercoll, to avoid falling into Walter's hands."

Syrella's eyes looked wet for a moment, then she approached, the heavy fabric of her dress swishing against the floor. "You do have something of Alice's features," she murmured. "So, the rumours were true. Who trained you?"

Elliot hesitated for a moment and the woman, who had stopped a few metres away, noticed. "Surely you had a Master, if you're capable of defeating a man like Reynald Karford."

"Roger Belet was my Master's name. He raised me in a village near Iovbridge."

Syrella Endor's eyes narrowed again, losing their sad look.

"I cannot believe that this youngster overthrew Reynald," said one of the ruler's young counsellors.

Syrella glanced at the former Guardian Commander. Reynald met her gaze and did not deny what was said.

"Lord Karford? Is this true?" she asked.

The chained man looked at her grimly and, after a moment, nodded, surprising Elliot.

"I'd like to read the queen's letter," demanded the governor suddenly.

Selwyn held out the sealed letter, and the governor approached him. Syrella snatched the parchment and broke the wax seal. The governor frowned after reading the letter. "The queen names you a knight without mentioning your full name," she said, an accusatory tone in her voice.

"The queen doesn't know my full name, Your Majesty," Elliot admitted.

Suspicion grew in Syrella's face. "Are you telling me that you hid the truth from your queen and cousin but shared it with me?" she asked, outraged.

"Iovbridge is swarming with traitors these days, and it wasn't wise to reveal this information." For a moment, Elliot remembered his Master's words: *"You must not reveal your name sooner than is necessary."* He did not know if now was a good time, but it seemed necessary.

"It seems that we earned your trust quickly," Syrella responded, observing him. She turned and resumed her seat between the golden snakes.

"The queen's order cannot be accepted. Elmor will not take its men to Isisdor," declared the governor, sitting back.

"It's not an order but a request," he clarified, but Syrella didn't respond.

Elliot was about to speak again when a voice to his right boomed. "Wirskworth will turn its back on its oaths under your command?" yelled Morys. The guards tensed, and Elliot feared they'd be thrown out of the city if Morys didn't restrain himself.

But Syrella smiled. "Forgive me, Lord Bardolf. I'm not willing to sacrifice the lives of my men to save your queen. If my memory serves, her army did not appear on the battlefield when her cousin took your brothers' lives... Or did you forget that the sons of Elmor are your real brothers and not those of Isisdor?"

Morys's face contorted in anger. "My brothers died because their ruler wasn't wise enough in battle. I, too, would have died if I hadn't had the good fortune to be one of the few men chosen to guard Wirskworth's wall that day."

The governor sprang up, and her men drew their swords.

"Do you think that the Elmor blood in your veins gives you the right to insult me, Bardolf?" Her dark skin flushed. "My House has led this kingdom to glory since the First Kings, and the battlefield tactics are my decision."

"Then the blood of your people is on your hands and not on those of the queen." John's voice resounded like thunder. "She had to do right by her people when her allies put logic aside."

The governor looked at him like he was a poisonous snake. "It's been quite some time since we last met, Long Arm," she hissed. "So be it, the blood of my people is on my hands." With these words, she sat back in her seat. "I don't intend to fight for Iovbridge. It was a mistake that Elmor agreed to the union of kingdoms under George Thorn. Perhaps Knightdorn would have avoided decades of war without the institution of the one king."

"When Northerners and Southerners killed each other, and the Mercenaries of Vylor raped and looted every village and every city... Knightdorn was of course a better place," John sneered with sarcasm.

Elliot had to admit that John had all the wits of a clever advisor, if only he wasn't such a drunkard.

"I didn't know you were a proponent of the one-king institution, Long Arm," Syrella scoffed. "But you're forgetting what happened in Knightdorn when the First King ruled." Sarcasm was evident in her voice.

"I never said that the one-king institution would of itself bring peace to Knightdorn," replied John. "Only if there's a worthy king on the throne," he concluded firmly.

The governor stood again. "The queen is asking me to fight by her side and is sending a knight as a messenger, though the institution of knights has been banned for years." Her words were sharp, like knives, as she closed the distance between them once more. "And you claim to be the son of Thomas Egercoll, that you lived in a village with a Master whose name I've never heard of before," she continued, looking at Elliot. "You came to my city holding a Karford captive to show me that there's still hope, that the queen has strong soldiers, but if that were true, you wouldn't need my help. The queen should ask for my help without intrigue and trickery."

Selwyn took a step forward, and five blades were aimed at his neck. "The queen restored the institution of knighthood, anointing my father, Peter Brau, lord of the knights of Isisdor," he said.

The governor glanced at Selwyn.

"I don't know if he is an Egercoll, my lady," continued Selwyn, pointing to Elliot. "But I know that Walter Thorn may soon be outside the walls of Wirskworth, and this boy is your only hope!" His voice sounded imposing in the great hall. There was confusion in the bystanders' eyes—and fear.

"Is Walter coming to my city?" The edge in Syrella's voice had softened.

"I can't say for certain, but maybe," replied Selwyn.

"Why?"

"Because the queen tried to sidetrack him in Elmor." Selwyn looked down at the marble floor as he said the words.

"If that's true, you will be executed!" Syrella shouted. "The queen's letter calls for my army to march on to Iovbridge, honouring the Endors' old alliance with the Egercolls. It says nothing about a plan that would bring Thorn to my doorstep. If Sophie has conspired in such a way against my people, you are condemned for Isisdor's treason against Elmor."

Elliot dared to speak. "The plan was mine, Your Majesty. It was the only way we would have a chance of winning the war against Walter."

The governor looked frightened. "Explain yourself. What will draw Walter here?"

Elliot sighed heavily and laid out his plan to Syrella and the others present. He told them about the battle with Reynald, about the Sword of Destiny, about his opinion on how Walter would react to the news, as well as about the urgent need to quickly gather Elmor's villagers and food supplies in Wirskworth. "Even if Walter wants to leave some men in Elmor to guard Wirskworth in case you were to decide march for Iovbridge, it will be impossible for them to linger without the sustenance from the lands around the Forked River," he ended.

Fear had spread around the room, and Elliot saw horror in Syrella's brown eyes. "You sent your enemy to kill my people!"

Elliot raised his voice. "It was the only way Elmor's army could reach Iovbridge before the siege, if you decided to help us. If Walter walks into Wirskworth, and you follow the plan, he will be forced to retreat. No man in Elmor will die."

Syrella put a hand to her heart, then clenched it into a fist. "YOU HAD NO RIGHT!"

"Is there a soldier equal to Reynald Karford in Wirskworth?" John asked.

"What do you mean, Long Arm?"

"I have travelled across all of Knightdorn, even in the cities beyond it. I haven't seen a man equal to this young boy in years," John said coldly, without a trace of fear in his voice.

"Then maybe he should challenge Walter to single combat!" butted in one of the aged nobles. His large belly shook with the emphasis in his voice.

"I'm not ready to fight Thorn in a duel," Elliot said.

"So, you preferred to risk our lives," snorted the counsellor, annoyed. "If you were so worthy, you could have faced your enemy behind the walls of Iovbridge without our help."

"Lord Burns is right," Syrella said.

"No one can face an army like Walter Thorn's without enough men and supplies behind his city's walls. Just like he needs his allies, we need ours," said Elliot.

"The Royal Army turned its back on Elmor," Lord Burns continued.

"Why should we respond to your call?"

"Do you think Walter will let you live in peace if he takes the throne?" cried Elliot. "He will march on Elmor and kill every man, woman, and child as soon as he's crowned king."

"At least we will fight by choice and not let a queen who betrayed us decide for us." Lord Burns grinned now. "Even if you are an Egercoll, it doesn't matter... in Elmor, a name gives you neither strength nor glory if you don't earn them on your own. You're just a boy."

"Walter Thorn was *just a boy* once. He attacked half the kingdom when he was *just a boy* and sent the greatest warriors of his time to the grave when he was *just a boy*," John shouted again.

"The queen should have asked for our consent before deciding to carry out such a plan," the lord said again, ignoring Long Arm.

"There was no time for that," retorted Elliot. "And there is little time now. The Sword of Destiny must already be in Walter's hands. If he decides to march on Elmor, it won't be long before he arrives." his voice echoed across the room. "You must make your decision."

"Are you sure that if Walter marches on Elmor, he will do so with a small detachment of his army?" Syrella asked.

"Yes."

"Knowing Walter, I think he will ride to Elmor." Lord Burns spoke again. "He'll do what he can to prevent our joining with Iovbridge," he continued haughtily. "Nevertheless, it's strange that the queen entrusted you with this mission though she was ignorant of your name. If Iovbridge had a man capable of defeating Reynald, we would have heard of him a long time ago. Why would the queen trust a stranger?"

Elliot looked him in the eye. "It's true that I came to Iovbridge only recently, but the reason why the queen trusted me doesn't matter," he countered. "If Walter takes the bait, he will soon be on your land. You must quickly decide which path you will follow. The lives of Elmor's people depend on it." He wasn't going to give any more answers, as they would only lead to more questions.

"Why didn't the queen mention the plan in the letter?" Syrella asked.

"Our journey was full of danger," Eleanor said, speaking for the first time. "The letter could have fallen into the wrong hands."

The governor glared at Elliot. "Where have you been all these years? Why did you not go to your queen sooner?"

"I showed up the moment I was ready," he replied calmly unconcerned with Syrella's scrutiny.

"The counsellors and the governor must convene," Lord Burns said suddenly, and the ruler, who had been standing all this time, looked at him approvingly.

"Accompany our guests to the Tower of the Sharp Swords and take him to the dungeons," ordered the governor, pointing at Reynald.

"We're prisoners?" cried Morys, furious.

"You can leave if you want, Bardolf," Syrella hissed with indifference.

"I'd like to ask you not to reveal who my parents were to anyone outside this room," pleaded Elliot, holding Syrella's gaze. "The people of Elmor don't need another distraction right now," he added.

Syrella considered this for a moment, then responded with a brusque, "Very well."

Before they were escorted away, John's voice broke the silence. "As true lords of the south, could you welcome us with a little wine?"

Barlow's Honour

Sophie paced, trying to settle herself. It had been several hours since the Sword of Destiny had left Iovbridge, and anxiety churned her stomach. Had Walter fallen for her ploy? She also worried about the events in Elmor. The messengers should have arrived in Wirskworth by now, and it was questionable whether Syrella would decide to fight on her side.

Peter had sent some scouts to monitor Walter's movements in White City as Iovbridge prepared for the upcoming siege. If Elliot's plan succeeded, Walter and his cavalry would soon leave Ballar. Nevertheless, the informants had not returned, and as the hours passed, she felt fear flooding her heart.

Sophie came to a pause at her balcony, the moonlight caressing her feet and the floor, and her thoughts travelled to the sky, crossing the distance to Stonegate and the first victory against her cousin after twenty years of war.

A sharp knock interrupted her thoughts, and Peter's voice called from the other side of the door.

"May I come in, Your Majesty?"

It was the second night in a row that Peter had come to her chambers unannounced. Would the news be pleasing this time? Sophie quickly put on a robe and opened the wooden door, and the man walked in, flushed.

"What's going on?" Sophie couldn't contain her impatience.

"The scouts are back. Walter left Ballar with thousands of cavalrymen," replied the lord of the knights.

Relief surged in Sophie. She had hoped Elliot's assumptions would prove correct, but she had harbored doubts.

"A few thousand men remain in White City, and I would bet that Walter sent a messenger to his allies to wait at the Path of Shar until his return," murmured Peter. "He knows that it would be impossible for them to wait in Ballar."

"I can hardly believe it!" Sophie said. "Can we take Ramerstorm?"

"The scouts have informed me that Oldlands' men are reinforcing the city's gate," he replied. "White City must have about three thousand men from Gaeldeath, along with a thousand from Kelanger," he estimated.

"That's more than a few," Sophie acknowledged.

"If we try to besiege the city, we'll lose thousands of soldiers, and we don't know if we'll have Elmor's help," Peter said as he looked down.

Sophie was sure that he was anxious to hear from Selwyn.

"We need to find a way to enter Ramerstorm without besieging it." Sophie's tone of voice was resolute. "We shall act as Elliot advised us."

"We have to inform the council and Lord Ballard," said the general decisively. "Any remaining traitors here will not be able to reach Walter with a message in time, and the council along with the governor can help us find a way to enter Ramerstorm."

"If there are more traitors in Iovbridge, perhaps someone will try to warn the men guarding White City about our plans," Sophie replied.

"Maybe," agreed Peter. "Nevertheless, we can't attack Ramerstorm without informing the council. Even if someone sent a messenger to White City, not much would change—the number of the enemy's men would remain the same. Our main goal was to drag Walter to the south."

"If we find a plan to sneak into Ramerstorm without besieging it, it must not reach the ears of Walter's men."

"We will ban departures from the city," Peter suggested. "Only my trusted scouts will be able to leave Iovbridge."

Sophie sighed deeply. "All right. All that's left is to find a way to enter

Ramerstorm quietly."

Peter began to walk inside the chamber, pensive now. "The scouts informed me that Walter's slaves threw some new corpses into the stacks of the dead from the Battle of Ramerstorm."

"One of them must have been that of the Guardian of Stonegate," Sophie said. "He was sent to the enemy like a sheep to the slaughter."

The lord of the knights nodded, his pain at that loss clear. "My men saw a slave doing something unusual," Peter said. "While Walter's guards weren't looking, he tried to bury a corpse, and before doing so, he wrapped it in a cloak."

Sophie didn't understand. "What can a slave offer us? Will we ask him to fight?"

"He doesn't have to fight... He just has to open a passage to Ramerstorm for our army. I'm sure there are secret entrances to White City, and Borin must know them all. But I suspect we'll need someone to assist from the inside."

"We don't even know that slave's name," she pointed out.

"I think we do." His eyes met Sophie's. "My men described him as tall and scrawny, with red hair and a pimpled face. Only Tahryn's men used to bury their dead wrapped in cloaks."

Sophie closed her eyes with a sigh. "Giren Barlow," she whispered softly— Aghyr Barlow's only son was one of Walter's most notable slaves. Her heart twisted at the thought that they made him carry the corpses of the dead. Aghyr, the former Governor of Tahryn, had been murdered violently when Walter attacked Tahos. "This boy has already suffered so much. If they catch him, we'll be responsible for his torture."

"Your Majesty, this boy has already lost everything. I'm sure he'd rather die than continue to live like this," Peter said in a soft tone. "If we ask him to help us, perhaps we'll give him a new purpose. In any case, he can always refuse."

Sophie nodded slowly. "How will you talk to him? How will you know if he wants to help us? And how will you give him instructions about what to do?"

Peter breathed out wearily. "These are good questions," he said.

Silence grew between them until the man's eyes widened. Sophie knew that look.

The Tower of the Sharp Swords

Elliot woke abruptly, soaked in sweat, his breathing ragged. The nightmare lingered, and his heartbeat wouldn't slow down. Lately, the same images had been emerging over and over in his dreams, like a curse that wouldn't go away. A woman screaming, her eyes red with tears. A momentary peace filled her gaze when she saw him, but then new, even louder screams followed. This dream had scared him ever since he was a child and was almost always accompanied by the girl with the veil who appeared just before he woke up.

He had long thought the screaming woman was his mother—her pain that of childbirth, her peace the knowledge that her son was born alive. Still, he had no idea who the girl haunting his dreams was, and he had been visited by the nightmare more often since leaving his village.

Elliot had thought of visiting his father's tomb while in the City of Heavens, but he'd been unable to make himself do so. There was no body as Thomas's corpse had been desecrated, and no one had ever heard what had happened to it. Nevertheless, his Master had told him that the people of Elirehar had built a prominent tomb for him in the crypts of Pegasus Castle, next to where the rest of the Egercolls rested. His mother's body had been taken to Tyverdawn where, according to Walter, it had been buried with noble honours, but no one could be sure if this was true. His Master had also heard that Walter had buried the bodies of Emma Egercoll and Robert Thorn in the capital of Gaeldeath, deciding that this would be his parents' last residence, even though he had never loved them. Emma Egercoll was the only Egercoll ever to be buried in Gaeldeath.

Elliot's chamber was pitch-dark. The moonlight didn't filter through the small window to the left of his bed, and the candle on the wooden table had gone out. The chamber was dank and smelled of mould, and a wolf pelt hung opposite Elliot's headrest. He and his companions had been led to the east tower of Moonstone, the Tower of the Sharp Swords. Moonstone was the name of the House of Endor's ancestral castle. It took its name from the stone used to build Wirskworth as well as many other places in Knightdorn, such as the Palace of the Dawn. The men in Syrella Endor's personal guard, known as the Sharp Swords, lived in the Tower of the Sharp Swords, which was full of winding stairs and had walls of thick stone.

He got up slowly and approached the small window. The stars were dim behind the clouds that had grown more common on these autumnal days. A noise from beyond his chamber caught his attention, and Elliot put his ear to the door. footsteps.

The Sharp Swords guarded Lady Endor every hour of the day. *Perhaps the watch changed*. And yet that thought didn't sit right in Elliot. He knew it would be wiser to stay in bed, but he was restless after his nightmare. He tried to open his chamber door as lightly as he could and passed into the stone corridor. The stones were cold on his bare feet. His eyes grew accustomed to the dark as he moved. Elliot listened carefully, scouring for the source of the noise, but silence reigned now. He walked a little further and found himself at a crossroads. He knew that if he continued to the left, he would get to the staircase leading to the tower's entrance, near the guards' chambers, while the corridor to his right led to the rooms where his companions rested.

A faint light was reflected on the stone walls, and Elliot hurried on the path to his right. He slid through the darkness, staying close to the mouldy walls, and he continued patiently until he began to hear footsteps again. Shortly afterwards, he found himself at a new crossroads.

He knew that the left path led outside his companions' chambers, but he had no idea where the other led. The dim light reappeared, so he followed the path on the right again. He began to walk fast, full of excitement, yet a faint anxiety niggled inside of him. What if someone wanted to attack his companions? *Impossible*. If anyone had this purpose, they weren't in the right place.

He kept walking silently until a tall mass appeared in his vision. He quickly hid in a recess as the light of a blazing torch passed by, held by a hooded figure. Elliot took a quick look but couldn't clearly distinguish the frame of the figure without revealing his presence. Then the light disappeared and a soft clinking noise rang in his ears. He pulled half his body out of the recess and peeped out carefully. Two big, yellow-green eyes looked at him from below as if fixed on him. Elliot felt cold sweat wash his forehead and hid again, but the damage had been done. Now, it would be wiser to show himself. He was about to leave the recess when he realised he hadn't heard the slightest sound since the devilish eyes had fallen upon him. Did that gaze belong to someone dead? Anxiety flooded his heart. He hurried out of his hiding place. The two bright eyes had stayed put, so he approached, frightened. A gentle meow caressed his ears, and then he saw the white cat standing in front of the wall. *Damn you*, he thought and moved in the direction the figure had gone.

Shortly afterwards, Elliot reached a dead end. A stone wall rose before him, and there was no path other than the one that had led him there. Frowning, he looked at the cat, pensive—perhaps its shadow had confused him. However, this didn't explain the light that had enveloped the corridor. Elliot leaned against the surface of the wall again, gently stroking the rough stone. His fingers found two small recesses and then a steel ring, icy to his touch and so deeply embedded in the stony cracks that it was almost impossible to discern. He pulled the ring slowly and the wall began to shift, stone grinding against stone as it moved. Elliot squeezed his body through the opening that was revealed and stared at the mouldy wooden staircase beyond. His feet slipped on the old wood. He reached for his sword—only to realize that in the rush of the moment, he hadn't taken his blade with him.

Light flashed between the stairs below, and he began to carefully go down, trying not to slip. He felt his heart pounding and moved as fast as he could without making the slightest noise. He walked on tiptoes for quite some time until he heard footsteps yet again. After a while, the footsteps stopped, and he heard stone on stone again. Following, he reached the end of the stairs and listened carefully. There was no one around, and he was again at a dead end. He felt along the stone wall in front of him and caught a ring again. He pulled it gently and slid through the wall opening.

Elliot glanced around, realising he was in the tower's dungeon. Iron doors gleamed under the flame of a torch held by a man standing a distance away. Elliot tried to calm himself. He knew who was imprisoned in this place.

A voice broke the stillness. "I thought you wouldn't come, William." Reynald Karford's voice.

Elliot slipped into an empty cell and listened.

"I wanted to be sure that no one would follow me."

"Very well."

"I never expected to see you here, Reynald."

Elliot recognised the second voice—it was one of the Sharp Swords guards. Sweat trickled down Elliot's forehead as he understood that Walter Thorn truly had men in every corner of Knightdorn.

The cold, quiet sound of metal clinking against metal reached Elliot—a key turning in a lock—and then he heard the cell door swing open.

"The truth is, I didn't expect to be in Wirskworth again," Reynald spoke.

"I can get you out of the city," offered William. "I hope you will speak to Walter about my devotion."

"I don't intend to meet him," Reynald replied, aggravated.

Silence.

"I thought you'd ride to Ballar. Walter is in White City," said William, his voice muffled now.

"Walter will soon be in Wirskworth, you fool. He won't risk Elmor getting involved in the battle for the throne."

"Where will you go?" asked William.

"I'll return to Stonegate."

"You want to return to that miserable place instead of fighting for our lord?" Disapproval had set into William's voice.

"With Stonegate at his command, Walter will end the war more easily," contended Reynald.

"No one cares about those filthy Guardians," hissed William. "Every great army in Knightdorn is on our side! It's only a matter of time before Walter is crowned king!" Reynald didn't respond, and the man of the Sharp Swords spoke again. "What do you have to say about the boy, Thomas's self-proclaimed *son*?"

The former Commander of Stonegate sighed. "This boy's a fool. He condemned himself to martyrdom with that lie."

"How did he manage to defeat you?" William asked, but there was no reply. "Are you sure he's not telling the truth about his parents?"

"I must leave the city. Now," Reynald said, ignoring that question too.

"I will help you, but you must not return to Stonegate," William insisted. "Don't forget that it was your mistake to be taken captive and dragged here. If you hadn't lost, and the South Passage was still in our hands, perhaps Walter wouldn't have had to leave Ba—"

He was cut off mid-sentence by a thud. At first, Elliot thought someone had stumbled, but then Reynald snarled so wildly that Elliot was sure he had grabbed William by the throat.

"Watch your words, or I'll cut your tong—"

Elliot kicked a discarded chain, the sound reverberating through the dungeon and cutting Reynald off. Holding his breath, Elliot felt around for anything that could be used as a weapon, but to no avail.

"No one should be here," shouted William, and footsteps echoed through the dungeons, the torchlight bouncing through the darkness as William approached. There was nowhere to hide, and light spread over him in an instant.

"The boy!" exclaimed William, gaping. Reynald moved into the light, a sneer on his face. "He must have followed me," the guard mumbled. "Walter will reward us for your death," he said, laughing now. "A boy who caused you so much trouble! How fitting that he dies by your hand!" William pulled his blade and put it in Reynald's hand. The wound Elliot had given him did not seem to hamper the man's grip.

"Kill him!" William urged. "I'll tell the council that he tried to kill you, but you killed him and escaped from your cell. I'll claim that he stole my keys when I took him to his chamber."

Reynald took a step forward, the sword raised. His brown eyes met Elliot's.

"Are you the son of Alice Asselin?"

The question surprised Elliot.

"Answer me!" yelled Reynald.

Elliot understood why he asked. He knew the Karfords had hated the Asselins since ancient times. Reynald wanted to feel the joy of killing Alice Asselin's son.

"Yes," he replied with as much courage as he had left.

The blade carved through flesh with precision. William's breath rattled as he grabbed the wound, and his blood gushed from his neck to pool on the floor of the Tower of the Sharp Swords like lava.

The God of Death

Elliot sat in a chair, resting his fingers on its wooden arms as Syrella Endor paced about, dishevelled. She seemed unable to process what she had heard.

"William was one of Thorn's men? I cannot believe it," she said again. "He was in my guard for years. His family was poor, but he had stood out from a young age thanks to his exceptional skills."

Elliot had recounted what had happened in the dungeon, without concealing the slightest detail. The governor's counsellors seemed equally stunned as the sunrays pierced the windows around them. The clouds had disappeared that day.

"Why did Reynald kill William?" she asked for the fourth time.

"I don't know, Your Majesty. Reynald was about to kill me when he suddenly turned his sword on the guard," Elliot repeated one more time.

"I don't understand... Why did he spare your life?"

"He asked me if I was telling the truth about who my mother was and then—" Elliot hesitated.

Syrella Endor glanced at him and kept walking to and fro in the small room. At the far end, a fire in an imposing hearth gave off some heat, and a grim-faced statue seemed to watch over the room.

"The fact that your mother was an Asselin should have given him yet another incentive to kill you," said Syrella. "Asselins and Karfords have been enemies throughout their history, and the blood shed between their houses would fill entire volumes. Nevertheless, the Karfords never succeeded in taking over Oldlands until the time of Walter Thorn, and they were disappointed when Thomas Egercoll chose Alice as his wife over Jeanne Karford, Reynald's cousin."

Elliot mulled over this a while. "Perhaps Reynald didn't agree with the views of the rest of the Karfords."

Lady Endor guffawed. "Reynald was one of Walter's most ardent supporters and a member of the Trinity of Death," she said. "But you said Reynald killed William and returned to his cell without protest?"

"First, he said, *'Wake up the guards. One of their men is dead'*," Elliot added.

The governor was silent for some time until she spoke decisively. "Whatever he did, he's still Reynald Karford. One action is not enough to absolve him of his sins. He will remain in a cell."

Lord Burns—the elderly, flabby man—spoke up. "If there are other traitors in Wirskworth, we are doomed," he declared fearfully. "If Walter is heading for Elmor, we cannot defeat him with spies in our ranks."

"Walter would never succeed in entering Wirskworth with just a few thousand riders, Sadon," said a pockmarked man. "I believe we should—must—help Iovbridge," he suggested loudly.

Elliot glanced up in surprise. He hadn't expected to find support among the counsellors.

"If Walter takes the throne, it will be the end of us. We must fight," continued the pockmarked man. He had a thick moustache and a crooked nose, and his hair was turning white.

"I will think about your suggestion, Lord Reis," said Syrella, and all eyes turned to her. "I am enormously disappointed in Sophie Delamere, but we may have no choice."

"Your Majesty, we don't have enough men to help Iovbridge," a slender young man with curly auburn hair advised.

"Lord Lengyr is right." Sadon Burns took the floor again. "The only thing we'll succeed in doing is to send two armies to their death." The flabby lord was dressed in red and was the only counselor wearing a cloak over his jerkin.

Suddenly, the door was flung open, and Linaria walked soberly into the room with two women close behind her. One was her twin sister, whom Elliot had learned of from Morys. The other brushed her silvery-blue hair away from her face with a gentle motion as she walked. Elliot watched as all eyes turned toward the beautiful woman with the starry blue eyes.

"Mother, what happened?" Linaria asked.

"William of the Sharp Swords was a traitor," Syrella replied. "I can only hope the rest of the men in my guard are more loyal than he was."

"I can assure you of that, Your Majesty," confirmed a muscular counsellor in a white jerkin. "The men of the Sharp Swords have sworn their lives to you. No one else would commit such heinous perfidy."

"Thank you, General Jahon," Syrella nodded.

Elliot recognised this man—he was one of the guards of the Sharp Swords. He had guessed that he was in command of Syrella's personal guard. Upon observing him, he could also tell he didn't come from a noble family. Elliot would bet that Jahon was around fifty years old, but time had been kind to him—few white hairs had made their appearance in his dense hair, and his face was unlined with imposing eyes, dark skin, and a pointed chin.

Linaria's sister looked fierce. "We must interrogate the men of the Sharp Swords," she said in a rasping voice.

"Thank you, Merhya," Syrella muttered. "But that's Jahon's responsibility," she pointed out.

Merhya Endor may have looked like Linaria, but her face suggested she was more belligerent than her sister. Merhya and Linaria were dressed in leather trousers and linen tunics the colour of a cloudy sky.

Lord Lengyr rose to address them all again. "Rumour has it that Walter has sixty-five thousand men in his ranks. None of us can stop such an army." His face was full of terror.

"If you don't try to stop Walter's army with the men of Iovbridge at your side, how will you stop it on your own when he takes the throne and marches against you?" challenged Elliot. "For now, you just have to stay in the city, following the plan. We'll figure out how to deal with Walter in Isisdor later."

The governor scowled to remind him he had no say in her council. "Maybe we can find a better plan," she rallied, looking at her counsellors. "If Walter marches against Wirskworth only with Gaeldeath's riders, we may be able to attack him and defeat him."

"How many of your loved ones died the last time Walter attacked Elmor?" Elliot knew he was pushing his luck.

Syrella looked at him like a predator about to attack its prey. Such was her rage that her features hardened as the scar stretched on her face.

"If you follow my plan, no one will die this time." Elliot's words seemed to incite those present all the more. They exchanged angry glances.

"You have no right to express your opinion in this council!" Syrella thundered, her amber earrings trembling with her fury. Her bearskin cloak seemed to bristle with defiance. "As for our plan, don't you worry! This time the God of Souls will be on our side."

"No god will help you, only your good sense." Elliot wouldn't give in, and her anger hadn't scared him off.

A scrawny man with a black cloak and greasy, hawkish hair glared daggers at Elliot with his icy eyes. "Insulting the God of Souls, the divine lord of my temple is a punishable offence," he warned. "The signs in the heavens have shown me the truth, Your Majesty. Walter will ride toward us, and the snake will devour the tiger this time. We must attack him in the open," he concluded, ecstatic.

"Thank you, Edmund," Syrella spoke.

Elliot looked at Edmund—no doubt the high priest of Wirskworth. "I didn't expect a glorious city like this to be plagued by superstition," he lashed out. "It seems that reason is dead in Elmor."

"You are too young to pass judgement on our decisions or the power of the gods," came the governor's reply.

Voices hissed and raged as the counsellors broke out in tirades at his words. Elliot tuned out the ranting as they began to argue among each other, staring into the crackling flames. He felt the weight of eyes upon him and turned to see her—the woman with the incandescent blue eyes was looking at him with a mix of surprise and admiration.

Syrella called for silence, then addressed Elliot. "Thank you for telling me what happened in the dungeons. I don't know if Walter is heading towards my city, but my council and I will decide our course of action." With these words, she gestured to her left, and the young woman with the silver-blue hair walked toward him. Elliot understood. He got up and followed his escort, but before exiting the room, he stopped short and raised his voice, sweat beading on his brow.

"No one knows me in this city. No one thinks I'm telling the truth about who I am, and clearly no one would trust a stranger and a queen who didn't defend them. Nevertheless, the plan I confided in you is your only hope if Walter walks on your land, and if you leave the queen defenceless in the battle for the throne, your end will be the same as hers." He left the room, feeling their stares on his back.

The woman led him to Moonstone's large courtyard, and Elliot relished the feel of the sunlight on his face. The light of day had cleared the foggy landscape of the night before, and now he could see several manor houses, similar to small towers, on the lower plains of the city. The view from Moonstone's courtyard was so vast that he could see much of Elmor in the distance. The woman noted his gaze and spoke softly, a hint of aloofness in her voice.

"Lord Daryn Endark's manor house is in front of us. To the east, the tower with the pointed top belongs to Lord Shilor Penn."

"I've never met them," he said.

"They were the two counsellors who didn't speak," she said, and Elliot remembered their faces.

He continued to look at the manor houses. He knew that Elmor was one of the former kingdoms that had shown respect for its nobles, ignoring many of Thomas Egercoll's decrees. In truth the second king had looked past the ties of several lords with their rulers, as many houses had shed their blood alongside their leaders for centuries.

"Are there any lords of Elmor outside Wirskworth?" asked Elliot.

"Lord Hewdar left the city for his castle after the battle on the Forked River. He had an intense quarrel with Syrella, so he decided to leave the capital and Elmor's council." Her tone grew more animated. "Jacob Hewdar is a tough man, but the death of his son in battle shook him. Myril, his castle, is located north of Wirskworth, close to Snake Road."

If Syrella followed his advice, she would order her people to take refuge in Wirskworth, whether or not she chose to fight with Sophie. Elliot wondered if, despite this quarrel, she would send word to Lord Hewdar as well.

They kept walking along a narrow path. They had moved west, leaving Moonstone behind. They were now in a narrow sloping alleyway with a green courtyard that stretched before them. It was so big that it looked more like a little forest. The trees created an imposing labyrinth, and wildflowers dotted the landscape with colour. The morning light warmed Elliot's body under his green linen jerkin—the men of the Sharp Swords had supplied him and his companions with fresh clothing.

As the silence between them grew, Elliot couldn't help himself. "You don't look like any woman I've ever met," he said, his words coming out in a rush.

The young woman smiled. "I'm only half human," she explained. "My mother was an elwyn, and my father was Syrella Endor's brother."

Elliot had already guessed the truth as this woman had reminded him of Aleron the moment he first saw her. "You are very special," he mumbled, looking at the ground.

She weighed him up, as if she thought he was mocking her. "Few would agree with you," she said after a while.

"I've never heard of someone with an elwyn mother and a human father."

She averted her gaze. "Giants slept with humans throughout the ages. But the elves and the elwyn never loved anyone outside of their race. My mother was the only one of her kind to fall in love with a human."

"So, you *are* special," he said again, and then she peered at him carefully.

"I don't know if you're a good warrior, but you're certainly new to our world."

Elliot didn't understand, and she continued.

"The elwyn race has been decadent and cursed for centuries—your ancestors made sure of that," she muttered. "My father's family took it hard when he returned to Wirskworth with a baby from an elwyn mother in his arms. Had my name not been Endor, I might have been killed." There was some bitterness in her voice, though whether it was directed at his ancestors or her own family, he was not sure. Still, he was not responsible for actions his ancestors had taken centuries before his birth.

Her words brought forth questions. Did this mean the legends were true? Had Manhon Egercoll tied the Elder Races to the Mountains of the Forgotten World with his curse, and had they sold the mythical swords to his enemies all the while? He wasn't sure whether the elwyn were only to be found in the Mountains of the Forgotten World, since he had seen an elwyn with his own two eyes in Ersemor. Furthermore, if the legend of the curse was true, how had she managed to leave those mountains? Elwyn blood ran through her veins. It did not seem like the right time ask any of these things. He watched her, saw the silk shimmer in the sun, saw how it caressed her body. A few strands of hair blew across her face, and Elliot felt his heart race. "What's your name?" he asked.

The woman didn't answer immediately. She approached a curtain of dangling vines studded with white flowers and thorns.

"Velhisya," she stammered after a while and walked among the prickly flowers. Elliot tried to follow her but the thorns pricked his skin, causing him acute pain. Velhisya avoided the thorns with ethereal movements, but Elliot felt his flesh tearing more and more.

"Don't tell me that a warrior capable of defeating Reynald Karford in a duel cannot pass among mere flowers." Velhisya's laughter echoed in his ears, her delight clear.

Elliot tried to keep going, and then a memory flashed through his mind. It was a rainy day, and he was practicing furiously, like every day of his training. His Master had taught him to move like a tornado, and no one could compete with him in the small village where he grew up. Although he was only thirteen years old, tall, burly men struggled to nip him with the wooden swords they held. The little boy dodged their blows so fast that he seemed to be dancing in the midst of battle.

"I'm the best," he had shouted to his Master.

The old man had looked at him with a frown. *"None of these men has ever held a sword in their hands before. You take too much pride in too little a thing,"* he had said.

Elliot had felt outraged. *"They are twice my size and can't even get close to me,"* he had responded arrogantly, like a strutting peacock.

"If you could defeat them in difficult conditions, you might convince me."

"I can defeat them in any circumstances," Elliot had proclaimed with tenacity.

"Very well," the aged man had replied. *"What would you say to fighting in a place that I will propose?"*

Elliot was thirsty to prove his worth and accepted the challenge though he had no idea what the Master meant by *difficult conditions.* A few hours later, they were in a small forest where they used to hunt. He was holding the wooden sword, ready for battle, and in front of him stood a solidly-built stockbreeder, Alhen. Elliot waited for them to duel, but before the fight began, the Master gave Alhen a cloak so thick that it made him look like an elephant.

Elliot prepared for a duel. He knew that the cloak wouldn't save Alhen from his blows, but the Master had spoken decisively. *"One moment,*

Elliot. You're not in the right position."

Elliot was baffled and looked at the old man, then followed his gaze to a small passage thick with cactoid plants. Now he understood. The breeder's thick woollen cloak wasn't to protect him from Elliot's blows but from the thorns. He wanted to protest, but the Master had read the truth in his eyes before he said a word. *"If the enemy pushes you into a place like this, what will you do? Start crying?"*

Elliot turned his back and entered the pathway, carefully picking his way among the thorny trunks, not saying a word. The thorns didn't reach higher than his chest, so his neck was protected. However, if he made the mistake of ducking to avoid a blow, he could lose his eyes. Alhen's sword tore through the air, and Elliot tried to repel his blows, but in vain. With each attempt, the thorns penetrated deeper and deeper into his body. Shortly afterwards, he had accepted his defeat, weeping.

The old man had approached him that night, his eyes revealing his love. *"Are you angry?"* he had asked in a soft voice.

Elliot kept staring at the stars, not speaking.

"Do you understand what I'm trying to teach you?"

"To be humble," Elliot had murmured after a while.

The Master had smiled. *"This is a lesson but not the only one."*

"But—"

"Think," the man had insisted. *"What made you lose?"*

"The thorns!" shouted Elliot passionately. *"It's impossible to fight in that place without getting hurt."*

"Exactly," the Master had replied. *"You must learn to endure the pain. Pain frightens people, but you must not succumb to that fear. Some of the greatest knights I've ever known were so afraid of pain that their only thought was how to avoid every blow and not how to win the battle."*

"Maybe they were afraid that the pain of a sword would lead to their death," he had cried.

"Maybe," the old man had growled. *"But never fear death, Elliot! Welcome it as your friend, and then you will feel stronger than you can*

ever imagine."

"What should I be afraid of if not death?"

"A life without love."

The memory brought a tear to Elliot's eyes. He hadn't given any thought to those moments in a long time. With quick steps, Elliot passed between the vines. Velhisya waited patiently for him a few metres away. They carried on until they found a low stone wall before them. Elliot approached it and looked over it. The waters of the Forked River looked magical as he gazed at the view from the hill.

"What was your mother's name?" Elliot looked back at the young woman.

"Ellin," she murmured tersely. He waited for her to go on, and Velhisya seemed to understand. "The elwyn have only one name. There are no lords or nobles in their race."

Elliot knew that among humans, only nobles bore their house's name alongside the names they were given at birth. He had assumed that the elwyn had a similar tradition and that her mother came from such a family.

"My mother's name means *light* in the ancient elwyn language—the power of my race came from the magic of light. But that magic died centuries ago." Her eyes searched for his, as an accusatory note overshadowed her voice again.

Elliot felt irate—he was just an orphan boy who had nothing to do with the actions of his forefathers. He looked away, unsure how to respond, and caught sight of a strange tree, pitch-black, with branches that were coarse and ugly. He moved away from Velhisya to inspect it. He thought that some kind of disease must have struck its roots as its trunk had ugly bumps, resembling scaly eggs, and its top seemed about to split in two. He was about to move closer, but a hand grabbed him by the shoulder.

"Do not approach this tree," whispered Velhisya in his ear. "The Night Trees are drenched with poison from end to end."

Elliot shrank back. "Only the Endors would want such a tree in their courtyard. Now I understand why the people of Elmor are known as Poison Masters," he said.

"This tree has been here since the time of the Elder Races, before the Endors came to Elmor with their people," Velhisya retorted. "It's the only tree that wasn't planted by my ancestors, but they kept it in the city to study it. This little forest was created hundreds of years ago by the first King of Elmor. Most of its trees and flowers produce some kind of poison. It's true that the Endors and their people have been studying poisons and their qualities since ancient times. Nevertheless, the Night Trees have Orhyn Shadow in their branches."

Elliot hadn't realised he was in such a dangerous place. The sun's rays shone on the leaves of most of the flowers, creating a beautiful landscape in this rocky city. The view from the highest hill in Wirskworth was unique. Elliot saw hills and plains under the blue sky. The Forked River formed elaborate curves in the land of Elmor. The Night Tree was the only ugly sight in this little forest.

"What is Orhyn Shadow?" asked Elliot.

"The strongest poison in the world."

Velhisya seemed to read the question in his eyes. "This poison causes pain beyond imagination. The victim feels stabbing pain all over their body, so strong that they can't move. Yet Orhyn Shadow isn't deadly. Usually, the victim ends their life on their own, unable to bear the incomparable pain."

Elliot shivered as she continued. "The archers of Elmor always soaked their arrows with various poisons but never used Orhyn Shadow. Ylinor's men in the North beyond the North usually used it. Thomas Egercoll forbade all Knightdorn from doing so. Legend has it that Orhyn Shadow was made by the God of Death himself, one of the world's first gods, together with the God of Life."

Elliot smiled for a moment. "One would think that the God of Death's poison should cause the greatest harm: death itself."

Velhisya's eyes narrowed menacingly, hiding their crystalline blue colour. "Death is a blessing compared to the torment caused by this poison. There are worse things than death, Elliot Egercoll," she said contemptuously.

"I hope this tree is the only one of its kind," he said, ignoring her tone of voice.

"Of course not. The Night Trees grow on the Mountains of Darkness at the North Beyond the North," Velhisya said. "Gaeldeath has thousands of them. But the Night Trees are not the only ones that carry Orhyn Shadow. The white tiger's teeth as well as the thorns on the wyverns' wings are full of it."

Elliot's eyes widened. "Does Walter Thorn's tiger have this venom in its teeth?"

Velhisya gave him an exasperated look. "Of course," she replied. "A scratch from Annys's teeth is enough to make the victim incapable of fighting, allowing her to devour the unfortunate wretch." Velhisya turned her gaze up towards the sky. "There aren't many of these creatures left. The wyverns have been lost from the skies since the giants disappeared, and Walter owns one of the last tigers of the north. The white tiger has often been the companion of northern men for centuries. Nevertheless, the wyverns never followed any other creature other than the giants."

"Is there an antidote?" He had saved the most important question for last.

Velhisya stayed silent for a moment. "The flower of Myr contains the only antidote to Orhyn Shadow—Drowning Poison."

"A poison is the antidote to the strongest poison in the world?" he yelped, flabbergasted.

Velhisya nodded. "If liquid from the Myr flower is found in a human body soaked with Orhyn Shadow, the body will be healed. But a body free of poison will suffer the torment of choking with drops of Myr in its veins," she continued. "Nevertheless, the thorns in the Myr's stem contain the antidote to its own poison."

Elliot was astonished. A poison from the bloom of a flower could cure the strongest poison in the world, while the same flower had the antidote to the poison of its own blooms in its thorns! Suddenly, a rush of wings came from behind them. He turned to see Hurwig land on the branch of a tree with cherry-coloured leaves. Velhisya looked at the white hawk in wonder.

"Don't be afraid! It won't hurt you," Elliot reassured her, approaching Hurwig. He caressed the little head of the bird, which seemed to croon with joy. He felt the scent of the flowers in his nostrils when Velhisya spoke to him again.

"There was another antidote to Orhyn shadow, but it was lost centuries ago." Her tone betrayed her irritation again, as if there was an underlying accusatory note.

Elliot turned to her, waiting for the rest.

"The elwyn's magic was a valuable antidote to the poison until their power was forever lost."

Elliot felt anger welling up inside of him. "I'm not responsible for whatever happened to the Elder Races! Maybe they deserved it!" he yelled so loudly that Hurwig pulled away from his touch.

Velhisya's starry blue eyes turned fierce. "My father was considered even more lowly than a peasant when he returned to Wirskworth with me in his arms. A man who had slept with an elwyn. Even his family could hardly tolerate him." Elliot was sure that these words had festered inside of her for years. "Syrella's daughters have always been cherished, the beloved princesses of Elmor, and after the defeat in the Forked River, my cousin and my uncle's ashes were placed in the Temple of the God of Souls with honours never before seen in the kingdom. When my father died of a deadly disease, few honoured his body just because he had loved an elwyn. If my name wasn't Endor, the people of Elmor would have made me a prostitute and thrown me into the river as soon as they were finished with me." Her words were sharp as knives. For a moment, Elliot thought that she would attack him. “Do you think that my father and I deserved this fate?”

Elliot bent his head to her pain, understanding that she had needed someone upon whom to lay blame for her suffering. “I’m sorry, Velhisya,” he whispered. “I wish I could make up for my ancestors’ mistakes,” he continued humbly. “At least you had the chance to live close to your father, even for a short while. I never met my parents.” Elliot wondered where the girl’s mother could be but didn’t voice that question.

Velhisya’s cheeks flushed, as though she had not expected his apology.

“So, here you are...”

Long Arm’s voice made Elliot turn round.

“Apparently, trouble follows you everywhere.” John’s eyes gleamed as he spoke.

The Twin Enemies

John and Elliot left Velhisya behind, John leading him to where their other companions awaited, saying only that they needed to speak with him urgently. He didn't know what had happened, and anxiety stirred inside of him. Long Arm hadn't told him a thing. They kept walking until Elliot was sure they weren't on the right track.

"This road does not lead to the Tower of the Sharp Swords," said Elliot, stopping Long Arm.

"I know," he replied calmly. "I wanted to get you on your own."

Elliot was puzzled. "I thought you wanted to talk to me along with the others... I thought something happened—"

"Everything's fine," said John. "I just wanted to know what happened in the dungeons." His eyes lit up strangely as he uttered the last sentence.

"How do you know?"

"News travels fast."

Elliot gave him what he hoped was a piercing look. He took a deep breath and began to recount the events of the night before. John's eyes widened as he listened to him. Long Arm may have been a drunkard, but he had good judgment and knowledge that Elliot couldn't find in any of his other companions—for some reason he trusted him.

"Very strange," John said as soon as Elliot finished his story. "This man should hate you if only for your name, and you humiliated him inside his own castle. He passed up the chance to earn great honours from Walter for murdering Thomas's self-proclaimed only *son*. If I were you, I'd make sure I heard what he has to say."

In his surprise, Elliot stopped walking. "You think I should talk to him?"

"Of course."

"This captive was one of the most trusted soldiers of the man who killed my entire family!"

"In all honesty, you're a good lad, Elliot, but you can be hard-headed at times!" said John vigorously. "Reynald chose to spare your life, even knowing that you are the queen's only hope against Walter. He knows the full extent of the plan to trick Walter and he has seen you fight..."

Elliot was not convinced.

"In the name of the gods! Don't you have any curiosity to find out why he chose to save you and why he isn't riding like a demon to warn Walter?" John sighed. "I may not know much about wars and battles, but I do know that a man like Reynald Karford does nothing without thinking about the consequences of his actions. If the news that an Egercoll was saved by his sword reaches Walter's ears, Knightdorn will be too small to hide him."

"All right. But I think my time is better spent speaking to Syrella," grumbled Elliot. "I should be more insistent that she listen to me. With each passing day, our time is running out!"

"You have so much to learn, Elliot," laughed John. "The Scarred Queen will follow your plan..."

"Scarred Queen?"

"I'm sure you noticed the scar on her face," Long Arm replied. "This has been her nickname since she took over Elmor."

"Why are you so certain she'll follow my plan?" wondered Elliot, ignoring this titbit of information.

"Do you think she would have hosted you in her capital if she didn't intend to listen to you? She knows that no man in her region would stand any chance against Reynald, even if she hasn't said it out loud, and she's even more curious about your origins. I think she suspects that this plan doesn't come from the queen but from you. Iovbridge has never shown great strategic thinking in recent years, and the only one who could think of such a plan would first have to be sure that a man like Reynald could be defeated, and only you knew it was possible. I can't be sure if she will send her armies to Iovbridge, but she will follow the plan you confided to her to save Elmor's people from Walter's cavalry. After all, she has nothing to lose by gathering supplies and villagers in Wirskworth—the city can house hundreds of thousands of people."

Elliot frowned, not sharing John's optimism.

"Still, she must first persuade her council. In Elmor, they respect the great lords, as you must have already realised. Oftentimes, politics is harder than war." John smiled wide. "Now, you will forgive me, but I heard that there are amazing brothels in this city!"

Elliot descended into the depths of the dungeon. The sunlight didn't reach the bottom of the Tower of the Sharp Swords. Only some torches lit the space. He felt a touch of fear—would he like the words he was about to hear?

He walked until two men accosted him. Their armour covered every inch of their bodies, and their hands moved toward the hilts of their swords.

"What are you doing here?" barked one of the two guards.

Elliot weighed them up carefully—their long black-and-yellow cloaks shone in the dim light, and they wore thick, silver gaiters. The one had round green eyes and a strange triangular moustache while the other was shorter and flat-faced.

"I have come here to talk to Reynald Karford," Elliot said.

The shorter man seemed reluctant. "The governor ordered us not to let anyone near this prisoner."

"I caught this man myself and brought him to Wirskworth. All I ask is to talk to him," he insisted.

The two guards, certainly aware of what had happened in the Tower of the Sharp Swords the night before, exchanged glances, then one of them stepped aside. "Make it quick," he said abruptly.

Elliot nodded and hurried past. His eyes fell on the wall-opening that he had crossed the previous night but also on the small cell where he had hidden—the place where he had skirted round a most certain death. He grabbed a torch from the stone wall next to him and walked until the flames lit up the cell of the once hateful man. Reynald's hands covered his face as the light blinded his eyes. The man got up and walked toward Elliot, his movement easier than it had been. It seemed Syrella Endor had sent her healers to treat him.

"Did you come to thank me, Egercoll?" His eyes flashed under the torchlight.

Elliot observed him through the iron bars. "Why?" was the only word he heard himself say.

"Maybe I have another goal in mind, little one..." The prisoner smirked, still arrogant and stubborn.

"That could have been true if I weren't an Egercoll."

"You are?" Reynald's eyes glinted.

"You know the answer, Karford. I wouldn't have lied to you just before I died."

The man remained silent for a few moments. Elliot waited patiently, feeling a hint of anxiety about the words he would utter.

"I have nothing to tell you!" he snapped after a while.

Elliot was perplexed. "You saved my life!" he exclaimed. "If Walter hears of this deed, you're dead! You're telling me that you had the courage to save me, but you're afraid to tell me why?"

Reynald turned his back on him. "I..." He hesitated, guilt lacing his voice. "...I never wanted the loss of your mother," he said after a while, and Elliot froze in place at the sound of his words.

"I know what you think—I was one of Walter's most trusted soldiers...

a Ghost of the Trinity of Death..." Reynald's voice was muffled. "Even if I wasn't, the Karfords always hated the Asselins. Many in Oldlands called our houses the *Twin Enemies*—old texts attested to the fact that the Asselins and Karfords came from the same house, the House of Colsmith. Legend has it that this was one of the greatest houses in the west, left without male offspring over the centuries."

"I don't understand."

"I hated your father. He vented his rage on the noble families and stole centuries-old entitlements from our houses!" he shouted. "But your mother," his tone softened, "didn't deserve such an end. Walter had promised me he wouldn't look for her. Even if she were pregnant, no child could be a threat to him..." Reynald's bitterness about his former lord and master going back on his word was obvious. "Alice knew he was going to kill her, so she ended her life just before he got to her hideout."

That moment shook Elliot more than any other—Reynald's voice was broken, as if he had been crying. He watched the man's back through the cell bars, and thousands of thoughts swirled in his mind. *It's not possible... No, it could not be true.*

"Everything I did was for your mother, not for you."

Elliot tried to put his thoughts in order. "When your men caught my companions in the Land of Fire, you wanted to rape Eleanor! You asked for her to be sent to your chamber," he said, feeling out of breath. "Are you telling me that a man like you saved me for the sake of my dead mother?"

The man turned to face him. "If I had wanted to rape young girls, I would've stayed with Walter for the last seventeen years," he snarled. "I only wanted to protect her from Stonegate's men. The Guardians of the South don't show much respect for women prisoners."

"You attacked us." He raised his voice. "You threatened to kill her just before we left Ersemor."

"I was a captive," Reynald snapped. "I hadn't believed a word of what you said in the Centaurs-Land, and I didn't know what you intended for me—I had to flee to save my life!"

Elliot looked at Reynald, forcing himself to hold that gaze. "You saved me for my mother's sake...," he murmured. "Is that why you left the Trinity of Death and stayed in Stonegate all these years?"

The answer behind this question was a secret that Elliot was certain nobody else knew.

The man remained silent for a while, then gave a single nod. Elliot opened his mouth to speak, then closed it again, unable to make a sound. He wanted to leave. He wanted to be alone. He turned to go, but the man's voice sounded loud and bold behind him.

"Let me fight by your side."

Elliot turned slowly toward him and fixed his eyes on Reynald. "No."

A vein in Reynald's temple twitched. "If you tell anyone what I told you, I'll get out of this cell, and this time you won't escape, Egercoll!"

"We'll talk again soon, Reynald Karford," replied Elliot, and with these words, he squared his shoulders and walked away.

The Men of Rain

Giren felt ill on this cold morning. He was cleaning a spacious chamber and had a terrible ache in his stomach. Giren was wearing a lemon-coloured jerkin which had been mended many a time, and his body was very weak. He could barely walk, and the feeling of hunger drained him even more. The guards had followed their lord's instructions word for word, so all they had given the servants to eat the day before was the dead bodies of the men who had lost their lives by Walter's hand. The slaves hadn't touched the lifeless bodies, so Giren, along with some others, had asked the guards to allow them to stack the corpses with the rest of the dead lying outside White City.

The guards had smiled upon hearing this plea.

"The king ordered this to be your food," a Gaeldeath man had told Giren.

"No one wants to eat these corpses, but if they remain in the castle, they will rot. Do you want the slaves to get sick just before the war in Iovbridge?"

Giren's audacity had irritated the guard, but the possibility of illness inflicting the army right before it marched put fear in his eyes, he had accepted their request.

"As you wish," the guard had replied. *"If this is your will, you won't eat."* With these words, he had ordered Giren and the other servants to get out of his sight.

The result was that Giren and many more slaves went without food for more than a day. But the hunger was offset by the small act of defiance he had carried out the day before—bringing the body of the Guardian of

Stonegate to rest outside White City, first wrapping it in a cloak as a token of decency. He had tried to cover the body with dirt, using his hands. Better this shallow grave than being tossed over the walls of Iovbridge with all the other corpses.

Suddenly, the chamber door opened with a thud, and a large man came in. He was an Oldlands officer. Giren didn't know his name, but he was sure he was an officer, otherwise he wouldn't have been given such a large chamber. Coarse and imposing behind his long beard, he glanced at Giren. The man was armoured, a brown cloak with the Oldlands emblem hung from his back, and he looked strong enough to kill Giren with a wave of his hand. The officer walked over to a round table at the edge of the room and sat on the chair next to it.

"Would you like me to bring you some pork, my lord?" Giren asked quickly.

"I'm not a lord," came the man's answer.

"Forgive me," Giren replied with a deep bow. "What can I do for you?" he asked, without looking him in the eye.

"I knew your father. He was an honest, fair man."

Giren was both surprised and embarrassed. He hadn't heard any compliment about his House in years, and few knew who he was. Many of Walter's Ghosts knew his name, but they only used it to humiliate him, talking about the destruction of his House and the death of his father. "Thank you for your kind words, Commander."

"How did you know I'm a commander?"

"Only an officer would be given such a chamber."

The man smiled for a moment and continued to observe him. After a while, he got up from his chair and approached. Giren was afraid he would hit him but then saw a plate of figs and bread in the man's hands.

"Eat," urged the man calmly.

Giren remained rooted in his place. He was sure it was a trap.

"I won't hurt you," continued the man.

He was very hungry. After a moment of indecision, he grabbed the bread and started eating greedily. "What is your name, Commander?" he asked, chewing.

"I'm Devan, a captain of Kelanger," replied the man.

"No one should disobey the orders of the one and only true king... Walter ordered the guards to give the servants only dead bodies for food," murmured Giren, trying to understand why the officer before him was ignoring Walter's orders.

"Power is intoxicating, Giren. Many times, men with power lose their sanity," said Devan. "I am sorry for what you have suffered."

Giren pushed his dirty hair aside and looked Devan over. He hadn't felt respected by anyone for many years.

"Do you believe you are in the service of the wrong king?" Giren asked before he could restrain himself. He thought Devan would get angry, but the man from Kelanger turned his gaze away, looking into the void.

"I don't know," said the captain after a while. "It's true that the queen sitting on the throne of Iovbridge doesn't have the strength to rule Knightdorn, and Ricard Karford and Walter Thorn put me on the council of the Oldlands. Some might say I owe them gratitude," he murmured. "However, I've fought enough to know that a true leader shows his real face to his enemies, not his allies."

"Then perhaps you should leave the ranks of that king," Giren rejoined.

The man looked at him wearily. "I'm an Oldlands man! I must follow my governor's orders."

"I thought the true Governor of Oldlands—Aymer Asselin—died at the hands of Walter in dishonourable ways." Giren wondered where he had found the courage to say all that.

"No one can be sure of that—old Aymer's executioner was never found."

"I think everyone knows who the real killer was."

Devan seemed speechless when a loud knock shook the door. The captain got up and opened it. Saron Gray, a man from Gaeldeath, rushed into the chamber. Giren immediately lowered his head and left the bread on the wooden table. Saron always liked to torture slaves.

"What brings you to my chamber, Lord Gray?" Devan addressed the newcomer.

He ignored him and looked at Giren. "Here you are, you filth!" he yelled.

"I was tidying up the captain's room," replied Giren humbly.

Saron was stocky and ugly. He wore a silk jerkin the colour of blood. He walked swiftly toward Giren and grabbed him by the neck. "Who is Shyllan Vallero?" he roared.

Giren had no idea what he was talking about.

"Answer me, or I will kill you," shouted Saron, unsheathing a long sword from his belt.

Devan took a step forward. "What's going on, Saron?" he said, raising his voice.

The man scowled at this interference. "A messenger arrived on our land earlier, holding a letter."

A wrinkle appeared on Devan's forehead "And why are you here?" he wondered.

Saron took a step back, letting go of Giren's neck. "Before our king left Ramerstorm last night, he ordered me to read every letter that reaches the city," he informed him. "Only one letter arrived today, and the recipient is this filth here," the man pointed and turned his gaze to Giren. "If you don't tell me who Shyllan Vallero is, I will have your legs cut off," he thundered.

Giren stood riveted in his place, unable to speak. Saron's words sounded paranoid in his mind. He had never heard of that name.

The captain of Oldlands tried to put things in order. "A man arrived in White City and handed over a letter for this slave here?"

"Exactly," confirmed Saron.

Devan glanced at Giren, as if telling him to be silent.

"Do you have this letter with you, my lord? Maybe I could take a look at it."

Saron looked at the captain suspiciously. "Why?" he asked sharply.

"I'm curious," said Devan.

"King Walter ordered that only I read the letters reaching the city," Saron alleged.

"I am not questioning your authority, Saron. I'm simply curious," murmured the captain. "I believe that the devotion I've shown to our king is enough for me to have the honour of reading a letter from an unknown sender."

Saron watched him for a moment. Shortly afterwards, he pulled a crumpled parchment from his belt, along with a dirty cloth patched in several places. "I didn't know you could read," he said brusquely and held out his hand to Devan.

The captain grabbed the letter and began to read. When he had finished reading, he seemed confused.

"If you are exchanging letters with one of the traitors in Iovbridge, I will cripple you," Saron spoke again, looking at Giren.

"No slave could easily find ink and parchment, let alone a messenger to leave the city and head to Iovbridge," the captain said. "Plus, no enemy from the capital of Isisdor would send a messenger to our land since they know that a letter sealed with a coat of arms or emblem from our enemies' regions would be burned, and the man who carried it would be severely punished. Only someone with information from our allies would take the initiative to send a letter." The captain seemed skeptical.

"It's conceivable that in Iovbridge they have found out that we read all letters so long as they don't have the *queen's* seal or that of our enemy-rulers... The letter may contain a hidden message, and our enemies are trying to uncover information from this lecher," Saron seethed.

"A hidden message that only a slave could uncover." Devan sighed with annoyance. "This letter is simply a declaration of loyalty to our king."

Saron remained silent for a while. "It's strange," he muttered.

"His father was a descendant of Tahryn's first king, and many know that Walter has kept him in his ranks for years. Clearly, a man from Tahryn who moved to Iovbridge sent this letter."

"Every man in the kingdom knows that he's a slave. What fool would think that this rat fink would give our king advice?"

Giren stood there with his mouth open at these last words. The captain looked at him, but Giren could not read his thoughts.

"Giren," Devan spoke after a while, "are you sure you don't know the writing or the coat of arms on this man's seal?" Devan extended his hand toward the servant, trying to show him the letter, when Saron got in the way.

"What do you think you're doing?" cried the Gaeldeath man. "Our king would be furious if he found out that we allowed a slave to read a letter."

"If there is an ally in Iovbridge who rushed to send a letter to declare his submission to our king because of Giren, I think Walter would be glad. Maybe he'd think that Giren's position is not the one it should have been all these years," countered the captain. "Who brought this letter?" he asked.

"Some tradesman," Saron replied. "He told the guards that a lord in Iovbridge gave it to him five days ago, along with enough gold to have it delivered to Walter's men in White City."

"If this lord has that much gold these days, he must be very rich," cried Devan.

Saron glanced at Giren. "Can you read, you ruddy castoff?" he sniggered loudly.

"Yes, my lord," he replied. "I was taught when I was a child."

"Hmm, turns out you're not the most useless critter in this city reeking of goat bathed in manure, after all." Saron laughed and nodded at the captain.

Devan reached out to Giren, and he grabbed the letter. He began to read it quickly, but each word confused him all the more.

To Lord Giren Barlow,

It's been a long time since we last met, but I have never forgotten the friendship that has united us since our childhood. Time may have separated us, but my devotion to you remains alive, so I had to write these words to you, declaring my devotion to you but also to the king you serve. A king who has your support will always be my king too.

The self-proclaimed queen fears Walter Thorn's arrival. She fears that she will lose everything in a short time, knowing the full extent of the true king's unsurpassed power. Walter Thorn is the leader the kingdom needs, and this is why you are by his side. Walter Thorn is the one who opened the door to the rebellion against the Pegasi and their descendants who desecrated this ancient kingdom's traditions. It's a common secret in every part of Knightdorn that they pray for the coming of the true king, knowing that he's the only one who can pull Knightdorn out of the tunnel of its current rulership. The Pegasus Usurper has no worthy warriors. In the future, she will no longer have a place in the history of this kingdom. After Walter's arrival in Ballar, even the earth creaks because of His Majesty under Hawk's Nest.

I'm sending this letter to you, Giren, knowing that you're one of Walter Thorn's most trusted counsellors, to ask you to convey to your king, whose power is equal to the power in the legendary Seven Swords of this world, the devotion of a man loyal to you.

I am counting the days and nights to the time when the throne will belong to its true leader and thus, you will be freed from your thirst to take revenge on the Pegasus Tamers for the evil they brought to your lord's House.

This cloth was a gift from you to me when we were children. It's time for me to send it back to you hoping that you'll be holding it when we meet again, as the true king will be sitting on Knightdorn's throne, having destroyed the House of Pegasus once and for all.

If you and your lord need my help, don't hesitate to ask. It will be my honour.

May the God of Rain be with you.
Yours,
Lord Shyllan Vallero

Giren read the letter over and over but didn't understand a thing.

"Do you know this man?" Saron seemed to lose his patience.

"I don't thi—" He stopped mid-sentence as Devan gave a discreet nod.

Giren hesitated for a moment, and then Saron pushed him to the floor and kicked him in the ribs.

"I mean, I don't remember that name, but his words and this cloth prove that he is a son of Tahryn," he groaned. "I've forgotten my past, Lord Grey. Perhaps I knew this man when I was a kid. Perhaps my devotion to our king made him want to support Walter in his battle for the throne." Giren didn't know if he had said the right words, but he swore he had seen a gleam in Devan's eyes.

Saron was now content. "Maybe you're not so insignificant after all, Giren," he chirped. "If there are Tarhyn's men in Iovbridge who want to help us because of your devotion to our king, maybe we can use them."

Giren nodded slightly.

"Did you say that this cloth is proof that the sender is a man of Tahryn?" continued Saron.

"Yes."

"Why?" asked the lord with obvious curiosity.

"The first Shiplords of Tahryn used to wave these cloths to their loved ones when they left the port of Tahos for the Cold Sea. The ship that's worn out in the middle of the cloth is Tahryn's emblem," Giren replied.

The man brought the frayed canvas in front of him, unfurling it completely, and then Giren's gaze fell on the cloth's patches. He stifled astonishment, hoping no one had noticed. Then Saron Grey walked over to him and pulled the letter from his hands. Giren mustered as much courage as he could find in him.

"Can I keep the cloth and the letter?" His voice sounded shrill.

Saron looked at him disapprovingly. "I must show it to our king as soon as he returns. An ally in Iovbridge may be important information for him."

"I can deliver it to him or to you, my lord, when the king returns to the city," Giren murmured. "It's just a great honour for me to be able to help in our king's war," he added. "This letter and this cloth can remind me of this achievement." He prayed silently, waiting for the final decision.

The Gaeldeath man glanced at him and tossed the letter along with the ragged cloth toward him. "Be careful not to lose them, otherwise I'll take your life." With these words, he opened the chamber door and disappeared from sight.

Giren remained speechless, while a look of approval appeared on Devan's face.

"You did well," noted the captain after a moment.

Giren looked at him in wonderment.

"It was obvious that you had no idea who sent this letter—your eyes were telling the truth," said Devan.

"When Walter returns, I will have to explain to him how I know this man." Giren shivered with fear.

"You will say exactly what you said to Saron. Make sure you are convincing if you want to keep your head," murmured the captain.

He was still lying on the ground. He got up with a slight stagger as his ribs ached from Saron's kick. "Thank you, Captain," he said.

The man shook his head, as if telling him that he didn't need to thank him. "And who might the sender be?" Devan asked.

"Someone crazy, without a doubt. Many are looking for allies in Thorn's ranks, trying to gain favour with the future king," Giren answered, and Devan agreed with a nod.

"Why did you ask to keep the letter and the cloth?"

"I thought it would make me look more convincing," Giren said. "Do you need anything else, Captain?"

"No, thank you."

Giren bowed and moved toward the door to leave the room. His legs were stronger the rest of the day as he performed his duties. It was the eighth day that he was in this city and the first during which he felt a sense of optimism. He served the commanders in the great hall, soaped the wooden tables down, and fed the horses in the courtyard of Hawk's Nest.

A few hours later, darkness had fallen, and he was lying on the hard, icy floor of the stable where he was sleeping. The straw softened the pain he felt in his back when the candle that gently lit his surrounds began to flicker. Giren listened to the snoring around him and after making sure everyone was asleep, he got up quietly and walked on tiptoe. When he reached the small window at the end of the stable, the starlight illuminated his weary face.

His hands trembled as he pulled the patched cloth out of his dirty costume, bringing it under the soft night light. The Fairy, the ship of Tahryn's first king, was illuminated by the glow of the moon. Giren gazed at the galley of Mengon Barlow, his most famous ancestor. It had grown ragged and worn over the years, but Giren knew. The Shiplords of old knew how to hide their messages better than anyone. He took a small knife out of his rags. He had hidden it in his clothing while clearing the dinner table. Giren started snipping the patched parts of the cloth, working skilfully until several pieces of cloth fell to the floor and left holes in the frayed canvas. His breath quickened, excitement sweeping over his body as he placed the cloth over Shyllan Vallero's letter.

He staggered as the words revealed by the cutouts came into focus. He looked hastily around but no one had woken up, then leaned close to read:

The queen needs you
open the secret tunnel under Hawk's Nest in Seven nights

and you will be freed once and for all
May the God of Rain be with you.

Giren read the letter over and over, until he was sure his eyes had not played tricks on him. Iovbridge was asking for his help, and the queen would set him free if he succeeded. Although he had no idea where this tunnel was, he had enough days at his disposal to find out.

His mind travelled far from the dark stable, so far that nothing could imprison it anymore. His mother was feeding his sister when he became afraid of the loud sounds of an evening storm that broke out. His father noticed his expression and gently pulled him by the hand. *"Come with me, Giren."*

He walked beside his father, until they reached the castle's courtyard, and then he felt the rain covering every cell of his body.

"The first men of Tahryn, the Men of Rain, used to say that raindrops are our god's gift; the rain can wash away our hearts' weaknesses and fears," whispered his father, and Giren's small lips tightened as he broke into a hesitant smile. Shortly afterwards, his hand gripped his father's palm under the heavy downpour as the rainwater began to wash away all his fears.

Giren interrupted his thoughts, clenched the letter in his fist, and opened his tear-filled eyes. For a moment, he felt that he was there again, a little boy at his father's side as the rain cleansed his body, leaving his soul free to fly. His wet gaze fell on the moonlight again, and then he finally saw him—his father was smiling at him from the stars, arms outstretched, ready to take him into his arms.

The Cry of War

Elliot walked the halls of Moonstone, heading for the room with the large hearth and the statue of the grim man. Lady Endor and her council wanted to talk to him. *About time.* And yet it had been four days since he had spoken to Reynald Karford, and he had not yet been able to digest what he had heard nor shake those words from his mind. He had last seen the ruler and her counsellors on the day he visited Reynald, and if the plan had succeeded, Walter would soon be on Snake Road. Nevertheless, Elliot had heard that Syrella had ordered her men to gather every villager and crop from Elmor. He had seen with his own eyes thousands of people arriving in the city in the last days. So, all that remained was to find out if the ruler would go back on her initial decision and choose to march her armies to Iovbridge.

The days had passed slowly in Wirskworth, and his only company was the band of travellers who had accompanied him from Isisdor. Elliot thought that the ruler would have requested the presence of all five envoys in order to announce her decisions, but he was wrong. Peter Brau had told him that great warriors were highly respected in Elmor, so perhaps his victory over Reynald had given him more prestige—if nothing else, the queen had knighted him. Men like Selwyn were important, as he was the son of the lord of the knights, yet Elliot had since learnt that in Elmor you gained respect only for your own achievements and not for those of other men of your house. *Perhaps the ruler asked for my presence for some other purpose and not to announce her decision*, he thought.

Elliot kept walking, the long sword given to him by the men of the Sharp Swords hanging from his belt. After his adventure in the dungeons of the Tower of the Sharp Swords, he was always armed. He knocked on the correct door and was bade to enter. The chamber was quite full. Syrella Endor fixed her imposing eyes on him as he moved toward her. The ruler wore a snow-white dress, and her counsellors sat soberly, dressed in expensive jerkins. Elliot's gaze fell on three women seated with Elmor's council: the governor's daughters and Velhisya. Elliot hadn't seen the young woman since the day they walked in the courtyard and among the poisonous flowers. He wondered if she despised him for the name he bore. She wore a green dress with a gold-embroidered collar and beads decorating it. Her cousins wore dark leather clothes.

"I heard you were roaming in the dungeons a few days ago," a voice broke the silence.

Elliot looked at the Governor of Elmor in her ornate chair but didn't speak.

"Do you have any new information?" Syrella asked after a while.

Elliot shook his head.

"You're asking for my trust, yet you're lying before my very eyes," snapped the ruler. "The guards told me that you stayed in Karford's cell for quite some while."

"He didn't tell me anything of importance," responded Elliot. "I think the only important issue is the final decision of Elmor's ruler about the Queen of Knightdorn's request and not Reynald Karford." Irritation was palpable in his voice. Their time was running out, and Syrella had to make her decision known.

"You should speak with more respect," said Edmund in his familiar angry manner. "It is the ruler's right to judge what is important and what is not. You and your queen need our help, not we yours! It'd be wise to remember this and answer the governor's questions with reverence if you expect us to accept Iovbridge's call."

Elliot smiled for a moment. "I'd say we need each other," he replied with forcefulness. “Otherwise, Wirskworth will become a graveyard as soon as Thorn takes the throne.”

“Your opinion on this council is more insignificant than the night walk of an ant.” The high priest’s blurry black eyes filled with satisfaction at the insult.

Elliot’s gaze wandered around the room. It was exactly the same as in his last visit—except for a deer’s head nailed on the wall behind the high priest’s head. He was sure that the animal’s head had not been there four days ago. He took a step forward. “My opinion may be trivial on this council, but I’d say that a priest’s opinion should not sway decisions about wars and battles,” he said. “How many men of Elmor’s enemies has your sword taken, lord of the temple? How many times have you fought next to this city’s sons on the battlefield?” His voice came out thundering, and he could swear that Velhisya’s starry blue eyes looked at him with admiration.

Edmund seemed enraged. “The power of the god I serve is stronger than any sword, you fool!”

“If the God of Souls is so powerful, why didn’t you ask him to fight at the Forked River?”

“Enough!” Syrella stood up, and the high priest closed his mouth, cutting off what he wanted to say.

“I hope your sword is as sharp as your tongue, sir,” Syrella’s scar seemed larger as she spoke.

Elliot looked at her in silence.

“My counsellors and I have decided—”

Her voice trailed off abruptly as the door opened with a thud, and a dishevelled man rushed in.

“Your Majesty, a man from Myril has arrived in the city, asking to speak with you. He says it is urgent. He said that he saw Walter’s riders in Elmor,” said the newcomer.

Elliot remembered Velhisya uttering that name—Lord Hewdar’s castle. He turned toward the governor and guessed at the truth before hearing her words.

"Lord Hewdar!" Syrella's eyes were filled with terror. "I sent messengers to every corner of Elmor, except his castle!"

The counsellors looked around at each other. No one had thought of Lord Hewdar.

"Did this man come here by himself?" Syrella addressed the newcomer.

"Yes, Your Majesty," he replied.

"Bring him to me," she ordered.

Time seemed to pass torturously until the man returned, accompanied by a frantic lad with bushy black hair and a pale face.

"Your Majesty." The lad bowed sharply, looking at the ruler. "I saw men with banners of the white tiger riding toward Snake Road," he said with pain in his voice.

His words sounded like a dirge, and guilt was clearly visible on the governor's face. She turned to Elliot. Everything had gone wrong. His trick had succeeded, but at the same time he had managed to bring the most dangerous man of all time to Elmor's doorstep. Elliot was not to blame for the council's mistake, but he was sure they would charge him with it.

"What is your name?" asked Syrella after a moment.

"Tom, Your Majesty."

"Where did you see these men?" she continued.

"I rode south of Myril, trying out my new steed. I was north of the Road of Elves when I heard whinnying, and then I saw with my own eyes thousands of horsemen riding down Snake Road. The riders were coming from the Road of Elves and would soon be near Myril. Fortunately, they didn't see me, but I didn't have time to get to the castle and inform my lord. So, I exhausted my horse to get here instead. I wanted to inform you that Walter's men are in Elmor."

Syrella seemed contrite. "When did you see Walter's men?" she asked with a crack in her voice.

"Shortly after dawn," said the young man. "On my way to

Wirskworth, I intended to warn every villager and wanderer about Walter's arrival, but I didn't find anyone. Every village along my journey was deserted." A note of wonder was now in Tom's tone.

The governor was speechless. Quiet spread across the room until Elliot spoke. "Walter will be at Wirskworth soon." He had listened carefully to Tom's words. Walter had moved according to plan. Nevertheless, he had reached Snake Road earlier than expected. Reynald's sword couldn't have been in his hands earlier than five days ago. This meant that Walter had left Ballar immediately, as soon as he'd heard the news and was probably riding fast to get to Snake Road before the fifth day's sunset. "I'm sure he will let his men and horses rest for a while in Lord Hewdar's castle since it's the only place where he could have found food in Elmor. Then, he'll head to Wirskworth. If he starts before the break of dawn tomorrow, he'll be here before sunset."

Syrella's eyes fixed on him, full of menace. "Lord Hewdar will be attacked because of you!" she screeched. "The plots you and the queen contrived are responsible for this."

"I'm sorry, Your Majesty, but I told you to send messengers to every man in your land. If you neglected this lord, that's not my fault." Elliot humbly bowed his head.

"HOW DARE YOU?" Syrella's voice shook the room.

"Your Majesty, I understand your anger, but you know deep in your heart that I'm not responsible for what has happened," Elliot replied. "There's a chance that Walter will ride to Snake Road, and as soon as he realises that Elmor's army isn't there, he may encamp on a plain, ignoring Myril."

Elliot knew that the odds of that happening were slim. Walter would search for wanderers and villagers, trying to find out if Elmor's soldiers had crossed Snake Road. If he didn't find anyone, he would certainly visit the castle of the only lord far from the region's capital. The only hope that he might ignore Myril was if he didn't know that Lord Hewdar had been residing there in recent years. "Even if Walter attacks Myril, the right time will come for you to take revenge on your dead," he concluded, looking at the ruler and her counsellors.

Syrella turned her gaze away from Elliot. "Maybe now is the right time for revenge. Even if he doesn't attack Jacob, Walter Thorn has already brought a lot of death to my land," she said, as if to herself. "How many men did you see marching along Snake Road?" she asked, addressing Tom.

"They were just riders, Your Majesty," said the lad. "There must have been a little over ten thousand."

Syrella glanced at Elliot. He had told her that he expected Walter to ride south only with Gaeldeath's twelve thousand cavalrymen. "We will form our battle lines outside the city. If Walter takes the bait and approaches the wall, we'll slaughter his soldiers and Walter himself!" she stormed. "Our army is almost equal to his, and our archers will hurt his cavalry if they get near the city."

"You cannot defeat twelve thousand horsemen," Elliot shouted. "Walter didn't head south-east to take Wirskworth but to disband its army! If you meet him outside the city, the waves of his cavalry will destroy them, and he'll fulfil his purpose. The archers won't be able to help once the battle is joined, and Elmor has less than two thousand horses. The only way to win this battle is to wait."

"Your Majesty, I must admit that a battle against Walter could be fatal for this city's future. Perhaps we could capitulate, promising to abstain from the war in exchange for peace in Elmor," Lord Burns chimed in for the first time.

Syrella turned on Burns, more venom in her face than she had aimed at Elliot. "Are you asking me to capitulate to the man who sent my brother, my nephew, even your own son and my husband to death?" she thundered. "The people of Elmor would revolt if I made any kind of deal with a man like Walter Thorn!"

Elliot had been unaware that Syrella's dead husband was the son of Lord Burns.

"Forgive me, Your Majesty. My rage equals yours. I only thought we could secure the future of the people of Elmor," the counsellor said, bowing slightly. "Nevertheless, I think a battle with Walter is a bad idea. Elmor suffered a lot the last time it tried to fight this man." Lord Burns paused, thinking, then went on. "Walter may attack the City of Heavens to feed his army if he doesn't find enough food on our land," he pondered. "Elirehar is not far away."

"His horses are already exhausted from the trip and it would take him a while to ride to the City of Heavens, rest his horses, and head back to Stonegate. Elmor's army could cross the South Passage before he could reach them. Nonetheless, if Walter had time to attack the City of Heavens, he would find food for several days as the men of the city have gathered all the crops off their land," Elliot continued.

"But he may attack the City of Heavens on his way back, as his men will be starving," said Syrella.

"Why delay his attack on Iovbridge even further, exhausting his soldiers even more, to attack a city that's not a danger to him?" countered Elliot. "He needs the same time to get to the north-west of the Road of Elves, where he will find land capable of feeding his men and horses, perhaps not as well as the capital of Elirehar could, but as he'll head north, he'll find crops to feed his armies on the return journey. An attack on the City of Heavens would only be a waste of time, while the fertile lands on the Road of Elves are on his way to Ballar."

"How do you know that the men in the capital of Elirehar have collected the harvest of all the crops on their land?" wondered Lord Burns.

"I had to change my route on my journey to Elmor, so my companions and I rested for a day in the City of Heavens. The guards confided in me that the Grand Master had ordered them to gather all crops outside the city as he predicted that a severe winter was coming."

"Grand Master?" wondered Syrella. "There is no Grand Master in the City of Heavens."

"My companions thought so too, until they saw Master Thorold," explained Elliot. "He told us that he had survived Walter's battle against Elirehar and has lived in the City of Heavens to this day, while no one outside Elirehar has learnt of this truth."

Surprise flashed through Syrella's face and was mirrored on the faces of her counsellors. Sadon Burns looked at Elliot as if seeing him for the first time, and he wondered if he had just made a terrible mistake—perhaps he shouldn't have revealed that Thorold was alive when he himself had kept it a secret for almost fifteen years.

"The signs from the God of Souls have shown me that we can defeat Walter in a man-to-man fight this time, Your Majesty," persisted the high priest, not caring about Thorold and Elirehar. Edmund's eyes wandered to the statue of the grim man. Elliot finally understood who this statue represented.

"Then let's hope his sword contributes to the battle," Elliot responded in irritation.

"You've got a mouth on you, boy," shot Edmund. "Are we to worship you simply because you showed up with Reynald Karford? Who knows what trick you used to capture him," he challenged. "Maybe you're just a liar."

Elliot pulled the sword hanging from his belt as fast as he could. All eyes in the room watched in horror as the blade spun in the air, heading for the priest. The old man's eyes opened wide. Screams rang out. The point of the sword buried itself next to Edmund's left ear, in the deer head behind him.

The high priest looked at the steel, horrified, then turned his gaze to Elliot, eyes burning with hate. Elliot held that gaze, staring into those dark irises, but then he felt as though an inexplicable force enveloped the priest's skinny body, something malevolent and ancient. And Elliot would have sworn he saw the God of Souls in those eyes, staring back at him, ready to welcome Elliot into his icy embrace.

The Companion on the Fence

John's gaze fell on the glowing sunset outside the window in front of him, thoughts swirling in his head like annoying small insects, leaving him no time to calm down. They had just learned that Walter was on Snake Road. He had to run, run away. He had to save himself from the storm that would soon reach this glorious city. *This city withstood the attack of the giants on their winged monsters*, a little voice whispered in his ear. It was true. He was in the safest place. Nothing could better protect him from Walter than this inhospitable rocky city. Wirskworth's walls were stronger than any other in the world, built by creatures superior to humans. But the question that tormented his soul and mind, the question that had kept him awake for the last few nights, unless he was lost in the magical world of intoxication, was not his security, but whether he wanted to be in this place, surrounded by people he didn't trust at all. John had established Sophie Delamere's motives and character before moving to Iovbridge. This woman was a merciful queen in contrast to Elmor's ruler, who was quite authoritarian. Nevertheless, the Queen of Knightdorn didn't have the virtues and determination of a true leader.

Sophie Delamere had a pure heart, but life had taught him that the world wasn't made to be ruled by pure people, so he had decided not to waste his life for her sake when Walter attacked Iovbridge. *The Ice Islands would never forgive such a thing*, whispered the voice in his ear again. He tossed that thought aside in annoyance. Truth be told, he admired the independent islands' politics, just as Thomas Egercoll had. Positions of standing had not been inherited there for centuries, so power was not granted to anyone. But when a leader was chosen, everyone had to follow them to their death, even if they didn't share their ideals. He didn't mind following someone to their death, as long as they shared the same aspiration: a better world.

Lies! The little voice got so loud that for a moment he thought someone had entered the chamber. *You wouldn't risk your life for anyone! All you care about is yourself!* His demons didn't let him fool himself. But deep down he believed that he would put aside his self-centeredness when he found a suitable leader for this kingdom. The thought amused him sometimes. It sounded like the same answer he gave when asked why he had never married. *I haven't found the right one yet*, he always replied, laughing, knowing there was no *right one*, since he would always prefer to spend his nights with different women. The truth was that he could never really devote himself to a leader. Unconditionally supporting someone's aspirations and whims frightened him. *So, what should I do?* The question sat in the centre of his mind again, unwavering and unanswered.

Walter's army had reached Elmor, and perhaps the best idea would be to leave the city before the enemy's men reached its gates. *I need to talk to Elliot*, he thought. The boy had told him he could leave after reaching Wirskworth. But did he really want to leave? He put his face in his palms, closing his eyes. Elliot was the first man who had given him hope in decades—and he was only a boy, really. The lad moved a blade as if it were an extension of his hand. He was also courageous, incorruptible, and ready to give his life for those who stood by his side. He had seen all this with his own eyes. Intransigence and complacency had forgotten to touch this boy's soul, and experience had taught John that it'd be almost impossible to meet someone else like him for the rest of his days.

Elliot had much to learn and was still young, but his virtues were unique in these times. *He needs you*, the voice whispered in his ear again. He knew this, but it was impossible for him to decide if he should do something about it. Besides, he was among allies he didn't trust and in a city full of pain and rage for the death that had befallen it, death it blamed on Iovbridge. Moreover, he feared how many enemy spies were on Elmor's soil. That guard of the Sharp Swords wasn't the only rat in the city, and Walter's story was stained with countless spies. *How many more of them were there in Wirskworth, and how many would try to kill them even in their sleep?* John felt himself getting dizzy with all these thoughts. He was sure they would drive him crazy in the end.

As he moved to sit and calm himself, a knock sounded on the door. Before he could call out, the door opened, slamming the wall with force. Elliot stood before him, a long sword hanging from his woollen belt. This sword wasn't the one he had carried on their journey. John assumed that the men of Wirskworth had supplied him with a better blade, certainly better than those they had in Iovbridge these days. The old mines in Wirskworth, situated in the bowels of the rocky mountain range upon which the ancient city of elves was built, were well-known for the good-quality steel, silver, and gold ore they contained.

The lad's gaze seemed uneasy, accompanied by a good dose of anxiety he was artlessly trying to hide. "One would say your plan worked, Elliot," he quipped.

Elliot smiled. "True, my friend."

John felt even worse at that.

"I was wondering if you were all right, John," Elliot spoke again after a few moments.

John hesitated—his mouth was dry, and words wouldn't come out. Elliot peered at him, seeming to see something of the truth. He took a step into the room. "I know you're scared, John. I know you never wanted to fight or be in a city in danger of being besieged," he said softly, without a trace of anger in his voice.

"I'm not afr—" he began, but he stopped mid-sentence. Fear was a better answer than saying that he was nothing more than a guide and that their journey had come to an end.

"I remember our agreement," Elliot said, again as if reading his thoughts. "You would never fight on my side but only lead me to Wirskworth. Once I reached the city, you would have fulfilled your duty."

John watched the young man intently, and a wave of surprise swept over him when he realised that Elliot didn't look either angry or disappointed. "I just..." He couldn't utter a word, for heaven's sake!

"John, you are free to leave whenever you want, but..." The boy couldn't say what he wanted. John gave him a gentle smile, hoping to encourage him. "But I need you," admitted Elliot. "Your knowledge and advice about the kingdom are invaluable to me, and I will need both until the last moment. I want to ask you to stay in the city, and if the enemy retreats, return to Iovbridge with me."

Elliot had surprised John more than a few times—now he was astonished. Need? No one had ever needed John Long Arm.

"I understand that this may—" stammered the boy.

John cut him off. "I'll be by your side, Elliot." His words were rich with determination, a sound foreign to him.

Elliot took stock of him and was about to say something but stopped. John thought he saw emotions brimming in that face, then Elliot nodded sharply and took a step toward John and clapped him on the shoulder. "I won't disappoint you," he reassured him. He turned around and left the room before John had time to comprehend what had just happened.

As the door closed behind Elliot, John took a few steps and sat on the bed in a daze. He had said he would stay. His mind replayed the scene over and over, and a question took root in him. How could he have said such a thing without the slightest hesitation? He had never cared enough to stay. Anywhere. With anyone. Had he meant it? *Maybe I just didn't want to upset him*, he thought, but deep down, he knew the truth. He suddenly felt like Elliot was the son he never had. No one else had appreciated his words or thoughts, no one else had ever really needed him, and while he had devoted his life to the pleasures of the mind and flesh, he now felt that he had found a real purpose. "I'll be by your side, Elliot," he repeated slowly to himself, trying to memorise the words that had left more of a mark on him than an entire lifetime of naked cavorting, pirating, and telling stories, fictional or true.

"Have I made the right decision?" he whispered to himself. *You made the decision that your heart wanted and not your mind*, his conscience answered, and then he finally realised why his voice had rung with such conviction.

The Dance of Blood

Later that day, Elliot found himself wandering Moonstone once again, as the governor had asked for his presence in a chamber he didn't know in the western tower. The man who had informed him of Syrella's bidding had instructed him on the direction he should follow. Long Arm's words were still fresh in Elliot's mind, warming him, but he was troubled by what the governor might want with him. His act against Edmund had angered Syrella that same morning, and the news from Myril had prevented her from announcing her decision. He was concerned that the day's events had changed many things, and that perhaps Syrella wanted to hold him responsible for what had happened.

It was now dark. The moon had made its appearance in the sky. Elliot watched his reflection in the windows he passed, thinking of Walter until he found the room he was looking for. Elmor's emblem was carved on the wooden entrance. He took a deep breath and knocked.

Elliot entered when bidden and saw the governor was seated at a table, with her daughters and niece on her right. Beyond them, General Jahon was looking over a stack of parchment, while Sadon Burns sat, holding a cup full of wine.

"Ah! You have finally arrived," Syrella said lightly.

He was surprised to find most of the counsellors were absent and by the finery they all wore—gems and cloth far more expensive than their usual fare. Linaria wore a light pink silk dress, and her hair was combed and shiny while Merhya wore a fig-coloured dress full of colourful rubies around her bust. Moreover, the governor was dressed in the colours of Elmor's emblem, a diadem crowning her head. The shades in her dress matched her dark skin. Lord Burns wore a golden silk jerkin and a cloak as black as a crow's feathers. Jahon wore a blue tunic and a black-and-yellow cloak with two crossed swords hung behind his back. Finally, Elliot's eyes fell on Velhisya. Her dress was sewn with gold thread and what looked like thousands of rubies. Her shiny, silver-blue hair made her look like a fairy. He swallowed and tried to catch her gaze, but she didn't even glance at him.

"I wanted to talk about the city's defence as long as Walter is outside my gates," Syrella began. "Maybe you could help. That would be more useful than throwing swords at my counsellors." Her eyes sparked with controlled anger.

Elliot looked at her in surprise—he hadn't expected to hear anything of the like. Syrella had insisted that only she and her counsellors would decide on Wirskworth's defence. Elliot glanced around the small room. A large wooden table covered with parchment was lit by a few candles, and a round plate of pears stood decoratively in its centre.

"One would say the council has been diminished," mumbled Elliot.

"A few days ago, one of the men in my guard almost set Reynald free. Do you think we should keep every lord in Elmor informed of our plans?" responded the ruler.

"A wise decision," he remarked.

"Only those people of Wirskworth whom I fully trust are in this room," she went on. "The city's army has about ten thousand men, and every lord of Elmor has left his men under my command. Lord Burns has the most."

Elliot had momentarily forgotten that they had never obeyed all of Thomas Egercoll's decrees in Elmor. He knew that the ruler had allowed the region's lords to keep their men under their command, while they had vacated their castles for Wirskworth. He would bet the lords of Elmor didn't pay the taxes required to own those men. In truth, he didn't find Syrella's decisions in this matter prudent.

"These men belong to you, my dear lady," Lord Burns spoke, his voice melancholy.

She gave him a warm look. "General Jahon is the commander of the Sharp Swords, Elmor's army, and the City Guard. The City Guard will be on constant alert, and my daughters will assist him with the command of the soldiers," Syrella concluded vigorously.

Elliot observed Jahon and Lady Syrella's two daughters. He had understood that Jahon was the supreme commander of Elmor, and his responsibilities were the same as those of Isisdor's new lord of the knights. Nevertheless, the ban on the institution of knights had left him with the title general, like Peter Brau, before the queen's new decisions. What's more, Syrella's daughters were the captains of Elmor, and the rest of the ruler's council seemed to consist only of lords bearing the title lord counsellor and the high priest. Elliot was aware that Elmor's council didn't much resemble that of Iovbridge.

"All we need is patience," Elliot exclaimed, thinking at the same time that Syrella could now appoint knights in her region after the events in Iovbridge. "Even with all his forces, it'd take Walter months to take this city with a proper siege, and he doesn't have the time or the resources to conduct one. If his cavalry approaches, our arrows will stop them. As for the gate, it'd need thousands of men to fall." He remembered the snakeheads ready to spew oil.

"What if Walter manages to enter the city?" Lord Burns' soft voice reached his ears again.

"That would be impossible," Elliot said. "He has no siege engines, nor did he travel here to besiege the city. He knew from the beginning that if Elmor refused the queen's call, all he could do was let some soldiers patrol Wirskworth until he took the throne. He believed that the region's land would be rich enough in crops to feed his men for a long time," he concluded.

"Many in the past believed that many things would be impossible for

Walter Thorn, but he proved them wrong," protested Lord Burns.

Elliot took a deep breath. "If Walter's men manage to enter the city, we'll hold the battle at the gate. The width of the gateway will prevent the riders from attacking in large numbers. Thus, they will lose the advantage of their numerical supremacy."

"Right," Lord Burns acquiesced. "And our men will be able to defeat Walter's Ghosts?" He had let all doubts hang from Elliot's words in an exemplary manner.

"I guess not," Elliot replied without a trace of hesitation.

"Therefore, I go back to my original question—what will we do if Walter manages to enter the city?" repeated the lord.

"We will fight, and if we don't manage to stop the enemy, we'll burn the lowest layer." His voice came out hoarse, as if he were trying to sound older. "We will stack straw around the gate, while civilians will be transferred to Wirskworth's highest hills. The fire won't make the leap to the higher levels."

Syrella's nostrils flared and Lord Burns struck the table with a fist. "Have you lost your mind?" he hollered. "Do you want our soldiers to be burnt? Even if we do that, Walter will kill every man, woman and child left in this city."

"If Walter gets in, he won't spare anybody's life no matter what we do, my lord." Elliot raised his voice. "He won't like being forced to postpone taking the throne, and he won't allow Wirskworth to ever get in his way again if he gets the chance. His history has shown that he doesn't spare the life of civilians from the regions of his sworn enemies," he continued vigorously. "Nevertheless, if we burn his men, he'll remember the snake's end with terror, even if he's not near the battle. And if he's in it, our death will be a small price to pay for such a great victory."

Lord Burns seemed not to believe his ears, but Syrella didn't look angry. He thought he saw curiosity and admiration in her features.

"Where will you be if Walter's men manage to get past our army, behind the gat—"

"I'll be dead," Elliot butted in.

He knew what Burns was trying to do—prove that Elliot wanted to sacrifice their soldiers to fight the enemy that he himself had brought to their doorstep. Of course, Burns himself would take no part in any fighting, instead observing the carnage from afar. He had not accounted for Elliot choosing to be in the thick of the fighting. If the gate was engulfed by the blaze, Elliot would be enveloped in flames along with all the rest.

"Very well," rasped the governor.

Elliot glanced at her and thought John was right once again—Syrella Endor valued his opinion. Otherwise, she wouldn't have asked for his presence in this small council. He had foreseen the enemy's every move in the plan he had confided in her during their first meeting. Over the years, few had managed to predict Walter's moves. And while she might not be able to publicly approve of his confrontation with her high priest, he was quite certain she recognized skill when she saw it and could privately admire his audacity.

"The City Guard will be vigilant until Walter leaves Elmor's land. Double the numbers of each watch." Jahon took the floor. He had remained silent up to that point.

"We must be careful during the nights. Walter might try to use his favourite Ghosts to assassinate my aunt," Velhisya spoke for the first time.

"The watches on the towers' ramparts will be constant," came Linaria's reply.

"The walls are very high and quite smooth. It'd be impossible for anyone to climb," Elliot said softly. Velhisya opened her mouth as though to argue, but he went on, ignoring her glare. "Walter sends his Ghosts to assassinate when he is certain he can install a loyal ally in the victim's place. Elmor has sworn enmity against him, and no ruler could persuade the people of this place to side with him without provoking a rebellion."

The governor gave him one last look and, nodding sharply, got up from her chair, ready to leave the small room.

"One moment," Elliot insisted. "There's one more thing."

"This is not the time to talk about Sophie Delamere's request," Syrella snapped back.

"Of course not," he acknowledged. "But that wasn't what I had in mind."

The ruler crossed her arms, waiting for him to continue.

"Walter is smart and experienced, and he knows well that it'll be impossible to enter the city with his cavalry only. The lack of food on Elmor's land will ruin all his plans, making his journey a waste of time. Not being able to do the slightest thing to hurt Wirskworth's armies will infuriate him."

The governor didn't seem to understand.

"I'm sure he will try to enrage you and make you fight him outside of the city," Elliot said. "You must not let him do that."

The ruler held his gaze and then nodded after a moment. "You have my word," she said. "We must go. They've been waiting for us in the great hall."

"I'll go back to my chamber."

Syrella glanced at him once more as her daughters and niece got to their feet and joined her at the door. "Dance is one of our oldest traditions, Sir Egercoll. I say you should honour us with your presence. Your companions from Iovbridge will be there—I sent my men to inform them."

Elliot had no idea what she meant. "Dance?" he asked falteringly.

"Naturally," she responded. "Follow me."

Syrella walked out of the room with the rest following her. *Dance?* Elliot wondered. The governor led them to Moonstone's great hall. A stately melody reached his ears as they approached the entrance to the room. He frowned at the sight of dozens of people dancing in the centre, wearing elegant clothes. *A dance just before the enemy reached their doorstep? Elmor's people are insane.* He had never seen such a dance before. In his village, men and women would dance in a large circle, holding hands, while drunken, old-man Singar would sing out of tune to celebrate the arrival of spring.

The governor walked to the centre of the great hall, and Elliot watched the magical spectacle. The animal trophies had been removed from the walls and replaced with red and gold textiles. The lanterns and torches that lit the place looked golden red, as though the people danced inside a volcano full of lava. Elliot noticed that the ornate ceiling now looked black and red above the bright flames, while even the starry sky outside the large windows seemed to have a cherry hue.

Hundreds of people lined the walls and corners of the room as countless pairs of dancers twirled airily in its centre. Elliot noticed that many of Wirskworth's ordinary people were watching the spectacle reverently from their corner of the room, while lords and nobles danced gracefully before their eyes. For a moment, Elliot felt poorly dressed—he had been wearing the same brown jerkin since morning.

The attendants moved aside as soon as they realised Syrella was present. Elliot recognised several nobles as well as men of the Sharp Swords in the centre of the hall. The two large snakes coiled around the ruler's stony seat seemed to have joined the cavorting crowd, flashing in the light. He watched those dancing. The women wore soft silk dresses, and their partners wore expensive jerkins and cloaks. Minstrels played wooden harps. The slow melody was reminiscent of a dirge. Elliot's gaze fell upon the dancers. Their dance was artful. The men had one hand behind their back and held their partner's hand with the other. The couples danced in a circular motion round the floor.

Elliot's eyes then fell upon his companions at the far end of the hall. Morys and Selwyn smiled broadly when they saw him as Eleanor stood beside them watching the dance. She looked gorgeous in her white dress and her raven-black hair falling to her bosom. The two men were much better dressed than Elliot in their sophisticated scarlet jerkins.

Elliot approached them. "The decor reminds me of—"

"—blood," Morys finished off. "One of Elmor's oldest traditions is the Dance of Blood," he explained. "It is custom before any battle on this soil. This dance is an early tribute to those who will shed their blood in battle."

Elliot was flummoxed. "But if Walter retreats to Ballar, no blood will be shed."

"It doesn't matter," deflected Morys. "The people of Elmor had this tradition before moving to Knightdorn, back when they lived on Kerth's soil. Before any battle or siege, the tradition was honoured, even if no blood is shed. Don't forget, the ruler may yet decide to march her army to Iovbridge, and then many will shed their blood."

"It's a strange tradition," Selwyn remarked.

Elliot looked back at the young Brau. Something seemed to have changed about him in recent days. He could swear he saw a trace of sadness mixed with fear on Selwyn's face.

"I'm glad to see you, Elliot," said Eleanor happily, having just noticed him.

"As am I."

The young woman laughed playfully and hugged him. Elliot searched for John when a loud voice made him turn around abruptly.

"Morys?"

A woman, two young girls at her side, was looking at Morys searchingly.

"Good evening, Mother," whispered Morys, lowering his gaze.

The woman stared at him a moment longer, then ran to him without warning and hugged him. Morys seemed surprised by her reaction, but he reciprocated her embrace. The two girls approached and hugged him too, tears streaming down their cheeks.

"Where is Father?" stammered Morys.

The woman's face grew still and she hesitated, then said, "Your father... your father is dead." More tears began to flow from her brown eyes.

Morys swayed slightly, and the blood drained from his face. "How?" The word came sharply out of his mouth once he regained his composure.

"A stableman tried to rob the house where your little sister was with... with—" The words wouldn't come and Elliot thought he understood. Morys had told him that his mother had difficulty speaking of the mistress with whom his father had had an illegitimate daughter a few years ago.

"What happened?"

"They resisted and—"

"The stableman killed them and ran away." One of the sisters spoke up, her voice steady. "Father went to visit them and found Irien dead with Reyna in her arms."

Morys had grown still, his face white.

His mother took up the telling again. "Eluard found a piece of the stableman's jerkin, torn off during the struggle. He recognised the pattern, found the man, and attacked him without informing the City Guard, and... and..."

"They killed each other." The girl finished the sentence.

Tears welled up in Morys's eyes. Eleanor reached for his hand and gripped it. Elliot felt overwhelmed with sadness, and Selwyn seemed more devastated than Morys.

Morys's mother hugged him again. "I'm really glad to see you again," she cried. "It was impossible for me to write to you, Morys. Wirskworth doesn't have enough men to use as messengers these days, and no one wanted to go to Iovbridge with the South Passage blocked off. I heard that you were in the city a few days ago, and I assumed that someone would have told you the news about your father," she carried on. "I hoped that you would come to see us."

"When did all this happen?" Morys asked.

"About two months ago."

Morys hugged his mother, and the two girls again. Elliot looked away, wanting to give them a semblance of privacy, and his eyes fell on the governor, who had thrown herself into the dance with Lord Burns as her partner. Around them, the tearful scene had attracted quite a few indiscreet sniggers.

"What matters is that we are together again," Morys said after a while, wiping away his tears. "I'm sorry for not having visited you earlier. My arrival was somewhat... eventful," he apologised.

"Don't apologise. Eluard would be proud if he saw us," his mother declared, trying to hold back her tears.

"Mother, I have the honour of introducing you to Selwyn Brau, son of Peter Brau, Lord of the Knights of Isisdor," Morys said. Selwyn gently stretched out his hand to the woman. "This is Eleanor Dilerion," he continued. Elliot tried to move away but didn't manage to do so. "Elliot..." Morys stopped short. "A queen's knight," he then ended hurriedly.

On the day of his arrival, Elliot had asked his companions, as well as those present in the great hall of Moonstone, not to reveal his identity. The truth was that Elliot had regretted his impetuous outbursts. He had already twice reneged on his promise to hide this information, as he had also divulged the truth in Ersemor. He didn't know if the governor, her counsellors and the men of Sharp Swords had kept their word, while it had been proven that a man of the governor's guard was a man of Walter's.

Morys went on to introduce them all. "This is my mother, Rohesya; my sister, Roheria; and my younger sister, Relenia."

Rohesya seemed amazed. "So, the rumours are true!"

Morys looked confused.

"The institution of knights!" Relenia exclaimed.

The man was clearly relieved. "Yes, there have been some changes in Iovbridge lately," he mumbled.

"So here you all are!" a voice was heard, and Elliot turned abruptly. John stood behind them, wearing an apple-coloured silk jerkin. He looked embarrassed but cheerful at the same time. "I know how ridiculous I look in this costume," he added with a smile.

Eleanor hugged him, Selwyn shook his hand, and Morys was quick to introduce him to his family. Elliot was glad to be with them.

"I have to admit your sister is gorgeous, Morys," said John, looking at Roheria. Long Arm hadn't heard of the loss of Morys's father, so he immediately turned his attention to the beautiful ladies before him.

"And very young, John." Morys sidled in, his eyes flashing. Roheria looked much like Morys and her soft features blushed at the sound of John's words. She had a sweet face and playful eyes. A young noblewoman would never take to heart the sweet nothings of a man like John. But they were in Wirskworth as envoys of the Queen of Knightdorn, and John's attire, along with the fact that he was sober, gave him prestige anew.

"I believe that the beauty of youth could comfort an old man like me in this dance," Long Arm said politely, extending his hand. The young girl blushed and took his hand while Morys looked away in despair. They soon disappeared into the crowd.

Eleanor tugged Morys's hand. "Maybe we too could—" She stopped mid-sentence. Morys seemed overwhelmed by the news his mother had just told him, but he smiled at her. He hugged his mother and younger sister once more, took Eleanor's hand, and the two walked into the crowd.

Elliot nudged Selwyn, who had remained quiet. For days, Elliot had been looking for an opportunity to talk to him. The young man turned to face him with tear-filled eyes.

"Are you okay?"

"Yes, I just..."

And then Elliot understood. Morys's loss of a relative had awakened in him the pain he felt for his brothers.

Elliot was about to say something, but Selwyn spoke first. "Did you want anything else, Elliot?" he asked somewhat hurriedly.

"Well." He hesitated since it was obvious Selwyn didn't want to talk at the moment. "No," he spluttered.

Selwyn looked at him for a moment, nodded curtly, and walked over to Relenia, who was talking to her mother. Morys's younger sister didn't look like the rest of the family. Her skin was lighter, her eyes the colour of honey, and her hair straight and shiny. She wore a silver necklace and a linen dress.

"Forgive me, Lady Bardolf," Selwyn stuttered, blushing as he interrupted the two women. "I would like to ask your daughter for this dance," he whispered, turning pink. "If she so wishes," he added hurriedly and stretched his hand out, bowing slightly.

Relenia looked him over. Unlike her sister, she hadn't blushed. A few moments later, she took Selwyn's hand and followed his lead.

The two rushed to the dancefloor, and Elliot was left alone to watch his companions swaying finely in step with the crowd.

"A knight from a poor family!" Rohesya walked over to him. "My son didn't mention your House's name. I assume that you don't come from nobility, young knight."

"It's true, my lady."

Rohesya looked at him strangely, as if she knew more than she was saying. "It was a pleasure meeting you. Now, if you'll excuse me, I'd like to find some wine." With these words, she moved away.

Elliot turned his attention back to the dance, catching sight of Eleanor's black hair and then John nimbly leading Roheria round the floor. The girl kept laughing. No doubt he was an entertaining partner. Elliot would never have expected a drunken and sloppy man like John to dance with such grace, yet the latter pleasantly surprised him at every opportunity. Out of nowhere, he felt a gentle touch on his shoulder.

"An Egercoll, alone among the crowd." Velhisya's blue eyes looked at him playfully. Elliot looked around, worried someone had caught the name. "Don't worry! Nobody would bother to eavesdrop on an elwyn's words," she said, needling him.

Elliot felt a sting in his heart. She wanted to blame him once again for acts that weren't his. She looked beautiful in her golden dress, but sorrow swirled inside of him because of her words. He felt an incomparable tenderness for her, but while he wanted to be near her, something inside him pushed him away. The time would soon come when he would face the man who had deprived him of everything, and he would give his first battle against pain and death. On top of that, doubts about his motives and aspirations emerged like shadows in every city he had visited. They seemed like weeds slowly and torturously eating through his flesh, through his skin. Velhisya was rude and cruel to him, but he didn't feel indifference or resentment when he saw her, only sadness.

"Forgive me, Lady Endor," he cried softly and turned to leave, but her hand suddenly grabbed his.

"I wanted to ask you to forgive me." Her touch was a gentle caress. "You are not responsible for what happened hundreds of years ago. I apologise for what I said."

Elliot felt his soul fluttering for a few moments, as if it wanted to fly. He noticed the white skin above her neckline, her slender arms and straight shoulders shining under the fiery light that adorned the room. He wanted to say something, but his mind had numbed at the sight of her.

"Would you like to dance with me?"

He hesitated. "Oh, I..." She looked at him in confusion. "...I don't know how to dance."

Velhisya smiled and grasped his hand. "A knight and a great warrior who trembles at the sight of a dance!" Her delicate features sparkled as she laughed.

"Maybe some other time," Elliot heard himself say. The terror that came over him at the idea of dancing was greater than his fear of the ensuing battle.

"No one in this room would really want to dance with a woman like me. I'd say you owe me this dance," cooed Velhisya in a soft tone that exuded more willingness than accusation. Elliot swore that no man could deny her anything she asked for. She may not have been sought after for a wife because of her mother's race, but her beauty was unique.

"It's not that difficult. Just follow my lead," she whispered and pulled him gently into the whirling crowd.

He followed her hesitantly, holding her hand, and felt as though all eyes in the room were pinned on them.

Velhisya guided him slowly, and they began to sway rhythmically to the melody. They had locked eyes, as if it were impossible for them to be separated, and then, for the first time in his short life, Elliot felt that nothing else mattered—war, revenge, Walter, they all seemed like a distant dream. All that existed in this world were those glowing, starry-blue eyes gleaming in front of him.

The Wooden Horse

Elliot gazed from an old window at the highest point of the Tower of the Sharp Swords. It would not be long before dawn would make its appearance. He was still thinking about last night. Velhisya had danced with him in front of all of Wirskworth, and his heart pounded every time her eyes came to life in his mind. He was tired, unable to remember the last time he had had a restful sleep. Footsteps roused him out of the flood of thoughts that preoccupied his mind.

"You look awful, Elliot," Eleanor said as she joined him at the window.

"The dance exhausted me," he responded, smiling.

Eleanor wore an orange linen dress.

She approached him and gently rested her hand on his shoulder. "Whatever happens, it's not your fault," she whispered softly.

He turned to face her, puzzled.

"I know you're afraid that the enemy may enter the city."

"I'm not afraid of dea—"

She cut him off. "I know. But you're afraid that your actions may bring death to others who had no say in your plan... You're also afraid that your plan may have brought death to Lord Hewdar's castle."

Elliot turned his gaze to the void. "My plan," he whispered. The secrets he bore, that he could not share with anyone, weighted on him, driving him into loneliness.

"Elliot, what you did was our only hope of preventing the throne from falling into the hands of the worst man the world has ever known," she insisted. "You are one of the few men who would give his very life to protect the people of Knightdorn. Few would have the courage to follow such a dangerous plan and risk their lives so many times. You look a lot like Sophie, so I believed you were telling the truth about your parents from the very first moment. Over and above that, you're not only compassionate and courageous, but you also have unique skills in combat and battle tactics. It may be that you're the king we need."

Elliot looked at her in amazement. That she would speak such words despite how much she loved Sophie...

"I would follow you to my death," she added, looking him straight in the eye.

Elliot's eyes filled with tears. The devotion and faith she had just shown were unprecedented for him.

He jumped, startled, as a war horn howled in Wirskworth. There, through the window and beyond Wirskworth—thousands of horsemen approaching the city. Elliot ran, Eleanor behind him, heading towards Moonstone's courtyard, where the view would be best. Syrella Endor was already there, her daughters and counsellors with her.

"It seems you were right," Syrella said, her gaze fixed on the movement beyond her walls. "The enemy army consists of only a few thousand cavalrymen."

White-tiger banners fluttered in the dawn light. Elliot watched as a golden chariot drawn by two sturdy horses passed in front of each rider, a white tiger trailing after. The driver of the resplendent chariot pulled on the horses' reins and looked up at the wall and the peak of Wirskworth. Walter Thorn's long blond hair shone as he reached out to stroke the white tiger stretching its huge body next to the chariot. Walter's hand drifted to the hilt of the sword hanging from his belt, and a flame of hatred erupted in Elliot.

Walter swatted at the flies buzzing around him, anger raging through him. He now understood the queen's plan. His men were hungry and exhausted, unable to find sustenance along the Forked River. Walter raised his hand, and a soldier dressed in black approached him. The Ghost's black visor covered every part of his face, making him look like a messenger of death. Only the Trinity of Death and the Ghosts wore helmets with these visors, along with black armour that covered every inch of their body. Walter believed this attire provoked fear in his opponents.

Walter looked at the high wall again, and his anger grew slowly but surely. He shouldn't have left Ramerstorm. His gaze wandered to Moonstone at the peak of the city. He could see tiny figures there, watching him. Syrella Endor, no doubt, and the fools who followed her. Soon, their blood would be flowing in his palms, thick and scarlet, like the blood of all those who had defied him. He smiled—his greatest gift was knowing his opponents' weaknesses. Walter turned to the Ghost. "Tell the men to set up the tents and prepare the wooden horses before it gets dark," he ordered, his voice rolling like thunder.

Syrella Endor was in her chambers in the Tower of Poisons, when the light of sundown sneaked into the majestic chamber through some wooden windows. She looked at the bed to her right. Its canopy was draped with red silk, and its base was made of oak. Shortly after, she advanced towards a high elm chair next to a round table and sat down.

Syrella wore a light grey linen tunic and had a black leather belt around her waist. In truth she preferred military attire over beautiful silk dresses that were better suited to a ruler.

She remembered duelling with her brothers since she was a little girl even though her father never wanted to see her with a sword in her hands. Her daughters had become like her, which gave her great joy. The two girls were belligerent, and while they were now almost twenty-five, they weren't married, indifferent to the weddings and majestic banquets most noble women dreamed of. Nevertheless, her dead husband was never a skilled swordsman. He'd hated battles and loved banquets and majestic celebrations. He had not been a brave man, and she had never truly loved him. Sermor Burns, son of Sadon Burns, was every inch a lord, and his father had been an ally of hers since she had suckled at her mother's breast.

Her father, Edward, had gladly accepted when Sadon offered to have his only son marry Syrella. The House of Burns was the most powerful in Elmor, second only to the House of Endor, and Edward had always set his sights on the union of those two great houses. Though her father had married a woman of humble descent purely out of love, he hadn't sought the same for his daughter. Syrella always believed that her father was lucky to have followed his heart in choosing a wife, and while she had hoped the same for herself, Edward had disagreed. After the unification of the kingdoms and the election of George Thorn to the throne, her father wanted his former kingdom united, which required strong alliances. Edward Endor was one of the rulers who hated the fact that George Thorn had been crowned King of Knightdorn.

"You will marry Sermor Burns," Edward had told young Syrella on a cloudy morning. *"I will appoint you as my successor for Elmor's rulership and will resign from my duties."*

She was stunned. *"But you have two sons."*

Prior to Thomas Egercoll's reforms in Knightdorn, the eldest son of every ruler in the kingdom inherited the hegemonic title of his father, and if there were no male descendants, the title was passed on to the ruler's oldest brother. Patrilineal succession dominated in Knightdorn for centuries, but every king or ruler had the right to abdicate, and appoint a successor, all of which had been disallowed after Thomas's decrees.

"Your brothers are courageous yet foolish too—you're the only one who

inherited my wisdom." Syrella's father was very ill, and words came out of his mouth with difficulty. The healers had said that he didn't have much time left, and that his disease was unknown to them.

"But father, Sigor is older than me, and no region in Knightdorn has ever been ruled by a woman. You cannot appoint me as your successor," Syrella had countered.

Edward's hair had whitened on his temples. *"Knightdorn's law stipulates that after my death, Sigor will take command of Elmor, but I have the right to appoint any successor I wish while I'm alive. The law doesn't prohibit me from appointing a daughter—only tradition does—and I couldn't care less about traditions."* He wouldn't take no for an answer.

"If I take over the rulership of Elmor, I'll probably be the last governor named Endor," Syrella had replied. She was only fifteen but knew that her sons and daughters would be named after her lord-husband's House.

"No!" Edward had insisted. *"Your children will bear the name of the House of Endor, and you'll remain the Governor Regnant of Elmor after your marriage. I have agreed on everything with Sadon, and his son shall abide by our agreement."*

"I don't like Sermor Burns." Syrella had looked at her father pleadingly.

He had given her a stern look. *"Listen to me. George Thorn is a bloodthirsty king. His reign will soon bring friction. Elmor must remain strong and united, and a union of our House with the Burns' is the best answer."*

"My brothers will hate me," Syrella had shouted in a last ditch attempt to voice her objection.

"It's not their decision to make, but mine." Her father was not about to back down.

Thus, fifteen-year-old Syrella obeyed and married Sermor. A few days after the wedding, Edward passed away, surrendering to his illness. Syrella may have been in the land of the living for a little more than fifty years, but she remembered very well what happened after her father died, about thirty-five years ago. George Thorn had killed several of Elmor's people at an Iovbridge feast, together with her father's only brother. The lords of Elmor were all outraged by the heinous act of the First King and asked her to revolt against him, but she knew that it'd be impossible to win a battle against the Crown without allies. Nevertheless, having long been on the lookout for a pretext to revolt against George's reign, the Egercolls immediately raised the banners of war, and most of the governors of Knightdorn followed them. A few months after her father's death, Thomas Egercoll sat on Knightdorn's throne.

The years passed and peace reigned in the kingdom for the first time in the Age of Men, but Syrella hadn't managed to become a mother for a whole ten years after her marriage. Syrella hated this period of her life; she had miscarried four times, and the healers came to believe she would never bring a child into this world until she got pregnant with twins. Merhya and Linaria were born, giving her the joy that her marriage never did.

Syrella's mind flew back to her brothers. Over the years, her House became smaller and smaller. Her older brother, Sigor, had had a son before her with Amelia Reis, but Amelia died at birth. Then Sigor and his only child, Henry, lost their lives at the Forked River.

Aside from that, her younger brother, Arthur Endor, had committed one of the biggest sins in Elmor's history. Arthur loved adventure and at the age of twenty-five, he had remained unmarried, indifferent to Elmor's noble girls. Then, he decided to make a trip to the Mountains of the Forgotten World. Her brother had always wanted to see with his own eyes if the legends about the Elder Races were true. So, he left Wirskworth and did not return for over a year. Syrella was certain he was dead as none of her men had managed to trace him. That is, until Arthur returned to Elmor's capital with a baby in his arms, a baby from an elwyn mother. The oldest race in the world may have known great glory several centuries ago, but in the Age of Men, the Elder Races were considered cursed and decadent. Edmund had suggested leaving the baby to the waves of the sea, saying that the God of Souls would curse Elmor if it grew up on its land, and Arthur had threatened to kill him if he ever repeated those words again. Her brother had loved Velhisya more than life itself. No matter how many times Syrella had asked him where her mother was and why she hadn't followed him to Elmor, he had never answered. Nevertheless, the Endors had tried to keep the truth about Velhisya's mother a secret. In Elmor, many suspected the truth about Velhisya since everything about her betrayed her lineage, but some believed that she was just a woman of extraordinary beauty.

Syrella kept thinking about her family. Shortly after Thomas's death and Walter's rise, Arthur died of the same disease as their father. Their mother too, had died many years earlier at Arthur's birth. Thus, Syrella, along with her daughters and Velhisya were the last with the blood of the Endors in their veins. Syrella loved Velhisya, ignoring the rumours about the Elder Races, while envying her younger brother. Unlike her, Arthur had had children with the woman he longed for, just like their own father.

For a moment, Syrella thought of her dead husband. She had never expected him to fight at the Forked River. However, she didn't know that Sermor was convinced they had a perfect plan and that he believed that a victory against this enemy with him near the battle, would confer tremendous prestige upon his name. So, on the day of the battle, her husband had decided to journey to the Forked River, confiding neither to Syrella nor to his father of his intent. He consequently met with a tragic death alongside her brother and her nephew, breaking her heart in two. She may never have loved Sermor but had never wished for him to die either.

It was common knowledge that many blamed her for the death that had enshrouded Elmor at the Forked River, though there were some who believed that it was a heroic act of bravery. Nonetheless, Wirskworth had one of the largest armies in Knightdorn with about twenty-five thousand soldiers before that battle, but now had no more than ten thousand. When Syrella conceived of the Forked River plan, she thought that Walter would line his men up outside Wirskworth to besiege it, so she deemed it wise to hide her armies behind the trees, east of the river. That way, her men would attack the enemy without warning, the latter not having anticipated an attack outside the city. Most of her counsellors, along with her brother and nephew, found the plan ingenious, though several soldiers thought it was dangerous. Jahon himself had disagreed with her, but she didn't heed his advice.

Syrella carried out the plan, but Walter's men were the ones who attacked at the Forked River unannounced and ravaged her army. The enemy's forces pushed her men toward the river and annihilated them. Then they left Elmor, not caring about besieging Wirskworth. Walter knew that Elmor had lost the best part of its power and that the soldiers left in the area were no longer a threat to him.

She pushed all her thoughts out of her mind and touched the long scar that dominated her face, a souvenir given to her by a stableman's son at the age of thirteen as she trained for battle. Her father was furious but hadn't punished the young boy since it was his daughter who had asked for the duel—and with steel weapons to boot.

Suddenly, the chamber door opened with a thud, and Jahon hurried in. He was wearing the black-and-yellow cloak with the two crossed swords, the emblem of the Sharp Swords guard, over his leather jerkin. His normally stern features were bright with drunken lust. Jahon ran toward Syrella and embraced her tightly, pressing his mouth to hers. His left hand started caressing her breasts, and his right hand slid down between her legs. She got up with a swift move, pushing him away.

"Have you lost your mind?" she roared like a she-wolf.

"I've missed you," he responded gently.

Syrella walked away from him. "We are at war, you fool! There are guards right outside this chamber."

"There is no one! I took care of it." Jahon smirked and approached her again, touching her sweaty thighs under her tunic. She surrendered to his touch, feeling desire awaken between her legs. She pulled him closer, grabbing his muscular arms. Jahon may have been close to fifty, but her passion for him had never been extinguished since the day they met. This man was her sin. Syrella had been in love with Jahon since she was a little girl, and while she had tried to love her husband as much as she had loved her general, she hadn't been successful. Jahon came from a poor family, and despite his skills in battle, her father would never have accepted him as her husband.

Syrella and Jahon were the only ones who knew that her children were not Sermor's. When Syrella fell pregnant by her general, it was the only time she didn't miscarry, and she took it as a sign. Jahon was for her what sinew is for a hyena, water for a mermaid, or the stars for the heavens. However, after Sermor's death, she never considered marrying Jahon, not wanting to arouse suspicion about their relationship. There were those in Wirskworth who whispered that she had always favoured the general.

Jahon caressed Syrella's hardened nipples under the fabric of her tunic. But then the temple bell rang out like a war cry, and they separated in a rush of breath and desire.

"What's happening?" she asked, still trembling.

"I don't know," Jahon said.

They both knew that the temple bells only rang on the occasions of noble weddings, feasts, celebrations—or when something terrible was happening. Yet Walter had just arrived in Wirskworth, and the fatigue of the journey, combined with the lack of food on Syrella's land, should have been enough to force him to let his men rest for this day. And as Elliot had predicted, he had no siege weapons.

Syrella raced from her chamber, Jahon following as they left the Tower of Poisons and headed for the temple on the middle level of the city. They crossed the narrow path of the Snail Road. The sunset's dim light gently touched the edges of the white stone on Wirskworth's noble towers, creating the illusion that they were on fire. They continued walking, passing some stables and barns until they reached the Brass Road. The streets were empty and Syrella and Jahon hurried across the commercial quarter in Wirskworth until they found themselves in front of the temple. She saw a throng jostling along the width of the portico, and all the while, the bells kept ringing.

Syrella glanced at the statue of the God of Souls in the centre of the portico as she climbed a few steps. This temple was every Governor of Elmor's last residence as well as that of every Endor ancestor who had lived on Wirskworth's soil. She ascended the crescent-shaped portico, discerning countless people on her way up. Both noble and ordinary people were huddled here and there, but her eyes fell on her counsellors. A few metres away, the men of the Sharp Swords seemed to be at a loss. Elliot, along with the other messengers who had arrived from Isisdor, were looking beyond the city, aghast with terror.

In her haste to get to the temple, Syrella had neglected to look beyond the walls. She did so now, and the spectacle froze her soul. Four wooden contraptions shaped like horses had been displayed before her gate, and each bore a naked body, bound, flesh pale in the light of the setting sun. She now understood why the high priest had decided to ring the bells. Lord Hewdar, she realized, fear clenching her stomach, and his wife and daughters. At her side, Jahon motioned, opening his mouth to speak, but Syrella saw it too—heavy weights dangled from each of their legs, pulling them down onto the pointed back of their wooden mounts. Stacks of weights waited nearby, to be added one by one until—Syrella swallowed. Until the wedge of the horse carved through flesh and bone and killed them.

Edmund's thunderous voice rang out over the sound of the bells. "Look at your handiwork, knight of Iovbridge!"

His eyes looked hard at Elliot. The people of Elmor began to shout war cries. Once again in their history, a Thorn would cover their land with a veil of horror.

Syrella's eyes were fixed on Elliot's—tears gleamed there. Walter's men began to tie more weights on the captives' feet, and the Hewdars' screams blotted out every other sound in the ancient city of the elves. A wave of hatred flooded Syrella's heart, so vehement that nothing could stop it.

Medusa's Revenge

Walter looked at the perfumed, flabby lord with the fat cheeks and sharp chin. He reminded Walter of a placid bear, curled up in a wooden chair as he was, with his boots trampling the woollen kilims spread around the tent.

"I haven't seen you in a long time," he said indifferently.

Walter had rested his sheathed blade on a round table. A few candles flickered next to the elaborate sword, imparting a subdued glow to the surrounds.

"You may not see me often, but you know I'm your faithful servant," came the flabby lord's reply. His voice betrayed fear.

"Only because you want to govern Elmor."

"Not just because of that," the man justified himself. "I never wanted Sophie Delamere on the throne, and the Scarred Queen was the worst thing that ever happened to Elmor. Any other governor would have supported your battle against Iovbridge."

"Then why did you marry your son off to her?" countered Walter.

"I didn't know," admitted Sadon Burns. "I had no idea who she really was, so many years ago."

"You knew her father was an opponent of the First King and that an Endor would never side with a Thorn."

Burns quailed where he sat. "My lord, I couldn't have known what the future would bring, nor how foolish and narrow-minded she would turn out to be once she saw who the Egercolls really were."

"I would have expected you to blame me for your son's death," Walter remarked, ignoring his words.

"No," came the lord's reply. "You were not the one who betrayed me. All soldiers kill their enemies in battle. You and your men could not have known that my son was at the Forked River. Besides, you didn't even know what he looked like."

"Do you think they betrayed you?" Walter started removing his clothes, preparing to get into a wooden tub filled with hot water. He'd confiscated it from Hedwar's castle and lugged it to Wirskworth, determined to enjoy some measure of luxury.

"Of course, that whore always wished my son dead!" Sadon choked on his voice. "I had for a long time suspected that she didn't love Sermor. Finally, a few years ago, I saw her, with my very own eyes, in Jahon's arms." His fat cheeks had gone red with rage.

Naked, Walter slipped into the tub. "Are you sure that the Scarred Queen persuaded your son to fight at the Forked River?"

"Everyone knew that my son was not a warrior. He never fought in a battle," Sadon muttered in a daze. "I'm sure the whore persuaded him to fight, filling his mind with nonsense about the glory of victory. Even if she claims she was ignorant of his decision, I know she's lying. She always wanted him dead so she could stay with her lover."

"Yet you were the one who informed me about the Scarred Queen's plan. You sent my men to the place where your son was, ready to fight."

"I told you about the plan because I wanted you to put an end to the Endors' rule in Elmor. I was sure my son would be in the city and not on the battlefield. When I found out, it was too late... After the whore's failure, I thought the whole of Elmor would rise up against her. But I was wrong... Wirskworth must be completely destroyed for me to convince its people and council that the Scarred Queen doesn't deserve to lead this glorious land."

"Do you really think that Syrella Endor sent your son to the Forked River, where her brother and nephew were, intending to lead him to his death?" Walter wondered.

Sadon waved his hands about as if trying to chase away an annoying fly. "I'm sure she planned his death. Even if her plan had worked and her men had attacked your armies from behind, they'd have left Sermor unprotected in battle, ensuring his death."

"Your own granddaughters have the Endors' blood in their veins." Walter spoke in a pleasant tone; he enjoyed the suffering of the man before him.

"I told you they're not my granddaughters," Sadon said, puffing up his chest. "They don't look like my son—I know the whore has been screwing Jahon for years. Unfortunately, the Endors have enormous power in Elmor. Even if I'd revealed the truth, no one would have revolted against Syrella, and my own life would have been in more danger than hers. Elsewhere, I could have revealed her secret, and they would have punished that whore by impaling her. But in Elmor, a whore and her bastards have more power than anyone else."

"I always wondered why you never told your son the truth about Syrella and her lover. And why didn't you tell him about the plan or that you had sided with me and ask him to swear allegiance to me?"

"Sermor had a big mouth. I was afraid he'd reveal something. And if he had accused Syrella of adultery, he would have been killed," the lord muttered.

Walter stared at him for a moment. "I know you want me to kill the Scarred Queen and her daughters, to leave Elmor in your hands—"

Sadon stayed silent.

"—but I feel that you have no devotion to me, Knightdorn's true king," Walter went on. "The only reason you're helping me destroy the Scarred Queen is because you want to avenge your son and rule Elmor yourself."

Sadon seemed to muster all his courage. "I have always respected the magnitude of your strength, Your Majesty." His voice was barely audible. "For years, I've wanted Elmor to follow you in the battle against Delamere and you to sit on Knightdorn's throne."

"Why are you here?" Walter queried.

"To help you, of course," replied the lord. "I wanted to give you information, as I've been doing for years, sending you letters."

"I hope no one saw you leave the city tonight."

"No," Sadon insisted. "I know better than anyone how to slip out of the city."

Walter decided to believe him. Sadon was too scared to lie. "I don't think you can help me enter Wirskworth, kill the Scarred Queen, and destroy her army. Without siege weapons, I won't be able to break through. All you can offer me is a truce with Elmor so that they don't get involved in my fight with Iovbridge." He felt anger at this admission.

"I tried, but Syrella refused," Sadon confessed. "Besides, the Scarred Queen thought of fighting you outside the city, lining up her men near the walls. I was sure that many would disagree with her plan, so I called her words into question, not to arouse suspicion."

Walter smiled at that. Syrella Endor seemed to be truly foolish. "Will Elmor send its armies to Iovbridge when I leave?" he asked.

"The ruler hasn't yet made her decision, but I'm almost certain that she'll follow their call."

"Naturally. It was my mistake marching to Elmor," mumbled Walter. "But it doesn't matter. I will set off for Ballar at first light, and in a few days, I'll take the throne that belongs to me, killing every man of Isisdor and Elmor!" he added. "Nevertheless, if the Scarred Queen had accepted the truce you suggested to her, how would you have taken over Elmor's rulership?"

The question seemed to surprise Sadon. "I would wait for you to take the throne and force her to leave her office with some charge of treason. After all, once you wear the crown, you can change any of Thomas's laws."

"Elmor and its ruler would never obey my laws."

"Then you'd have the right to attack Wirskworth, and after the death of Syrella and her supporters, you could let Elmor appoint a new governor."

Walter grinned again. "Even with Syrella dead, do you think Elmor's council would choose you as the new governor? Medusa never ruled Elmor, and the ruler has daughters." He enjoyed speaking of the House of Burns' emblem with a note of disdain. "In this region, people like to be ruled by the Endors, even by the women of their House—they would hardly support a ruler who would side with me, especially after Syrella's death."

"Once she dies, I will spread the truth around. No one is devoted to her daughters—only to her. With Syrella dead and Elmor conquered, they'll opt for whomever you wish. Fear won't let them do otherwise. You can even put a stop to the choice of the governors by a council vote, instating those of your liking in each Knightdorn region," Sadon replied.

"It's smart to give people the illusion that their opinion matters," Walter noted. "But don't worry, Sadon, I've given the rulership of several regions to the men I wanted over the years. Still, I'm wondering how you can help me right now. Any land with crops capable of feeding my army is too far from Wirskworth. If I ride with all my men toward fertile grounds, Syrella might get her men through Stonegate, heading to Iovbridge, and I won't be able to catch up with them before they cross through. I also can't let soldiers to patrol Wirskworth for days without food while I return to Ballar."

The lord took a deep breath. His thick palms seemed sweaty—Walter liked his fear.

"Wirskworth uses the Forked River's waters," Sadon said hesitantly.

Walter jerked upright, sending a wave of water down the tub, and looked intently at the man for the first time since he had entered the tent. "I thought the city's tanks were filled with rainwater. But rain is rare south-east," he mumbled, more to himself.

"The Forked River is the main source of water for Wirskworth and the City of Heavens. The basements of Wirskworth have a dam, built in the time of the Elder Races." Now Sadon spoke boldly. "When the tanks are empty, the dam goes down so they can be refilled," he pointed out.

Walter nodded at him, feeling a pinch of excitement, and allowed him to go on.

"The water level is low, but in the disturbance brought on by news of your impending arrival, the governor and her counsellors have forgotten." A sardonic smile formed on the lord's ugly face.

Walter remained silent for a brief moment, then he stood up, got out of the tub, walked across the tent, and threw a tunic over his wet body.

"But if you conta—"

Walter cut him short. "I understand what you're suggesting. But if we were to wait for this plan to come to fruition, my men and horses would still be exhausted from hunger. The wisest thing to do is go back to Ballar and destroy Iovbridge and all its supporters, and that's what I will do. But there is more I want to find out from you," he said. "There are rumours that Wirskworth is hosting envoys from Iovbridge, messengers who managed to take the South Passage and arrived in Elmor's capital with Reynald in captivity. What do you know of this? And who gave the Scarred Queen the idea to pick every crop from her land? Who was waiting for me to come to Elmor?"

Sadon seemed frightened. "It's true, Your Majesty," he replied. "Some messengers from Iovbridge arrived with Reynald Karford as their prisoner. The conquest of Stonegate was such an important affair for Syrella that she gave a hearing to the travellers and considered Isisdor's request." He grew pale. "The plan for Elmor's crops was suggested by one of that party, a boy named Elliot, yet it wasn't written in Delamere's letter which only called for an alliance with Elmor.

"And Syrella listened to this boy?"

Sadon nodded. "Elliot confided the plan to her and the council, implying that his words were his queen's words though they weren't in the letter. The boy told us that it was probable that you would march to Elmor, wanting to prevent its involvement in the battle for Iovbridge. He believed that by sending you the Sword of Destiny, you'd be convinced that Elmor was about to send men to Isisdor and that'd make you head south."

"How did Reynald fall?" Walter asked angrily.

"Elliot defeated him in single combat—a boy that Delamere knighted in her letter."

"A boy managed to defeat Reynald? An unknown boy was honoured with a knightly title?" *If nothing else, the Stonegate messenger told the truth.*

"A lot of peculiar things have happened in the last few days." Sadon lowered his voice. "The Crown restored the institution of knights, naming Peter Brau Lord of the Knights of Isisdor and knighting that boy. Karford himself didn't deny the defeat. Also—"

"Also?"

"Also, the boy claims to be the son of Thomas Egercoll and Alice Asselin."

It was as if time had stopped. Walter stood still. "How did this boy get to Iovbridge?" he asked in a calm voice.

"He told us he grew up in a village a few miles away from Iovbridge and was trained by a Master whose name I have never heard before," said Sadon. "He also said that he arrived in the capital some time ago for the first time, as he didn't want his name to be revealed in the kingdom before he was ready. His Master's name was Roger Belet."

The steel of the Blade of Power was unsheathed in a flash and touched the juicy flesh on Sadon's neck. Walter punched the man in the jaw with his other hand. "If I find out that your words are false, I will feed your limbs to the dogs."

"My lord... Your Majesty...," Sadon pleaded, groaning in pain. "I swear to you, those were his words," he whined. "And on top of that, a man of the Sharp Swords was presented with the opportunity to kill him, but Reynald saved the boy."

Walter frowned and drew back. "William tried to kill the boy, and

Reynald killed him?"

"I don't know exactly what happened, Your Majesty," Sadon cried. "Elliot claimed to have heard noises during the night and found William trying to free Reynald. But William ferreted the boy out and was about to kill him when Reynald cut his throat, saving the boy's life."

Walter withdrew the sword from the man's neck and remained pensive for a while.

"Why didn't you order William to kill the Scarred Queen, Your Majesty?" asked Sadon.

Walter looked at him disdainfully. "William began to serve me after the battle on the Forked River. Elmor was full of discord after that battle, and it no longer had any intention of helping Iovbridge. Why would I kill its ruler and turn the entire region against me? It'd be impossible for Elmor to be governed by an ally of mine after a fraudulent assassination of Syrella. Elmor won't bow to me until I've sown death throughout Wirskworth, cowing them into submission." Walter paced the tent for a moment. Nevertheless, William would never be able to kill the ruler. The Scarred Queen is never guarded by one man only, and her general even checks whether her food is poisoned. William was the one who gave me all this information. It was useful to have a guard near Syrella under my command, even if he couldn't kill her," he added. "But I wonder why news of the existence of a descendant of Thomas hasn't reached every corner of Knightdorn... Iovbridge would have rushed to spread this truth, trying to attract allies to its ranks."

"Elliot told us he hadn't revealed who he was to Sophie, fearing word would be out sooner than he wanted."

Walter fixed Burns with a stare. "Is there anything else you should tell me?"

Sadon nodded weakly. "Master Thorold is alive."

"Impossible," Walter growled.

"Nobody knew. The messengers from Iovbridge informed us that they had found him in the City of Heavens. He has survived all these years and stayed there, keeping it a secret that he was alive."

Walter moved away, lost in thought. Everything had finally been revealed, all the conspiracies they had set up behind his back all these years. He would kill them all. And they'd suffer so much that they'd wish they had died years earlier, rather than lived and plotted against him. If they thought he would go back to Ballar, having achieved nothing, if they thought they had defeated him, they were fools.

"Guards," he shouted.

Two Ghosts with masked faces entered the tent.

"Bring me the Trinity of Death and choose two thousand horses."

"Your Majesty, all our horses are exhausted," said a Ghost.

"Do as I say," he roared. "And let the men know that we're staying in Elmor. No one leaves Wirskworth!"

"But Your Majesty, there is no food on this land! We can't stay here!" the other Ghost spoke.

"You shall do as I say!" Walter screamed. "Any man who can't withstand his hunger is free to kill his horse, eat its flesh, and return to Ballar on foot." Then, he turned to Sadon. "Go back to Wirskworth and find a convincing excuse for your face," he shouted, indicated the growing bruise on the man's fat cheek.

Sadon Burns got up, his legs unsteady, sweat beading on his hairline, and rushed from the tent, pale as a ghost.

The Secret of Pegasus

Elliot woke up soaked in sweat, his dreams darker than ravens' wings. He wanted to get up but felt a pinch in his chest. For a moment, he thought he was going to vomit, but he managed to sit up, trembling. The screams of the Hewdars, dead because of him, still haunted him.

As the soft morning light licked his face, he noticed a large spider that had climbed on the window. Its long, slender legs moved slowly and carefully as if it were afraid of being attacked at any moment. Elliot sat on the hard mattress, watching it, until a loud knock on the chamber door made him jump up.

He got up and opened the door. He was confounded to see who his visitor was. Syrella Endor stood before him, grim, with black circles around her eyes. It was obvious that she hadn't been able to sleep.

"To what do I owe your visit, Your Majesty?" he said, startled.

The ruler hurried into the chamber and looked at him in a strange manner. Elliot didn't speak. Perhaps the Hewdars' loss had convinced her to throw him out of Wirskworth.

"I need to talk to you." Her voice had its familiar sharp tone. "As you can imagine, I have trusted men watching every move in the city, and when you informed me that Walter could march into Elmor, I doubled the number of informants."

Elliot didn't understand why she was sharing such information with him. "My lady, I don't understand—"

"Listen to me!" she ordered, and he obeyed. "My daughters, my counsellors... they all thirst for glory, for blood, or to satisfy my will, showing their devotion to the Governor of Elmor. But it's obvious, Elliot, that you have the courage of your opinion in front of any leader or nobleman, and while I don't know if you're telling the truth about who you really are, you've earned my respect. The plan you confided to me as soon as you arrived in the city was one of the smartest I've heard in years, and if it succeeds, it will be our best hope to fight Walter."

She paused for a moment. "I know this plan wasn't the queen's or her counsellors'. Iovbridge has never been so shrewd in all these years," she continued. "The reason I want to talk to you is because I need your opinion about some news that has reached my ears, and I dare say you're the only one who can advise me wisely at this time."

Elliot hadn't expected to hear these words from Syrella. Her words indicated that she had decided to send her army to Iovbridge. He gave an imperceptible nod, waiting for her to go on.

"My informants notified me that someone entered the city from an underground passage on its west side, which most Wirskworth residents don't even know about. The intruder had a key to the passage door, which was strange," she murmured. "My guards didn't recognise him, and he stole away as the watch changed, slipping out of sight before they could follow." Now, there was evident irritation in her voice. "I was told they caught sight of him at the last minute, while the intruder himself probably didn't even realise they had seen him."

"One of Walter's soldiers?" Elliot felt scared.

"I doubt that," came Syrella's response. "Even if someone knew of this passage, it'd be impossible to know the guards' watches or traverse it unseen, unless they had done it several times before. And only a man from Wirskworth could possibly obtain the key."

Elliot thought carefully—only one explanation made sense.

"I think someone from Wirskworth managed to get out of the city and they were spotted upon their return," she said, echoing his thoughts. "It would be impossible for an unknown soldier to approach me and kill me, but a man from the city, someone close to me, might try. I believe that this is possibly the intention of this traitor, and that's why he has come back to the city."

Elliot nodded, feeling the weight of the uncertainty that faced them—and of a secret.

"However, the truth is that everyone in Wirskworth knows that I'm always guarded closely, which would make an assassination attempt on me by a single man almost impossible," she carried on. "But even if the goal is not my assassination, maybe someone gave Walter valuable information and then returned to the city to continue his work as a spy."

For a moment, his Master's aged figure came to life before Elliot's very eyes. If Walter had uncovered the information Elliot feared, he wouldn't leave Elmor's land that easily. How could he have behaved so foolishly? "Who knows about this secret pass—?"

Syrella answered before he could finish his question. "My counsellors and some guards, along with the Sharp Swords. Yet, no man of the Sharp Swords was gone from the city even for a moment. I have spies watching them at all times after the incident in the dungeons..."

"Maybe the high priest," suggested Elliot.

Syrella breathed out wearily. "I doubt he'd have the courage to do such a thing. Much as you hate him, I don't think he would follow a man like Walter."

Elliot was in turmoil. Whoever left the city could have given Walter valuable information and remained there under his wing. His return showed that he had a further task to accomplish. Unfortunately, Syrella couldn't share this information with her council; if any one of her counsellors were the traitor, he'd be more careful if he knew he'd been spotted. Elliot was convinced that a prominent man from Wirskworth was the traitor, explaining Walter's faultless tactics at the Forked River's battle. He was certain that this man wasn't William of the Sharp Swords. The governor's personal guards didn't belong to her council, and whoever informed Walter of Wirskworth's tactics had done so days before the battle. Only a very trusted man would have known so much, so early. Clearly William was nothing more than a rat, informing on the ruler's guard and would only try to kill her if there was no other option. Just like Walter, Elliot knew that Syrella's assassination would unite Elmor. Walter had probably only used William to find out the details about who guards Syrella at all times.

"There's another thing," she suddenly said. "The guards at the city battlements informed me that about two thousand men left Walter's camp just before sunrise and that they rode along the Road of Elves, heading toward Elirehar."

Elliot felt a pinch of panic as he realised he'd made another mistake. "You're right, my lady. Only a man from Wirskworth could accomplish what you described. I believe that your guard must be doubled, and your family needs to be guarded as well. We can't know if the traitor only gave information to Walter or sought to carry out a murderous plot against you or other members of your family. However, I'm sure that the traitor has some ultimate purpose since he returned to the city."

Syrella nodded in approval.

"I must also leave the city as soon as possible," Elliot suddenly said with a note of haste in his voice.

Syrella raised an eyebrow. "Leave?"

"Walter has killed every Grand Master who ever lived in Knightdorn," he murmured. "I told the council that Master Thorold is alive. I don't know if the traitor is a man on the council, but if this information has reached the enemy's camp—"

Syrella's eyes widened for a moment and then she grew serious. "If you think Walter has led his men to the capital of Elirehar, you must stay here! You can't fight him in the City of Heavens. Its walls are weak, and its soldiers are fewer than five hundred."

"I have to make sure... If Walter went to Elirehar, I must save the Master," Elliot stressed. "I need to take him away from the capital. He's the last one left, and I think he knows—" Anxiety stopped his tongue.

"Assign your protection to your most trusted men. I'm going to need a fast horse," he said with determination.

Elliot glanced out the window of his chamber window in the Tower of the Sharp Swords. If Walter had started before dawn, he'd reach Elirehar before nightfall. He would have taken only the fittest and strongest horses after his journey from Ballar, and he wouldn't stop for a moment's rest.

"I will speak to your companions," said Syrella.

"No," Elliot said. "It will be safer for them to stay here."

The woman looked at him with pity. "You remind me of my little brother— brave and daring, but foolish. He always tried to protect others, forgetting about himself. No one can survive on their own, Elliot!" Her eyes searched his.

"It's dangerous—" He stopped mid-sentence. The image of a girl popped into his mind, a girl with blonde hair. "I must leave right now, and I must leave alone," he repeated.

"Very well," said the ruler. "I will order a horse to be prepared in the stables east of Moonstone. You'll leave the city through the Water Gate. You must ride south of the Forked River to avoid encountering Walter along the Road of Elves. It is our good fortune that the enemy troops are not near the bridge leading south of the river. You will cross carefully to get to the opposite bank, and the trees will help you ride to Elirehar unnoticed."

Syrella was right. It would be impossible for him to get to the south bank of the river if the enemy had set camp a little further east. He and his companions had used this bridge on their journey to the capital of Elmor, and he remembered its location. He nodded sharply, and Syrella glanced at him one last time, a hint of sadness in her eyes, before leaving the chamber.

Elliot put on his boots and secured the breastplate he had procured from Iovbridge over his chest. He then fastened a belt around his waist and sheathed the sword that the men of Wirskworth had given him a few days earlier. Finally, he threw the blue cloak of Isisdor over his shoulders and, with tousled hair, left the chamber. When he reached the stables, he found more people than he'd expected. Morys, Selwyn, John, and Eleanor had already mounted their horses and a young skinny stableman was holding the reins of a black horse. Annoyance overcame him as soon as he saw them, dressed in the same rigging they wore on their journey from Iovbridge. If nothing else, Syrella had informed them very quickly of what had happened.

"What are you doing here?" Elliot asked.

"We heard that you're leaving the city," came the reply from Selwyn.

"This trip might be my last, Selwyn," Elliot said, his voice sharp. He did not want them to risk their lives for him.

"I'm honoured to walk beside you," replied Selwyn.

"I promised to protect you." His gaze wandered to all four companions. "If we come across Walter, I won't be able to keep my promise."

"I'll be honoured to die by your side, Elliot," Morys said, his voice solemn and sure.

Elliot almost choked. He had no time for this. He had to leave as fast as he could. Walter would ride to the City of Heavens without pausing to rest. "You can't follow me! If you die and I survive, guilt will haunt me until the end of my days," he burst out. He searched Selwyn's face for the fear he had seen there in the past few days. It lingered in his eyes yet, but the young man seemed resolute.

"I'll follow you no matter what you say, Elliot," Eleanor chimed in. Elliot noticed that she had a bow and arrows on her back in addition to the sword hanging from her waist.

"As will I," Morys seconded.

"If you want to lead one day, you must know that a prudent leader never drives away those loyal to him." Long Arm's words were like a lance to his chest. He had never expected John to risk his life to follow him, but the man had surprised him yet again. Elliot wanted to shout that he had never wanted to lead, but they had no time to lose. *Damn you, Syrella,* he thought and mounted his black mare.

"We'll leave the city through the Water Gate and ride south of the Forked River," he spoke hurriedly, and his companions offered no comment or question. Apparently, Syrella had informed them fully. "We must leave Wirskworth quietly. Nobody must find out that the queen's envoys are leaving. It'll sound like we're running away. Morys, can you lead us there without drawing attention to us?"

The man nodded sharply and kicked his horse. They began to descend, passing through quiet alleys. Elliot turned his gaze and noticed the Temple of the God of Souls, visible from afar. The horses continued to gallop, whinnying as they descended towards the low hills of the city along deserted paths. The companions rode for a few moments until Morys suddenly turned his horse. The five riders passed through a portico hidden in a corner. The portico led to a tunnel that Elliot would never have noticed it unless someone showed it to him. They began to traverse the tunnel, the way growing dark. They were at the foundations of Wirskworth. Suddenly, Elliot felt his horse slip, and he pulled its reins hard.

"Watch out for the water." Morys's voice echoed around them.

Elliot looked more closely and then understood why the atmosphere was humid. A huge cistern was located inside the mountain on which the city had been built. Elliot glanced at the cistern—its water level was low. Likely there was an underground passage that allowed the water of the Forked River to fill the cistern every time it emptied, and this passage was probably blocked by a dam, raised when necessary. That was the only logical explanation, so that there was always water in a place where rain was rare. Their horses crossed the perimeter of the tank, and Morys stopped his horse abruptly. Elliot almost fell on him as his own horse stumbled.

"Dammit, Morys!" screamed Elliot, pulling the reins hard, his feet slipping from the steel stirrups.

"Sorry," the man apologised.

Elliot's eyes fell on a sliding gate, forged from steel. Its chains were placed in pockets with vertical grooves on the rocky mountain walls and then passed through a small winch.

"Who are you?" The guard's angry voice startled them, as the man had appeared out of nowhere.

"We want to leave the city," answered Morys, looking at the guard who had raised his sword.

The guard looked at them with suspicion. "The governor has forbidden anyone from entering or leaving the city. How did you find this passage?" he shouted.

"Let them pass, Yoren!" A panting man suddenly appeared behind Elliot and his party, running. "The governor ordered us to let them go."

The guard seemed peeved, but he went to the winch and started pulling the chain. The steel was raised with a rattling sound, and the five companions went through the arch, leaving Wirskworth.

The companions rode quickly along a cobbled alleyway, and the Forked River was immediately visible in front of them. They reached the bridge and crossed to the south bank, Elliot glancing regularly around him. He remembered that the trees on both sides of the river were quite dense, so the enemy wouldn't be able to see them.

The companions began to distance themselves from the city. They continued in silence for hours until the hot midday sun took the place of the soft light of dawn. Elliot didn't halt his mare for a moment, mud flying from beneath the horses' hooves as they churned the path next to the river. After a long stretch of the journey, the sun slowly began to disappear from the sky, and the moon appeared faintly in the dim light of sunset. The ground was slippery, full of slime, and countless leaves covered its brown mud. Elliot listened to the rustling of leaves and smelled autumn as they approached the City of Heavens, when a strange sound reached his ears.

"Stop!" he hissed, trying to keep his voice as low as he could.

The companions pulled their mares to a halt.

"Listen!" he cautioned.

At first there was only the sound of the breeze, but then a gentle splash reached Elliot's ears, while a faint voice, chuckling, he thought, filtered through the whirl of the wind.

Elliot rode toward the river, passing through some trees, and looked carefully. Some men could be spotted a little further off, on the opposite bank, and he heard a second splash. But the tree trunks were too close together to allow him a view of what the men were doing. Elliot put his finger to his lips, nodding at his companions to stay silent, and jumped off his mare. They were next to one of the wooden bridges leading to the northern bank. He remembered this bridge as it was the second closest to Elirehar's capital. He crossed the bridge in silence, each of his friends following one by one. The tree trunks were quite dense in this part, and the Road of Elves dominated a little further north. Elliot walked slowly among the tall trees as the voices grew louder. He came to a halt and tied his mare's reins to a small tree, his companions following suit, then ducked between a pair of gnarled trunks, kneeling to stay low and out of sight.

He peered through the gap in the trees, catching sight of men in scarlet cloaks and breastplates bearing the tiger. Walter's soldiers were by the river, carrying human corpses.

"The Scarred Queen won't expect this surprise!" A hoarse laughter resounded.

"Even the dead have their uses," called another voice.

He counted ten men. A battle with them could be fatal. They tossed another lifeless body into the calm waters.

"Who would've thought the Hewdars would be so valuable?" cackled a sadistic voice. "They gave us food and their prostitute wives, and now their rot will trouble the Poison Masters' stomachs."

Morys jumped out from behind the trunks, screaming. The soldiers spun to face him and froze, goggle-eyed. The closest drew his sword in time to block Mory's swing, and another raised a bow and arrow, aiming at Morys. An arrow whistled from Elliot's side as Eleanor let loose, piercing the archer's shoulder, and the bow slipped out of his hands.

"Take cover! There are more among the trees," someone shouted.

One of Walter's men ran toward Morys, and cries and howls sounded as the fight began. The soldier attacked furiously, but Morys avoided his blow and pierced him on the shoulder with the tip of his blade. The strike didn't punch through the armour, though, and the soldier punched Morys, who stumbled back, blood running from his nose as a second man rushed him from behind. Elliot leapt into the fray, shoving Morys out of harm's way, then sweeping his sword through the air to cleave the throat of the first man. His companion screamed and started brandishing his sword at Elliot. He turned his body, repelling the blow and plunged his sword through the soldier's open mouth.

Seven of Walter's men surrounded them, their swords raised, hatred on their faces. Morys had recovered, and he and Elliot stood back to back.

"There, behind the two trunks!" shouted one of the scarlet-cloaked soldiers, and two men ran toward Eleanor. Another arced his sword down on Elliot's head, who dodged and stabbed into the man's elbow, where a joint in the armor left him unprotected. The man screamed, and Elliot cut his throat. Elliot turned his head and in horror saw Morys running toward Eleanor, following the two men who had rushed toward her.

"NO, MORYS!" he screamed, but then a huge man attacked him, lowering his sword with tremendous force. Elliot moved swiftly, avoiding the blow, and struck the man's neck, severing tendons and arteries. The three remaining men hesitated now, clearly less certain their superior numbers would allow them to prevail. Their swords flashed in the subdued light of the growing dusk, and Elliot moved with tremendous speed, dodging and striking back at every opportunity. The clanging rang in the air. Elliot spun, his sword extended, and all three men fell lightly to the ground, their throats spewing blood, the hiss of their last breaths rustling like leaves in autumn. He turned and saw the two soldiers who had run toward Eleanor on the ground. An arrow protruded from one's skull while John drew his sword from the other's.

"What on earth were you thinking, Morys?" roared Elliot.

The man looked at him, panting, his nose still bleeding. "They were trying to pollute the river!" he replied. "They were trying to pollute the water of Elmor and Elirehar with our people's corpses! They didn't give them the slightest honour even after their death!"

Elliot tried to control his anger. "John and Selwyn were waiting behind the trees. If anyone managed to approach Eleanor, they would take them by surprise," he exhaled furiously. "Why did you run toward them, damn you? You left my back unprotected! If they had a second archer, you'd be dead! You were too far from Eleanor's field for her to protect you!"

Morys lowered his head humbly.

"Don't let your emotions carry you away! You are a soldier, Morys!" Elliot reprimanded him.

"Speaking of which, you didn't seem to need Morys's protection," murmured John, looking at Elliot.

A sound caused Elliot to spin with his sword raised. Selwyn emerged from between the branches, his face white with fright. Elliot turned his attention to the bleeding archer Eleanor had hit. The man was around thirty, short, big-nosed, with sparse hair. Elliot grabbed him forcibly. "What were you trying to do? Where are the rest of Walter's riders?" he shouted.

The man spat in his face, and Elliot punched him. "If you don't speak, I'll take to Wirskworth and subject you to the same torture as the Hewdars!"

Fear crept into the man's eyes. "Our king rode to the City of Heavens, intending to besiege it," he cried. "He also instructed me and nine other men to dump the Hewdars and their men's bodies into the Forked River to pollute its waters," he finished, panting.

"How long have you been here?" he asked.

"Long enough. We decided to rest for a while before returning to Wirskworth, and we threw at least ten bodies in the river. There were only two left."

Elliot's eyes saw two violated bodies near the river and felt a flame of hatred awaken inside him. "Which road did the other riders follow?"

"They rode north of the river, on the Road of Elves, heading toward Elirehar as fast as possible," whispered the man. "My lord strained the horses so much that they must have reached the City of Heavens by now. He also ordered some men to cut a large trunk by the Forked River last night. He wanted to build a battering ram." It was obvious that the wounded soldier was giving as much information as he could in an effort to save his life.

The man's words filled Elliot's soul with fury, and though the archer was unarmed and harmless, he couldn't contain his rage. His sword flashed, and the man's head fell to the ground with a thump.

"Selwyn, go back to Wirskworth! Ride as fast as you can and tell the governor that they need to fill the cistern at the Water Gate before the contaminated water spreads across the river." Elliot's words were sharp. "The rest of you, follow me or go back to Wirskworth!" He hurried to his mare.

"I want to remain by your side," Selwyn said.

"You swore to obey me. It's time to honour your oath."

Elliot mounted his horse and angrily pulled the reins. He heard his companions following him as he crossed the small bridge, heading south of the river again. He knew he had to walk this path. If Walter had arrived in the City of Heavens a while ago, they could possibly cross paths with him as soon as they approached Elirehar's capital, if they rode on the Road of Elves. The City of Heavens would fall quickly, and the riders would be on their way back to Wirskworth. Elliot intended to cross again closer to the city, after first scouting to see if the enemy was still there.

Elliot heard the hoofbeats of Selwyn's horse as the young man sped away in the other direction, and he continued on, the rest of the companions following him. The four horsemen tore through the wind, and darkness soon settled upon them. They continued for some time, anguish nesting in Elliot's soul. What would he face upon reaching the City of Heavens? The moon illuminated their path, filtering between clouds that had blown out of nowhere, and Elliot lost his sense of time until a strange crackling noise reached his ears. Elliot kicked his horse. He would soon see Elirehar's capital above the tall trees. The night seemed brighter, and Elliot understood why—the City of Heavens was ablaze, and the white clouds in the sky had hidden the black smoke.

Elliot's mouth went dry, and his heart began to pound in his chest as he watched the red hyenas swallow everything in their path. The low city walls looked like incandescent trunks, and the gate had been dismantled. He didn't hear any whinnying. The enemy had left once the work was done. Elliot crossed the bridge over the Forked River and rode toward the gate.

"ELLIOT! NO! COME BACK!" He heard John's voice, but ignored him.

He saw a pointed trunk lying next to the shattered city entrance. A dozen arrows appeared to the left and right, nailed to the barren ground, but none had found their target. Elliot scanned the scene. Hundreds of men lay dead behind the gate, their bodies strewn at unnatural angles. Elliot rode into the city as flames devoured everything in their path. He felt the heat envelop him as he headed for the Temple of the God of Life, next to Pegasus Castle. His breathing grew laboured, the air dwindling in his lungs, and he felt blinded by the smoke as he tried to reach his destination.

His horse seemed to slip, and Elliot held the reins tighter, trying to stay upright in his saddle. At last Pegasus Castle appeared before him through the smoky air, and he got off his horse, holding the reins tightly. The ground beneath him was wet, sticky even, and he reached down to touch it. His palm came back red with blood. He could see little through the smoke, but then heavy raindrops started beating on his head. The clouds had now covered the sky, like friends bringing aid, and the rain poured down on the flames that looked like fiery spirits dancing in the dark. The fire began to subside, but now Elliot could see the horror that had embraced the City of Pegasus once again. Men, women, and children lay dead in front of the Temple of the God of Life, stacked like slaughtered sheep. Many bodies were headless, and around the temple's entrance there were dismembered and burnt bodies. Tears welled up in his eyes, and he started coughing and vomiting as the downpour whipped his face.

A hand grabbed him by the shoulder. "We must leave." Morys tried to pull him away, but an agonizing scream echoed through the rain.

"NO, NO, NO!"

Elliot pushed aside Morys's hand and ran toward the sound, pulling his horse. The cry sounded again as he passed burnt out buildings.

"NO, NO!"

A small stone house with its wooden door knocked in smoked lightly, a few metres away from Pegasus Castle. Elliot tied his horse to a broken gate and ran inside, pushing aside the smashed door. Master Thorold had knelt on the ground, his hands clasping those of a young woman, blonde and dressed in blue. Selyn, Elliot remembered numbly. The dress had turned scarlet with blood, and there was a stab wound in her chest, level with her heart.

"Master Thorold!" he shouted.

The old man raised his head and glanced at Elliot, then turned back to the young woman, heedless of the smoke, the rain and Elliot's voice.

"Master Thorold!"

"NO, NO, NO!" the man kept screaming.

Morys, John, and Eleanor crowded into the house. Elliot leaned over Selyn. Her eyes were closed, and her face was serene and beautiful, as if asleep. He stroked her hair gently and noticed a knife by her side.

"SHE KILLED HERSELF!" Thorold shouted. "She chose suicide rather than fall into their hands, and I... and I... wasn't here to protect her!" Grief racked his body as he sobbed.

Struck by something he could not name, something he saw in the dead woman's face, Elliot grabbed the old man and lifted him to his feet.

"What are you doing?" John tried to restrain him, but Elliot pushed him violently.

"WHO WAS SHE?" screamed Elliot with all his might.

"Elliot!" Eleanor gripped his left hand but couldn't free the old man.

"YOU KNEW WHO I WAS FROM THE FIRST MOMENT! YOU RECOGNISED ME! WHY? HOW?"

Thorold didn't say a word, but his eyes filled with tears.

"I feel as if I know her. WHO WAS SHE?" He shook the Master hard, the old man's bones like a plaything in his hands.

"Your twin sister."

Elliot released his grip, no longer in control of his limbs. He knelt on the floor, his eyes filling with hot tears. Rage, stronger than ever, awakened in him. He felt anger and hatred enveloping him, drenching his body with an insurmountable force. The time for revenge had come.

The Eyes of the Dead

The wind dispersed the smell of scorched grass to every corner of the City of Heavens. Morys walked quietly on the dark, cobbled streets of the city, feeling poisoned air churning in his lungs. Few houses were left untouched by the fiery demons, blackened by soot, their walls smoking in the night. The flames had embraced every corner of the once glorious city of the Egercolls, except for the home of the God of Life.

A few hours earlier, John had searched for houses that hadn't been scorched and ruined by the flames. He had found a small manor house largely intact, so they decided to spend the night there and head to Wirskworth the next morning. Morys had swept the ashes from the stone floor on which he'd lie. He had taken off his cloak and armour before trying to sleep, but his sleep proved to be shallow. When he woke to a crackling noise, he saw John was dozing next to him, but Eleanor had disappeared from the large chamber they had given her. Morys grabbed his sword with a sharp motion, wondering if the girl had gone to look for Elliot. John had told them to leave the young man alone, as he was sure he was in shock, but Morys knew he was wrong. John may have travelled the world, he may have boundless knowledge of the kingdom and its people, but he didn't know much about soldiers and men of war. Elliot's eyes flooded with hatred when he heard Thorold's words, and Morys's experience suggested he'd surely do something reckless. The boy had unparalleled abilities but lacked life experience, and this combination was quite dangerous. It was often fighting skills that drove great men to their death. A man who doesn't know how to grasp the blade will only think of running away at the sight of a man like Walter Thorn. But capable soldiers often overestimated their strength and ended up in the arms of the God of Souls. Elliot hadn't spoken after Thorold's revelations. He had taken his sister in his arms and left the little house without saying a word, and no one had tried to follow him. Morys and Eleanor had taken the distressed Master to the manor, leaving him in a room next to the wooden kitchen benches. Thorold cried and mumbled until he fell asleep in his lament.

Morys continued to walk in the dark and suddenly felt the ground soften under his boots. Soil had taken the place of stone, and a small forest was revealed in front of him, on the south side of the city. Some branches were blackened, and dry grass grew here and there in the rain-soaked soil. He was sure that there was no one around him, yet he felt thousands of eyes fixed on him. The quiet of the landscape, the rustling of leaves, and the icy breeze made him shudder. His eyes wandered for a moment to the sky, and then he realised why he felt like someone was watching him—the stars were the Eyes of the Dead, as his father used to say. The souls who had left Elirehar's capital a few hours ago were shining, looking at him from above. The rainclouds had moved on, but a cloud of black smoke clung over the city and stretched for miles beyond.

The sound of something being dragged distracted him, and he raised his sword under the moonlight. He strained to listen, but the noise was gone. He moved hesitantly, looking left and right, and then heard a strange sound, like a sob. He had finally found Eleanor.

The girl was sitting under a tall lemon tree with creased branches and faded brown leaves. Her face was hidden in her palms, and her spindly knees touched her chest as she cried, crouched in the dark.

Morys didn't want to scare her so he walked slowly toward her, lowering his sword. He put his hand gently on her shoulder, and she jumped in fear.

"It's me!" he cried.

The girl looked at him angrily. "You scared me."

"Sorry," Morys apologised tenderly, and his eyes met hers. They were swollen and red. "I saw that you were gone, and I went out to look for you," he continued.

"So many dead, so many children..." The words dried up in Eleanor's mouth, and tears welled up in her eyes again.

Morys threw his sword to the ground and hugged her. "I know," he whispered softly in her ear.

"Is that what my parents looked like when they were killed by Walter's men?" she sobbed. "Is that what the people of Felador looked like after the Battle of Aquarine?" The pain had overwhelmed her.

"Do not think of what they looked like. Don't pity the dead, Eleanor."

She pulled away from his embrace and took stock of him for a long moment. "Have you seen Elliot?" Her voice sounded as if she had said something that was forbidden.

"No. I don't know where he is. I can't believe what Thorold told him," he breathed out.

"Neither can I," she agreed. "Queen Alice gave birth to twins, without anyone knowing... What do you think Elliot will do?"

"Hard to say," Morys responded, "but I do know that pain and anger are poor advisors."

A moment of silence covered them as the moonlight fell on Eleanor's black hair.

"Why did you want to duel for me?" Eleanor's voice was steady, and she looked him in the eyes.

Morys frowned, confused.

"With Karford," she added.

"Well... I..." His gaze wandered in the void for a moment. "It was my duty to protect you," he said daringly as he met her gaze.

A star streaked through the sky above them as they leaned toward each other. Their lips were united like two raindrops. Morys tasted the salt of her tears and smelled the scent of her. He pulled her close, their bodies a passionate tangle as they became one under the Eyes of the Dead, who bathed them in their eternal blue-white light.

The Oath of the South

His horse galloped and snorted as Elliot retraced the path that had led him to Elirehar. His mind thrummed with questions. Who was responsible for what had happened? At first, he had blamed his own father. How could a king have entrusted the fate of his wife and children to a Master? If he had trusted his counsellors, they would never have let Elliot and his sister separate. Once he had grown tired of blaming Thomas Egercoll, his hatred was redirected toward the man who had raised him. He wished he could bring his Master back to life and unleash all the rage that had accumulated within him. The man he would have given his life to protect, the man who was the only family he had ever known, both a Master and a father to him, had not only deprived him of his sister but had also kept countless truths from him all these years.

Last night was the most torturous he had ever experienced. Elliot tried to vent the rage on the trees, flaying them with his sword, until he accepted it was useless to curse men who were no longer in this world. Then his gaze had fallen on his sister's tangled blonde hair. Her face was serene, and her white skin looked pearly in the moonglow. He had found a shovel in a small stable and had, for an hour, dug under some trees behind the Temple of the God of Life. He knew that the Egercolls' ancestors were buried in the crypts of Pegasus Castle, but he wouldn't carry his sister there. They had grown up cut off from their ancestors. So should they remain even in death. Elliot had wrapped the girl in his blue cloak before placing her in the ground. After covering the body with dirt, he remained alone under the starlight. He stared at the sky until hatred wrapped his soul so fiercely that he now knew what he had to do. After all, he had trained for it all these years.

Shortly before dawn, Elliot had mounted his horse and slipped silently out of the City of Heavens, then crossed the bridge leading south of the Forked River. He had started early, wanting to be sure that no one would follow him. This battle was his. A few moments earlier, he had found himself at the spot where he had fought Walter's men the night before. It seemed to him that an eternity had passed since then.

Wind ripped through his hair as he rode low over his horse's neck, though he glanced up when a squawk caught his attention. Hurwig flew over his head, flapping his white wings, his cry like a mourning dirge. It was as if the white hawk could feel the pain overwhelming him. Elliot rode and rode, urging his horse ever onward. He wanted to get to Wirskworth before sunset. He heard Hurwig screeching furiously. He glanced up and then was met with darkness.

He awoke to an awful headache, and his eyes burned so much that he thought they would jump out of their sockets. He tried to lift his eyelids, but the light was too strong. Elliot felt hands supporting him. He realised that his feet were dragging on the hot ground.

He heard a voice to his right. "We caught him south of the Forked River by hitting him on the head with a rock, and a little later we found these scumbags."

Have they caught the others? Elliot wondered.

"It was probably them who attacked Egin and the rest," came a second voice full of hatred. "Take them to our king."

Only one man could be called a *king* in these places. He didn't know what had happened, but even so, he was where he wanted to be. He half-opened his eyes, and the sunlight instantly blinded him. The sun was still high in the sky; he had not been unconscious for long.

"Elliot!" The voice made him shiver.

He winced as he turned his head, already knowing what he would see.

Eleanor's lips were swollen as though she had been struck, her cheek bruised, and Elliot could see more familiar figures next to her. They had caught everyone, even Master Thorold. His companions must have silently followed him, keeping their distance, and they had taken the Grand Master along with them. He hadn't noticed he was being followed. He ought to have noticed. Guilt overcame him, and the hatred roaring through him began to evaporate. How could he have behaved so foolishly? The people he had promised to protect would die a torturous death, and it'd all be his fault. He remembered his Master's words: *"Killing a man in order to protect the kingdom is completely different from killing him in order to avenge yourself. Revenge will make you seek him out. Your heart will be filled with rage and hate, so you will risk lives to get to him."* Blinded by revenge, Elliot had failed to act upon what he had been taught. He hadn't expected his companions to be able to follow him, but that didn't mean he hadn't failed.

The men dragging him came to a halt and dropped him to the ground.

"This vermin was caught south of the Forked River, and we're bringing them before the king," announced a voice.

Elliot raised his head and noticed multiple figures looking at him with cold calculation in their eyes. The men were dressed in scarlet cloaks, with a tiger engraved on the breastplates of most. Dizziness swept over him as he pushed himself to his feet, and his legs ached from being dragged. They had taken his sword, but the knife he always hid in his boot was still there, its weight a comfort as he straightened.

He took a step, staggering, and dozens of swords were raised to point at him. His gaze fell on his companions. His sister may have left the world, but they were the siblings life had granted him. Morys looked worse than Eleanor, his face black from the blows, blood soaking his hair. John was unharmed, as if he had surrendered right away, and although Elliot would have expected him to be both frightened and furious that he'd die because of Elliot, he only seemed despondent. A little farther off, Master Thorold seemed on the verge of death—he was on his feet, but barely, white-faced under the heat of the sun.

Elliot turned and looked toward Wirskworth. He had figured out where they were. His eyes fell on the middle hill of the city, where the Temple of the God of Souls was located. Their souls would soon fall into his hands, and the governor would watch their death from afar. At least Selwyn would live.

Footsteps approached, and several men shuffled to the side, creating an opening in their ranks—and Elliot saw him at last, the man he hated most in the world. Walter Thorn's long blond hair caressed his shoulders, bathed in the sunrays. His armour glistened, and two gold, tiger-shaped clasps held a long, fire-coloured cloak on his shoulders. It was so heavy it didn't wave about at all as he walked. Elliot's eyes fell on the sword hanging from his waist. The Blade of Power had a dazzling hilt, thicker than that of the Sword of Destiny. Elliot took stock of him—his palms, legs, neck, and head were uncovered by his armour.

Walter Thorn smiled as he looked at the captives, and a huge white tiger prowled into sight behind him. Their eyes were the same icy blue and full of malice. His smile grew wider when his gaze fell on the Master.

"Where did you catch them?" he asked a man on his right.

"The boy was riding fast, south of the Forked River, and the others were following him a few miles behind. We also found Egin and his men, Your Majesty," replied the soldier.

Walter stood in silence, waiting for him to go on.

"They're all dead." The man looked frightened as he spoke.

Walter walked toward the captives, and Elliot noticed the company that had arrived with the blond man. The Ghost Soldiers were dressed in black with armour that covered their entire bodies and helmets that hid every inch of their faces. Moreover, there were three soldiers next to Walter whose armour was the same as those of the Ghosts, but instead of black, they wore blood-red cloaks. Elliot observed the three members of the Trinity of Death: one enormous man, another a little taller than a dwarf, and the third a man of medium height. His gaze was fixed on the winged creature carved on the tall soldier's chest. It resembled the wyverns Long Arm had told him about. Finally, he saw a Ghost in a black cloak, standing right behind Walter. The soldier's form was petite, and Elliot knew it was Berta Loers. His Master had told him about her.

"Master Thorold, it's been years since we last met." Walter's voice dripped with malevolence. He had not reacted to the news of his dead men.

The old man didn't answer.

"As soon as I heard you were presiding over the City of Heavens, I rushed to visit you, but you didn't welcome me... Turns out though, it was written in the stars that our paths would cross again!" His voice was drenched with sarcasm. "Won't you look at me, my old friend?" Now Walter's tone of voice carried a veiled threat.

"Leave him alone." Elliot's words made everyone freeze and Walter turned slowly toward him.

"Who are you?"

Elliot felt anger simmering inside of him. "My name is Elliot."

Walter remained silent for a moment. "You must be the self-proclaimed *son* of Thomas Egercoll, the boy who caused me so much trouble." A susurrus of hushed voices broke out after these words.

For a moment, Elliot forgot his fear and guilt and was overcome by his wrath. "It is I! My name is Elliot Egercoll," he announced stonily.

The man's long hair fluttered as he cast a contemptuous look at him. "Was it you who fought Reynald Karford?"

"Yes!"

"And you sent me his sword?"

"Yes!"

"And was it you who killed my men at the Forked River?"

"Yes!"

"And you tried to get Elmor to take up the war against me once again?"

"YES!" cried Elliot aloud for the fourth time. He wanted to pounce on him, to torment him, to kill him.

"Very well, then." Walter seemed quite serene as his armour sparkled in the sunlight. "You have confessed your crimes before me. I sentence you to death! As for the people of Wirskworth, I will show generosity and leave their city unscathed if they walk by my side in the war to overthrow the usurper, supporting my claim to the throne."

Elliot felt a hatred he had never felt before. "A MURDERER LIKE YOU WILL NEVER BE A TRUE KING!" he screamed. "YOU ATTACKED A CITY WITHOUT AN ARMY! YOU MURDERED WOMEN AND CHILDREN!" The words dried up in his mouth. "You killed... you killed..." No, he wouldn't say anything more, he wouldn't give him the satisfaction of gloating over another Egercoll's death. "The governors, along with the council of Iovbridge, chose Sophie Delamere to rule Knightdorn. You are just a murderous rebel—nothing more than that!"

Walter remained calm. "I think you don't know the whole story, boy," he remarked. "Few governors wanted Sophie Delamere on the throne, and those who didn't support her were ousted, unable to participate in the election of the new ruler of Knightdorn after Thomas Egercoll's death. I've heard that even the governors who voted for Delamere were threatened with death in order to—"

"You're a liar." Elliot could barely finish his phrase before the gigantic man in black lashed out, a huge fist meeting Elliot's jaw. Elliot dropped to the ground.

"No one interrupts a king," Walter said with disdain. "Most Knightdorn rulers now want me on the throne. Delamere's refusal to hand over Iovbridge is a betrayal of the kingdom."

Elliot tried to get up. "The law stipulates that royal rights end only with death. The queen can neither lose nor relinquish her office." His voice remained steady.

"This law was the decision of a single man, stupid boy..." Walter was now right in front of him. "Thomas Egercoll took the throne that belonged to my grandfather by force and then changed laws that had existed for centuries, violating and desecrating traditions. He made his decisions without the consent of rulers and nobles, turning himself into one of the worst tyrants Knightdorn has ever known." Malice was evident in his every word. "And when his end was approaching, he made sure that the throne remained with a foolish girl. He tried to ensure that the kingdom would not return to its old and noble traditions. His betrayal, as well as that of Delamere, who took the throne in the most deceitful of ways in Knightdorn's history, must be punished, and the crown must be returned to the house it belongs to."

Elliot took a step toward Walter, and the giant man was about to lunge at him again when Walter stopped him with a nod of the head.

"I know the lies and rumours that you've spread throughout the kingdom all these years to tarnish the second king's memory." Elliot spat out his words. "However many men you kill, however many cities you conquer, however many lords you buy, you will never get to be a true king. A king inspires devotion, not fear, and a man who killed his own father, the true Governor of Gaeldeath, will never inspire devotion."

The Blade of Power came out of its sheath at lightning speed. "My grandfather was the true Governor of Gaeldeath and Knightdorn, not my father," Walter yelled. "Your refusal to bow before me, the true king and successor of the First King, is punishable by the most dishonourable death."

"A king who just burned a city full of old people and children," scoffed Elliot.

"A king has the right to punish traitors as he sees fit."

"What was their treason?"

"That they didn't stand by me in claiming the throne, in acceptance of the fact that Thomas Egercoll was a tyrant."

"My father was the king you will never succeed in becoming," Elliot shouted.

Walter looked at him for a moment, then started laughing out loud, and his men followed suit. "The cowardly Thomas Egercoll whose life was taken by my sword while he begged for mercy," he cackled. "I wonder if there's even anyone who can attest you are who you say you are." He had now lost his cheerful tone.

Elliot remained silent after that.

"Your Majesty, this scum attacked our men. It's enough for us to sentence him to death by torture with the wooden horse," the voice of the Trinity man of medium height was heard.

"Wise words, Brian, but there's another thing I need to know," Walter said. "Who trained you?" he suddenly snapped.

Elliot looked him straight in the eyes, with no trace of fear. "Roger Belet," he declared.

"You should know that I don't forgive lies," Walter reminded him. "Strip the girl." His eyes turned to Eleanor.

Morys moved as some soldiers approached Eleanor, but a Ghost Soldier punched him and held him by the neck.

"I will cut off her arms, her legs, even her breasts, until you tell the truth!" The Blade of Power rose in Walter's hand. "I'm sure you would like to spare her from that. Something tells me that all the prisoners my men captured are your friends."

Elliot's mind spun. He had to protect his companions—though it would mean revealing information he had sworn to keep secret. But he had no reason to hide the truth now that his death looked him in the eye.

"I challenge you to single combat," Elliot declared after a few moments, looking at Walter. He had wanted to ask for this from the beginning, but his mind had been paralysed by all that had happened. His original plan was to get to Walter's camp alone and challenge him to a duel, spewing his outrage over his sister's death. Single combat was the only solution left to protect his companions—and his secret, at least as long as he stayed alive. Elliot still felt dizzy after the blow to his head, but he had no other option.

"I would never do a traitor like you such an honour. You don't deserve to duel with me." Walter glanced at his men who started untying the girl's breastplate.

"TELL THEM TO STOP," Elliot yelled.

Walter looked at him with a smirk—he had found a weak spot. "Your only hope is to tell me the truth."

Elliot hesitated as the soldiers removed Eleanor's breastplate and leather clothing, leaving her bare-chested on the ground. She struggled to free herself, wriggling, and Elliot's eyes filled with tears, hearing her screams, along with those of Morys by his side.

"There never was a Master named Roger Belet, and only two Masters could train a boy who could defeat a man like Reynald Karford—the two Grand Masters I never found," said Walter suddenly. "One was hiding in the City of Heavens for years, and the other was never found, though many think he died by my hand. I know Thorold didn't train you. The news of a skilled soldier growing up in the City of Heavens would have travelled to Knightdorn, and I'm sure the man who trained you knew that very well. TELL ME WHO TRAINED YOU, OR I'LL ORDER THEM TO CUT HER BREASTS OFF."

Elliot looked at Eleanor and took a deep breath. "Althalos Baudry." The words filled the air, and all eyes turned on him, stunned.

Morys seized the opportunity and yanked his captor's sword free. He lunged at one of the men holding Eleanor, but Short Death was faster. Morys collapsed to the ground, bleeding from a wound above his pelvis, his shout of hatred turning to a cry of pain.

Eleanor started screaming. Elliot could hardly think. It was as if his life had lost all meaning in a matter of moments. "I CHALLENGE YOU TO SINGLE COMBAT IN EXCHANGE FOR THE CAPTIVES' LIVES," he screamed, looking at Walter pleadingly. He had failed to protect even those who had believed in him.

Walter sized him up, smiling. "Even if I gave you the honour of fighting me, combat only makes sense when you have something to offer, stupid boy. I have the largest army in the kingdom. I'm the Ruler of Gaeldeath and the future King of Knightdorn. What do you have to offer in return, after your defeat?"

"I'm an anointed royal knight and protector of Knightdorn," responded Elliot. "Your fear of fighting me only proves the Crown's supremacy."

His words cut deeper than any profanity. The Trinity men and the Ghosts drew their swords. Walter raised his hand with a smile. "Very well... it's been years since I last killed a knight who was trained by my beloved Althalos," he sneered.

His words filled Elliot with fierce hatred. Walter pulled a sword from a Ghost's sheath and gave a subtle nod to the men who held Eleanor. The soldiers threw Eleanor's clothes over her, and she grabbed at them as she crawled, weeping, to Morys's side. Walter tossed the borrowed sword at Elliot. "Until our combat is over, your friends will be guests in my camp. If you win, all my armies will belong to you, as the Gods are my witness. But if you lose, you will all be tortured on the wooden horse."

Elliot raised his sword and brought all his training to mind. If he could control his emotions, there might still be hope. Walter came for him so fast that Elliot barely had time to react. The blow was so strong that he feared his blade would bend. He countered, but Walter avoided him nonchalantly and hit him on the head with his sword's hilt. Elliot stumbled as a second blow aimed at his legs. He spun, avoiding the sword, while the tip of his own sword scratched Walter's fingers. A murmur of surprise spread around them. The blond man raised his hand to the height of his eyes. The Blade of Power was still in his palm, and while his leather glove was cut, there was no blood on his skin. Elliot looked at his hand in surprise, and Walter's eyes narrowed menacingly.

Walter's blows fell like lightning. Elliot threw the sword to his left hand, trying to attack with new angles. Walter repelled him with the hilt and struck again. The tip of the Blade of Power sliced the flesh on Elliot's left leg. He tripped, and Walter struck. Elliot repulsed the blow, but the sword slipped out of his hand, and Walter raised his blade again, ready to finish him off. He bent down, avoiding the blow, and pulled the hidden knife from his boot. He stabbed toward Walter's leg—and screamed as the tiger bit at the wound Walter had given him.

Poison.

Orhyn Shadow spilled into his blood. He tried to get up, but his every move caused him unbearable pain. Only stillness helped. He didn't care even if he remained paralysed, as long as this torment was over.

Walter kicked the knife that had slipped out of his hand. "I gave you the honour of duelling with me in a fair fight. You chose to fight fraudulently." His hand caressed the tiger's head. The man sheathed the Blade of Power and glanced at the Trinity of Death. "Time to go back to Iovbridge. The queen is waiting for us, and we must not disappoint her," he smiled sardonically.

"What about Elmor's army?" Short Death spoke.

"We'll follow the plan I had before I found out about this scum," Walter answered, looking at Elliot disdainfully. "We'll return to Ballar and attack Iovbridge, killing anyone in our path. No army will be able to stop us. I won't wait any longer. I've already waited for too many years. Perhaps the death of this foolish boy who gave hope to the filthy Poison Masters will convince them that it'd be wiser for them to stay in Wirskworth." Walter glanced toward Elmor's capital. "Have five wooden horses erected and put these scumbags on them," he continued, looking at the prisoners. "Half of us are leaving for Ballar now. Half will remain here until they breathe their last. As soon as they're dead, they'll follow."

"The Governor of Elmor may order an attack on our men if she sees only six thousand cavalrymen outside her walls," responded the giant Trinity man. "Even at that disadvantage, we might defeat them if we were properly rested, but our horses and men are exhausted from hunger and fatigue."

"She is not going to attack," Walter rejoined. "The smoke from the

City of Heavens last night reminded her of my might. I'm sure she suspected what happened, since her men must have seen me ride toward Elirehar—the smoke came from the west, and there's only one city there. And the Hewdars' martyrdom will be another reason for her to be intimidated," he said. "I am also sure that my men in the city will persuade Syrella not to slip away from Wirskworth, and she will obey. Fear will prevail over her courage. But still, order the men to stand in battle formation as soon as the wooden horses are set up."

The Trinity listened to the orders carefully. "Should we give the girl to the men?" asked Short Death.

Walter looked at him angrily. "I want all the prisoners dead before dusk. No distractions," he yelled.

The Trinity members moved hurriedly as Walter left them, without even a glance at Elliot. He tried to get up, but pain tore through his limbs. He turned his eyes, helpless, and his gaze crossed with that of John. Long Arm's face was full of sorrow and disappointment. Elliot could no longer bear the pain in his body and soul and surrendered to its vortex.

Elliot opened his eyes to a commotion around him, pain searing through his eyelids as they moved. He had fainted, he didn't know for how long, but he was still alive. The pain had only grown worse, but he shifted his gaze left and right while keeping his head still. He couldn't see any of his companions but noticed the wooden horses skilfully set up by Walter's men. Little time had passed, then. Tears brimmed in his eyes.

Hoofbeats pounded close by, and he slowly turned to his right. Walter and half his men were ready to ride to Ballar. The blond man approached in his chariot. "Pick him up," he ordered.

Two hands grabbed Elliot by the shoulders and lifted him violently. Pain tore through his body, but his legs supported him.

"Where is Althalos?"

Elliot gathered all his remaining strength and looked at him without fear. He wouldn't give him that satisfaction. "He's dead."

Walter remained silent for a moment, as if lamenting, when suddenly a faint smile formed on his lips. "The old man had lost his mind if he thought he could save you from me, boy," he snorted contemptuously. "He lost the king, he lost the knights he trained, he even lost my mother, along with Alice, pinning all his hopes on you... A boy with a dead name..." With these words, he flicked the reins and drove away, and the other men followed suit.

Elliot was spun on his feet by his captor, and then he saw his companions. Morys was lying on his back, motionless, Eleanor next to him. She had her clothes on, and her face was full of tears. A little further on, John was standing, grim, next to the teetering Master whose life seemed to be ebbing away. Elliot closed his eyes. He couldn't bear the sight of his companions. He couldn't bear John's utterly disheartened look. He felt a new wave of pain wash through his body and wished to die as soon as possible. His mind travelled far and wide. For a moment, he thought he was dreaming as Althalos Baudry appeared before him with a face full of pity. Now, he finally understood what Althalos had tried to teach him, but it was too late. Darkness began to envelop him when a loud sound shook the very ground they stood on.

A war horn howled from Wirskworth, and the towering door of the ancient city of the elves opened with a deafening thud. Hundreds of horses rushed out like wild beasts while countless men behind them ran on foot, looking like frantic hyenas. And they were not alone. There, to the north, sharp spears and white banners. The Guardians of the South had come.

Thousands of cries followed. Walter's men raced to form ranks as officers screamed orders. Elliot searched for Walter, catching sight of that blond hair; he hadn't had time to get away. Elliot heard his cries. "Go on, don't stop!" he yelled furiously.

"Now is the time to wipe them out, Your Majesty," Brian yelled, on his horse.

"The men are exhausted. Half of them are not even on their horses and we're not in battle formation, you idiot! MOVE!" screamed Walter, lashing the two horses that pulled the chariot. Six thousand soldiers who were ready to follow him on horseback started riding. "PROTECT THE RETREAT," he shouted again, addressing the rest of the men.

The riders who were to stay in Wirskworth until the prisoners died hollered left and right, trying to find their horses and to line up, giving the horde following Walter time to retreat.

Pain needled him endlessly, but he punched his captor in the gut and grabbed the sword from the man's belt. Swinging down, Elliot split his skull, and the soldier dropped. He tried to move toward Eleanor, constantly losing his balance as chaos prevailed around him.

Wirskworth's army, alongside the Guardians of the South, clashed with the enemy men who had been ordered to remain in Elmor until the prisoners died. Clouds of dust covered the battlefield, and the ground grew slick with blood. Elliot's eyes had filled with dust. He was trying to move toward his companions and was forced to avoid an attack, dodging a swinging blade. He was about to retaliate when a spear was nailed into his opponent's neck. Elliot saw the Snake of Elmor on the chest of the rider who had just protected him. He continued walking until two men in black appeared in his visual field. In one glance, his eyes swept over the scene. Two Ghosts had surrounded Eleanor, who was grunting as she struggled to lift Morys's weight. John lay on the ground next to her, covered in blood. As the one Ghost was about to finish him off, a figure darted in to protect him. Linaria looked fearless in her armour. She attacked furiously, her hair fluttering behind her. The Ghost repulsed her attack, and his fellow soldier tried to repel her.

Elliot tried to run, but the pain choked him. His leg was torn, and Orhyn Shadow flowed in his veins. He felt the need to retreat, to wrap himself in the arms of darkness, but the image of a villager in a thick cloak safe from the thorns that scratched at a child stuck in his mind. A knight's true power, he remembered, was not to take lives but to endure pain without fear for as long as he could.

Linaria repulsed the Ghosts' blows but could not counter. The men in black, with the covered faces, had circled her. She attempted a clumsy blow, and a sword cut her arm, making her blade slip out of her hand. The black-clad soldier raised his sword to the sky, and Linaria looked at death with courage, but then a fierce cry resounded on the battlefield, and the Ghost's sword glanced off steel, the blades shivering against each other as Elliot stopped the blow.

Elliot felt the power of the Pegasi in him as he faced Walter Thorn's Ghosts. The steel began to dance furiously. He avoided the blows despite the pain piercing his body. The men in black attacked with rage, but he read their movements. They swung their swords down in heavy arcs, but Elliot turned his blade to meet them both, halting their strikes above his forehead. Their hot breath washed over his face as their momentum carried them close, but then Elliot shoved, sending them back a half-step. As swift as lightning, Elliot spun, sword extended, the point slicing through their throats. The two men fell to the ground.

Elliot's legs trembled, and the sword slipped out of his hand. He stared at the battlefield for a few moments before returning to Linaria. "It looks like we won," he mumbled and sank to the ground.

The Freeing of the Slave

Peter Brau's ears prickled at the rustling of the leaves as he moved stealthily, crouching among the trees. Several hundred men followed him silently in the rainy night. They had snuck from Iovbridge a few hours before and had managed to kill Walter's scouts in the Vale of Gods. Peter's men had no horses or siege weapons, but if their plan succeeded, they wouldn't need them either way.

Peter tripped on a stone, and a hand grabbed him by the shoulder.

"Watch your step, Peter," snorted Frederic, supporting him.

Peter nodded sharply and continued carefully, hoping this plan would succeed. It was the first time something inside of him filled him with optimism instead of the familiar feeling of fear that overwhelmed him before each battle with Walter and his men. White City had four thousand soldiers guarding it, and he had taken only two thousand men from Iovbridge, for if they failed, Knightdorn's capital would need every body it could muster as soon as Walter returned. What's more, only two captains had followed him, leaving the rest by the queen's side. Merick and Frederic walked behind Peter silently, followed by the other men. Two thousand would be enough to accomplish what they needed to here—if all went well. For a moment, Peter's mind wandered to the enslaved son of Tahryn, and doubts unfolded within him once more.

They continued to walk silently, like predators approaching their prey, till White City appeared before them in the dim moonlight. Borin had given him detailed instructions on which path to follow. Peter had decided not to take Ballar's men with him and to keep this plan a secret. After the assassination attempt in the palace, he was suspicious of Ballar's soldiers.

The point they were looking for should have been close, but panic started to spread through Peter's chest as his doubts surfaced. Had the letter reached Giren? Had he understood the message? He might have burned it in fear before revealing the secret message. They could be risking Iovbridge for nothing. They could be walking into a trap.

"It must be here," Merick whispered.

Peter looked carefully and saw the entrance to the secret passage which led to the tunnel under Hawk's Nest, through the trees. Borin had given him the right instructions. Peter looked at the ramparts of the White City wall. There were no guards above, while a sliding iron gate blocked the secret passage. There was no sign of Giren.

Peter waited for a moment, his uncertainty growing. "Retreat," he whispered in Merick's ear. "There's nobody here."

"For heavens' sake, Peter," Frederic said in a low voice. "Did you expect the lad to stand outside the gate to greet you?"

"Even if the letter reached his hands, he wouldn't know whether it was a trap. Perhaps he's hidden behind the gate, waiting for a signal," Merick added.

"If an enemy decrypted the letter and set a trap, we'll all die if we draw their attention. I don't want to approach the gate," Peter said.

"Throw a stone."

Peter was astonished. "Are you crazy? Do you want the guards to hear us?"

Suddenly, a wolf's howl resounded in the dark, and Frederic smiled at this stroke of luck. He grabbed a pebble and threw it against the iron. The pinging sound it made was loud but the wolf had continued its song. Peter closed his eyes, trying to breathe, his heartbeat growing louder and louder. Nothing happened, and Frederic was about to throw another pebble when Peter grabbed him by the shoulder.

"Stop!"

"In the name of the Seven Swords." The captain tried to free himself from Peter's grip.

"Frederic, I'm ordering you to stop," Peter whispered.

The captain opened his mouth, angry, when a pair of eyes appeared behind the latticed grille of the sliding gate. "I didn't think you'd come," said a voice.

Frederic opened his mouth in surprise, and a smile was painted on Giren's lips.

Giren raised the gate, producing a long grating sound. The wolves began to howl again, muffling the noise, as if luck could not abandon them that night. Peter looked at the sky for a moment, and then he knew—this battle belonged to him.

The men passed through the opening of the gate and found themselves in the tunnel, under Hawk's Nest. They walked silently, like spirits of the night, moving through arched passageways and up stairs, walking fast behind Giren. They were now inside Borin's castle, and Peter couldn't hear the slightest noise until loud laughter and applause reached his ears. They had arrived outside the castle's great hall, and the voices betrayed the feast set on the majestic tables of Borin Ballard's home.

Peter looked at his captains and drew his sword, then, with a nod, he rushed into the great hall, men pouring after him. Walter's men leapt from their seats, pewter mugs and platters spilling to the ground in their shock. Peter's voice echoed in the great hall of Hawk's Nest.

"IN THE QUEEN'S NAME, YOU ARE UNDER ARREST."

The Green Gold

Elliot knew only pain and sorrow. They tormented him in an unyielding whirlpool. Everything around him appeared red, red and mournful as if death had enveloped him. He had no idea where he was. Was he dead? And if so, why did he feel pain? He always believed that pain left with death. He tried to leave that place, to fly away. He tried over and over, but in vain. Did he still have a body? He didn't know. Perhaps he was a spirit.

The void lurched, and he felt like he was drowning, as if his lungs were full of water, and then the images in front of him changed. An old man showed him how to hold a small wooden sword, but the old man's figure quickly disappeared, and a little girl with blonde hair covered by a veil appeared before him. The pain inside of him overwhelmed him.

"No, no," he tried to shout, but he didn't know if he had a voice anymore. Nevertheless, he was sure that he had heard his voice. The world vanished, and a young woman with fairytale eyes and silver-blue hair sprang up in front of him. The pain began to subside—perhaps the afterlife was not just sorrow and suffering, after all. Elliot wanted to hug her, kiss her, and tell her how he felt about her, but moments later the woman disappeared into a grey cloud.

The scenery changed again. A woman with black hair resembling a crow's feathers stared him in the eyes. She was lying naked on the ground, screaming.

"NO, NO, HELP, ELEANOR!" Everything became dim.

Someone threw a cold cloth over his forehead, and Elliot half-opened his eyes. Candlelight flickered in his blurry vision. He tried to move.

"Not so fast, my lad, the poison has not yet left your blood," murmured Thorold.

"How long have I been here?" Elliot felt little spasms in his body. The pain was not so strong, but it got stronger with his every move.

"Only a few hours, it will be dawn soon," replied the old man.

"Where is Eleanor? Where is—"

"Everyone's fine. You must rest," Thorold cut him off. The old man was wearing a black tunic. "You're lucky you're in the only city with the antidote for the poison that entered your body."

"Where is Morys?"

"You must rest, my boy!" The old man's tone seemed to change at the sound of this name.

Elliot tried again to get up, and Thorold pushed him back. "You must listen to me if you want to get well."

Elliot was so weak he couldn't resist. "Why are you here?" he wondered, glancing at the room he had woken up in. A table next to the Master held a handful of glass vials, and shelves on the opposite wall contained many more.

"To heal you," Thorold replied.

"You're not a healer."

"I can confess to you that I know more than many healers." The man smiled faintly.

"Will Morys be all right?"

Thorold didn't speak. He turned to the table with the vials and started looking for something.

"Talk to me." Elliot raised his voice. "You owe me several truths, Thorold."

The Master sighed sadly. "Elliot, I'm sorry that—"

"Not now," Elliot cut him off decisively. He would hear this story another time. "Right now I want to know if Morys will be fine."

The old man didn't move for a while. "His spine can't be healed," he said suddenly.

Elliot felt his heart tear in two. "Will he die?"

Thorold sighed wearily. "No, but he will be crippled for the rest of his life. He can't move from the neck down."

Silence fell across the room, and a knot tightened Elliot's stomach. It was his fault. He was to blame for everything.

"He asked to see you as soon as you recover," the Master informed him, without looking him in the eye. "But not now! Now, you need to rest."

Elliot mustered all his strength, trying to lift his body. He knew that maybe Morys wanted to blame him, but he didn't care. He deserved to suffer. His muscles twinged as he got up. They had dressed him in light white linen clothes.

"Take me to him," he asked as soon as he straightened up his body.

Thorold raised an eyebrow and looked as though he would refuse, but he didn't speak and instead opened the small chamber door. Elliot followed him out into a narrow corridor with dozens of fixed torches and many doors. Thorold stopped at one and opened it.

Eleanor stood by Morys's headrest, his crying mother and sisters kneeling by the bed at her side. Black dominated their linen dresses, while Eleanor was dressed in green silk. Morys had a cold, distant look, as if he didn't want them near him. The bedcovers covered his whole body, and his face was tired and pale. Everyone's eyes turned to the newcomers. Elliot wasn't ready for this moment—he wasn't ready to face the Bardolf family.

"I want to be alone with Elliot." The reclining man seemed to come alive when he spotted him.

Morys's mother's gaze lingered on her son, but then she wiped her eyes and gently pulled her daughters away. Eleanor didn't move from her place. The three women headed toward the door, and as they passed in front of Elliot, their eyes met.

"I'm sorry," Elliot cried. His voice was barely audible. To his surprise, Morys's mother hugged him and left the room, her daughters and Thorold following.

"I know what you want to do," Eleanor said when only the three of them remained. "You can't... I won't let you..." Her words were drowned in tears.

Elliot didn't understand what was happening.

"I love you," she whispered, leaning down to wrap her arms around Morys.

"I love you too," replied the man who could not return the hug, but his eyes filled with tears in her arms. "But I want you to let me talk to Elliot," Morys added after a few moments.

Eleanor caressed him gently and kissed him, then she headed towards the door.

Elliot wanted to tell her something, but he was bereft of words. Eleanor rested her hand on his shoulder consolingly when she approached him and, with a pained look, left the chamber.

Before he could restrain himself, Elliot broke the silence spreading in the room. "I didn't know that..." He wavered mid-sentence.

"No one had time enough to find out." Morys was pale as a ghost in the candlelight.

"I'm sorry." Elliot humbly bowed his head. He didn't have the courage to look at him like a man, even though he had ruined his life.

"It's not your fault, Elliot."

"It is. I should have protected you... I acted like a fool..." Tears burned in his eyes. Why didn't Morys hate him? He should hate him. His serene voice made Elliot feel even worse. "I failed," he whispered after a while.

"You didn't fail," replied Morys. "In war, there are always losses. If anyone's responsible for what happened, it's Walter Thorn and his men."

"I put you in danger... I risked your lives... I didn't tell you the truth about—"

"Listen to me," Morys interrupted him in a loud voice despite his ashen face. "It was the first time Walter Thorn retreated on the battle-field, it was the first time his men watered the ground with their blood, it was the first time the south united in seventeen years!" The man spoke with fortitude. "None of this would have happened without you, Elliot. If I'm sorry about something, it's that I won't have the privilege to fight at your side again. Althalos would have been proud of you."

Elliot stared at him. "It doesn't matter," he muttered. "All that matters is that you're alive. I don't need your sword."

"Unfortunately, that was all I could offer you," said Morys with a smile. "To be precise, I can no longer offer anything to anyone."

"Morys—"

"I'm neither a Master nor a healer, Elliot. I'm a soldier, and the gods have given me the honour of fighting next to one of the greatest warriors of my time," he said in a steady voice. "But now, my time has come."

Tears began to flow from Elliot's eyes. Now he understood. Now the words Eleanor had uttered made sense. She had understood, though Elliot was sure that Morys had not confided his thoughts to her.

"All I ask of you is to give me the honour of leaving this world as a soldier."

"No!" Elliot's voice trembled.

"Please!" Now it was Morys's turn to cry. "I can't live like this!"

"Do you want me to kill... to kill... a brother?"

"I don't want you to kill me," the man said firmly. "I want you to deliver me from this torment."

Elliot was lost for words. "Eleanor loves you, Morys."

"She is worth more than that... Think about it... Would you like the love of your life to see you helpless, forever?" he argued.

"Your mother... Your..." He couldn't go on—it was impossible for him to do what his friend asked. But he knew that he would want the same.

"I beg you, Elliot! You're the only one who can help me... No one else would—" Morys stopped. "I want you to be the one to do it. It'll be my honour," he whispered.

Silence held sway, and the two men remained speechless until Elliot looked up. "How?" It was one word, just one word, yet the most difficult he had ever uttered.

"Just grab the vial of green liquid." Morys's eyes pointed to the right.

Dozens of shelves to his left held countless vials. Elliot searched with his eyes and then saw it—the green liquid in the vial glowed like a torch. He stretched out his hands and grasped the glass receptacle. Its surface was cold, and the liquid inside it seemed thick.

"What is it?" he asked.

"Green Gold, a poison that brings the most peaceful death, without any pain."

Their eyes met for a few moments, and he read the truth in Morys's gaze. He was ready to say goodbye, forever. Elliot pulled the little cork and walked over to Morys, trying to hold back his tears. "Having a man like you by my side was an honour!" he cried.

The man looked at him with a smile and half-opened his mouth. Elliot hesitated, then poured the poison between Morys's lips. Relieved, Morys closed his eyes and licked his lips. After a moment, he opened his eyes and said, "Tell Eleanor I love her."

Elliot nodded, looking at him, without speaking. He knew that if he said anything, his voice would break.

"You are the only king I would follow to my death," whispered Morys, taking one last look at Elliot.

Tears streamed down Elliot's face like rivers, and Morys's eyes wandered into the void, unable to see anything anymore.

The Path of Justice

Elliot had curled up in a chair, unable to restrain his tears. John stared at him, patiently sitting on a bed across the room. The morning light had made its appearance, but Elliot hadn't been able to sleep a wink the night before. Morys's lifeless gaze constantly tormented his mind. John had come to his chamber in the Tower of the Sharp Swords a short while ago, knowing what had happened. He had told him that Thorold had given Eleanor a sedative herb, immersing her in an enchanted sleep, as the girl had howled and cried for hours. He had also told him that Selwyn wanted to talk to him but had hesitated, believing that Elliot didn't want to see him.

"Did you think you'd fight the greatest warrior of all time without losing a thing?" Long Arm spoke suddenly.

"I should have protected you all... I should have—"

"I told you when I met you, Elliot. No one can protect anyone!" John declared. "Nevertheless, your anger did make you behave foolishly."

"I didn't expect you to—" Elliot hesitated. It was difficult for him to talk about what had happened.

"You didn't expect us to follow you?" John snorted. "It wasn't hard," he muttered. "Eleanor and Morys were awake early and heard you leave the City of Heavens. Then they ran to the house where Thorold and I slept. I was a bounty hunter for years. It wasn't difficult to follow your traces."

"Why follow me?"

"Because we thought you'd do something stupid. Of course, we had no idea what exactly, but as soon as we found out you were heading to Wirskworth, I was almost certain you wanted to challenge Walter to single combat. I wanted to stop you. Still, a part of me hoped that you wouldn't behave so foolishly," John remarked.

Elliot felt shame and guilt overwhelm him.

"Nevertheless, you surprised me once again," John continued. "I've seen many complacent though skilful lads in my time, killing for pleasure and bragging about their misdeeds, but in the face of death they shrieked like puppies..." Long Arm looked him straight in the eye. "It was impossible to beat Walter in the situation you were in. You had been beaten by his men, and although you could have begged for your life, you tried to fight to save your friends. I've also seen knights and officers writhing and weeping with Orhyn Shadow in their veins, but you managed to fight with this poison in your blood." He shifted his gaze, looking into the void. "No longer do you have the luxury of wallowing in self-pity, Elliot. After yesterday, there are too many people out there who believe in you."

"Why?" Elliot retorted. "I failed."

"Did you really?" John remarked. "The people of Elmor saw a boy standing bravely before Walter Thorn! They saw a man who had been invincible for almost twenty years flee! They saw Ghost Soldiers lose their lives by your sword! They saw Gaeldeath riders falling dead onto the soil, exhausted from hunger and hardship! The rumour that it was your plan that brought all this about flies through the city!" John's eyes flashed as they turned to Elliot. "And most importantly, they witnessed with their own eyes, an Egercoll, trained by Althalos Baudry, saving the life of an Endor!" he blazed. "Everyone heard your cries when you revealed your Master's identity to Walter outside Wirskworth. By now, the whole city knows who you really are... I don't know when or how, but I heard that it was the governor who revealed the secret."

Elliot sighed, hiding his face in his palms. "I don't know if I can go on, John... I don't know if I have the strength."

"You must go on... If you can't do it for Knightdorn's people, do it for Morys."

At the sound of the name, Elliot's stomach tightened. "Eleanor will never want to see me again," he mumbled.

"Do you think she holds you responsible?" asked Long Arm.

"Of course!"

The man snorted contemptuously. "Morys would have ended his life with or without your help. At some point, he would have found a way. It was better for him not to have been alone at the final hour. Eleanor knows this truth as she knows that she'd never have found the courage to do what you did. I'm sure she's glad that it was you who was by his side during that final moment."

Their eyes met, and John stood up with a jolt. "We're late! We must go to the temple," he growled. Elliot frowned, and Long Arm explained. "The governor will sentence the prisoners of yesterday's battle to death, and she wants the execution to take place as soon as possible. The Guardians of the South remain in the city to watch the punishment," John said. "Syrella's men wanted to inform you at the first light of day, but they found me earlier, and I assured them that I would do it. I intended to see you as soon as I woke up. I thought you'd be in the chamber where Thorold had been sent to heal you, but I heard you had come here before dawn."

"Execution?" Elliot wondered.

"Have you forgotten who governs Wirskworth? Did you think Syrella Endor would spare the life of any of Walter's men who survived?" John remarked. "Only a leader like Sophie Delamere would consider such a thing..."

"When will the execution take place?" Elliot asked.

"Soon," replied John.

Elliot got up off of his chair and rushed out of the room. He was still dressed in the linen clothes he had woken up in. "We must hurry!" he flung at John.

Elliot walked with long strides despite the pain in his wounded leg, and it didn't take them long to leave Moonstone. They continued, crossing Snail Road and Brass Road, and approached the temple. The roads were deserted, and as soon as they approached the temple's portico, Elliot understood why.

All the people of Wirskworth had gathered around the Temple of the God of Souls, while the prisoners, fewer than one hundred in number, were gathered in front of the statue in the centre of the huge portico. Elliot spotted Edmund, the repugnant high priest beside the prisoners—he wore a black cloak. Next to him stood Syrella Endor, dressed in green silk and satin, with yellow trim. A little farther off, the elaborate armour of the men of the Sharp Swords shone like rubies, their long cloaks trailing behind them. The counsellors looked nervous beside the men of the Sharp Swords, staring at the vast crowd gathered around the temple. Elliot's eyes fell on the sun banner with the spears. Stonegate's men stood under the portico but closer to it than anyone else. He pushed through the crowd to reach Syrella.

Sophie Delamere looked down the length of the Royal Hall feeling powerful—for the first time in her life she had won. The lord of the knights, along with some guards, marched toward her, accompanying the captives. The latter were all Oldlands men, as none of the Gaeldeath soldiers had survived. Only thirty men had arrived in Iovbridge as prisoners, asking for mercy from Isisdor's soldiers.

Peter trod soberly beside the prisoners, wearing a grey cloak and a white jerkin with the Pegasus and the Seven Swords sewn on his chest. The men of the council watched gloomily in their silk costumes from their seats below her. The Royal Hall was flooded with people, nobles and soldiers tightly-packed in every corner. The captives were led before the elevated throne with the majestic wings. Hundreds of contemptuous glares turned in their direction.

Peter approached Sophie. The prisoners knelt before her, silent, still dressed in battle clothes. Sophie got up from the throne abruptly.

Syrella Endor saw the boy approaching her. She had heard his cries among the crowd. She was glad that he had managed to come to the temple—he deserved to see the spectacle that would follow.

The banner of the snake fluttered all round the portico. Syrella glanced at the kneeling captives, and her heart skipped a beat. She would finally get a modicum of revenge for the death of her people, another victory after the one they had just achieved the day before.

The captives were ashen-faced and filthy, wearing woollen rags. Her men had taken their armour off and dressed them in cast off clothes. The crowd cheered in ecstasy. Its shouts grew louder as soon as Elliot approached her, recognizing the young man.

"I'm glad you're here," Syrella said in a hushed tone. "It's time for justice."

"No," replied Elliot with flashing eyes.

"What?"

"I ask that these men's lives be spared," he continued.

"Have you lost your mind?" she shouted while the cheering of the crowd drifted in the air.

"I know these men are responsible for countless crimes, but if we take their lives, we will be no better than Walter," Elliot argued. "By executing them, we won't bring our dead back to life!"

"Walter Thorn never spared the lives of any of his enemies!" Syrella thundered.

"We must show Knightdorn that Walter's enemies are better than him," Elliot said in a pleading tone.

Syrella felt anger. She couldn't do what he asked for. Her brother, her nephew, Lord Hewdar... They all passed before her eyes, and her soul was filled with more and more hatred.

"These men only followed orders," Elliot continued. "The only way to show our enemies a better path is to follow it ourselves."

Sophie knew what she had to do. The council had decided to spare the captives' lives a few hours earlier. Most counsellors believed that they shouldn't provoke Walter any more, otherwise his rage would break out relentlessly in Iovbridge. They thought that if Sophie spared lives, he'd do the same if he conquered the capital of Knightdorn. Frederic and Merick had disagreed, asking for blood, but the lord of the knights had sided with the majority. It was one of the few times Peter believed that the opinion of most was reasonable. He had argued that the men of Oldlands had only followed their ruler's orders, and that they weren't responsible for Walter's actions. If Sophie spared their lives, she might create discord among the enemy's ranks, as many Oldlands soldiers would see that she was merciful in contrast to Walter. Sophie had agreed to follow the majority's opinion, ignoring Frederic and Merick.

"King Thomas, but also the entire House of Egercoll, has always shown generosity towards prisoners of war throughout its history," Sophie's voice echoed loudly in the Royal Hall.

Syrella Endor looked at Elliot. He could not read her expression. He prayed she would do the right thing. After a few moments, Syrella turned to the crowd and raised her hand. The cheering stopped at once.

"We have achieved a great victory against the men who have watered our land with blood and death several times in the last twenty years. These men killed, raped, and looted, and they deserve to be punished for their crimes," she announced.

Her eyes fell momentarily upon Elliot.

"Nevertheless, Elmor will never be like its enemies," she shouted. "The captives will be held in cells, and they will pay for their crimes, but they will not pay with their lives."

The crowd had gone quiet, but now it swelled with fresh vigor as an enraged outcry swept over them, blotting out every other sound in the ancient city of the elves.

Sophie looked at Peter before continuing. "But I'm not an Egercoll!" she suddenly roared. "KILL THEM ALL!"

Peter's eyes opened wide, and he turned towards the guards, but it was too late. The Oldlands men's blood spilled like thick lava onto the floor of the Palace of the Dawn, and Peter knew that Knightdorn would be covered in pain and death for many more years to come.

The Last Plan

Sophie felt the cold air whisper over her skin as she walked down a cobbled street, gazing at the Scarlet Sea. This alley had been her favourite in Iovbridge since she was a child. She had left the palace a while ago, wanting to walk beside the stormy waters, letting her thoughts travel far. The Scarlet Sea was like lava that morning. *How fitting the name given to these waters*, she thought.

Her eyelids were heavy. Much as she had tried to sink into the world of dreams last night, she hadn't succeeded. The sound of steel plunging into human flesh loomed in her mind. Screams, cries of pain, begging, and blood—red and thick—were her only thoughts. Was that the price of revenge?

The Oldlands men deserved to die. They had betrayed Aymer Asselin the day they decided to follow a Karford. They had even betrayed the memory of Alice Asselin with their decision. They had also betrayed Sophie herself. Yet her guilt just wouldn't diminish. Sometimes she wondered how Walter had taken so many lives without going mad with guilt.

Sophie always believed that her life had far more death than she wished, and yet, when given the opportunity to choose between life and death, blood and forgiveness, she had chosen the justice of steel. Her parents, her uncle, countless men who had sworn allegiance to her... They all had passed before her eyes, and rage had flashed in her like a vicious reptile. *Had the souls of the dead calmed after her act?* She didn't believe so. The dead didn't care about what was happening in the world of the living. So the joy of revenge had turned to ashes inside her.

"Your Majesty." Peter had appeared behind her, like a shadow.

Sophie didn't want to see him. Not yet. "I'd like to be alone."

"We need to talk," he insisted. "We have no news from Wirskworth..."

She closed her eyes, feeling the taste of the sea in her mouth. If she could, she would never talk about battles or war again in her life.

Suddenly, a loud caw sounded on her left, and Sophie turned to see a white hawk with broad wings perched on the stone ledge beside her. There was a white scroll in the hooked talons of its right foot. Sophie walked over to the hawk and pulled the letter free.

"Only centaurs can order animals—only they used to transfer letters that way," Peter remarked.

Sophie noticed the sealing wax—the Endor Snake shone in the sunlight.

The queen opened the scroll and began to read, unblinking, as if time had stopped. Peter waited impatiently until she raised her head with a vague look, as if her mind had left the world.

"What's going on?" asked Peter in angst. He needed to know.

The woman didn't move.

"Walter... occupied Wirsk—" He couldn't even say it.

"Once again, you were right, Peter."

"What do you me..."

"The boy... the boy..." panted Sophie

The queen took a deep breath and began to read aloud.

"'Elliot Egercoll, son of Thomas Egercoll and Alice Asselin, knight of Queen Sophie Delamere, protector of Knightdorn and the glorious race of men, managed with the help of Wirskworth and the Guardians of Stonegate to protect the south from Walter Thorn's attack.

"The Oath of the South came to life in the soils of the south-east, and the alliance of Elmor and Isisdor glowed again, like fire, ready to burn everything in its path.

"I, Syrella Endor, Governor of Elmor, invite the queen and the Governor of Ballar to travel with their people to the ancient city of the elves. Only united behind the strongest walls in the world will we stand a chance to defeat our enemy.

"The light of the skies may have been extinguished on Egercoll soil, but in Elmor, the alliances of the past will be reborn from their ashes as fearless as a pegasus.'"

Peace enveloped Peter's soul. His son had to be alive, otherwise Syrella would have mentioned something in her letter. "The light of the skies may have been extinguished?" he mumbled after a while, confused.

"The City of Heavens has been shrouded in darkness for decades," Sophie said.

"Elliot Egercoll... son of Thomas. I can't believe it," Peter exhaled, constantly losing his train of thought. "How is that possible?"

"He was trained by Althalos, as you correctly guessed."

"But how do we know?"

"The truth was right in front of our eyes, Peter... Who could have achieved what this boy has achieved?"

"But—"

"He managed to take Stonegate, he managed to convince us to attack Ramerstorm, he managed to protect Elmor from Walter, while his real plan was always what you, too, wanted from the very start... Nevertheless, Althalos knew. He may not have seen me since I was a little girl, but he knew that I wouldn't agree to retreat to Elmor without an invitation," she said.

Peter couldn't comprehend the facts. "How do you know Althalos trained him?" he remarked dazed.

"'A leader full of love and compassion for his people will always have allies who believe in him, no matter how powerful his enemies are.'" Sophie brought the parchment up to his face, showing him the last sentence, the phrase she had just uttered.

Peter stared, the Grand Master's face filling his mind, telling him to support Sophie after Thomas's death. Peter had believed that Althalos had lost his mind. He had tried to explain to him that nobody would support the little girl; even if some did, they would sooner or later betray her by taking the enemy's side, as Walter's power was incomparable. Nevertheless, no matter what he had said to the old man, he hadn't been able to argue against the weight of those words.

The Rider of Fate

The sunset had made its appearance, accompanied by a fragrant, calming breeze while thousands of colourful leaves rustled in tune, reminiscent of a melody on the harp. Elliot had great affection for the little forest next to Moonstone.

"I didn't expect to find you here."

Elliot was surprised to hear the voice. "This place is peaceful," he proffered calmly, looking at Velhisya who had appeared out of nowhere. He smiled and took her in—she was so beautiful.

She wore a diadem adorned with gems on her silver-blue hair, and her silk dress was the colour of lemon. It was as if the dim light of the setting sun incandesced upon her as she walked toward him. For a moment, Elliot thought she was wearing the sun, even as her hair glowed like the halo of the moon.

"All the Endors loved this place," she said, sighing, looking at the little forest.

Elliot smiled. "Apparently, some Egercolls can admire its beauty too," he jibed.

She approached him, hesitation reflected in her eyes. She seemed to want to speak, but something was holding her back, so he looked at her encouragingly.

"I'm grateful you saved my cousin." Her eyes searched his.

"I am the only one who should be grateful. Elmor's men saved me from certain death."

They walked a few paces before she spoke again.

"Master Thorold wants to talk to you."

Elliot never expected the Master to send Velhisya to find him. "How did you know I was here?" he asked in a hushed voice.

Velhisya laughed softly. "I didn't," she replied. "I just thought... I like to come here too, when I feel melancholy...," she murmured.

Elliot took a step toward her and felt untold emotions. He wanted to take her in his arms and kiss her. "Where will I find him?" he asked after a few awkward moments.

"He's waiting for you at the Water Gate."

He took one last look at her, then turned away, mustering all his strength to leave her presence. He swore that her eyes lit up strangely as they parted.

His wounded leg ached. It had only been two days since Walter and his tiger had attacked him. Still, it wasn't long before he reached the secret passage next to the long narrow cistern of Wirskworth. Elliot was surprised when he came across the spectacle that awaited him. The Water Gate was open. Having pulled the rusty chain, a guard lifted it and looked like he had been waiting for him. Elliot wondered what was going on when a whinnying broke the silence.

"Follow me, Elliot," a voice was heard, and Thorold emerged behind him on a horse, holding the reins of a second brown mare in his right hand. The Master rode with unexpected grace for his age.

Elliot mounted the brown horse in a flash, and the two horses passed through the gate at speed as night began to make its appearance. Shortly afterwards, the wan moon was visible in the sky as they crossed a path north of the Forked River, a little further south of the Road of Elves.

The hours passed, and after much time, Elliot noticed Ersemor's outskirts to their right. He had no idea where Thorold was leading him. The Master turned his horse with an abrupt move and started riding toward the forest at high speed. Elliot followed him, and after a few moments, they reached Ersemor. They rode incessantly, passing fallen trees and small clearings, and Elliot felt increasingly mystified about their final destination, until the Master stopped abruptly and dismounted his horse. He followed suit.

"What are we doing in the Centaurs-Land?" exclaimed Elliot, observing Thorold's thick woollen cloak. He only wore a beetle-coloured linen jerkin, and the night breeze made him shudder.

"Ersemor hides much more than the Centaurs-Land," countered Thorold. The landscape was dark, but the moonlight shone on the Master's face. "As you said, I recognised you immediately, as soon as I saw you in the Temple of the God of Life," Thorold confessed unexpectedly. "I didn't expect you to pass through the City of Heavens," he continued in a voice that came out hoarse. "However, I couldn't tell you anything. I promised Althalos that I would speak to you only after Walter had left the south."

Elliot had already guessed that the two men had been in communication. But there were other things he wished to know. "Why were my sister and I separated?" he spoke loudly.

Thorold sighed. "That was Althalos's idea," he murmured ruefully. "I was the only Grand Master, apart from him, who had survived and whom he trusted. So, he gave me Selyn when she was still very young because he wanted you to split up early, so that you wouldn't remember her... But he knew that memories of her had remained in your mind," the elder remarked. "After Walter's attack on the City of Heavens, Althalos knew that his old apprentice wouldn't busy himself with the former kingdom of the House of Egercoll again, so the City of Heavens would be safe. Then he gave me the girl, and I decided not to train warriors again and to raise her as if she were my blood."

Elliot turned away in anger.

"You have to understand... Whatever Althalos did, he did because it was necessary. He cared about you more than anything else in the world!"

Thorold's words infuriated Elliot. "HE HID EVERYTHING FROM ME!" he screamed. All the anger that had accumulated inside of him erupted.

The man closed his eyes forlornly, then opened them again. "He had no choice."

Elliot was about to protest, but Thorold spoke faster. "Althalos knew that you had to stay away from every member of your family in order to complete your training. Boys trained by Grand Masters always had to make sacrifices."

"HE NEVER EVEN MENTIONED HER EXISTENCE!"

The old man exhaled wearily. "If you had known, your only concern would have been to find her and make sure that she was safe. You'd have done anything for her... But the future of Knightdorn depended on you, and you had to be trained believing that you had lost everything. Only then would your mind be fully focused on your undertakings, which were profoundly difficult."

"He could have trained her too," Elliot retorted. "He could have taught us both, without separating us."

"As I told you, you had to train on your own, believing that you had lost everything. The Grand Masters always trained one warrior at a time. Althalos also believed that it'd be best if only one child was trained, and the other lived peacefully, away from fighting and death." Elliot was steaming. "Deep down, you know that Althalos was right."

"I don't care!" he grunted. "He kept so many secrets from me! He made me carry out a plan, hiding countless bits of information that would have helped me accomplish it more easily!"

"Part of your training is to find out for yourself how to achieve your aims," Thorold said.

"It doesn't matter anymore," Elliot mumbled, looking at the starry sky between the trees. "I failed... I didn't follow Althalos' advice."

"The important thing is not whether you failed to follow his advice." The old man spoke kindly. "The important thing is whether you now understand the reasons why he gave you such advice."

Elliot was speechless for a moment. "I'm certain now that you knew the plan," he flung back.

"Yes," Thorold admitted. "But still, I'd like to hear it from you and find out which points you disagreed with, but also whether you have changed your mind now..."

Elliot felt as if he had passed a test and Thorold wanted to see how much he had learnt from it. For a moment, he felt like he had his old Master before him. "Althalos was informed of everything going on in the kingdom throughout the years he was in hiding. He came to know the characters of several notable figures in Knightdorn well. Based on that information, he tried to set up a plan to deal with Walter," he began. "Althalos knew that Iovbridge would easily fall under siege since the Royal Army was much smaller than the enemy's forces.

"The only region with a combat-worthy army that could easily ally itself with the palace was Elmor. Althalos knew that Syrella would forget the past and help Sophie. Still, even if Elmor helped Isisdor, it'd be difficult to hope for a victory in Iovbridge. Knightdorn's capital does not have strong walls. Thus, Althalos concluded that Wirskworth, the city with the strongest walls in the world, was the best place for a battle against Walter and his allies and decided to try to lure the two rival camps there for the final encounter.

"As soon as Althalos had thought through every detail of the plan, he told me that I had to go to Iovbridge and confess part of his plan to Sophie while simultaneously asking for some companions who would ride with me to Elmor. I'd also take Stonegate for the queen, defeating Reynald in single combat. He also wanted me to succeed in getting a letter from Sophie, in which the queen would ask for an alliance from Syrella Endor. Then, I would send the news of Reynald's fall to Walter, dropping the bait so that he would march to Elmor. As soon as I arrived in Wirskworth, I'd advise Syrella to pick every crop from her land. Althalos had told me not to reveal the whole plan, not even to Syrella, before the right time. So, I would ask her to march her armies to Iovbridge, instead of inviting the queen to Elmor."

Elliot sighed heavily for a moment. "Once I heard the plan, I had thousands of doubts... Firstly, I couldn't believe that Althalos expected the queen to listen to and heed the advice of a stranger. The same was true for Syrella. And I doubted whether Walter would take the bait. I asked the Master how I would persuade the two women to hear me out, but he didn't answer. In his opinion, I was to solve this riddle by myself. He was also sure that Walter would ride south as soon as he heard that Reynald had fallen and that Stonegate had submitted to Iovbridge's orders, while some of the queen's messengers would head for Wirskworth. Knowing his character, he was certain that he wouldn't want Elmor men involved in the Battle of Iovbridge. Althalos believed that his old apprentice would fear that Reynald's fall, along with an alliance between Isisdor and Elmor, could bring friction to the ranks of his allies, given that the devotion of many of them was based solely on fear. Elmor's involvement would also make Iovbridge's siege quite difficult, even if the chances of winning were still on Walter's side.

"Althalos was convinced that his old apprentice wanted to take Iovbridge quickly, showing his power throughout the kingdom. That way, no one would ever question him again. However, Walter didn't want to try to assassinate Sophie slyly. That would make him look cowardly and weak, and many were already whispering that he had failed to subdue Oldlands and had therefore conspired to assassinate Aymer. Althalos had thought it possible that Walter would doubt whether it was worth going south, since Elmor might possibly not follow the call. However, Althalos believed that Walter would conclude that Syrella would accept a new alliance—even if she didn't, he could leave some of his men on her land to stop her army in case she changed her mind. Thus, the scorched earth tactic was the best plan for Elmor in Althalos' head.

"Listening to my Master's thoughts, I was convinced that Walter would take the bait and decide to attack Elmor's army on Snake Road. Any other tactic would have been risky or impossible after Stonegate changed commander." Elliot paused for a moment.

"Once I was convinced that Walter would be misled into going to Elmor, I again asked Althalos how I could persuade Syrella and Sophie to listen to me. My Master replied that Syrella actually wanted to fight Walter. All she needed was a nudge from Sophie, and if the Stonegate hurdle were out of her way, it'd be easy to make the decision to ally with Iovbridge. But I still had to find the words I'd say to her to make her follow my plan and accept a new alliance. Althalos believed that I would find a way to persuade Sophie and told me that if I failed, I'd have to leave Iovbridge no later than three days after my arrival and try to carry out the plan, leaving the palace out of it. In that case, I'd ride alone to Elmor, without a letter from the queen, but I'd inform Iovbridge if I managed to defeat Reynald and convince Syrella of a new alliance with the Crown by sending messengers." Elliot took a deep breath before continuing.

"I thought about Althalos' words for a long time and one day I took issue with him. I thought the plan was risky, and the only way to succeed would be to reveal my real name to the queen and the Governor of Elmor. Thomas Egercoll's son would be more easily accepted than an unknown boy, and even if this information reached Walter, he wouldn't care. After all, my father's name was now dead. I agreed, though, that I had to hide my Master's identity, otherwise Walter could have reversed all his decisions in the face of the revelation that there was a living man who was a descendant of Thomas Egercoll and, what is more, had been trained by Althalos.

"I also believed that since our real goal was to get the people of Iovbridge to Elmor, it'd be better for me to confide the true plan to the queen from the start, so that she and her people would head to Wirskworth as soon as Walter left Ballar. With Stonegate in our hands, the people of Knightdorn's capital could go south. I'd also inform Syrella of their arrival while they waited at Stonegate until Walter made his way back to Ballar, leaving the way to Wirskworth open." Elliot's voice now bore a hint of indignation.

"Althalos told me that I was wrong. In his view, I had to persuade the two women to hear me out, using only my words and not my name, otherwise I would've failed to complete my training. And he argued that even if I revealed the truth about who I was, it wouldn't convince either Sophie or Syrella to listen to me, unless I inspired their confidence in me.

"He also believed that Sophie would never accept a plan to retreat to Wirskworth without Syrella herself inviting her. Otherwise, she would have retreated to Elmor a long time ago. The Master believed that the reason Sophie didn't want to back down was that she didn't want to force Syrella to protect her, putting her people in danger. On top of that, a retreat shortly before the battle for the throne would make her look cowardly throughout the kingdom. Moreover, Althalos was unsure of the decisions Syrella would take. He may have believed that she'd accept an alliance with Sophie, but if he was wrong, then the queen could have found herself exposed in the Land of Fire in the unlikely event she decided to retreat." Elliot glanced at Thorold, who nodded for him to continue.

"Finally, Althalos told me that if Walter heard that the soldier who defeated Reynald was the son of Thomas and Alice, he'd immediately realise the truth about who had trained him. Walter was the only one who knew he hadn't killed his old Master and that Thomas would have trusted only Althalos with his only son. According to Althalos, this was where the most danger lay, because if Walter found out the truth earlier and concluded that Althalos had trained me, he could reverse his decisions and destroy everything. In short, my Master believed that the revelation of my name would offer me nothing of substance, neither in Isisdor nor in Elmor, but it would imperil us all. That's why it was very important that I didn't reveal the slightest thing until Walter had left Wirskworth for White City." Elliot stopped talking for a moment, unable to keep from dwelling on how he had failed to follow this directive.

"Truth be told," he went on, "I didn't agree with Althalos, but I agreed to follow his instructions, telling him that I should ride to Iovbridge earlier. That way, I'd have more time to find a way to convince the queen and set off for Elmor sooner. But Althalos disagreed with this too. He believed that I had no hope of being heard by the queen before Walter had almost arrived outside her walls. In his opinion, the only way Sophie would hear me out and give me guides and witnesses for my victory over Reynald was if she was desperate. Otherwise, I wouldn't be able to persuade her and would be forced to leave Iovbridge alone, without a letter from the queen to the Governor of Elmor, which would make my mission even harder...

"I didn't expect Althalos to die the moment I was to set out. I knew he was sick, but I wasn't read—" Elliot's voice broke. He may have been mad at his Master, but the lose still filled him with pain.

Thorold put a hand on his shoulder, waiting for him to go on.

"Althalos guessed right about everything," Elliot admitted, straightening and recovering himself. "He was right about Sophie and Syrella, while my stupidity in revealing my name made Walter change his plans, just as Althalos had feared. I'm sure Walter intended to return to Ballar as soon as he found scorched earth in Elmor, deciding to take his revenge in Iovbridge.

"But it seems a spy from Wirskworth revealed everything about me to him, so he decided to stay in the south, trying to pollute the waters of the Forked River. That way, the people of Wirskworth would have been forced to fight outside of the city. Wirskworth's guards failed to catch the spy and it's certain that it was he who informed Walter that you were alive," he ended, looking at the Master with a sense of guilt. "I was the one who revealed the truth about you to Elmor's council. If I hadn't opened my mouth..."

Thorold sighed deeply at those last words. "It was my mistake to reveal myself to your company. I thought that secret would be safe. Sadly, I was wrong. Old age has made me forget that young people are often impulsive, even if they don't have bad intentions," he in turn admitted.

Elliot was pensive. "I don't think Walter was that interested in you," he remarked. "If you had been training warriors, the news would have reached him a long time ago. I think he was just outraged after hearing several secrets he had been ignorant of for years, and so he decided to kill us both."

"I agree."

"But my stupidity in revealing that you were alive cost the lives of all the people of the City of Heavens!" Guilt gnawed at Elliot's soul.

"That's not true," the Master rebutted him. "Only Walter is responsible for that."

"As soon as Walter left Elmor, I could have revealed the whole truth... Althalos believed that if we reached that point, I could confide the real plan to Syrella and urge her to invite the queen to her land, she would agree, and Sophie would accept the invitation.

"Besides, if I managed to repulse Walter from the south, take Stonegate, and help Iovbridge attack the enemy forces remaining in Ballar, I would've proved my worth to everyone, compelling them to listen to me. At the same time, I would've dealt a great blow to the reputation of the power of the enemy. The queen may have conceded the throne in the end, but she would have done so as a victor, not as a coward. Plus, she would have retreated with an invitation from Syrella, which was the most important thing for her," he remarked.

"Truth be told, I was afraid that the queen may have taken too long to retreat to Wirskworth, as soon as I revealed the real plan to her," Elliot went on. "If I sent her a messenger as soon as Walter left Wirskworth, it would have been days before the message reached Iovbridge. Moreover, she would need time to travel south-east with her people. I was afraid Walter might find out she had left Iovbridge and find a way to attack her in the open.

"Nevertheless, Althalos assured me that the tired horses of Gaeldeath would need many days to get to Ballar. He was also sure that the men of Iovbridge would have managed to kill the enemy soldiers guarding White City. So, when Walter returned to Ramerstorm, he wouldn't learn what had happened while he was away. It was clear that Sophie would travel through the south-east path, and there are no villagers or wanderers in the Land of Fire. Walter wouldn't have been able to find out that the queen had left the city until the moment he attacked it." Elliot paused. "When I discussed all this with Althalos, I didn't know I'd have Hurwig," he added suddenly.

Thorold nodded with a smile.

"Althalos wanted me to reveal my truth when it could no longer have an effect on the outcome. Once Walter had left Elmor and Sophie had set off for Wirskworth, the plan would have succeeded. When Walter returns to Ballar and attacks Iovbridge, he'll figure everything out. Then, he'll get even angrier and decide to attack Wirskworth with all his forces, in order to destroy his enemies once and for all. The truth about me and my Master would change nothing at that moment except serve to tarnish his reputation even more," he concluded.

Thorold nodded thoughtfully. "I think you now know why Althalos did what he did. Even if you're mad at him," he noted.

Elliot didn't speak for a moment. "He kept me in the dark even concerning the legends about my family. He never told me the story of the Seven Swords." A note of irritation crept into his voice.

"Some truths we must discover ourselves, Elliot."

"I almost destroyed everything," Elliot breathed out wearily, letting his anger slide away.

"You were lucky in your misfortune," Thorold remarked. "Walter should have killed you right away when you appeared before him, but he was arrogant. Now he won't make that same mistake again. Moreover, his rage over the secrets he found out about made him disregard his men's fatigue and hunger. His decision to ride quickly to the City of Heavens resulted in the exhaustion of even his strongest horses, while he had neither the time nor the carts to carry supplies to Wirskworth. He also neglected to consider the stubbornness and courage of Syrella. Walter's actions against the Hewdars and Elirehar enraged her instead of scaring her. As soon as she saw the smoke coming from the west, it was more than certain that she would try to avenge herself and Elirehar's people. And he never would expected the Guardians of Stonegate to attack him. They may not have been large in number, but everyone knows what worthy warriors they are."

"I never found out why the Stonegate soldiers decided to march to Wirskworth," Elliot said. He had met Jarin in the city briefly before the Guardians had departed but had neglected to ask him about it. The day's events had killed his curiosity.

"The Guardians of Stonegate saw that Syrella was gathering crops and villagers into Wirskworth," the elder replied. "When Walter attacked Myril, a Guardian riding near the castle saw the attack and raced to warn Stonegate. The Guardians were furious as soon as they saw how cruelly Walter behaved towards Jacob Hewdar and his people. Jarin decided to ride with all his horses to Wirskworth and watch from a distance to see whether Elmor's army would attack. He had assumed that Walter would be there, as this was the only explanation for Syrella's gathering food and villagers off of her land.

"After you left for Elirehar, the Guardians arrived in Wirskworth and waited north of the city. Syrella had noticed their presence, as Wirskworth's high hills provide a very good view," the old man remarked. "As soon as Wirskworth opened its gates and rode out to meet Walter, they knew it was their chance to join. They also killed some of Walter's men who had visited Stonegate a few days earlier, as they insulted Jarin and tried to attack him when he refused them entry."

Elliot had listened intently and remembered Walter's men arriving at Stonegate when he was there. "Whatever happened, the truth is that I failed," he lamented after a while. "I revealed the truth about myself even to the centaurs!" he exclaimed.

Thorold smiled. "You didn't fail, my good child," he said. "You may have got carried away by your hotheadedness, but you showed unparalleled courage and devotion towards those who believed in you. Althalos would have been proud of you. Nevertheless, don't be afraid of failure.

Failure makes us wiser. As for the centaurs, they, much like Aleron, knew who you were from the moment you set foot in Ersemor. They just wanted to see what kind of person you were. Truthfully, though, they were disappointed, but you still have time to convince them," he encouraged Elliot cheerfully.

Elliot looked deep into the trees around them. He had suspected that the centaur Leghor had known a lot about him. And it had been clear that Aleron did.

"You told me I had to train alone, believing I had lost everything," Elliot said suddenly, "but since Althalos believed that only one child should be trained and the other live peacefully, why did he choose to train me and not my sister?" He had finally uttered the question that tormented him all this time. "Was it just because I was a boy?"

Thorold closed his eyes. "It's time for you to learn this story," he murmured after a while. "Follow me."

Something twisted in Elliot's stomach, but he obeyed.

"Have you heard about the legend of the Rider of Fate?" asked the old man, as they walked.

"No," he replied.

"I'm sure you've heard of the story about the Elder Races and the curse of Manhon Egercoll by now."

"Yes!"

"This story is true," Thorold said. "The Elder Races betrayed the Egercolls by selling the six swords that had been watered with pegasus blood to their enemies. There upon, Manhon took the seventh sword and cursed them to remain in the Mountains of the Forgotten World forever."

"It's true?"

"Manhon avenged the death of his brothers and was the last man to ever ride a pegasus," Thorold continued. "The seventh sword, the Sword of Light, remained in the House of Egercoll for countless generations, but no one ever found out about the fate of the last pegasus... Many think it died after Manhon's death, while others refuse to even believe in the existence of pegasi," cried the old man. "Besides, many legends claim that the pegasi died as soon as their riders lost their lives, but that's not absolutely true."

The knot doubled in Elliot's stomach, though he couldn't have said why. He felt like a child listening to a scary story.

"A pegasus dies the moment its rider dies but is then reborn through the light of the God of Life, ready to be attached to a new master. The truth is that there were never more than seven pegasi, and the only objects ever made that could kill them were the legendary seven swords that left the world in the dark. Before the existence of these swords, the pegasi were immortal." Thorold's voice was barely audible this time.

"There's one more legend, the legend of the Rider of Fate," the Master spoke again, and Elliot's stomach tightened in anticipation. "According to that legend, Thindor, Manhon's pegasus and the last pegasus in the world, felt the light of the God of Life slowly die out when his brothers were slaughtered, and the Elder Races' power withered. It was the moment when the darkness of the God of Death haunted the world, swallowing life. So, after Manhon's death, the last pegasus disappeared, refusing to unite with a new rider. Thindor awaits the Rider of Fate, the only man who can awaken his powers and break the curse that holds the Elder Races trapped by resurrecting the power of light."

An exasperated sigh escaped Elliot's lips. "I don't believe in fairytales," he scoffed. "But even if I did, the Elder Races may have deserved this fate." He felt bad as soon as he spoke these words, his thoughts turning to Velhisya.

"If the Elder Races deserved this fate, have you ever considered what the race of humans deserves for their sins?"

Elliot fell silent upon hearing Thorold's words.

The old man continued to walk, passing through some thorny branches. Elliot followed him silently. They turned left and right several times, until the trees thinned out, and a clearing shone in front of them.

Thorold kept going, but Elliot walked hesitantly. This place reminded him of the Path of Wishes, but they were much further south. Ahead of him, the Master turned abruptly and disappeared from Elliot's sight. He picked up his pace, and as the clearing extended before him, he heard a soft sound to his right. Elliot turned his gaze, and he was struck with wonder.

The pure white creature looked at him from afar with its golden eyes—its wings were broad and long, full of silver feathers, and its legs were slender strong. Thorold stood beside the pegasus and with a soothing motion gently caressed its head. The pegasus closed its eyes, purring, as the human hand stroked its white hair.

Elliot walked toward the creature, the golden eyes still watching him. The pegasus took a step toward him. Elliot could have sworn that the Master was holding his breath, but after a few moments, Thindor snorted and stepped back.

"How...? How is it possible?" Elliot stammered.

"Now only two people know this secret," said Thorold. "When Walter arrived in the City of Heavens, I was here."

Elliot couldn't believe what he was seeing.

"Althalos trained you because of the truth that the centaurs had read in the waters of the Lake of Life," said the Master. "Althalos had known Aleron, the eldest of the elwyn race, for years. He wanted to free the Elder Races from Manhon's curse. But Thindor had never chosen a new rider after his last master's death, and legend has it that he'd follow the Rider of Fate on his own, as soon as he was born.

"When Thomas dethroned George Thorn, united the kingdoms under many years of peace, and concurrently changed countless laws that had plagued Knightdorn for centuries, Althalos believed in him, even though Thomas wasn't one of the boys he had trained in the past. Nevertheless, the Grand Master didn't divulge the secret about Thindor to him. A few years later, Althalos concluded Walter's training, and as soon as he took over Gaeldeath and exiled his father, Althalos knew he had made a mistake in choosing him as his apprentice.

"In all his life, Althalos had never met another man with abilities as deadly as Walter's. He knew that no one could stop him. Then, at Aleron's insistence, he decided to reveal Thindor to Thomas. At the time, Althalos was the only human who knew the greatest secret of the Age of Men, as the centaurs and Elder Races who knew the truth hadn't told anyone else. Althalos had wanted to liberate the Elder Races for years, regardless of Walter's rise, but he hadn't managed to find a way. He knew that no one would stand any chance against his former apprentice without the help of creatures superior to humans. So, he thought that perhaps the need for help against Walter's power combined with the need to liberate the Elder Races was the key for an Egercoll to awaken Thindor's power and break Manhon's curse.

"Thomas couldn't believe his eyes when he saw Thindor. Then, Althalos told him to go to the Mountains of the Forgotten World to try and liberate the Elder Races. Your father was an Egercoll, and he had the Sword of Light, and legend had it that only an Egercoll with that blade could awaken Thindor's power and break the curse.

"Thomas made his way through the Mountains of the Forgotten World but failed to free the Elder Races, and Thindor never followed him. Althalos and Aleron were disappointed. They knew that legend said Thindor would follow the Rider of Fate on his own, which hadn't happened in all the years Thomas was alive. But they believed that as soon as the second king reached the Mountains of the Forgotten World, Thindor's power would be awakened, and the pegasus would choose him as his new rider.

"Both turned out to be wrong. Nevertheless, the centaurs decided to follow Thomas in the war against Walter, even if he had failed to liberate the Elder Races." Thorold faltered for a moment. "After Thomas's failure in the Mountains of the Forgotten World, the waters of the Lake of Life revealed the truth to the centaurs."

Elliot noticed Thorold's hesitation, remembering John's words. Long

Arm had said that the centaurs could read the future in the waters of the Lake of Life.

"The centaurs saw that only a male Egercoll, born during an alignment of the moon with the sun, could liberate the Elder Races and unite with Thindor," the Master continued. "Althalos and Aleron didn't know this before sending Thomas to the Mountains of the Forgotten World. When they found out, they never sent anyone there again as in the last three hundred years no Egercoll had been born during that kind of alignment. A phenomenon such as this happens once every fifty years." The old man stared at him.

Elliot stared back, and then terror penetrated his body. "Me?" he stammered, unable to believe it.

"You are the only male Egercoll born during an alignment of the moon and sun, so Althalos decided to train you, having deemed it better that your sister live in peace, away from the life of a warrior."

Elliot stepped back in shock. "Why didn't he tell me?"

"You weren't ready. You had a lot to accomplish, and the idea that you were special wouldn't help. Your Master thought you shouldn't know this before you managed to carry out his plan. If nothing else, Althalos never had absolute faith in the truths of the Lake of Life," Thorold replied.

Elliot felt as if the world had started shrinking around him. "Who else knew?" he asked after a while.

"Althalos confided the secret to me shortly after you were born, and he thought it wise to reveal it to Selyn too. Now, only you and I know."

"Althalos thought my sister should know the truth, but not me?" Elliot couldn't believe it. "When did you intend to tell me the truth about the existence of my sister?" he asked, still trying to digest the facts.

"After Walter was dead," came the Master's answer. "Before that moment, the truth would have been just another burden for you, and you already had enough to carry."

"Did she know?" Elliot asked after a moment. "Did she know I was her brother?"

Thorold exhaled wearily, "Yes," he said while watching him. "But she had sworn she wouldn't tell you."

Thorold paced to the side and then back again and met Elliot's gaze. "I had agreed with Althalos to find you and talk to you as soon as Walter left Ballar, but I was not to reveal anything about your sister's existence. Nevertheless, Selyn had to know everything. Althalos and I had aged, and if we died, someone had to know these secrets. If I died before Walter left Elmor, Selyn would talk to you instead of me. She'd tell you everything, except that she was your sister, until Walter's death."

Elliot looked up at the sky. "Is there anything else you should tell me?" he asked after a few moments.

Thorold closed his eyes and nodded, then opened them again. "You need to go to the Mountains of the Forgotten World. You have to do what your father failed to do, and what's more, you must ask for alliances from any region that is not on Walter's side."

"You want me to leave Elmor a little before Walter comes to the south with all his forces for the final encounter?" he yelled. "As soon as he realises what has happened, he'll head to Wirskworth with sixty-five thousand men. The queen needs me!"

The old man seemed sad. "Althalos failed to mention that without more allies, it'll be impossible to win this battle, even behind Wirskworth's walls," he responded. "But now you have enough time to get to the Mountains of the Forgotten World before Walter brings his armies to Elmor. Nonetheless, remember that the war against Walter is a war of the humans, not of the Elder Races. The Elder Races must be freed, regardless of whether we need allies to defeat our enemy and survive," he said solemnly.

"What would have happened to the Elder Races if Walter hadn't fallen into the trap and stayed in Ballar? What if Syrella hadn't agreed to invite Sophie to Elmor or even help her?" Elliot wondered. "If any of this had happened, Iovbridge would have had no other ally, and I would have had to fight alongside Sophie. I wouldn't have had time to head to the Mountains of the Forgotten World."

"If Walter hadn't taken the bait or if Syrella had refused to either help or host Sophie, then I'd have advised you to return to Iovbridge as soon as I met you," replied Thorold calmly. "If you failed to persuade Syrella to listen to you, you'd certainly fail to liberate the Elder Races, while if Walter hadn't taken the bait, your fate would have been to fight in Isisdor. As I told you before, Althalos didn't unequivocally believe in the truths of the Lake of Life, and if the enemy didn't move according to plan, your fate would have been to fight alongside the queen, even if it meant your end. No one can be absolutely certain that you would be able to liberate the Elder Races, but you would certainly be able to help Sophie." He smiled gently, seemingly aware of the great burden of his words.

Elliot exhaled wearily. "If I go to the Mountains of the Forgotten World, who will be sent to ask for alliances from the regions that aren't on Walter's side?"

Thorold's eyes sparked. "I think your recent adventures have given you enough people you can entrust with this mission."

"I need you to swear something to me, Thorold," Elliot implored after a while.

The Master looked at him for a moment before nodding in agreement.

"When we leave this place, you and Althalos will keep no more secrets from me."

Thorold weighed him up. It was impossible to read the thoughts behind his wizened face. But then the Master nodded sharply.

"Do you think I am the Rider of Fate?" Elliot suddenly murmured.

The man smiled. "That, no one can know. At any rate, you must not reveal the truth about Thindor to anyone, and if you're ever tempted to do so, remember: Thindor is the last pegasus in the world, and there are seven swords that can take his life."

Elliot felt alone, just as he had when Althalos had confided the plan to him. "How will I make it?" he blurted after a while. "Thindor has never chosen to come to all these years, and I don't have the Sword of Light."

Lines of sorrow spread on Thorold's face. "The answers will find you on their own, Elliot. Only you can find the way to become Thindor's rider, if, of course, that is your destiny," he said in a voice that was barely audible.

Elliot glanced at the old man. He could have sworn that Althalos had come alive again in the expression Thorold wore.

The Company's Separation

Apprehension filled Elliot as he walked. He was in the Tower of the Sharp Swords, looking for a large chamber in its west wing. Syrella had assured him that his companions were waiting for him there and that he'd recognise it from an elaborate sword engraved on its entrance. He went through several hallways until he found the door he was looking for and mustered all his courage before going inside.

John stood, seemingly carefree, gazing here and there, while Eleanor was huddled in Selwyn's arms. The men's jerkins were the colour of walnut, and the woman's linen dress had a lilac hue. Elliot walked in unobtrusively, but three pairs of eyes fixed on him at once. Awkwardness engulfed him. It seemed as if decades had gone by since the last time their company had been together.

"We need to talk." Elliot had thought of many different introductions, but now they had flown out of his mind.

For a moment, his eyes met Eleanor's. He searched for hatred or even anger, but all he saw in them was sadness.

"Your plan succeeded, Elliot Egercoll, or rather Althalos Baudry's plan," John said. "Are there any other truths you are now ready to share?" He hiccuped, but John had proven that he could think while drunk.

"I'm sorry I couldn't reveal the truth..." Elliot's voice trailed off.

"Is there something you needed to ask of us?" John spoke once more.

Elliot was full of hesitation. "I need help, and you are the only ones I would trust to—"

"I cannot fulfill Althalos' wishes," Long Arm cut him off. "Believe me—neither would he ever want a man like me for this purpose," he continued, choking a burp.

"Althalos's last plan has been fulfilled. Now I need your help to fulfill one of my own," replied Elliot. "The queen will ride to Wirskworth, along with the people of Iovbridge and White City, conceding the throne to Walter," he said, before anyone interrupted him.

His words seemed to make everyone freeze.

"The queen will leave Iovbridge?" Selwyn's eyes narrowed as Elliot nodded affirmatively. "But how...?"

"The governor sent an invitation to Sophie."

Selwyn and John seemed surprised, and Elliot told them everything they didn't know but needed to. "I swear I won't hide any secrets from you again. Unless I can't do otherwise," he finished.

Silence spread across the room. The three companions seemed discomfited, looking at Elliot.

"I will fight. I'll fight to the end, as he did..." Eleanor broke the silence, and Elliot welcomed her words with a gentle smile, thinking of Morys.

"I disappointed you, Elliot," Selwyn suddenly spoke up. "I was a coward..." His voice broke. "But I wasn't afraid for my life. I was thinking of the pain in my father's face. I was thinking of my mother screaming at the sight of my dead body if I lost my life..." His eyes filled with tears. "My parents have suffered a great deal, and I wanted to save them more pain, but I won't get cold feet again. I'll be with you till the end." His last words came out boldly.

Elliot looked at him, moved. "No, Selwyn. I disappointed you, all of you—"

"You're a fool," John cut in, glancing at him with a fond grimace.

Elliot smiled. "In order to stand a chance against Walter, we need new allies. Only you can help me build new alliances."

"New alli—" started Long Arm.

"You'll go to Aquarine," Elliot addressed Eleanor, interrupting him.

The girl seemed confused. “There is nothing there... Felador has no soldiers after the Battle of Aquarine. Everything on its soil died that day.”

“It may not have soldiers, but it does have people who need a new leader. You can help them. You can give them a new purpose,” Elliot suggested.

“They cannot fight,” came Eleanor’s response.

“No, they can’t right now, but war is not the only thing of value when in pursuit of an alliance. Felador has been without a governor for a long time. You are the only one I would trust for this purpose.”

“How do you know they will choose me as their governor?” Eleanor asked. “Do you think they’ll give me Felador because I come from one of its dead noble houses, or because the queen was in love with my brother?”

Elliot smiled. “They will not choose you for your name but for who you are.”

Eleanor seemed surprised. She looked at him for a few moments, moved, before nodding in agreement.

Elliot turned to Selwyn. “I know your father is expecting to find you here, but you have to get to the Black Vale.”

The young man’s eyebrows shot up. “They won’t fight for us,” he argued.

“You will ride to Vylor, bearing gold. You will assure them that if they ally with our army, they will be paid handsomely.”

“Thomas abolished the Black Vale’s rights, depriving each governor of the right to vote in the election of the King of Knightdorn. And Queen Sophie never restored their rights, and they now have a ruler who believes in nothing but gold. He will never fight on the side of the weak,” John said.

“Tell them that if they help us, their rights will be restored, and they will be given lands and titles,” Elliot continued, ignoring Long Arm.

“Why should they believe me?” rebutted Selwyn.

“Sophie Delamere has never made false promises throughout her reign. They know she would never send a messenger to them without meaning what she says she intends to do."

Selwyn looked troubled but didn't speak, and then he nodded sharply.

"As for you, John, I'll give you what you've always wanted."

"Will you send me to the Sea of Men to mingle with the mermaids?"

"No, I think the Ice Islands are more suitable for you."

John scoffed. "They won't fight against Walter. The Ice Islands keep their word."

"Tell them what happened in Elmor and let them decide," Elliot replied. "I'm sure they know well who my father was and how violent and tyrannical Walter is. Tell them that the kingdom my father built is what the queen and I are trying to protect, and we need all the help we can get."

John remained pensive for a while. "Perhaps the news that a son of Thomas, trained by Althalos, having appeared in the kingdom would arouse their interest. You are more cunning than I thought," he muttered.

Elliot limited himself to a smile.

"It seems we'll be doing the dirty work while you'll be commanding the armies of Isisdor and Elmor, behind Wirskworth's walls," said Long Arm pointedly.

Elliot looked him in the eyes. "I'm going to a place where I think no one else would want to go at this point in time."

All eyes fixed on him, puzzled.

"Unfortunately, no one should know about this," Elliot warned.

John chuckled. "Of course! Another secret you can't share..."

Elliot remained silent.

"So be it," Long Arm breathed out. "You're asking for alliances that have been dead for decades or never even existed. I hope you're capable of building one on your own at least."

"I'll try to build one that's not dead but has been cursed for centuries."

John opened his mouth wide, and Elliot smiled again at his companions. It was his duty to entrust this secret only to them. But one other thought rumbled in his mind. *Would he ever see them again*?

The Return of the Ghost Soldier

The horse was whinnying furiously behind the latticed gate, and Reynald tried to calm it down. He had no idea why he was there. A little earlier, some guards had taken him out of his cell, blindfolded him, and taken him out of Moonstone. He was waiting for an invisible blow when suddenly the guards put him on a horse. After a while, the horse had unexpectedly stopped, and then he felt hands pulling him to the ground. His captors had taken the chains off his hands, freed his eyes, and left him, along with the horse, behind an underground sliding gate, next to a huge cistern. The guards left without giving him the slightest explanation.

"It's pleasing to see anxiety in your face."

Reynald turned around, terrified. Elliot, dressed in a jerkin in the colours of the sky, was standing before him.

"What are you doing here?" he asked.

"I think you know."

A shiver went through Reynald's body. There was humidity in Wirskworth's galleys, and he was dressed in rags.

"I have a mission for you, Reynald," teased the boy.

"I knew what you wanted from me when you refused to let me fight for you, but it's impossible," he murmured.

"Did you love my mother?"

The question surprised Reynald, but he churned it into anger. "You don't understand. He'll kill me instantly."

"Not if you say the right words," Elliot disagreed, getting closer to him.

Reynald scoffed. "I saved your life. I killed one of his spies. Do you think he'll take me back with open arms?"

"You saved the life of the self-proclaimed *son* of Thomas Egercoll. You didn't know if it was true. You wanted to earn his trust, to find out who trained him... a boy more capable than a former Trinity member..."

Reynald wasn't convinced.

"You're the only one who can do it," Elliot insisted.

"No one has ever been able to spy on Walter Thorn," Reynald remarked. "And why would you trust me? If I leave, I may find myself against you on the battlefield. I may forget everything."

"I have faith."

"You're a fool," Reynald jeered.

"I hear that often," Elliot admitted.

"Walter may order me to find you and kill you. If I get the chance, I'll have to do it, otherwise he'll cut my throat," he flung back angrily.

"I'm sure you'd seize the opportunity to prove that our first duel was simply a mistake," Elliot smiled.

Reynald looked at him. "How did I manage to escape from Wirskworth?" he asked after a while.

"You didn't escape..."

Reynald shook his head furiously at this madness. "You want me to tell him the truth?"

"Only half the truth. He'll believe that I trusted you. He knows that this has always been the Egercolls' weak spot."

Reynald observed him for a long moment, then rode the mare next to him, skeptical. "If I do what you're asking, I won't be doing it for you."

Elliot looked at him without an ounce of surprise in his eyes.

"No one can ever know about this," Reynald added.

"You have my word," the boy reassured him.

"Remember that, Egercoll, otherwise I'll find you and kill you with my own two hands."

Elliot didn't respond; he moved with confidence toward the winch with the heavy chain. The sliding gate rattled open upwards, the sound of grinding steel echoing through the cavern. Reynald took one last look at Elliot before grabbing the reins. Then he and his horse sallied forth like a tornado into the black veil of the night.

From Gregory Kontaxis

If you enjoyed the story, please consider reviewing on Amazon. It would mean so much to me. And if you are on Goodreads, would you share your thoughts with friends and followers?

You can also find the latest news by subscribing to my website at https://www.gregorykontaxis.com.

About the Author

Gregory Kontaxis was born in Athens. He studied Informatics and Finance in Greece and the United Kingdom, and he has worked as a Financial Analyst in Vienna and London. He currently resides in London, where he is occupied with investment risk management and writing. *The Return of the Knights* is the first book of his pentalogy, *The Dance of Light*.

Printed in Great Britain
by Amazon